TO BEAT THE DEVIL

A Mick Murphy Key West Mystery

Michael Haskins

Early praise for To Beat the Devil from other writers.

"The Russian Mafia, gunfights, a harrowing in-air plane crash all capture the violent world Mick Murphy inhabits. Michael Haskins makes me wonder if I ever want to visit the Keys again. He takes the laid-back Key West culture and ratchets it up to where you can't turn the pages fast enough. Another breathtaking tale from Haskins and Murphy."
Don Bruns, author, *Hot Stuff, Stuff Dreams Are Made Of, Stuff to Spy For, Don't Sweat the Small Stuff, Too Much Stuff and the Sever Music Series.*

"Michael Haskins does for Mick Murphy and his sidekick Norm in **Beat the Devil** what Robert Crais did for Elvis Cole and Joe Pike in **L.A. Requiem**, deepening the characters and their relationship in an engaging and thrill packed story."
Jochem Vandersteen, author of the *Noah Milano Series.*

TO BEAT THE DEVIL
A Mick Murphy Key West Mystery

ISBN-13: 978-1484850183
ISBN-10: 1484850181

Trade Paperback

Published in 2013
Fenian Bastard Press
Michael Haskins
www.michaelhaskins.net

Dedication

As always, this book is for the men and women, boys and girls, of my family because without them, I wouldn't give a damn. And for those children that have yet to arrive and I may never meet, may my stories help you discover my secrets and dreams.

VAYA CON DIOS

It seems that I am attending more funerals these days, saying farewell to friends, than weddings. That's usually a sign that I have been in one location too long. Saying a permanent goodbye is one the things I hate about life. Death doesn't discriminate, but I wish it did. There are those I'd rather hear the banshee crying for than know another friend has gone forever.

Rev. Séamus Ward SJ left a piece of Ireland whenever he preached in Key West. His sermons came from the heart and he didn't need a written script. He explained the scriptures so people would understand them. If central casting saw him, he would've been cast as Padre Thomas. I wrote the character long before I knew Father Séamus, maybe because of heavenly intervention. There isn't a Sunday that goes by that I don't miss him.

Phil Hogue was my friend long before he was my banker. He helped my wife and me buy our house in the Keys and we shared many lunches together, sometimes with the 'lunch bunch' and sometimes alone. If Wall Street bankers had men like Phil in its ranks, we wouldn't be in the economic crisis they've caused. I walk into his bank and miss his greeting.

Richard Collins was one of the first friends I made in Key West. What can anyone say about him? He was truly a Key West character with a heart bigger than the state of Texas. Richard's stories about the Keys and politicians knew no end and the ones that didn't make tears of laughter come, made you cry anyway. Richard, anyone that knew he would say, never met a bar tab he wouldn't pick up. If we all anteed up what we owed him, he would've been too rich to die. At the end, he proved himself above all of us by keeping his sense of humor.

Freddy Cabanas should have had a bigger role in this story. Fate wouldn't have it and the one man that made flying an adventure to so many Key Westers and tourists alike, died in a plane accident while I finished writing the book. He was a family man, a brother and a friend to many. He fought with the Conch Republics Air Force, and with loaves of stale Cuban bread saved the island and sent the US Coast Guard on its way – all in the spirit of fun. Fun might've been Freddy's middle name.

These four friends are missed but the loss is more than mine, it's mankind's, because they were fun, loving and caring people that gave of themselves to enrich the lives of others. Who will take their place?

Acknowledgements

Many people had a helping hand in my writing this. I have probably played enough with the information they gave me to make it unrecognizable, but that doesn't make their contribution less appreciated. I tell them it's poetic license and they pretend to believe me.

Thanks to Jim Linder for all his background on intelligence agencies and flying, especially seaplanes. Couldn't have got off the ground without him. His knowledge of firearms kept me shooting straight.

A true debt of gratitude to Captain Pat DeQuattro USCG and Captain Jim Fitton USCG (retired), for taking the time to listen to my plots and answer my questions. They set me right on a number of items and any mistakes with the information they shared are mine alone.

I want to thank my editor, Nadja Hansen, for making the words work and to Jen Musselman for taking a sliver of an idea and creating a great cover. Rob O'Neal's photo of me must have spent time in PhotoShop. It's good to see Rob back on the streets with his camera, after his accident.

I have great friends who let me bounce ideas and problems off them, Bob Pierce, Burt Hansen, Bill Lane, and Texas Rich, who also deserves credit for the many reads and corrections he did! I think he can quote the book from beginning to end.

Thanks to Shirrel Rhoades and Bill Murphy for taking time to do an early read and giving me feedback.

Thanks to the Casa Marina critique group for showing me my waywardness as well as when I got it right, Mike Dennis, Jonathan Woods, Sara Goodwin-Nguyen, and Jessica Argyle.

Larry Lumpkin was invaluable with supplying me information on the P-51 Mustang and if I had to hedge his information, I apologize but sometimes the story refuses to cooperate with the facts. Not too often, I hope. Any errors are mine, not Larry's.

Real friendship is shown in times of trouble; prosperity is full of friends.

Euripides, 480 - 406 BC

There is nothing on this earth more to be prized than true friendship.

Thomas Aquinas, 1225 – 1274

Friendship is a common belief in the same fallacies, mountebanks, and hobgoblins.

H. L. Mencken, 1880 – 1956

A friend in need . . .

PART ONE

NORM'S STORY

What's friendship's realest measure? I'll tell you. The amount of precious time you'll squander on someone else's calamities and fuck-ups.

Richard Ford, author

Chapter One

The Russian mobster sat naked in the old office chair, his cloths discarded in a pile on the warehouse floor. Duct tape secured his wrists to the armrests and more tape forced his legs backward, attached to the wheel spokes below the seat. Welts and open bruises, red, purple and black, covered his chest and stomach, blood flowed from his broken nose, both eyes were swollen closed from the beating, and on the left side of his head, he had a torn ear. The mobster breathed through his opened mouth and I could see broken teeth and blood. His engorged scrotum looked like a red and purple softball.

My friend Liam Mick Murphy stood in front of the condemned man, a three-foot length of rubber garden hose in his hand. The hose still had its new-bought shine except where blood stained it.

I stood about twenty feet away and slowly scrolled through the mobster's cell phone.

"He's not gonna talk," I said, but kept my attention on the cell phone. "He knows you'll kill him if he does. If you don't kill him, Alexei will." I looked up.

"You tell me what I want and you can run and hide from Alexei," Mick Murphy said to the man.

The mobster said nothing.

"I think what we want is in his cell." I held the phone up and pointed to the screen. "Names and numbers. He has eight on the speed dial. One and two are men, the others are clubs."

"And what does that tell us, Norm, that this fucker won't?" He raised the hose and brought it down hard on the mobster's shoulder. A moan squealed from the man's bloody mouth.

"How do you arrange the names on your speed dial?" It was a rhetorical question because we prioritized our speed dial.

"Is one of the names Alexei?" He hit the mobster again.

"No." I didn't expect it to be, neither did Mick Murphy.

"Then how the hell does it help us?" His words came slowly, angrily. Torturing a man tires you and Mick Murphy needed sleep, but he was frantic and wanted to find Alexei and kill him. It was a difficult task, finding and killing him, but Murphy was determined and for reasons that would've made me determined too.

I've known Mick Murphy for more than twenty years and I've seen him caught in situations between leftist guerrillas fighting government soldiers, and Mexican drug cartels fighting everyone, and know he can be tough and defend himself.

I tried to tell him before this crusade to find and kill Alexei began that being the aggressor was a whole different world than using violence to defend yourself. He would be responsible, I told him, for what went down, not someone else, because he was the initiator. What he wanted to do would close doors that would never open for him again. I don't know if he heard me, or if he cared. I talked from experience.

He lived in a world of hurt and thought killing Alexei, the guy who put the play in motion that killed his fiancée, sunk his sailboat and all but killed him, was what he needed. His physical wounds took six months to heal but his head was somewhere else, far from the carefree, Key West, sail-bum/journalist I know, and far from healing. He used vengeance as a painkiller. I watched his detachment as he beat the mobster.

"We're moving up the food chain." I read the names to myself. "Two men. He reports to one of them, maybe both. One and two on the speed dial."

"We done here?" He grunted the words with rage and frustration.

The mobster turned his head slowly and looked toward me. He couldn't see with the swollen eyes, but he knew the direction of my voice and his fate.

"Yes." I put the cell phone in my jacket pocket.

"Let's go climb that food chain." Mick Murphy dropped the hose and walked to the exit door. "Coming?" He said it as a dare.

"Be right there," I said.

Mick Murphy walked outside and when he opened the

door, the harsh South Florida sun shot into the room, blinding me. He closed the door and the warehouse was dim again.

The mobster's damaged stare followed me as I walked toward him.

"Alexei will kill you both." The words spit from his mouth between bloody bubbles. "And not so quickly."

"He'll try," I said, and shot him between his swollen eyes with a small twenty-two semi-automatic. He couldn't see the gun but knew the shot was coming. It was his destiny and he accepted it. The shot's report was lost within the empty warehouse as his screams had been.

Chapter Two

Mick Murphy sat impatiently in the SUV, as I exited the dark warehouse and into the scorching June heat. Even in the morning, the mugginess of Fort Lauderdale was high. I stopped in the empty, fenced-off parking lot and dialed my cell phone.

"SoFlo, fifteen," I said when the call was answered. "Cleaning crew." I hung up.

The warehouse was one of many safe house locations a well-kept, secret branch of joint military intelligence agencies controlled around the country. The address, for my purposes, was SoFlo, fifteen. It meant Southern Florida, number fifteen. When we returned, the body would be gone.

This industrial complex that housed the warehouse, took up a few city blocks in a once-thriving area on the fringes of Fort Lauderdale, but companies found cheaper labor outside the country and now only a few buildings had occupants. It was the perfect location for our purposes, not many inquisitive neighbors.

The agency kept most of its safe houses empty, though a few stored items that came from or went to Mexico or Central America. We needed empty and this was available with no questions asked. It was a favor owed and now paid.

Mick Murphy sat with the door open, looking straight ahead. He could've started the engine and had the A/C running, but he lives in Key West and likes the heat. Maybe he's preparing for his time in hell. I got in and had the A/C on high right away. If Mick Murphy thought he was taking me to hell with him, he was mistaken. I live in Southern California where the heat isn't usually as brutal, but my time spent in Central American countries helped me adjust.

"What now, Norm?" Mick Murphy is a get-to-the-point kind of guy.

He was in a hurry but didn't have a clue as to where he was going. I've spent the last six-months trying to help him get well, to slow him down, control his anger, set a direction. This kind of shit, seek and eliminate, is what I do for the military, for the decision makers in Washington, but I do it outside the country where laws and rules were a lot more flexible. The golden rule is don't get caught. I have no delusion about what would happen if I were caught, the brass and decision makers would deny involvement with me.

"We go back to the hotel and sleep," I said. We had hotel rooms in South Beach because that's where Alexei and the Russian mob had its private clubs. "I call the clubs on his speed dial." I drove toward the freeway.

"And then?" He played it like a chess game and always thought two or three moves ahead of where he was. At least that hadn't changed. Yet.

"Either Viktor or Yakov run the clubs. I call, ask for them and someone will tell me when to call back."

"Simple as that?"

"No," I said. Kidnapping Russian mobsters is never simple, dealing with them is near impossible. "But someone will tell me and then we'll know which club to go to."

"Late, like with this bird?"

"They show up when the action begins, so, yeah, late. Maybe before midnight."

"And this gets us to Alexei how, Norm?"

"One of these guys runs the clubs in South Beach. He knows when Alexei is expected. He's in Alexei's outer circle, maybe knows his local routine because he wants to be impressive, and that gets us closer. Both these guys want to be in the inner circle, that's where the power and money are. One of them is on top of things, to look good to the boss. Maybe even knows where the boss is. Alexei protects himself with layers and doesn't trust too many, even in his circle. You don't get to be an old KGB agent if you're too trusting."

"How come Alexei walked up to me in Key West, if he's so cautious?"

"You weren't a threat to him," I said. "He wasn't alone. He's never alone and that's going to make taking him difficult. Messy."

"You think there's a better way to do it?"

"No, not if you want to face off with him."

"I want him to know it's me." Mick Murphy's words came out hard, determination pushing them.

"It'll take time and we have to be as cautious as Alexei," I said and turned onto I-95 and hit bumper-to-bumper traffic. "I'm not interested in a suicide mission."

"You're right, Norm." Mick Murphy slumped in the seat.

"What's wrong?"

"Tired, I guess."

"You having second thoughts about interrogating these guys?"

"Whatever it takes to get Alexei," he said and closed his eyes. "I've got no problems with it."

"It's gonna take more than you and me," I said and Mick Murphy grunted a reply. "Whichever one these guys we go after, it could be hard to grab him. They'll have security."

"I'm not afraid of hard, I'm afraid of failure," he said without looking at me. "What about your spook buddies?"

"I'm off the radar," I said, only a half lie, and traffic moved forward a few feet. "We're lucky to get the warehouse."

I'm with Mick Murphy because he's a friend in need. I owe him for saving my life a long time ago. I'm indebted and spent the past few years paying him back, though he never asked me to. He has never asked me why I'm there for him, either. Then again, I've never asked him why he's shown up in my life the few times that I've needed him.

My usual array of magic tricks that were called-in favors from the intelligence agency when in trouble, were less available to me now. All I could offer him for sure was my experience and support.

"You've always have a plan, what is it?"

"Someone to do surveillance for us. You with the red hair and beard stand out too much and I don't want to run into any Russian thug that might remember me."

"I trust Pauly."

Pauly is an ex-drug smuggler friend of Mick Murphy's who retired to Key West. I, personally, have a hard time thinking he's retired, or even liking him, but he's Mick Murphy's friend and proven it a few times. Trusting him, from my point of view, is a whole other issue.

"If Alexei thinks that you're looking for him, it's as good as over. You understand that, right?" The words sounded cynical because I was repeating the warning for the hundredth time.

"I've spent the last six months listening to you," he said, matching my sarcasm. "If I didn't believe you, I wouldn't be here. You do this for a living. I'm along for your expertise and expect to get Alexei. I'll do the rest. You tell me what to do and I'll do it, no questions asked."

"Mick, you don't know how to not ask questions." He's a journalist, and like cops are always cops in and out of uniforms, Mick Murphy is always a journalist in his ways.

"I'm learning from the best," he said and smiled to himself, but I caught it. "I'll call Pauly if we ever get out of this traffic and back to the hotel. Then we'll get some sleep." Three cars stopped at a red light in Key West is traffic to Mick Murphy, not like on I-95, it was making him anxious. "When I wake up, I want to know your plan."

"So do I." Traffic moved at a snail's pace. It reminded me of Los Angeles and that put me in my comfort zone.

Chapter Three

I found myself hopelessly entombed with doubt while looking for a possible way Mick Murphy and I could locate and snatch the Russian. A rap on the hotel door startled me. I wasn't expecting anyone, not at ten P.M. I grabbed my Glock off the table. Could the Russians be this lucky? Shit, I hoped not. Why would they bother to knock?

In the quiet that followed, I heard street commotion outside, car horns blaring and high-spirited crowds strolling South Beach. Nothing came from the door. I waited. Another rap. Looking through the peephole could get me killed, so I stood off to the side.

"Yeah." I waited to see if someone shot into the room.

"Pauly," the voice called quietly.

I don't know Mick Murphy's friend Pauly, the ex-drug smuggler, well enough to identify his voice, and I don't trust him one-hundred percent, so I left the security hinge on the door and cracked it open with my Glock ready. Pauly stood there, a duffel bag hung from his shoulder. I recognized his shaggy strawberry-blonde hair, close-cropped beard, and crooked smile. I closed the door, slipped the hinge back and reopened it.

"You're here," I said.

Pauly walked in, ignoring the Glock. "Mick called late this morning."

I relocked the door. The smuggler wouldn't have been my first choice for help.

He dropped the duffel bag and it made a loud clanging noise, even on the thick carpet. "Told me he needed my help."

"That it?" I sat on the sofa and he took a chair.

"Yeah, Norm, that's it."

"Help with what?" Maybe Mick Murphy was smart in not telling him.

"Damn it, I haven't heard from him in six months." Pauly leaned forward, resentment in his tone and a hard stare for me. "I'm the curious type. He's my friend and last time I saw him he was half-dead. He calls, asks for help and here I am. Like I said, I'm curious. For chrissake, let's stop playing mind games." Pauly looked around the room. "Where is he?"

"Sleeping." I pointed to the door that connected our rooms.

"Is he okay?"

"Yeah. He's healed pretty much."

"But what?"

I tapped my head. "He's on a quest."

"To kill that asshole Alexei?"

"Yeah."

"How long have you been in Florida?" The animosity was back.

"Alexei's businesses are here," I said.

"Your resources are that good? Alexei's a goddamn enigma. But you found his businesses?"

"We found one guy. He's led us to two more," I said, ignoring his questions. I don't like answering questions. "It took us a week to get him."

"How long has Mick been back?" He was demanding as well as curious.

"Mick's choice not to contact anyone," I said, trying to sound responsive.

"I'm not just anyone," he protested. "I'm the guy who pulled him and Tita off the damn pier during your gun battle with the cartel, saved their asses. I'm the guy that stopped the Russian sniper prick from getting that third round off and killing him in Key West."

"I'm not arguing, Pauly," I said, holding my hands in a surrendering position. "I ain't calling the shots. But he thought of you when we needed help. He's changed and you should be ready for that."

"Shit Norm, what happened that night would change anyone." Pauly scratched at his bearded chin. "You need my help for what?"

"Viktor and Yakov," I said. "One of them runs Alexei's

clubs. Viktor shows up around midnight. I'm thinking he's the one. Yakov is probably second in the pecking order."

"But?"

"No idea what either looks like."

"Why don't you or Mick go in?" Was his curiosity getting the better of him, or was it caution?

"I've had run-ins with the Russian mob. Someone might recognize me." I said. "Mick's a wild card these days. It wouldn't work."

"You want me to go in and ID these bastards."

"Yeah, but it ain't that easy." I leaned toward him. "You get picked up at a bar by one of the Russian girls. She escorts you in as her guest. And then you need to figure out a way to ID Viktor."

Pauly laughed. "Gettin' in is easy. All I've got to do is flash a damn bankroll that would choke a horse or a wallet full of credit cards. ID-ing him might take time. I'll have to come up with something once I'm in the club. The bar downstairs part of the girl's routine?"

"Good as any." From what he said, Pauly knew something of how the clubs operated.

"Where's the club?"

"Two blocks. The South Beach Social Club."

"Damn original." He laughed.

"Where are you staying?"

"Suite upstairs. I've got the Town Car, so I can play the part."

He wasn't playing the part, he was the big spender, the go to guy.

I pointed to the duffel bag. "Your wardrobe?"

Pauly looked toward the door to Mick Murphy's room. "You know Padre Thomas, right?"

I nodded.

"He biked to my house in Key Haven a few weeks ago and that's a long way for an old fart to ride." He kept his voice low, as if there were others in the room. "He told me Mick would call and ask for my help. He didn't say why, only that Mick was in trouble. He's a strange one. Seems to know things he shouldn't."

"Very strange," I said.

"I asked him questions about Mick, but his answers were vague. All I got out of him was that it's dangerous. I don't know why I believed the padre, but I did. I half expected the call, but it was a hell of a surprise to hear Mick's voice." He paused and slowly shook his head. He pointed to the duffel bag. "I'm here and that is one of two. I brought firepower, not knowing what I was getting into."

"This Viktor might have protection. Extra firepower will come in handy." Ex-drug smugglers can be good for something.

"Identify him and then what?" Pauly said.

"We follow him. Figure a way to grab him."

"Mick knows Bob's an ex-SEAL," he said. "He's been trained to snatch people. He'd be better at this shit than me." Snatching someone seemed to make him edgy.

"Mick's calling the shots and he chose you." I knew he was right, but I hated explaining myself, especially to someone like Pauly.

"You're not bringing him back here." Pauly looked around the room.

"To a warehouse in Lauderdale."

Pauly frowned, understanding. "Tonight's a good night to begin."

"Mick should be up soon. We'll be your backup, just in case anything fucks up."

"Later, I'll help keep an eye on Mick too, if you want," Pauly said. "He can be a character when things are normal, but he's got a good head on his shoulders."

"Yeah, but things ain't close to normal, Pauly. You need to know this. I watched him torture a man. Beat him senseless and he didn't show any emotion. I don't want him like that."

"To enjoy it, you mean."

"Yeah, that too. I know Alexei. He's avoided Interpol for years." How much should I tell him? I decided to tell him the truth. "Our chances aren't too good. If we find him, getting close enough to kill him might be impossible."

He nodded toward the closed door. "Have you told him that?"

I shook my head. "If he goes without some control, it's a suicide mission."

"Why are you doing this?" Pauly asked. "Why are you risking everything for him?"

"It's a long story." Pauly waited for me to say more. "I met Mick in Central America. He was doing a story on the Colombian cartel. I was after its leaders. Mick got into a tight spot and I pulled him out. We've been friends ever since."

"There's more to it than friendship."

"You're wrong." I lied. "You're here out of friendship?"

"Sure. Mick's been my friend for fifteen damn years," he said. "I can count my friends on one hand and still hold a cigar. Friendship and trust is everything to me."

"I was held by a leftwing group in Nicaragua. They had me dead to rights," I said, deciding to add the most important piece of why I was there. "Mick convinced them I was working for him. On his word, they let me go."

"So you owe him."

"Yeah, you could say that. We owe each other. Is that good enough for you?"

"Norm, you don't like me much, I've picked up on that," he said and grinned, kind of a challenge. "My past bothers you. Can you put it aside for this?"

"Mick needs your help, so we're beginning over tonight, Pauly. We're helping a friend." I kept my words as impartial as possible. We needed him. "We have no past between us. I can make that work. Can you?" I wondered if his answer would also be a lie.

"Okay," he said, his hostility gone, and stood up. "Let me get ready and we'll find this fucker and move forward. Midnight, okay?"

"Midnight, in the bar," I said and closed the door behind

him.

Pauly left the duffel bag of weapons on the floor. Had I made a deal with the devil?

Chapter Four

Pauly came back close to midnight, all spit-shined and ready to go. I'm not a slave to fashion, but even I could see that his clothing was expensive and his Rolex shined as only gold can. The shirt probably cost more than my handcrafted, cowboy boots. He was the perfect mark for the bar girls. Of course, what's money to a retired drug smuggler?

Pauly and Mick Murphy greeted each other as if it was just another day and no time had passed. No animosity on Pauly's part and no explanation from Mick Murphy about his long absence.

"How we gonna work this, Norm?" Mick Murphy had his usual get-to-the-point attitude.

"Pauly, no gun, right?" I said.

"Clean," he said.

I walked them to the coffee table. "These are earpiece receivers." I pointed to two small round objects on the table. "And mikes." The two button sized transmitters sat next to the earpieces.

"Only two sets?" Pauly said.

"You go in clean," I reminded him. "They might have metal detectors or jamming equipment. They don't want anyone armed or wired inside."

"Other than themselves." Pauly frowned, knowing his life could depend on us.

The earpiece fit like an expensive hearing aid, almost invisible. The mike got pinned to the inside shirt collar and powered off the receiver's battery. Amazing what intelligence agencies engineers come up with or can buy off the private sector.

"The receiver is good for twelve-hours." I took the small earpiece, closed the tiny battery holder, and slipped it into my ear. "The mike goes inside the collar." I made sure Mick Murphy was paying attention. "We stay within a half mile of each other, we're okay."

Mick Murphy picked up the device and followed my example.

"What about me?" Pauly said. "How do we keep in touch?"

I handed him a piece of paper with a phone number and a four-digit code on it.

"Hell, I've gotta phone for help?" He knew better, but he wanted an explanation, to know our plan for his safety.

"Call that number. When you hear the beep punch in the four-digits," I said.

Pauly dialed. "Now what?"

"We can hear you, but your phone has to stay on," I said. "Keep it in the coat's breast pocket."

"How do I hear you?"

"You don't. If things go south, just say help."

"Help," Pauly said into the phone, not pleased with the situation.

"Loud and clear," I said, ignoring his concern. "It's as if we're on a conference call."

"But I'm muted."

"Yeah. You'd draw their attention talking to yourself. They won't leave you alone inside and it'll probably be too noisy to hear anyway."

"I'll go to the damn john."

"You won't be alone," I said. "They may jam cell phone signals."

"Great," Pauly growled. "Then what?"

"Mick will watch the entrance. I'll watch the alley. Those are the two exits. We'll know when you come out."

"Forcibly or on my own," Pauly mumbled and put the phone in his jacket pocket. "Stay close and pay attention." He left the room without looking back.

* * *

We gave Pauly a half-hour and then Mick Murphy and I went down to the bar. A scattering of people sat around drinking, getting ready to join the busy mid-week nightlife of South Beach. I wore scruffy old tennis shoes, jeans and a western shirt. Mick

Murphy could've been my twin if it wasn't for his red hair and beard.

We took seats at the bar, just as we came in off the lobby, and ordered beers. Pauly and the two women with him were in our view. Because of our earpieces, we had heard the women approach Pauly in the bar. The young women positioned themselves on either side of him, and all three were eating shrimp cocktail appetizers. I know how expensive the appetizers are from having lunch at the bar and even Mick Murphy said he could buy a large bag of head-on shrimp at the docks on Stock Island for the price of one shrimp cocktail. Three appetizers would pay for what I was wearing, and maybe a new pair of cowboy boots.

Both women had shoulder-length blond hair and closer in age to girls than they were women. They spoke English with moderate accents. Probably college girls earning extra money hustling for the Russians. They were from Eastern Europe. That meant their families came from the old Soviet bloc and knew how the Russian mob worked. The girls received a stipend for bringing the mark into the club and maybe a portion of what he spent. It wasn't unusual for a bill to be a few thousand dollars when the evening ended.

"I'm going to find a party," Pauly said as he finished his shrimp cocktail. "You girls like to party?"

The girls laughed. Maybe it was more of a girlish giggle. It came naturally or from experience and almost sounded honest.

You've got to give the Joint Special Ops Command credit for its technology. If we were standing in front of Pauly, we couldn't have heard better. These devices beat hell out of the shit I've borrowed from the CIA and DEA.

"We like this hotel because it is not so crowded," one girl said. "You like crowds?" She pouted to show Pauly she didn't.

"I like parties," he said. "Big parties, small parties. I like good times and fun, don't you?"

Giggles again from the girls.

"What's so funny?" Pauly played into their game.

"Our friend has a club down the street." The other girl

spoke up. "He is wealthy, and opened it for only members."

"And membership costs what?" Pauly sounded skeptical.

"Nothing," the first girl said with a sexy smile she must have practiced in front of a mirror to make it so perfect. "We are members and you can come in as our guest. The food is good too, if you like steaks."

"I like steaks and champagne," the second girl chirped like a caged bird.

"Who doesn't?" Pauly winked at them, buying their story. "Can we walk?"

"Maybe not after too much champagne," the first girl mouthed in a sultry voice and a devilish grin that made promises she knew she didn't have to keep.

Pauly peeled off a few bills from his bankroll, making sure the girls saw it, and left the cash on the bar. "Let's go party," he said as each girl grabbed an arm. They walked past without a look but we heard Pauly whistling.

"Plan in motion," Murphy said, excitedly. We drained our beers.

I've run my adult life on pre-made plans and realize that no plan works entirely. It's only a guide to follow because humans are involved and humans will fuck up a wet dream without even thinking about it.

Most plans needed tweaking as you go to keep on track and I learned that the hard way. Some of my plans, just a few, worked so smoothly that I got results sooner than expected. But most turned to shit somewhere and I usually had the human element to thank. Some plans could be fixed after the screw up, and went on to work, while others blew the fuck up in my face and left good people dead.

Mick Murphy's plan in motion comment didn't make me smile. I paid for the beers. We went outside on the busy street and watched Pauly walking away with his arms around the two blonds. He looked like he was enjoying himself. I wonder what we were walking into other than a group of crazy Russians. Mick Murphy has the uncanny ability to bring out the pessimist in me.

Chapter Five

The South Beach Social Club had a small courtyard in front that set the main entrance twenty-something feet back from the busy sidewalk. A short wall and shrubbery offered additional privacy to the building. A narrow, gated walkway led to a door with a sign above stating it was a private club.

Mick Murphy and I peered over the wall and watched as the door opened for Pauly and the two women. A large bouncer blocked the entrance, said something to the women and let them in. He shook hands with Pauly, nothing like making the mark feel welcome.

"Thank you," we heard Pauly say in reply to whatever the bouncer had said, thanks to our earpiece receivers.

The club took up the bottom floor of the three-story building. The top floor windows were dark, but lights shone through gaps in the curtains on the second floor.

Reception from Pauly's phone was good but noise from inside the club made me strain to understand him.

"You know where to go?" I said to Mick Murphy.

He nodded and pointed toward the parking garage, almost diagonally across the street, between slow moving vehicles, jay-walking pedestrians and us. "Third floor spot, Norm. Hell, I parked, why would I forget?" He looked at me and I could see doubt on his face.

"Wanted to make sure," I said. "You've been tired, hoss. Said so yourself."

"I'm awake, now." He looked back at the courtyard and then at the parking garage. "With the binoculars I should be able to see right into the yard. See who comes and goes."

"Pauly's our concern," I said. "When he comes out the front, he's okay."

"With the girls?"

"I doubt it." The Russian mob's prostitutes worked the other side of Miami. These operations were about thousand-dollar bottles of liquor charged on a credit card from an out-of-town businessman.

The scheme isn't illegal. Officials have investigated, but since the clubs are private, they didn't violate any existing laws by charging extravagant prices. Buyer beware, as the old adage goes.

"With all the background noise I can't hear Pauly too clearly," Mick Murphy said.

"Listen for him to call for help. Otherwise assume he's okay."

"How much danger is he in?"

I was surprised at the question. It was as if Mick Murphy cared. The only thing he's cared about in the last six months is revenge. "All he's gotta do is pay the bill."

"If it all goes south?"

"I'll be in the alley. If they're throwing Pauly out, it'll be to the alley," I said. "If that happens I'll need the car there fast. You get to me pronto."

"Crossing that street might take time."

"The stop light works with the garage exit, I checked," I said. "Use the horn, and try not to hit anyone."

"No problem, as long as they get out of the way." He slapped me on the shoulder. Was he serious or lightening up?

Mick Murphy joined the jaywalkers and crossed the street. I turned and walked toward the cross street and the alley.

With Dumpsters against the wall, a rubbish truck could move down the alley with barely enough room for the driver to get out and help move the large containers for emptying. If the men didn't put the Dumpster back tight against the wall, nothing else would make it down the alley. Openings at both ends enabled delivery trucks to come and go.

I stayed in the shadows. Enough dim light shined over the back doors of businesses so employees could see to empty the garbage at night. The rest of the alley was shadowy at best. The bins stunk. They might've been emptied early each morning, but it smelled as if cleaning them wasn't a priority.

Lights seeped through curtains on the top floor off the alley, as well as the second floor of the building. It was one-thirty

A.M. and the noise from the busy street filtered back. Twice, back doors opened and employees emptied trash into the Dumpsters. The Russian's back door never opened.

"I'm here," Mick Murphy's voice rumbled into my earpiece and mixed in with the club's noise. "Clear view."

"I'm in back," I said. "Tomorrow you get the alley. It stinks and I hear rats."

"Russian or American?"

"Rats are rats," I said.

We stopped talking and listened to Pauly. A band played somewhere in the club and the music was amplified. The background noise often garbled what we heard. Pauly and the girls ordered a bottle of champagne and steak dinners. Along with their kickback, the girls would eat well tonight. Maybe they ate that way every night.

"It's awful loud," Pauly yelled. "Is there anywhere less noisy?"

They finished dinner and were on a third bottle of champagne. The girls were difficult to hear over the noise but I heard enough to know they made unrecognizable toasts to various things and swilled the bubbly like water. They must've been brought up on vodka shots at home. Pauly played along. I was concerned how he'd play it when the bill came.

"We can take the champagne to the backroom," one girl said in a tipsy voice.

"Let's do that," Pauly said.

Someone spoke Russian and one of the girls replied. Music blared though my earpiece and then softened. Pauly and the girls moved into the backroom. Another bottle of champagne ordered, giggles, and less distracting background noise in the earpiece from the private room.

From the mixture of voices I heard, there had to be others in the room. The loud music had stopped and laughter took its place.

"Excuse me," Pauly said and a man answered. I couldn't hear him clearly, because the background laughter and conversation blocked him out. "I'd like to see Viktor when he's free."

Oh shit! What was he doing? This was supposed to be about surveillance not confrontation.

A garbled reply.

"Of course you know him, he runs this place," Pauly said after the man said something I couldn't understand.

Muddled voices came back, two men or maybe three were talking close to Pauly.

"Thank you," Pauly said to the man. "Something wrong?" It sounded as if he was speaking to the girls. Both girls were talking hurriedly at the same time, their accents more distinctive in their native tongue. I couldn't understand them, but it didn't sound like party chatter.

"No, no," Pauly said to the girls. "We have a mutual friend. Nothing to worry about." He tried to calm the girls.

"Mick, get the car started." I walked past the club's rear door and two doors down I pushed a Dumpster away from the wall to stop through traffic and cover my ass as I waited with my Glock ready. Nothing good was in the immediate future, thanks to the ex-drug smuggler.

Chapter Six

"I can get up myself," Pauly said calmly to someone. I heard the scraping of chairs against the floor in my earpiece. "I don't need help," he yelled. "Get your hands off me."

Shit. It wasn't supposed to go down like this. Not so soon. No way of knowing what we were up against.

"Mick, bring the car."

"I heard," Mick Murphy said.

"Turn left onto the street and take the first right," I said. "Back down the alley. I've blocked the other entrance."

"I'm moving."

"Get the M-4, we may need it. This is going to shit."

The Colt M-4 is a cut-down version of the military M-16. It is suitable for us because opened full-length it was only thirty-three inches and had a thirty-round magazine. We had the fully automatic version and the magazine would empty in seconds.

"It's sitting next to me, Norm."

I heard a loud voice speaking Russian through the ear-piece and realized the background chatter had stopped. The men had cleared the room, including the two girls, I assumed.

"There is no Viktor here," the man said.

"Tell him I'm a friend of Alexei," Pauly said, staying calm.

"Do not know Alexei, do not know Viktor."

The talker mentioned Alexei ahead of Viktor and that told me he knew them. Boss always comes first. Pauly might have noticed it too. They were following a pecking order. But what the fuck was Pauly thinking?

"So why would Alexei ask me to give Viktor a message at this address?"

"Do not know," the man said. "Time to go."

"Tell these baboons to let me go, I don't need help."

"They will show you the way out."

"I know the way out."

"Not this way out," the man said and I could hear menace

in his tone.

Pauly moaned as his breath escaped in an uncontrollable whoosh, and I understood why the two thugs held onto him. I heard a loud smack, fist against flesh and bone, and knew someone gave Pauly a quick going over. One punch to the stomach, one to the face; not a beating as much as a way to establish who was in charge. Pauly's cell phone made a loud cracking noise as it hit the floor and then all communication between us died.

"Mick, where the fuck are you?"

"Trying not to hit jaywalkers," he sighed.

The club's back door opened. A man stepped out, looked both ways and signaled in the direction I had walked into the alley from. A car came out of nowhere and drove toward the backdoor. I held my Glock and stayed behind the Dumpster as cover.

Two very large men kept a bent-over Pauly from falling in the doorway. The car stopped and the trunk popped open. Not a good sign. The driver got out holding a roll of gray tape. More bad news. Another wet dream gone to hell, thank you, Pauly. I crouched between the Dumpster and wall and brought up the Glock, knowing I'd need to use it. They spoke Russian casually. Maybe this was a nightly occurrence for them.

When I looked toward the door, Pauly stood erect, struggling to free himself. The two thugs fought to keep hold of him. With a speed that surprised me, Pauly kicked his right foot into the knee of the man on his left. The guy had a moment of disbelief and then grabbed toward his leg with both hands as he crumpled to the ground. The guy on the right didn't seem aware of what happened until Pauly's left jab hit him in the throat. He grabbed his neck. Pauly turned the man toward him, hit him in the stomach and as the man bent over, Pauly grabbed his head, brought it down and slammed his knee into the man's face. He crashed to the ground, unconscious.

When the second man fell, both men by the car had drawn their handguns and so had the man with the shattered knee. Pauly quickly took that gun and kicked the man in the head, as I shot the thug standing closest to him. The man from the car looked toward me, which was his mistake because Pauly shot him. Both shots echoed in the alley before the noise from the street swallowed it.

I ran toward Pauly as Mick Murphy backed the SUV down the alley.

"What took you so damn long?" Pauly said. He stood next to the two injured men on the pavement.

I raised my gun and shot both Russians in the head. The reverberating booms sounded louder than before and rang in my ears. We had no time to waste. We had to get out of there.

"I was waiting for Mick." I pointed at the stopped SUV. "We've gotta move. It won't take them long to know where the girls met you. Come on." We rushed toward Mick Murphy, who held the Colt M-4, and the SUV.

I was concerned other Russian thugs might show up in the doorway, more than I worried about the police arriving. The Russians weren't going to call the police and we didn't need a shootout in South Beach.

"Yeah, you're right." Pauly looked back at the two dead men. "Where to?"

"The warehouse. It's safe."

"Man, I've got a comfortable damn suite, how about changing hotels?"

"Die in comfort. Your choice."

Pauly had the beginnings of a black eye.

Chapter Seven

Mick Murphy drove around the jaywalkers and traffic sensibly but fast enough that we were back at the hotel before securing our seat belts.

He parked in the rear lot. I ran up the backstairs with Pauly, and we returned to the SUV in less than five minutes with a suitcase and the second duffel bag. No official checkout. Pauly pulled his Town Car behind the SUV and we were off.

The Russians would put a priority to finding Pauly and now, with four dead bodies in the alley behind their club, they knew he wasn't acting alone.

The drive on I-95 had few cars at four in the morning and we kept up a good speed. There was no time to waste. We dropped off Pauly's belongings inside the warehouse, parked the Town Car, and headed back to South Beach. From the duffel bag, we grabbed two more Colt M-4s and a shitpot full of 30-round magazines. Pauly came prepared. I liked that, but said nothing to the ex-drug smuggler.

We had to be in place when Viktor left and we didn't know what time that was.

"You're sure he was Viktor?" I asked for the tenth time.

"Hell, yeah," Pauly said from the back seat. "He was in charge. No doubt about that and by the look of things in the damn alley . . ." He paused and shook his head. "They wanted to know what I was up to and planned on taking me somewhere to make me talk. Then they'd kill me. Orders like that had to come from that fucker Viktor."

"Putting you in the trunk, it wasn't a good sign." I agreed with his assessment.

"He didn't believe asshole Alexei sent me," Pauly said. "What does that say?"

"He communicates with him, maybe just did," I said. I knew we were getting closer to Alexei. "Describe him again."

"Six-foot, clean-shaven, black hair, and in damn good

shape. Muscular, in his late forties."

"His punches hurt?"

Pauly touched his black eye. "Hell, yeah. He's hit people before. I didn't see it coming, he's that good."

I looked at my watch and it was almost five A.M. "Pauly, you and Mick watch from the parking garage. I'll watch the alley."

"Going back there, is that wise?" Mick Murphy said as he pulled into the parking garage.

"They're looking for us. Won't expect us to be chasing them."

"He could have a reserved spot in the garage," Pauly said. "He's not gonna waste time looking for a damn parking spot every night."

"Mick, check it. His name. The club's name. Then talk to me." Mick Murphy and I put the earpieces back in and went our separate ways. He parked in the same spot of the third level as before. We checked out the front of the Russian club before I left. Nothing.

Pauly was right. Viktor had his black, shiny Beamer in a reserved spot on the first floor. It was almost six when Viktor left the club and crossed the still-busy street to the parking garage. He walked alone and I hadn't expected that.

Mick Murphy picked me up on the corner and we followed the BMW as it got on I-95. He went a short distance but the car didn't bother to slow as it exited the Interstate. We thought he might have made us, but he slowed after the sharp turn and continued into Fort Lauderdale. Maybe he worked off frustration speeding around in his shiny car.

Viktor pulled into the side parking lot of a ten-story building. The first floor held a gym.

"Christ, four of his guys just got killed and he's gonna workout," I said. "What a caring guy." I would've been chasing the killers, but I ain't a Russian mobster.

"No wonder he hits so damn hard," Pauly said as we looked at the large windows that put the people working out in the gym on display.

Viktor walked from the parking lot carrying a gym bag. I looked around and he didn't seem to have any back up. "He's alone," I said.

"Could be meeting them there," Pauly said. "New crew, fresh and alert."

"Or maybe everyone's burying bodies," I said.

"You've got a point." Pauly leaned forward. "Take the son-of-a-bitch here, when he comes out."

"My thoughts exactly. Drive into the parking lot," I said to Mick Murphy." Let's see what we've got."

Parking spots in the lot all had "reserved/gym" stenciled on them. Of thirty spots, twenty had cars in them. Mick Murphy backed the SUV into an empty spot four cars from the Beamer.

"I'll check the gym," I said.

"He'll be in there for a couple of hours," Pauly said before I opened the door. "He's a damn workout freak. Two hours minimum. I know a lot of workout freaks, guys with too much time on their hands."

"Even with all that went down?" I asked.

"Hell, yeah, it's his religion."

I checked the GPS and found a Starbuck's two blocks away and left Pauly and Mick Murphy in the SUV. I was back with three expensive coffees within a half-hour. There were no empty spots in the lot and it wasn't seven A.M. yet.

"Nothing," Pauly said taking his Latte. "At least another hour, trust me."

I began to like him, but I wasn't to the point of trust yet, but he was probably right.

Mick Murphy took his coffee. "How do we do it?"

"Quickly," I said. "Catch him putting the gym bag in the trunk."

"Put him in the Beamer's trunk." Pauly said. "I'll drive and follow you to the warehouse."

"Works for me," I said and sipped my coffee.

"Me too, unless he comes out with someone." Mick Murphy toyed with the M-4, removing the thirty-round magazine and putting it back a few times.

"Then we follow him. Get our chance somewhere else," I said, staring at Mick Murphy, not wanting a shootout in downtown Fort Lauderdale because it would involve the police and then we were really fucked.

We waited in silence and drank our coffee.

At eight, I stood in a doorway close to the gym. At eight-thirty Viktor left, talking on his cell phone. I don't know what he said, he spoke Russian, but his words were hostile and he got louder and angrier before he hung up. I let Mick Murphy know we were heading to the parking lot.

Viktor closed his cell and didn't notice me behind him, he was preoccupied with something. He rushed to the BMW, popped the truck with his keypad just moments before I smashed him on the head with my Glock. He went down but not out.

Mick Murphy and Pauly were on him like a house cat on a mouse. Pauly gave a swift kick to his face. Viktor looked up, his nose bleeding, stunned. He said something in Russian and from the tone, I knew it wasn't a compliment.

"You gonna put me in a trunk, asshole, and then what?" Pauly kicked him again. "Now it's my turn. You go in the trunk."

"We need him alive," Mick Murphy said as Paul was about to kick Viktor again.

Mick Murphy and Pauly forced the dazed Viktor to his feet and tossed him into the trunk without any trouble. I went through the gym bag but found nothing interesting other than his wallet. I took his cell from his pocket.

"No gun?" Pauly said as I tossed the gym bag under the BMW parked next to him.

"No," I said. "But it's Viktor." I held up his driver's license.

"Let's get out of here, now." Pauly looked around. "He ain't alone. Sweet dreams, asshole," he said and closed the trunk. He used the keypad to open the Beamer.

Mick Murphy and I ran to the SUV and headed out of the parking lot. Three men walked from the gym, stared hard at the

Beamer with Pauly driving, and began yelling. One pulled a handgun but his two friends stopped him from shooting. They ran into the parking lot.

I didn't know if we'd have three cars or one following us. "Get lost, quick," I said to Mick Murphy. "They'll be behind us any minute now."

"I-95, right up here, two blocks."

"Step on it." I looked out the back and Pauly tailgated our bumper.

I was beginning to like this ex-drug smuggler. If we made the Interstate before the Russians caught sight of us, we might lose them. If not, we had to avoid the warehouse and prepare for a shootout on I-95. I kept the possibility of it all going to hell to myself. I watched the cars behind Pauly and Mick Murphy held his foot down on the gas. We were rollin'.

Chapter Eight

We moved along on the Interstate at seventy and Pauly stayed less than a car length behind. I watched the on ramp until it was out of sight, but everyone was speeding, so I couldn't tell if anyone followed us or not. I didn't know what car I was looking for anyway.

"Just keep going," I said. "Don't get off for the warehouse."

"Pauly doesn't have his cell." Mick Murphy kept his eyes on the road and signaled lane changes so Pauly would follow when cars or trucks got in his way.

Shit, I forgot that. "He'll follow us. This ain't his first rodeo."

"How far do you want to go?" His eyes jumped to the rearview mirror and then back to the road.

"Sample Road. Get off, turn west and pull into the first gas station."

"And you know this how?" Mick Murphy wondered aloud.

"Too much time on my hands." I didn't like explaining myself, not even to friends, but he knew I wasn't fond of Florida in general, and questioned how I knew my way around. "Surveillance. I always know the territory. You remember Panama City? Always have a couple of exit strategies planned ahead to time." I gave a little and left it for him to fill in the blanks.

"Just in case?" He said and I nodded.

Pauly followed but didn't leave room for another car to get between us. He didn't tailgate because if a bored cop pulled him over, how would he explain a mad Russian in the trunk? Hell, how would he explain driving that mad Russian's car?

He followed us onto the Sample Road exit ramp and into the gas station. We pulled next to the station's automated car wash, stopped and met between cars.

"He making noise?" I wondered about Viktor.

"No. Maybe the asshole's passed out."

"We should've checked the trunk," I said. "He might have

a weapon in there. He had nothing in the gym bag."

"If he's got a damn gun he could be playing possum and waiting for us." Pauly lit a cigarette. "What are we doing?"

I watched the traffic pass the station and carefully eyed the few cars that came in for gas. "Lookin' to see if anyone followed us."

"Those had to be his buddies as we left," Pauly said. "We might've lost them. Gym clothes on, they'd have to dig to get the damn car keys, give us an extra minute or so."

"One of them didn't dig too much to get his gun," Mick Murphy said. "Why didn't he shoot?"

"Viktor," I said. "His friends stopped him. No one wanted to take responsibility for shooting the boss."

"Not finding the asshole alive is one thing," Pauly said, still angry at the thought of Viktor's plans for him. "But trying to explain shooting him is a whole other problem."

I agreed. "Here's the plan. I'm riding with Pauly, that way we can communicate."

"Earpieces?" Mick Murphy asked.

"Cell," I said. "We'll go first. This is the car they're looking for."

"Couldn't we switch him to the SUV?" Pauly stubbed out the cigarette. "Leave the damn Beamer on a side street and not worry about them finding us?"

"What if he's got a gun, or any weapon?" I kept watch on the street and the cars entering. "If we've got to shoot him, here's not the place."

"Good point," Pauly said.

"You're our back up, Mick. Meet at the warehouse," I said.

He nodded.

"Give us five minutes then head south on the Interstate. We'll be too far apart for the earpieces, but if anything happens I'll call."

"If they pull you over somehow?" Mick Murphy, the pessimist, said.

"Come in like the cavalry."

He nodded and a small grin appeared.

In Florida, someone can have three M-4s in the back seat of a car and not worry about anyone caring. Seems that Florida residents love their guns almost as much as Texas residents do. Mick Murphy handed us two M-4s with extra thirty-round magazines. I put them into the back seat of the Beamer. If anyone noticed, they didn't show it.

"Five minutes," I reminded him. "You have any problem, you call."

"Try not to get lost." Mick Murphy walked into the station's convenience store as Pauly and I drove off.

Chapter Nine

The tension in the BMW was obvious as Pauly and I searched the snail-like traffic for would be attackers. Viktor was quiet in the trunk and I thought that maybe Pauly's kick had killed him. Pauly focused on driving. His jittery finger drumming on the steering wheel got on my nerves.

"Norm, I might not be the right guy for this," Pauly said, his eyes on the road.

"For what?" I was seeing the edgy side of the smuggler for the first time.

"You know why I'm an ex-smuggler?" He used a question to answer my question.

"Never crossed my mind?" I lied.

"The damn Mexicans," he said. "I was the best, no shit. Water or air, I was the goddam go to guy and they paid well."

"The Mexicans?"

Pauly nodded. "There was this waterfront warehouse on the east coast of northern Mexico, outside of Tampico," he said slowly. "All the shit was stored there and I'd pick it up in my go-fast or plane." He drummed his fingers on the steering wheel. "There was a small shed off the warehouse." He stopped talking.

"And?"

"They'd interrogate there. Other cartel members." He turned to me and wasn't smiling. "The used electrical drills and saws."

"I've heard."

"I got tired of the screams," he said, eyes back on the rush hour traffic. "The guys who did it, you knew them because of their eyes. Otherwise, they looked like you and me."

"Dead eyes," I said.

"Yeah, that's a good a fuckin' description as any," he said.

"I knew men like that."

"Yeah, well, these fuckers didn't get excited about anything until they had work to do," he said. "Then they'd get all animated and their eyes would blaze. Scared the shit out of me. I didn't want to be around any longer. I left with my last load of coke, said adios, motherfuckers!"

"Pauly, I need you on this," I admitted. "Mick needs you."

He nodded and his damn fingers kept drumming. "I didn't think it would lead to this. I thought we'd locate the guy and . . ." he fumbled for words. "I guess I didn't think too much."

"I'm doing this so Mick doesn't get those dead eyes," I said. "I don't want him to crossover that edge, and he ain't too far off. I'm not enjoying any of this. I wanna do it and get it over with."

I'm not the kind of guy who'd put his heart on his sleeve, so I didn't tell Pauly how I'd been in too many small sheds or been the cause of people's deaths, sometimes finding out afterward that they were innocent. I know what it killed in me, and I didn't want Mick Murphy, the one friend I've kept close over the years, to die inside, not even a little bit, and it had already begun.

"How long will it take?"

"I doubt I can control Mick for more than a day or two," I said. "With your help, maybe three days. I've got to be brutal, Pauly, to break this guy. Time ain't on my side."

"I'll help as long as I can take it, but I ain't cut out for this shit!" His words came out harsh. "I'll keep at it as long as I can, for Mick."

"I know I'm not cut out for it, either. I'm in it to help Mick, too," I said as we pulled up to the warehouse and remembered the screams I'd heard from small sheds in the jungles of Central America.

As I opened the roll-up door at the warehouse so Pauly could drive the Beamer inside and out of sight, Mick Murphy pulled in. Less than five minutes, which meant he sped. I didn't like that, he was in too much of a hurry. People in a hurry miss things. In this game, you can't afford the luxury of Monday morning quarterbacking.

Inside, the body and chair were gone. In fact, there was a new chair. A lingering smell of bleach covered the floor where blood had puddled, the burnt-brown stain it left gone. The cleaner had done a good job, but I expected that.

Pauly gazed around the large warehouse interior. "Safe?" He lit a cigarette.

"Yeah," I said, knowing he understood this was a safe house.

Off to one corner Pauly's stare stopped for a moment at a six-foot square holding cage, fenced on four sides and on top. Opposite the cage, against another wall, a small interrogation closet where a prisoner could only stand erect and a small storeroom took up space and didn't require a long stare. There wasn't much in the storeroom, but I had built a waterboarding platform and it was in there with towels, buckets and two garden hoses, Mick Murphy's cut-up hose and the other for the waterboarding, and a few uncomfortable cots for sleeping. If we had time to sleep, being uncomfortable wasn't important. Overhead lights dimly lit the large space and black-tinted windows kept out the daylight and prying eyes.

The bathroom and shower took up a small space at the other end of the warehouse and an office setup of sorts, an empty desk and chair, were there too, in the open, no walls. A picnic bench and an old refrigerator sat a few feet from the desk. To avoid possible detection by those searching for safe house residents, there was no communication equipment anywhere in the warehouse. Any safe house I've ever used, you brought what you needed or went without. It kept things simple, when everything around was chaotic. Simple. Safe.

Now, added to the interior with Pauly's Town Car was the shiny BMW.

"How do you want to do this shit?" Pauly said after finishing his onceover scan of the surroundings.

"We want him alive," Mick Murphy spoke before I could answer.

"That's the plan," I said without mentioning how plans fuck up. "You got the clicker, right?"

Pauly held it in his hands and showed me. He crushed out

the cigarette on the cement floor.

"Mick, stay to the right, I'm to the left and Pauly stand center. Use the clicker to open the trunk," I said. "If he comes out shooting . . ."

"Damn it," Mick Murphy said, and banged on the trunk. Viktor banged back. "You want out?"

"Yeah," he said.

I shook my head, upset with Mick Murphy's blindness to the possible seriousness of the situation. Why had he been so quiet during the ride? If Viktor had a gun, he could kill one of us before we killed him. Pauly and I took up our positions.

"We gotta talk, Mick," I said. "He could be armed, so be alert."

He nodded his head and frowned like a spoiled child as he arched his shoulders. "If you kill him, he can't talk."

"If he's got a weapon, he's a dead man," I answered. "Just be careful."

Pauly and I held our guns at the ready while Mick Murphy held his down along his side, not wanting to shoot. Pauly pushed the release button and we heard the trunk unlock. Viktor opened it with his knees. Blood, the result of Pauly's kicks, covered the front of his sweatsuit and his swollen nose gave him a clownish look. Both his eyes were purple, turning black due to his broken nose. It had to be painful. He'd used his sleeve to wipe his face, but streaks of dried blood smeared across his cheeks and chin. He needed a shave, but wouldn't get it here.

A black eye for a black eye; I saw Pauly smirk as he stared at Victor.

I watched Viktor's hands when he began to climb out. Damn Russian, he acted as if getting in and out of a trunk was something he did daily. He was cold, calculating and dangerous, with or without a gun. Viktor stood up, no weapon in view, leaned against the Beamer and gave us each a stare. His creepy smirk concerned me.

Viktor looked at Pauly. "You! What do you want?" He glanced at Mick Murphy and then glared at me. "Do you know who I am?"

I nodded and gave a roguish smile of my own.

"I leave now and maybe you are not dead man," he said, never losing the malicious grin.

"I've been a dead man walking for a long time," I said.

"You answer my questions and maybe you're not a dead man," Mick Murphy lied and caught Viktor's attention.

"No questions, no answers," he countered.

"Game's over, Viktor," I said and got his attention back to me. I raised my gun. "Strip down."

Viktor gave us each another quick, appraising look. If he had a weapon, it was time to use it. Nothing. Cocky son-of-a-bitch thought he was untouchable. That left him unprepared. He stood on the other side of the gun this time and he knew the routine.

"Strip," I yelled.

He shook his head slowly because the swollen nose hurt.

I grabbed my Glock by the barrel and took a step toward him. He stood his ground, eyes darting about looking for an alternative. There was none.

Slowly he pulled off the bloody top, careful not to put pressure against his nose. I could picture his mind working, looking for a solution, an escape.

"What do you want?" He dropped the top on the floor. "This is not necessary. You do not know who I am. You want money? I got money. Name price."

I pointed toward his pants.

"Not money? You want to know something. Maybe I tell you and go away." He smirked, keeping his attention on me. "Ask me."

"Pants," I said.

When you interrogate someone, having them naked takes away more than their clothes, it strips them of their dignity and leaves them feeling vulnerable. It creates a feeling of failure and has a terrorizing effect on a prisoner. Naked, a captive feels helpless and usually breaks easily.

Viktor knew this, as I would if the situation was reversed,

and his mind had to be searching for possible ways to avoid the inevitable. He looked for ways to escape, maybe even to die quickly. If he lunged toward Pauly, Viktor would be dead. Mick Murphy would fight with him and I would try to shoot him in the leg. He didn't know this, but he wondered.

He dropped his pants.

"Tennis shoes," I said.

He used his feet to remove them. "You pay for this. Slowly," he said.

"Shorts."

Viktor scowled. "This is not necessary, we talk, agree on something. You do not know who will revenge me."

I shook my head and pointed the gun at his underwear.

He removed the baby-blue jockey shorts.

I walked to him as he faced me and I used heavy duty, military-issued tie wraps to secure his hands. I felt his strength as he put pressure against the tightened restraints.

"What do you want?" he yelled. He was feeling defenseless. "You do not want to do this."

"Alexei," Mick Murphy said as he walked up to where I was standing. "Where is Alexei?"

He looked over his shoulder toward Mick Murphy. "Alexei?" He laughed. "You do not want Alexei. You find Alexei, he wants you to be dead man."

I looked at Pauly. I needed him to keep an eye on Mick Murphy and our prisoner. Both posed potential though different problems. It was too soon for the cleaner to come back. Pauly nodded.

From the back of the SUV, I took a black hood, opened it fully, and walked up behind Viktor and slipped it over his head. He shook his head repeatedly trying to make the hood fall off. I pulled the hood's tie strings tight against his throat. Victor moaned because of the pressure on his broken nose.

Chapter Ten

The hood took away Viktor's sight. He was helpless, hands restrained, as he stood naked, and anxious. He had only his hearing left for evaluating the seriousness of his situation. He knew enemies surrounded him in a strange location and little else. Sounds that were explainable when seen would now leave him confused and uneasy. In most cases, that confusion in prisoners turns to instability and fear. That's what I hoped for. Would it get Mick Murphy the answers he wanted before his interrogation of Viktor began? I hoped for that too.

No doubt, Viktor had been the aggressor in these kinds of situations before, so that added to his torment. He would recall what he had been proficient at and assume that was what lay ahead. I'm sure he was capable of more brutality than I could conjure up, but then again, maybe not.

Viktor knew this would end in his death. The sooner the better for me and, for other reasons, for him too. Quick was better than painful. I didn't want to let Mick Murphy beat him, torture him like the earlier victim, because I feared he was going to cross the line and become something he had always fought against as a journalist. Revenge is a lethal drug and Mick Murphy had the first signs of addiction.

Viktor's KGB training included tactics to withstand waterboarding and other tortures, as had mine. That concerned me.

However, in the end, there are no tactics that worked other than premature death. Time is on the side of the torturer. It wasn't a promising scenario unless Viktor had a fear of drowning. The longer he held out, the less control I had of Mick Murphy. Time was not a luxury I had.

I brought out the waterboarding equipment and passed the garden hose to Pauly. "Attach this over there." I pointed to a water spigot against the wall and raised my finger to my lips, to keep Pauly and Mick Murphy from talking.

Viktor's fear should've been getting the best of him, because I could've been talking about plugging in a battery charger.

That would be in his game plan, no doubt. The KGB always wanted a speedy conclusion and electrical torture got that.

I lay the board down and put an eighteen-inch block of wood at the end to keep Viktor's feet higher than his head. Pauly walked back with the hose. I saw the concern on his face as he handed it to me.

I motioned Mick Murphy and Pauly to meet me away from where Viktor might overhear us. "We'll have to force him down. Hard and fast," I whispered. "The harder we are, the more frightened he'll be."

They nodded.

"I'll kick his legs out from under him and you two force him onto the board. It could get difficult," I said. "Hold him down and I'll put the strap around him."

"Will it hold?" Pauly said, giving me an edgy stare. "He's a strong son of a bitch, Norm."

"There's rope in the SUV, if we need more restraints."

"Why not use the chair?" Mick Murphy whispered. "It worked before."

"Did it?" I said. "Really, Mick? We got Viktor because of the guy's cell phone, not because of your beating him."

Mick Murphy moved away without saying more. He got on one side of Viktor and Pauly the other. I hoped he got my meaning. I doubted it.

That Viktor stood without speaking surprised me. Usually, silence brought concern to the prisoner. They nervously asked questions, kept talking, and their captor's silence added to their anxiety. Viktor had discipline.

I kicked the back of Viktor's knees hard and as he collapsed, Mick Murphy and Pauly forced him onto the board. He fought them because that's what his training had taught him to do. His nakedness, his vulnerability, and his lack of sight set aside, his survival instinct kicked in. Mick Murphy placed a knee on Viktor's chest and Pauly used two hands to keep his shoulder down. I pulled the restraining belt as tight as I could across his chest and it forced his arms up tight on his stomach.

"What?" he screamed. "What you do?" He squirmed like a trussed hog.

I put my finger to my lips, again, and no one answered. I pointed at Pauly to stay close to Viktor. Mick Murphy came with me. No one spoke as I filled six, two-gallon buckets with water.

I put the towels in the bucket and when they were soaked took two out and tossed them onto the hood over Viktor's head. He continued to squirm. The pressure of the wet towels must have hurt his broken nose.

"What?" he yelled. "Talk to me!"

I pointed to Viktor's legs. Pauly went and held onto them. I began to pour water onto the towels, slowly at first. Viktor shook his head violently, hoping to avoid the water. It only took moments for him to begin gagging.

Waterboarding simulates drowning. As the water flows over the hooded prisoner's head, into the towels, the first reaction is to stop breathing, to hold your breath. The towels slowed the water but also kept the area moist, frightening the victim as water slowly continued to trickle after the initial flooding. The prisoner closes his mouth, but he can't close his nose, and water begins to enter the lungs and he gags, spitting it out into the hood, as best he can. It's not unheard of for a prisoner to drown during waterboarding. I used the buckets so I could control the amount of water. Others I know would rather use the hose, but it presents the possibility of using too much water and I didn't want to lose Viktor, not just yet.

After the first two-gallons of water, I waited a long minute and began the procedure again, all the while not saying anything. Silence allowed the victim's thoughts of his own mortality to go uninterrupted.

Each time Viktor tried to speak, he gagged, even after I stopped pouring water. The soaked towels dripped water onto his face and with each drop, his head moved in an effort to avoid what he thought would follow.

It was time for Viktor to hear a question. Pauly continued to hold his legs. I mouthed short and put my palms close together and hoped Mick Murphy understood the sign. Conversation, even angry conversation, would help Viktor escape the isolation he had to be feeling.

"Alexei!" Mick Murphy yelled.

Viktor shook his head. Did he refuse to answer or did he try to avoid dripping water? I couldn't tell. It didn't matter. What did matter, what concerned me was he might withstand a few waterboarding attempts. I didn't have the luxury of days to interrogate him.

"Alexei and this stops," Mick Murphy yelled again.

I lifted another bucket and motioned Mick Murphy to stop. He pulled back. I began to pour a steady stream of water onto the towels. Viktor gagged. I wanted him to answer, because the next procedure was the closet and as bad as waterboarding is, the closet seemed crueler.

Chapter Eleven

I'd finished waterboarding Viktor. He choked, retched, shook violently, but did not answer questions. His KGB training had prepared him well. I now faced the dilemma of what came next. I knew it had to be the closet and if that didn't work, I had no more wizardry in my bag of tricks to keep Mick Murphy from taking over the interrogation.

We left Viktor secured to the plank so he could worry about what was coming next, and sat at the table, taking our first break in hours. Pauly chain-smoked. He looked relieved for the time off, but his side-glances during the waterboarding told me Pauly had almost reached his breaking point.

"I'm hungry," Mick Murphy said, and looked at his wristwatch.

We hadn't eaten in more than twenty-four hours. In the past weeks, he never seemed to care about food, so why now?

"For what?" I said.

"When did we last eat, Norm?"

"Forever ago, Mick," I said. "There's the fast food joints down the road."

"Chicken or pizza?" He looked at Pauly.

"I don't care." Pauly stubbed out his umpteenth cigarette in a Styrofoam cup. "We need bottled water and a couple of packs of smokes. The hose water tastes like warm piss."

"A pizza, chicken, cigarettes, and water," Mick Murphy recounted as he stood. "I'll go."

"Come right back." It concerned me when he was on his own. "This ain't over."

"Not by a long shot." He almost laughed as he walked away.

I'd seen a small change in Mick Murphy since Pauly's arrival. A good change. That he had shown concern for Pauly's safety inside the Russian's club surprised me. Up until then, he had no concern for anyone's safety, including his own.

It could be that Pauly brought that Key West latitude with

him – that mystical line on nautical charts that brings with it an attitude adjustment to slow down, lie back, relax and enjoy yourself. Once that latitude hoodwinked you into being a believer, it was hard to lose it and it seemed to go with you wherever you went. I didn't understand the attraction, but I knew it existed.

Mick Murphy and I go back a long time to Central American revolutions and Mexican cartels. Good times in bad situations, if I recall correctly. He didn't connect me to his island paradise. Instead, he connected me to violence with a wide-range of latitudes, none of them relaxed or fun. By being there, I offered him a comfort zone. With me, he had bad times to remember and no need to consider anything else. The evil we witnessed and sometimes participated in, brought him a gruesome form of support for what he was doing now.

Pauly, on the other hand, brought memories of exciting adventures in paradise, on the water, fooling corrupt Bahamian customs officials, cold beer at waterfront bars, rainy afternoons in Key West that made you lazy and even hurricane parties that helped take the fright out of howling winds.

I saw the change in Mick Murphy's expression when he caught Pauly watching him during the waterboarding. The smile, the smug look of satisfaction disappeared from his face because Pauly was there.

Two days before, the three-foot piece of rubber hose Mick Murphy held in his hand fanned the embers in his eyes, and it grew in intensity each time he struck the victim. Embers of hate grew with each blow and he enjoyed it. I saw it again as the Russians died in the alley.

The fact that he at least tried to hide this fire of hatred and pleasure from Pauly gave me hope that it was extinguishable. Take what you can when it's offered, is my opinion, and I'd grasp at straws as long there was hope mixed in with it that Mick Murphy hadn't fallen into the abyss. Yet. He's my friend; I couldn't stand by and do nothing.

"Pauly, you gonna be okay?" I watched him smoke another cigarette.

"Yeah," he said without too much enthusiasm. "How much longer before the asshole breaks?"

"I'm gonna put him in the closet," I said and Pauly frowned. "I've got a psychedelic mixture to shoot him up with."

"What will that shit do?"

"He'll see Timothy Leary, for one thing." My joke didn't make Pauly smile. "It should speed things along, make him confused and lose control of time. All to our advantage, I hope."

"I can't believe the fucker hasn't broke." He put the cigarette out and lit another. "I would've. For chrissake, what's wrong with him?"

"His training, it prepared him for this," I said. "Alexei will be tougher."

"Will you get a chance to find out?"

"I doubt it."

Pauly nodded. "Let's move him to the closet and get this shit over with."

I took the syringe from the bag in the desk drawer. "He'll pass out or be sluggish right away," I said. "We've got about three minutes to get him in place. When the juice kicks in, he'll be a wild man, seeing things in his head that he can't believe on his magical mystery tour."

Pauly stubbed out the cigarette. "Ready when you are." He walked with me toward Viktor, ignoring my attempt at gallows humor.

Chapter Twelve

Mick Murphy called as he pulled into the parking lot and asked me to open the door, his hands were full. I unlocked the security bolt. He walked in, almost smiling, and I took the pizza box. His expression changed quickly from relaxed to angry as he saw that the waterboarding plank lay empty on the floor, the black hood on top of it. He turned to me, his hands holding four plastic bags from the fast-food place and Quick-Mart down the road.

"I moved him, hoss," I said and looked toward the closet. "Next step."

"I hope it works, Norm." The words were cold and challenging. He placed the bags on the table. He handed Pauly a carton of cigarettes and a grin came to his mouth.

"Thanks." Pauly tore open the carton and a package of cigarettes, then lit a new one. He sucked down half a bottle of warm water. "Shit, should've told you to bring ice too."

"Sorry." Mick Murphy apologizing? What a swing in attitudes. "Where are we?" He nodded toward the closet and took a slice of pizza, his expression still cold.

Pauly nibbled on a chicken leg, but never finished it. He lit a second cigarette and drained the bottle of water.

As we ate, I explained about using the LSD mixture on Viktor. Mick Murphy nodded his approval as he took a third slice of pizza.

Pauly went to the bathroom and we could hear him vomit.

"You okay?" Mick Murphy asked as Pauly walked back.

"Damn Russian steaks," he said and gave us a weak laugh. "I think the fuckers poisoned me." His stare fell briefly on me and I understood he was close to his limit.

"We're all tired," I said. "But so is Viktor."

"Great observation, Norm, but how's that get us closer to finding Alexei?"

I motioned Mick Murphy to follow me. A large cabinet hung on one of the closet's walls. Inside, a flat screen television sat next to an array of smaller panels and switches. I took the TV remote and turned it on.

"Closed circuit," I said. A grainy, black-and-white image of Viktor came onto the screen.

The hood was gone and Viktor remained naked. A line attached to his tie-wrapped wrists went through an eyehook on the ceiling, then tied off to a cleat by the doorway, and raised his arm above his head. He stood on a small box. His body shook, his head moved and we saw his mouth open and close. I left the sound muted. We couldn't hear his screams.

"He's on his trip," I said. "In an hour or so he'll calm down." I pointed to a small mike attached to the cabinet wall. "We can ask questions without going inside."

"Lights are off?" Mick Murphy said.

"A small red light is on. The walls are soundproofed and covered with tin."

"Why the tin?" Pauly asked.

"I can make the room cold or hot." I pointed at the thermostat. "The tin holds heat or cold, so if he tries to relieve the pressure on his shoulders and lean against the wall, it hurts just as bad. He should feel hopeless in a couple of hours. Do anything, say anything to stop the pain."

"Do you think he'll talk then?" Mick Murphy asked. "The waterboarding would've broke me." He shook his head, not understanding why it didn't break Viktor.

"He's been trained to withstand torture," I said. "But the body can only withstand so much. The KGB, hell, the CIA and all intelligence agencies know that, but the training gives agents confidence. Everyone talks or dies."

"Why are we waiting?"

I turned the thermostat to heat and moved the dial to ninety degrees. I took a cool soda from the six-pack and drank it. I checked the time. In a few minutes, the room would feel like an oven.

"He's on a trip to hell and in an hour the room would be just as hot," I said. "Let's get some rest." I pointed toward Pauly. His head lay on the table, he snored, as he slept. "We all need it. A little is better than none."

Mick Murphy pulled the cots out of storage without saying another word. He lay down and I did too. We left Pauly alone. I wouldn't sleep. I was too afraid of failing.

Chapter Thirteen

The smell of Pauly's cigarette smoke woke me. Mick Murphy tossed and turned on his cot. Nightmares, how restful can that be? I sat up. Pauly nodded. I nodded back.

"Didn't want to wake you," I said, explaining to Pauly why we let him sleep with his head on the table. I checked my wristwatch. Almost an hour had passed.

"Couldn't sleep, anyway." He coughed, making that hacking sound that longtime smokers do when trying to clear their lungs. "Nightmares about Mexico."

"Sorry about this shit," I said. I was sorry for all of us.

"I love Mexico, it's a beautiful country." His words carried sadness with them, as he crushed the cigarette in the already full-of-butts-and-ash Styrofoam cup. "You know, the beaches, the pyramids, the food, the people. They're great."

"Yeah," I said, but didn't agree. Too hot, too crowded. I wanted a taste of Mexico I went to downtown LA. Good tacos sold by street vendors and no need to cross a border. Downtown LA is Mexico City, only smaller, but just as crowded and hot, with a lot fewer gringos. Hell, if I wanted to spend time in a Third-World country with chickens running loose on potholed streets, I'd go to Key West. No border checks and lots of chickens.

"If I never get there again, it'll be too soon." A thin smile formed on Pauly's lips. "Chrissake, what they do to each other is terrifying." He lit a cigarette, took a hit and then held it between his fingers and watched it burn. He was quiet for a long, uncomfortable moment. Confession might be good for the soul, but it's tough on the confessor.

"The last time . . . I picked up a shipment . . . they held half dozen gunmen from another cartel . . ." He stared at the smoke swirl from the cigarette, chasing his thoughts. "I heard the whine of the chainsaw and then the screaming . . . fuck." He dumped the butt into the cup. "I was getting ready to leave and the assholes came by with a trash bag of heads . . . blood dripping from it . . . wanted to show them to me. Why the fuck would I wanna see them? I took off, made the drop and I've never been back."

"Probably a smart move." I understood the ex-smuggler a little better, now. I've witnessed horrific acts on the job, but never walked away. Wanted to, but couldn't.

"Yeah, I guess," he answered without looking at me.

"Pauly, you can leave," I said. "No reason for you to sit through this." The brutality between the drug cartels increased as the profit margins rose and that profit ratio expanded the competition. A vicious, unending circle. "It's all downhill from here. Mick and I can handle it."

"Bullshit, Norm," he said. "If the asshole doesn't talk, you'll need help. Mick's ready to go over the edge, you were right about that."

"All I'm saying is the doors aren't locked, Pauly."

"Thanks. I appreciate it." As he stood, he lit another cigarette. "What's next?"

We walked to the closet wall and I switched on the TV. A grainy image of Viktor in the dark came onto the screen. I turned the lights up and a harsh glare filled the small area. Viktor squinted into the brightness, his naked body shiny with sweat.

"Tell me where Alexei is and I have cold water for you," I said into the mike.

Viktor looked up, as if there were a window and he could see us, and slowly shook his head.

I turned the lights up full and the brightness almost washed out the TV picture. I changed the thermostat to fifty-five degrees. A posted list on the wall indicated sound effects and had numbers next to it that matched numbers on the dial above it. I chose Cats Fighting and turned the dial to number four. A screeching noise filled the room, forcing Viktor to look around the best he could. He was tired and slow. I muted the sound for us, left it ear piercing for Viktor, and walked away.

"How long?" Pauly asked. He dropped his cigarette on the concrete floor and stepped on it.

Mick Murphy sat up and shook the weariness from his

head.

"Fifteen minutes," I said.

"Then what?" Mick Murphy had been watching. He stood and stretched.

"Then we approach him again."

"And if he doesn't talk?"

"He's hot. In a few minutes he's gonna be cold. The light's blinding him, the LSD is in his system and with the cat-fighting noise, he'll be tripping again," I said. "Hard to think rationally with all that happening in your head. It's gonna add to his confusion. The past hour he's been tripping and lost track of time. Right now, his life is full of pain. We'll find out how long he can take it in fifteen minutes."

"All this isn't going to kill him, is it Norm?" Mick Murphy took a bottle of water and drank. "I don't want him dead, yet."

"Let me do my job, Mick, like you promised," I said. "Remember?"

"Yeah," he said. "You feel any better?" He turned to Pauly.

"Some," Pauly lied. "Tired, hungry for real food." He opened a new package of cigarettes and lit one. "I think I want this over with more than you do."

"I doubt that," Mick Murphy said and finished the water. "Fifteen minutes, Norm?"

"Yeah, I'll keep making changes of the sounds and temperatures every fifteen minutes, if needed," I said. "I told Pauly he could go back to Key West. Whatever comes next, we can handle."

Mick Murphy gave me a puzzled look and turned to Pauly. "You going?"

"Not just yet," he said, exhaling smoke.

I drank a bottle of water and went to the restroom to relieve myself and throw cold water on my face. The man looking back at me in the mirror was older than I remembered and tired. He wasn't impressive.

We walked to the closet wall. The TV had an almost

washed-out-image of Viktor shaking from the cold like a side of beef that still had life in it. I unmuted the TV sound and the loud screeching of fighting cats deafened us. I turned the sound track off and lowered the intensity of the light.

"A blanket and something warm to drink," I said into the mike. "Where is Alexei?"

"Alexei . . ." Viktor mumbled as he moved his head from side to side, dodging something only he could see. "Alexei . . . where is . . . Alexei?" His head kept bobbing. "No," he shouted at whatever moved inside his head.

Then he began babbling in Russian. He moved his shackled hands and moaned, screamed from the pain it caused. He gave an insane laugh and stopped.

"He tripping?" Mick Murphy asked.

"My guess," I said. "Alexei. Where is Alexei?" I spoke into the mike and heard my words come back at me from the TV. "Tell us where Alexei is and it will get warm. The images will go away."

Pauly had stepped back, turned away and crushed his cigarette on the floor.

"Never tried LSD." Mick Murphy stared at the TV screen.

"Lucky you," I said.

"A little grass in college," he confessed. "But I'm Irish. I've got enough problems controlling John Jameson, I don't need another addiction."

"That's how we keep the Irish from ruling the world," I said but didn't get any reaction from him. "Jameson's, Guinness, Harp."

"Yeah, Norm, I get it," he said. "God created liquor to keep the Irish from ruling the world."

Viktor's slurred words came out of the TV speakers. He spoke in Spanish, which surprised me and got Pauly's attention.

"What the fuck?" Pauly walked back to us.

"Listen. See if we can make out what he's saying," I said. "Maybe he thinks he's back in Cuba with the KGB."

Viktor swayed like a marionette and mumbled more Spanish between howls of pain.

"Tampico . . . alto . . . Tampico . . . alto . . . Alexei . . ." Viktor got our attention and then went into Russian or gibberish or something we couldn't understand.

"Stop Tampico?" I said, translating the Spanish.

"Tampico Alto is a city south of Tampico," Pauly said. "My last run was in that area." He frowned at the memory and shot me a quick look. "Alto also means upper or higher in this case."

"Is Alexei in Tampico Alto?" I turned the thermostat to seventy-five and lowered the intensity of the light as I spoke into the mike. "Is that where Alexei is"

"Tampico . . . alto . . . Iraní . . . Iraní . . . traficante . . ." Viktor slurred the words.

"You know what he said?" Pauly lit a cigarette. "Damn it."

"What's wrong?" I said, trying to put meaning to the words.

"Alexei is in Tampico Alto meeting Mexican and Iranian drug traffickers." Pauly exhaled smoke. "Or something to that effect."

"Christ," I moaned. "We need that like we need another Russian gang on our asses."

"He didn't say that, did he?" Mick Murphy said. He grabbed the mike from my hand. "Is Alexei in Tampico?"

Viktor's body shook, even though the heat was on. He laughed like a mad man with a secret in his head that only he knew and then went back to Russian gibberish.

"Mick, you have to read between the lines," I said, taking the mike back.

"How do you connect all that shit?"

"Mexico and drug traffickers are logical. Alexei wanting drugs, it makes sense he'd deal with Mexican cartels," I said.

"Where do the Iranians come in?" he said.

"That's the scary part, Mick," Pauly said, his back to the closet wall. "Iranians have been dealing with the cartels for years.

What better way to sneak a terror cell into the country? They've got tunnels dug under the border, a great way to move drugs or people."

"Alexei and terrorists, it's a possibility," I said. "A scary one, with his reputation of getting things done."

"We have to go to Tampico," Mick Murphy said. "Right now, before Alexei leaves."

Pauly looked at me, there was no excitement in his expression only dread.

"What if it's a trick or he's delusional?" I said. "Give me more time."

Mick Murphy paced. "Pauly, do you think it's possible? Alexei's in Tampico?"

"Sure it's possible," Pauly answered. "He's a crime boss and there's profit in drugs and people smuggling. Especially terrorists. I think it would be big money, 'cause he's got no political cause he's fighting for. But Norm's got a point too, it might be a trick. More time isn't a bad idea."

"It's a lead Norm," he turned to me, ignoring Pauly.

"You want to follow it?" It was a flawed lead because it came during the early stages of interrogation. Victims tell interrogators what they want to hear, to stop the abuses. Viktor might be playing games, but following the lead would put an end to what we were doing and I didn't think we'd ever get close to Alexei anyway.

"Bet your ass I do."

"Let me make some calls and see what I can arrange, okay?"

"Yeah, yeah, great," Mick Murphy said.

"Let me make a call first," Pauly said walking to the table. "I got a person or two in Tampico that will still talk to me."

"You sure?" I said.

Pauly turned to me and he wasn't smiling. "No I'm not sure, but I can get this over quicker than you can." He gave a hard stare toward Mick Murphy. "If any Russians are there, my contact will know. And, Mick, Russian doesn't mean it's Alexei."

"Yes, it does." Mick Murphy rubbed his hands together barely about to contain his excitement.

Pauly looked at me and shuddered.

Chapter Fourteen

Inside, the closet reeked of muck and urine. I expected a violent reaction, a hardness to Viktor's attitude, as I cautiously lowered him into a folding chair. His submissive behavior surprised and disappointed me.

Viktor's hands remained tie wrapped and attached to the cable that raised him, but I allowed him a limited amount of arm movement. He drank quickly from the bottle of water I gave him. Too quickly. He should've sipped it. He could get stomach cramps from gulping the water so fast. But, of course, that probably didn't seem too important to him.

I don't know if his eyes had adjusted to the light or not, but he stared in my direction with a vacant look. I wondered if he'd given up hope. The often-touted KGB training hadn't worked too well, if he broke so soon. Or maybe he wasn't such a tough guy on the other side of the gun.

"Do you want more water?" I said. He shook his head.

I left the room and sensed his stare on my back. I felt lucky it was only that and not a knife or bullet.

Mick Murphy and Pauly cleaned up the trash. I closed the door to the TV wall.

"What about the Beamer?" Pauly said.

"Leave the keys in it. Breakdown the M-4s and take them with you."

Pauly nodded. "I need to make that call, Norm."

"Yeah, we both need to make calls," I said. "But not here. Let's go somewhere else."

"Where to?" He was as anxious as I was to get away.

I looked at Mick Murphy and wanted to take him back to Key West, but knew he wouldn't agree to go. Not yet. "We gotta get you out of here."

I checked the time, it was almost six P.M. We were tired. Mick Murphy ran on an adrenaline rush of revenge, for the time being. How long before he'd crash for a long needed sleep? He thought we were getting closer to Alexei and that kept him going.

I wasn't sure, but stranger things had happened. It would be damn good luck on his part, if Alexei were there. Maybe there's some truth to Mick Murphy's spouting: *God loves drunks, fools and Irishmen*. He's batting a thousand, if that's true.

The possibility of finding Alexei gave another reason for us to get a good night's sleep before making a decision on what to do. Getting close to Alexei had similarities to the Celtic Banshee wail. They both implicated death.

Pauly had an excuse for not wanting to return to Tampico Alto. I thought that counted him out, leaving Mick Murphy and me to find a way to the Mexican port city.

"We need to check out of the hotel," I said.

"They've probably got some asshole watching it," Pauly said.

"They've got people everywhere looking for Viktor and you," I said. "Best thing is get out of town as fast as you can. Did you give your plate number at the hotel?"

"No," Pauly said. "I didn't use my real name either, but they've got me on the security camera."

"The Russians know you from the club, so fuck the camera," I said. "Get on the turnpike and head home."

"Meet you in Key West?"

Mick Murphy turned to us. "No! We don't need to go there. We need to get to Tampico."

I ignored his outburst. "Turnpike ends in Florida City. Choose a hotel and call us. Book us a double room."

"About two hours," Pauly said.

"We should be there an hour after you, no later," I said. "There's a Mexican restaurant as you get off the Turnpike, make a right at the light."

"Rosita's?"

"Yeah, you been there?"

"A few times."

"Get the rooms and we'll meet you at Rosita's about nine," I said. "Okay?"

"If I can go that damn long without eating, Norm." Pauly

never asked about Viktor's fate.

We were ready to go. I opened the roll-up door so Pauly could move his car.

"I'll start the SUV," Mick Murphy said as Pauly drove away. "Ready?"

"Get the A/C running and I'll be there."

He left the warehouse without replying.

I opened the closet door. The stench seemed worse. Viktor looked at me. His eyes had adjusted to the light, and contempt had replaced his blank expression.

"You will pay," he growled the words as I walked behind him. "Alexei, my avenging angel." He accepted his fate, and didn't beg. He showed his anger, his defiance. It was all that he had left.

"We all pay in the end, Viktor." I shot him in the back of the head with the twenty-two semi-automatic, and the report vibrated loudly in the small room. I picked up the shell casing while the small bullet bounced around his brain, turning off the switch to life.

I shut the closet door behind me. "SoFlo fifteen," I said when my cell phone call was answered. "Moving out and need a spring cleaning." I hung up, wiped my prints off the semi-automatic and placed it on the table where the cleaner would find it.

Outside, Murphy had the A/C on in the SUV, but kept his door open and let the heat in. He enjoyed his own hell. The fiery sun lounged in the sky, not ready to set, and the humidity was high. I wanted to sleep. What I needed was very hot Mexican *salsa* and a few cold Bohemia beers to wash away the bile in my throat and loosen the knot in my stomach.

Chapter Fifteen

Mick Murphy took Pauly's duffle bag of weapons and our rolling pieces of luggage from the hotel room to the SUV, while I checked out. I didn't see a menacing Russian loitering in the lobby, but knew someone, somewhere, observed those that came and went.

The Russians would never find Viktor's body and after a while, there'd be an in-house fight to impress Alexei, to see who'd replace him. That change wouldn't bring Pauly any escape from the Russians; they would always be on the lookout for the shaggy-haired American, trying to put a name to the images they had from security camera footage.

And Viktor was right, if they found Pauly, his fate would go a lot worse than Viktor's, but with the same result. A bullet in the head wasn't necessarily the Russians' means to closing an interrogation. Pauly realized this and that he stayed, amazed me. I never thought I'd respect the ex-smuggler, but I'd been wrong.

Mick Murphy peppered me with questions about Tampico and Tampico Alto on the ride to Florida City. Neither of us had spent much time there. We didn't know the local government's politics, or what influences the cartel had with the cities. An international airport and a Mexican navy base were on the outskirts, we knew that, and it was close to the Gulf coast and a few large lakes. Pauly knew the underbelly of the city and that knowledge was good enough reason not to return. *Los Zetas* ran the drug trade and that was another good reason not to go. The *Los Zetas* drug cartel is made up of deserters from the Mexican Special Forces and its trademark is brutality. Pauly had witnessed the brutality firsthand.

His "what if" questions were annoying, but Mick Murphy's frenzied high was in full throttle. He could smell Alexei and I was hesitant to break his bubble. My call to the Agency would fill in the gaps, but I left it unsaid because I didn't want to give him more encouragement or end the enthusiasm until I had facts.

I found it easier to say, "I don't know," to his laundry list of questions. After dinner, I hoped his manic high would crash and he'd sleep. I know I wanted to.

Pauly waited at Rosita's for us. He drank a cold beer, and ate *salsa* and chips that were on the table, as we walked in. It was dark now. The sun had set but forgot to take the humidity with it. I ordered three beers as the young Latina brought menus.

"No problems?" I looked over the menu.

"Not even fuckin' traffic, Norm," Pauly said. Away from the warehouse, his mood had improved.

We finished the plate of chips and bowl of *salsa* before the waitress returned. We ordered our meals and another round of everything.

"Florida Keys Motel, down US1, on the right." Pauly gave us key cards for the room. He couldn't smoke in the restaurant so the beer and chips kept his hands busy. "A new place. Big rooms. Booked in as Casey and Youngblood."

The waitress smiled as she delivered our beers and *salsa*. Young, innocent and pretty, she had a lot to smile about, unlike that man in the mirror I'd met.

"How long have you booked the rooms for?" Mick Murphy had a mouthful of *salsa* and chips, but only one thing on his mind.

"I said two days but that we might extend." Pauly helped himself to the fresh *salsa*. "Mick, you're Mr. Youngblood."

"I'm Mr. Casey?" Pauly nodded. "Did you make your call?" I sipped from the new beer.

The *salsa* was good and a jar of pickled jalapeños sat with the other condiments. Adding a jalapeño to the chip and *salsa* made the spicy bite almost satisfy me.

"Yes," he said and hesitated.

His hesitation suggested to me what he'd been told.

"And?" Mick Murphy said.

"My contact is checking for Russians in the area," he said. "Remember, there's a time difference. He'll call me back."

I had a feeling Pauly lied, as he waited for verification of what his contact had said. It's what I would've done.

"When?" Mick Murphy was anxious. He needed something to help move his thirst for revenge forward.

"When they fuckin' know something." Pauly tried following my example by adding a jalapeño to his chip and *salsa*. "Sooner would mean they're not thorough."

Pauly's good mood seemed to be fading. What was bothering him, now?

Our food came and we ate like starved prisoners of war, which, in a sense, we were. We did what was necessary to survive.

"When are you going to call, Norm?" Mick Murphy looked at me as he ate.

"When we know there's a reason to." I added *salsa* and jalapeños to my tacos. "I'm not chasing rumors, Mick."

He looked toward Pauly, ignoring his tacos.

"I can't make the damn phone ring, Mick," Pauly said, between bites. "Eat."

Mick Murphy picked at his food.

"If Russians are in Tampico or Tampico Alto, I can fly us there," Pauly said, surprising me, again. It had to be the last place in the world he wanted to be. He'd told me that. Making the decision had changed his mood. "I have a plane at the Marathon Airport. Maybe you don't need to make that call." He looked at me.

"There could be intel I can get." I added more jalapeños to my tacos and wondered what other surprises I could expect from Pauly. The heat helped me swallow as I wondered why he'd offer to fly us somewhere he dreaded. "A drug plane's not the safest way in."

"It's the only way in," Pauly said with an attempted smile to cover his angst. "But this ain't a drug plane."

"What is it?" I finished my dinner.

"A Beechcraft Starship," he said.

I whistled, because I knew the turboprop plane was rare and it cost around three million dollars, when you could find one. My agency had one, but traded up to the Piaggio P180 because of its faster speed, longer range and it carried more passengers. That and the company stopped making the Starship. "You gotta have one of the few left in private hands."

"I don't think there's a dozen in the air today."

"Maintenance and parts gotta be a problem."

"I bought as many spare parts as I could afford in 2004, when Raytheon cleared out their stock and sold them to Beechcraft owners," he said.

"Will it get us to Tampico?" Mick Murphy said, only one thing on his mind.

Pauly looked at me. "Yeah, in about three, three and a half hours from Key West."

"I don't want to go to Key West!" Mick Murphy said.

"Marathon," Pauly said. "The plane's in Marathon."

"We can leave tonight?"

"No, Mick." Pauly pushed his empty plate away. "I need to get some sleep and have the plane fueled and checked. Tomorrow night."

"A night arrival?" Why did it surprise me? Smugglers preferred night landings and take offs.

Pauly almost grinned but couldn't pull it off thinking about the destination. "If we get the go ahead, yeah, a night arrival. Old habits die hard. We'll be going in armed and illegal, remember that. *Los Zetas* don't like *gringos*. There's that, too."

"They like money," I said. "You remember where to go?"

"Hell, better, I may know who to pay off," Pauly said. "That's the call I'm waiting for."

I nodded, but thought about the bloody war between *Los Zetas*, the Gulf Cartel and Mexican Army. Leaving me little to smile about.

Chapter Sixteen

After I unpacked, I told Mick Murphy I needed a shower. He lay down on one of the hotel beds, leaving his suitcase unopened and Pauly's duffle bag of weapons on the floor, ready to move out with a moment's notice. Revenge is a hell of a motivator.

"Good idea. I'm next," he said. "I ate too much at dinner, Norm. I didn't realize how hungry I was."

"Good and spicy, like the joints we used to eat at in Tijuana." Dinner had almost washed away the bile in my throat and the knot in my stomach. Almost. I fought the temptation to tell Mick Murphy he didn't realize shit about anything, but kept my mouth shut. If I was going to vomit, I didn't want it to be unkind words to a friend.

When I came out of the bathroom, Mick Murphy lay there snoring. I didn't wake him.

Running on manic energy for the past twenty-four hours, he'd sleep for a while now that he was down. I dressed and went out into the hallway to call Pauly on my cell.

"I'm in the bar," he said, answering.

"Be there in a minute," I said.

The bar looked like a million hotel bars I'd been in. Dark with dimly lit booths off in the corner, faux candle light flickering on round tables for two, and a mahogany bar with bottles of liquor lined up on shelves like toy soldiers, all reflected in the large mirror behind them.

The bar closed at one A.M. It was close to that and we were the only customers. The bartender brought us our rum and cokes and went back to his closing chores.

"Mick?" Pauly said, sipping his drink, wondering about Mick Murphy. He looked as tired as I felt.

"Sleeping." I couldn't taste the rum in my drink.

"I'm not waiting on a call back." Pauly turned to me, admitting his earlier lie. "I didn't know what to tell him."

"The Russians are in Tampico Alto?"

"Fuckin' A."

"The Iranians, too?" I wondered what the significance of them being there together was.

"Together like flies on horseshit."

"Why'd you lie?"

"For chrissake, are you kidding?" Pauly put his drink down.

"Bad memories?" I thought I knew the answer.

"Fuck no!" He looked at me with an expression I can't explain. I'd say it made him look lost, but I doubted Pauly ever felt lost. "Well, yeah, there's that, but I'm talking about Mick, not me. We're three gringos flying into areas belonging to *Los Zetas*, who are fighting a bloody war with everyone and don't trust gringos."

"I know all that, Pauly, I live in LA and the Times is full of cartel news."

"You read about it," he said, showing his anger. "I've seen it!"

"Don't come." I wanted him to believe I meant it, because I didn't. My idea of reverse psychology. His knowledge of the drug operation there was important, it was essential to our success. If he chose not to fly us to Tampico Alto, we were in trouble. We'd be like two blind men with a three-legged mutt leading us across the LA freeway.

"If you and Mick go, I'm coming," Pauly said, drumming his fingers on the bar. "Damn it, if it's Alexei and he's mixed up with Iranians and *Los Zetas* . . ." He took a long swallow of his drink and looked around for an ashtray. Either the bartender had cleaned and put them away, or it was a no smoking bar. He placed a wrinkled pack of cigarettes down. "If Mick goes off half-cocked, he's dead."

"I told him I won't go on a suicide mission."

"I met Alexei in Key West, with Mick, once. You know him."

"Know of him," I said, correcting Pauly. "We've met briefly, but not under the best circumstances."

"Great!" Pauly took a deep breath that came back on him

as a yawn. "The guy Mick holds responsible for Tita's death, and wants to kill, will recognize all of us! No problem sneaking up on him." His sarcasm lost in a yawn that turned into a frown.

"Won't happen," I said. "The only chance of killing Alexei is from a distance. That's as close as Mick will ever get and live. Problem is he's not a good shot."

"Are you?"

"Better than some, not as good as others."

"What the fuck's that mean, Norm?" He put his empty glass down. The bartender ignored it.

"I'd have a chance of taking him out, if the conditions were favorable," I said.

"But?"

"But Mick wants to be the shooter."

"Fuck!" Pauly banged the empty glass and the bartender came to us.

"Last call," the bartender said, looking at his wristwatch.

"Sure, one more and we're out of here," Pauly said.

The bartender returned with our drinks and this time mine was heavy on the rum. He picked up the money I'd placed on the bar. "Keep the change." He nodded.

"I can tell him the Russians were there but left," Pauly said.

"He'd still want to go. Follow the scent like a hound dog. It's a trail."

"Tell him they're there?"

"Do you know it's Alexei, for sure?" I had my doubts.

"No, my Mexican contact said there are four Russians, four Iranians and they are dealing with the local boss. Something to do with an airplane."

"For smuggling drugs or people?" It was a rhetorical question, but got an answer.

"Both, I guess." Pauly looked at me. "What's wrong? I can see it on your face." He read people better than I'd given him credit for.

"The Iranian intelligence service is smart, well trained and financed," I said. My mind started spinning, looking to grab onto something I knew about VEVAK, the Iranian intelligence agency. "I don't see them hanging out at a drug cartel's airport buying cocaine and dealing with the Russian mob, not so openly that people knew about it. They're after something else."

"You don't show up at this airport unless you're part of the operation. My contact is close to the top, but he's scared shitless of *Los Zetas*."

"How does he know they're Iranians?"

"*El jefe* told the men Iranians and Russians would be meeting at the airport with *Los Zetas honchos* and everyone was to be on their best behavior. Doubled security, too."

"We're missing something," I said. "Iranians wanted drugs, they'd go over the mountain to Afghanistan, not Mexico."

"Maybe they're terrorists and want to be smuggled into the states."

"VEVAK would arrange student visas or diplomatic status for them," I said. "That's how they work. No, there's something else going on." I finished my second drink. "I think we'd better go to Tampico Alto and see for ourselves."

Pauly finished his drink and didn't seem overly excited. "We should leave Marathon at midnight tomorrow. The plane's ready to go."

He had lied about the plane needing to be prepared. I hoped that was the only lie he'd told about this trip because the knot in my gut got bigger and my gut never lied. Something bigger than drug smuggling and killing Alexei was at hand.

Chapter Seventeen

Pauly had booked the rooms for two nights, so we stayed the next day and used the time to clean the weapons in the duffle bags, our own semi-automatics and double check to see all magazines were loaded. For lunch, we returned to Rosita's and then went to Wal-Mart to buy extra clothing, preparing for God only knows what. Killing time until midnight reminded me of waiting in a dentist's chair.

Mick Murphy wanted to get to Mexico as soon as possible, and Pauly was edgy because he really didn't want to go. It all made for an interesting afternoon as the two tried to control themselves. Or maybe it was what the conversations between us lacked that concerned me. Small talk, bullshit that avoided the big question: what the hell were we doing? We checked out and headed south on US1 at seven P.M.

For dinner, we stopped at the waterfront Islamorada Seafood Company Restaurant, and finally pulled into the Marathon Airport's general aviation area a little before ten. Mick Murphy stopped to stare at the strange looking Beechcraft Starship.

"It flies?" He said to Pauly.

"Like an eagle."

The Starship's airframe is made of carbon fiber composite and has two turboprop engines in the rear of the plane, referred to as pusher engines because they push the plane instead of pulling it, as regular front-located prop engines do. A few years back the agency I work for had one and I'd flown on it a number of times.

The plane requires only one pilot, but has a seat for a copilot. The cabin capacity is six and the cruising speed is 335 mph, with a range of more than 1,500 miles. Its flight ceiling is 41,000 feet. I thought Pauly would fly a treetop hugger. The Starship was more than adequate to get us to Mexico.

Inside, Pauly checked the digital instrument panel that reminded me of a video game on a plasma TV, while Mick Murphy and I made ourselves comfortable in the cabin.

"I checked the weather," Pauly said, coming into the cabin

and sitting, facing us. Two of the four seats faced each other, the two behind these faced forward. "We can expect weather turbulence as we get close to Tampico, but most of the flight should be smooth."

"How long before we land?" Mick Murphy questioned landing and we hadn't even taken off.

"We're cleared for landing between three and four," Pauly said. "We leave here at midnight we should arrive in plenty of time."

"Someone's gonna clear us through customs?" I said.

"As long as we get in on time, Norm, we'll be okay," he said. "It'll cost."

"You're talking about landing at the international airport?"

"Yeah. It's like here, part of the airport is set aside for general aviation," Pauly said. "They get a lot of air traffic from Texas, so they're accommodating to private planes that arrive early in the morning." He smirked. "We'll need to show our appreciation."

"Do you have it?" I had contingency cash in my money belt and some stuffed in my bag.

"Yeah. You might have to show your gratitude for the customs checkout."

"No problem."

"Couldn't we leave now, arrive a little earlier?" Mick Murphy's impatience showed.

"Chrissake, Mick," Pauly sighed. "You want to arrive at a Mexican airport with our cargo of weapons? This ain't your first ballgame. We follow the plan."

"Until the plan falls apart," I said and no one smiled.

"If it falls apart, we're gonna be in a Mexican jail for a long time," Pauly answered.

"Or dead," I said. "How do you make it look like you're coming in from Texas?" The subject needed to be changed. "I've never flown with a real smuggler before."

"Ex-smuggler." Pauly got the flight chart and showed me

the route we'd take, heading toward the Texas-Mexican border and then swinging south, over the Gulf and call the tower at the Tampico International Airport.

"Simple as that?" Simple sometimes got complicated in my life.

"Flying the coastline at night is easier for smaller planes," Pauly said. "You fly from Texas and there aren't many landmarks to follow, because it's mostly desert, but along the coast there are villages and towns."

"Going north?"

"Treetop it to the border, Norm" he said and grinned. "There are private airports in South Texas that don't have air traffic control, so you pop up in the sky close to one and call the nearest airport with ATC and give them your flight plan to New Orleans, or wherever."

Mick Murphy remained antsy. "What's gonna happen when we land?"

Pauly looked at me and I nodded, not knowing what else to do.

"We taxi to the section of the airport we're directed to, and my contact will pick us up," Pauly said.

"And take us to Alexei?" Mick Murphy's one-track mind was in full motion.

"Mick, I told you there are Russians, I never said Alexei."

"Too coincidental."

"No Mick," I said. "To you Alexei is the only Russian gangster, but he ain't. We know he's got businesses in Florida and reports to New York. But the Russian mob's also in Texas and that's more logical, if Moscow wants a Mexican connection."

"Explain the Iranians. Call me stupid, Norm, but I can see Alexei sucking up to the Iranians and the cartel. It's him." Saying it as if he knew the Russian mobster personally.

"Why's he sucking up to the Iranians? And why in Mexico? Moscow is tight with Tehran." My questions went unanswered. "But say you're right. How do you expect to get close enough to shoot him?" I said. "He's met all three of us. We aren't gonna be welcomed."

"I don't know, Norm," Mick Murphy sighed and looked frustrated. "We look for a weak spot, like we did with the others . . ."

"Damn it, Mick, if he's got weak spots, he has 'em covered," I said. "The two guys we got in South Beach were amateurs compared to Alexei. They ran nightclubs, extortion rings. There's no comparison."

"He'll be in a confined area," Pauly said. "Heavily armed people all around him. Maybe a sniper could get him, but walking in would be signing your own death warrant. Hell, the fuckin' *Zetas* take on the Mexican army and they're protecting him."

Mick Murphy sat back and the color drained from his face. He ran his hand through his beard. "I need to see for myself," he said. "I don't expect you two to put your lives on the line for this. But it's something I need to do."

"I'll fly you there," Pauly said. "You do something stupid, I'll leave you there." I knew he lied and wondered if Mick Murphy knew it too. "Take the sniper shot. Be satisfied you killed him and walked away alive."

"I'll see what's what and if there's no other alternative, I'll take the shot," Mick Murphy lied, too.

Chapter Eighteen

Pauly had the plane in the air as the second hand on my wristwatch ticked in the new day and date. He called the Miami Air Traffic Control tower because Marathon didn't have one and the Key West tower had closed for the night. He gave his destination as a private airport south of Houston. It took minutes and the ex-smuggler flew legally across the Gulf of Mexico.

"What's wrong?" I asked Mick Murphy, because I felt his uncomfortable movements in the otherwise plush seat.

"Do you think Alexei's there, Norm?" His words carried self-doubt. "I want to kill the fucker so badly!"

"I know you do," I said. "I don't fault you for that."

"What do you fault me for?" The self-doubt had gone and now his words challenged me. His manic moods swung like a pendulum.

"Chasing a ghost."

"Fuck it, Norm, Alexei is flesh and blood. He's no ghost!"

"Somewhere, yeah, he's walking around," I said, trying to ignore his coldness. "But you hear the word Russian and translate it to mean Alexei."

"Viktor said it."

"Mick, getting at the truth with torture is iffy, at best."

"You don't think it's the truth?"

I took in a deep breath and realized that he had me as a captive audience for the next three hours, so the best thing was to deal with him. "Viktor probably had KGB training. If I'm right, he broke in a very short time, hours instead of days, which his training would've prepared him for."

"You're better than he was," he said, but the sharpness of his words took away the complimentary meaning.

"I'm not that good. I'd rather be lucky." I've known too many people that were good at their jobs, but their luck eventually ran out and now they're dead. "At best, what we have is a fifty/fifty chance that Viktor told us the truth, and that's giving us the benefit of the doubt."

"You don't think we'll get to find out for ourselves?" His timbre mellowed, again.

"Hell, Mick, if Alexei's there, he's being protected by *Los Zetas,* because of whatever deal they're working on," I said. "The Mexican army couldn't help us. You've kept tabs on the drug war down there, so you know it too."

"Yeah." He seemed to sink further into the large seat as he turned and looked out the small window. "Dark as my heart out there."

His statement surprised me. I hadn't been sure if he knew how crazy his quest was, but now I thought he might realize the futility of it. I also feared that the chase might be the dying act of a friend.

"We're over the Gulf. Nothing to see out there but black water and we've both seen a lot of that." I regretted the words as soon as I'd said them. Would he think back to our sailing on the Fenian Bastard, the boat Alexei's gunmen sank? That would lead to recalling Tita's death and only reinforce the reason for his pursuit.

"I miss being on the water." He kept his stare out the window. I wondered what he saw on the other side of the darkness. Maybe he could see Tita's ghost.

"I'm going to sit with Pauly awhile." I stood up and left Mick Murphy with his head pressed against the glass. "Get some sleep."

The plane's digital instrument panel's image reflected in the windshield. The whole setup looked like a video game I've seen kids play along the pier at Redondo Beach. I sat across from Pauly and put on the headphones. I looked out and stars filled the sky, much like what I'd seen when sailing the Fenian Bastard in the Caribbean with Mick Murphy.

"You a pilot, Norm?" Pauly turned to me.

"Don't drop dead," I said. "I'm not sure I could land this."

Pauly laughed. "Don't worry, if I'm gonna die today it'll be at the hands of some crazed Mexican with a chainsaw."

I didn't see anything to laugh at. "I'm sure you've got all

the bases covered."

"Two more hours," he said as if it were a death sentence he spoke of.

"How long before we see lights?"

"An hour and a half," Pauly said. "Jet stream stayed north of us, so we're making good time. No head winds to fight." He sat back and looked straight ahead.

The waiting before an operation always tore me up. You'd think with all the waiting required in my work I'd be more adjusted, but I'm not. Not knowing frightened me more than the action of an operation. As a kid, hearing the piercing sound of the dentist's drill always frightened me. Expectation of what's to come has usually proven to be more frightening than the action itself.

* * *

If drug smuggling was as easy as this trip appeared, I thought I might change careers. Pauly called the ATC tower at Tampico International Airport and received instructions to land. No problem.

"Seatbelts," Pauly said as he prepared for the descent.

I went back to the cabin. "We're landing, put your seatbelt on," I told Mick Murphy, pulling him away from some reverie.

We sat facing forward, looking into the cockpit, and watched the airport lights grow brighter. The plane descended and I realized we never hit the reported turbulence. Maybe it went with the jet stream.

The plane touched down with a soft meeting of tires and tarmac. Pauly spoke into the mike and listened as his instructions came through the earphones. He turned and nodded, his right thumb upward, shooting us an everything-was-okay signal.

From my seat, I could see out the windshield as a lit up electric cart led Pauly along the tarmac, away from the main terminal. The engines slowed and then stopped as the plane moved into a shadowy area at the far end of the runway between other private planes.

"We're here." Pauly took off the earphones. "Now we

wait."

Mick Murphy had his Sig Sauer semi-automatic in his hand. He dropped the magazine, checked it and put it back in the gun. The duffel bag of weapons lay on the floor behind his seat.

"You think you need that?" I kept my voice neutral.

"Better to have it and not need it . . ." His words trailed off and he smiled. "Right, Norm? How many times have you told me that?"

"Yeah," I said.

Pauly joined us, taking the seat that faced me. "My contact's name is Jorge. He and I go back a long way. Back to the days when he grew pot on his farm and I ran it by boat to Loo-ze-anna and South Florida."

"Long time ago," I agreed.

"A few lifetimes," Pauly said. "Then the fucking Colombians came with their coke and guns. Now the Mexican cartels have taken over, changed the whole ballgame."

"Do you trust him?" I said.

"Yeah," he stammered. "Kind of."

"Meaning?"

"*Los Zetas*, put them in the mix and I don't trust anything," he said. "Jorge was el jefe before the cartel wars broke out. I don't know his standing with *Los Zetas*, or their standing with him. If he helps us, he'll want something in return."

"I've got money."

"So does he and probably more than you and me together, Norm. I don't see money being what he wants."

"What then?"

"He may need me to make a delivery," Pauly mumbled without a smile. He patted the crumbled cigarette package in his shirt pocket.

"Promise him anything, then we take off and you're free."

"Ain't that easy. I've burned most of my bridges down here. I can't burn them all."

"Why? You plan to come back?" His concern was hard for me to swallow.

“My past is all I have,” he said. “I don’t want to lose it. Not all of it. Jorge is probably the one friend I have left here. I’m the godfather to his youngest daughter.”

“I hope he feels the same.”

“Me too,” Pauly said.

“Will he know if Alexei is here?” Mick Murphy broke his silence and turned away from the window.

Pauly pointed toward the front of the plane where two headlights grew brighter as they approached. “We’ll know in a minute if he’s a friend.”

“Or if he’s alone,” I said.

Chapter Nineteen

Pauly stepped outside to meet his friend Jorge. It felt like another trip to the dentist, waiting for him to walk back in. I became concerned because I didn't know what was going on and uncertainty is a killer. Pauly finally returned with Jorge following. I remained cautious and liked the feel of my .45 against my back.

Jorge wore a brown Stetson, a western long-sleeve shirt that showed off muscled arms pushing against the fabric, clean jeans and lizard-skin cowboy boots. Expensive boots, I could tell and looked down at my beat-up, old boots. I couldn't say how tall he was because of the boots and hat, but guessed close to my height, six-five, in his stocking feet. Jorge had to be in his early sixties, and he looked fit. His bushy, salt-and-pepper mustache highlighted a reddish-clay tanned face, and his dark brown eyes gave Mick Murphy and me a quick onceover. The grip of a semi-automatic stuck out over his cowboy belt. A real *vaquero*.

"Mick, Norm this is my friend Jorge," Pauly said.

Jorge didn't move. He looked at Pauly and then back at us. His smile came and went.

"DEA?" he said in accented English.

"No," Pauly said. "I already told you that, Jorge."

From Pauly's annoyed tone, I guessed that's what they were talking about on the tarmac.

"It is okay, *entiendo*, Pablito," Jorge said. He stepped forward and shook our hands. "I am here to be of service."

I looked to Pauly, hoping for an explanation but only saw a frustrated look. Were we being tested? If he thought we were DEA, what was our life expectancy?

"Look at him." I pointed to Mick Murphy. "How long would *el rojo* last as a DEA agent in *Méjico*?" A true statement but would it be believable to a drug smuggler?

Jorge seemed to ponder the question. "Maybe not in *Méjico*, but in Florida it is good to look like a gringo and not a *Mejicano*." He smiled. "I have seen red-haired gringos make drug buys."

"Pauly?" I needed him to explain what was happening, to ease my anxiety.

"Jorge thinks I've been in jail, so I'm helping the DEA, now."

"Did you ask him about Alexei?" Mick Murphy blurted out.

"*Quien es* Alexei?" Jorge said. He looked toward Pauly with squinted eyes. "*Quien es,* Pablito?"

"We're looking for a Russian named Alexei. That's why we're here. You told Pauly there were Russians at your airfield," Mick Murphy said without regard for the possible seriousness of the situation. "Are there?"

"*Ruso*?" He took off his Stetson and ran his hand through thinning hair. "*Sí, cuatro rusos y cuatro árabes . . .*" He stopped speaking abruptly. "*Y Los Zetas.*" He spit out the words.

"What do you know about them? Why are they here?" I asked, before Mick Murphy said too much and alienated us. From the way Jorge's voice wavered when mentioning *Los Zetas*, maybe we were discussing mutual dislikes.

Jorge sat down. He looked up toward Pauly. "No DEA?"

Pauly shook his head.

"Why do you want us to be DEA?" I sat across from him, now more curious than concerned.

Again, he looked toward Pauly. "My wife, Mora, is in England visiting our daughter. She is a doctor now, Pablito."

"Congratulations," Pauly said. "Salma will be a fine doctor."

"Yes," Jorge said. "Mora is with our youngest, Anna, *su ahijada*," he kept his stare on Pauly. "They will be in New York City in a few weeks to visit my son, Alfonso the lawyer."

"Excuse me, Jorge, but what does this have to do with wanting us to be DEA?" I said.

"My other son, *Miguelito*, is an attorney in Denver," he said as if I hadn't asked a question.

Pauly stood behind Jorge's seat and used hand motions to have me slow down and wait. I nodded.

"You want information of *los rusos y los árabes, sí*?"

"Yes," Mick Murphy said before I could answer.

"*Bueno*. I too want something."

"Name it," I said.

"I will help. You cannot get onto the airfield or the base, or too close. I will be your ears and eyes, *sí*? *Los Zetas* are all over. It is dangerous, even for me. You want what from *los sustantivos*?"

"We need their names, what they are doing, and why they are here together," I said. "And for helping, you want what?"

"I want to leave with you," he said, surprising me. His eyes squinted, again, as he looked to Pauly. "If DEA, I want witness protection. No *importante*. I am done with this. Like *mí hermano*, Pablito, I have had too much death. I have money in the states. A new identity. I can live with my family there. I leave with you, *sí*?"

Pauly stood behind Jorge and nodded at me. "If Pauly says you can come."

I could care less who came back with us, as long as we got back, but his request surprised me and surprise always concerns me.

Jorge turned to Pauly. "Pablito?"

Pauly smiled at his friend. "*Por qué no?*"

"I know one thing, maybe you want," Jorge said. "*Los rusos enseñar los árabes el avión.*"

"I don't understand," I said. "What about teaching the airplane?"

"*No sé*. Each morning *los rusos* and *los árabes* fly," he said. "They go to the desert, west and come back, maybe two hours gone. Maybe more."

It was my turn to look up at Pauly. "What are they doing?"

"Learning to fly?" He answered my question with a question. "Unless the Russians are showing the Iranians how easy it is to cross the border. But that doesn't make sense."

"Who is flying the plane when you see them?" I turned to

Jorge.

"*Los rusos*," he said. "When I see them, but I do not always see them."

"What the fuck!" I said.

"My thoughts exactly," Pauly said. "You're right, we're missing something, Norm."

"The *reason* for them getting together."

"I know there are local pilots that could teach the Iranians to fly."

"Why aren't they doing it, then?"

"Jorge, how close can you take us?" Pauly said.

"One and a half kilometers," he said. "We cleared the small hill that looks over the base, but the adobe house that was there didn't burn too good. Parts of the walls remain and the brush has begun to return. I can take you there, but I do not know when I can return."

"Who would check on the hill?" I said.

"Me," Jorge answered. "I would send someone. Maybe today I forget."

"That would be good," I said. "We'll need binoculars, water and some food."

"I've got two Bushnell binoculars." Pauly pulled a wrinkled package of cigarettes from his pocket, then put it back.

"I will get you water, a few tortillas and beans," Jorge said.

It was almost four-thirty and I knew the first gray light of dawn would be forcing the night away soon. "How long from here?"

"An hour," Jorge said. "Do you have weapons?"

"I thought we would be safe." I wondered why he was concerned about weapons.

"*Sí*, but I do not control *Los Zetas o la marina de guerra*," he said, talking of the Navy's special forces.

"There's a chance they'll attack?" I wasn't counting on another enemy.

"Always a chance." Jorge frowned. "*Cómo se dice?*"

"Navy," Pauly said.

"The navy soldiers are most dangerous for *Los Zetas*," he said. "The cartels fear them more than *la policia.* We have contacts within *la policia.*" He grinned.

"How have you remained safe for so many years?" I wondered who he'd paid off over the years.

"Norm," Pauly said, "Money talks and that's all we need to know."

"No, Pauly, we need to know if the Navy's in the neighborhood and we gotta worry," I said. "We don't need *Los Zetas* and the Navy after us."

"*No hay problema*," Jorge said. "*Los Zetas* will kill you and Navy will put you on TV to show how Americans drive the drug cartels. Maybe kill you later." He smirked at his own joke.

"That's good to know," I said but my sarcasm didn't seem appreciated by anyone.

Chapter Twenty

Jorge made a call and arranged to get Pauly's plane refueled later that morning. Mick Murphy put the duffel bag of weapons and binoculars in the back of Jorge's dusty Hummer, took a seat and waited. As usual, he was in a hurry, tapping on the window to get our attention. Pauly sat in front, we sat in back. A policeman opened the gate, waved us through, and we were on the eerie thoroughfare to somewhere.

The shadowy two-lane road had no streetlights. Large delivery trucks came toward us, headed for Tampico, their headlights cutting into the morning dimness. About forty-five minutes into the ride, Jorge pulled onto a dirt road and after a short distance stopped in front of a colorfully painted yellow-and-red adobe hut. He came out a few minutes later carrying a six-pack of water and four covered containers stacked atop each other, held in place with plastic netting.

"Homemade and good," Jorge said, handing everything to us in the back seat.

The sun slowly rose, pushing away the gray dawn, as the Hummer stopped beside what remained of the burnt-out hovel on a hill. We unloaded our arsenal and stored everything behind the wall furthest from our viewing point of Jorge's compound.

"You have my cell number," Jorge said to Pauly. "I will call when I can. If you must, call me but I may not be able to talk."

"Entiendo y gracias." Pauly hugged Jorge, a Mexican *abrazo*.

"If we need to leave, what do we do?" I said.

"In daylight, it is dangerous," Jorge said. "I have routine to follow, especially now. I will be in contact." He got into the Hummer and drove off without answering me. It looked as if we weren't leaving anytime soon. I didn't like the plan. We had no escape route.

Mick Murphy loaded the M-4's and stacked the extra magazines and boxes of ammo. Pauly and I scanned below, using the Bushnell binoculars. I kept the thoughts of being trapped to myself. To the far left of the encampment, a large lake began to take shape in the daylight.

"You see the lake?" Pauly said.

"Yeah."

"Seaplanes land there. One of my first flights," he said. Pride came with his statement. "A long time ago."

"I thought you were the go-to boat guy."

"Plane or boat," he said. "I never drove on land, too dangerous."

I wanted to laugh at his comment, but didn't. We had different ideas of danger. I searched the compound for the airplane and found it. "The airstrip at the far end?"

"Should be. Packed dirt. What it's always been. Can you make it out?"

"Yeah, a twin-engine plane, all by its lonesome back there." It looked like a toy from our vantage point.

"Can't tell what kind." Pauly scanned the compound below.

"Too far away."

Three large motorhomes sat close to the airstrip. "The motorhomes normal?"

"Not that I remember," Pauly said. "Brought in for the guests?"

I skimmed over the half dozen buildings. "Any other living quarters?"

"Each warehouse has a small room with cots," he said. "If you want to call that living."

"Office and five warehouses?" I guessed aloud. "Alexei wouldn't want a cot."

"Offices and supplies, but I only knew of two used to store product, back in the days of square grouper."

"Were there six buildings before?"

"I think so. They load the drugs from one of the warehouses onto a truck and deliver it to the Gulf at night, if it's a water delivery," he said. "I was trying to think which of the buildings they used to . . ." he paused. "You know, to cut off those heads."

"Not important, Pauly." I needed him focused on the now, not yesterday. I checked the time, it was almost seven. "We should watch the motorhomes. If they're gonna fly this morning they should be up and about soon."

"Fly in the morning and most afternoons," Pauly recited what Jorge had told us. "If it's flying lessons, they're getting a lot, quickly." He lit his first cigarette in hours.

"Maybe Jorge will come back with some good information."

"Can you make out anything?" Mick Murphy brought us each an M-4. I wondered if this would end up the Mexican version of the OK Corral before it was over.

"You going to war?" I said, taking the rifle.

"Never can tell." He reached for my binoculars and I let him have them. He studied the area. "We can't tell if it's Alexei with these. We need to get closer."

"Unlikely," Pauly said. "You heard Jorge. Security is tighter than a constipated asshole, so we stay put."

"Fuck," Mick Murphy cried. "This sucks. We're so close. There's gotta be something . . ."

"Mick, sit tight and let's see what Jorge has to say when he calls," I said. "Who knows, we watch the planes and maybe get a better idea of who the Russians are."

"Yeah, sure, then what?" he said.

"We figure out why they're teaching the Iranians to fly," Pauly said, still looking through the binoculars, the cigarette dangling from his lips.

Chapter Twenty-one

Pauly lit another cigarette. At this pace, he'd be out of smokes before the afternoon. I opened a bottle of water, took a drink, and scanned below before Mick Murphy wanted the binoculars to look for the elusive Alexei. Men and women scurried around the compound, moving into or out of buildings. Armed men patrolled the fenced-in grounds and guarded the main gate. No one approached the airplane.

The morning sun began to heat up and shade was at a premium on the hillside. None of the adobe walls were higher than five-feet, most were less than three-feet, and the roof had burned well, it was mostly gone. Scrub brush grew around the perimeter and a few bushes had sprouted up within the walls, but none were good for shade against the June sun.

Below, the compound's lakeside dock was empty. No seaplane meant no smuggling, I guessed. Smugglers not smuggling, Russian gangsters and Iranians, what was it about? I thought it interesting, it made me curious, and I had questions that I hoped Jorge had answers to. Alexei or not, something disturbing was taking place below.

Other than a couple of parked pickup trucks and a few Hummers, the only other item of interest was the airplane on the dirt tarmac. I watched as Jorge drove through the gate, said something to the guards and parked outside of one of the warehouses.

"Jorge's arrived," I said.

Pauly crushed his cigarette and picked up his binoculars.

We watched Jorge leave the Hummer and enter a warehouse.

"Offices?"

"That'd be my guess," Pauly said. "It's been a couple of years, Norm, so I ain't sure what's what down there."

"Three motorhomes," I said.

"One for the Arabs, two for the Russians?" Pauly put an unlit cigarette between his lips.

"Four Arabs in one, three Russians in another and Alexei

in the third. That sounds plausible."

"Why not two and two Russians? Who's the important party here?"

"Alexei's the boss and takes every opportunity to show it," I said. "He'd want his privacy to take care of business on the phone. His deal, he's priority." Then I thought about the Iranians. "Pauly, you know the Iranians aren't Arabs, they're Persians."

"They're all Arabs to me." He lit a cigarette.

"Maybe to Jorge, too," I said and it gave me one more thing to consider.

"What do we do now?" Mick Murphy said. "Sitting around here all day is fucking stupid."

"So's dying," Pauly said. "Come on, Mick, you've been on god-damn stakeouts, they're boring, but necessary. Think of it as research for one of your news stories, boring but necessary."

"It doesn't mean I need to like it!"

"You could've stayed in Miami." I wanted my harsh tone to cut through his bullshit. "Or on the plane. This was your damn idea and this is the way it's done."

"Okay, okay," Mick Murphy yelped and walked toward our arsenal. "Let me know if anything happens."

"Don't drink all the water!" I called after him. He shot me the finger without bothering to turn around.

Boring was not a strong enough word for how it went. Pauly impressed me, again, with his determination. Other than to light a new cigarette, or sip water, he kept his binoculars moving on the compound, checking vehicles and people. He let me know when two pickups arrived together.

I paced the hilltop, checking the land surrounding us. The two-lane road we came in on continued west but I couldn't see any landmarks for at least two miles. It might have been farmland once. Maybe it still was.

Our food consisted of cold rice and beans, chicken with peppers, but when mixed and rolled in the tortilla, the taco tasted good. Or perhaps I was hungry. Pauly enjoyed his taco too. We both sipped water.

"Where's Mick?" Pauly looked around.

I circled the burnt out adobe walls.

"Fuck," I bellowed and grabbed the binoculars and started looking below.

"He wouldn't!" Pauly joined the search.

"Keep looking." I rushed to where Mick Murphy had stored the duffel bag. Everything was there. "See him?"

"No," Pauly called back.

I took the extra ammo magazines and gave half to Pauly. He didn't smile as he accepted them.

"I'll check the perimeter," I said. "If you see him, yell."

"If he's gone down there . . . after Alexei . . ."

"They'll be up here like ants on a carcass."

"Why'd he do this?"

I made sure the M-4 was loaded and left Pauly pondering the question. I wondered the same thing, as I walked down the other side of the hill. Brush and weeds filled the old trail. A few burnt tree stubs remained while sprouts of new growth shot up everywhere. The afternoon sun filled the sky and I was sweating after only a few steps. On this side of the hill, you couldn't hear the muffled noise from the compound or traffic on the road. I stepped downward slowly, scanning the area, my finger on the trigger of the M-4.

"Norm," Mick Murphy called out from a knot of bushes.

I turned, the M-4 leveled in his direction. "What are you doin'?" I yelled.

"Taking a piss." Mick Murphy walked out of the scrubs zippering up. "There a problem?" He looked at the M-4 I pointed at him.

"Yeah!" I said. "You!" I pushed the barrel of the rifle into his stomach. "Why the fuck did you walk off without saying anything?"

He swiped the barrel away with his hands. "I need permission to take a piss?"

"Jesus, Mick," I said. "This ain't a game. We're not in Key West and there's no one covering our asses!"

"What the fuck?" He turned and began walking up the hill. "I'm not stupid."

"Then stop acting stupid." We were on the hill and had Pauly's attention. "There's three of us against the world right now."

"I needed to piss, for chrissake." He looked to Pauly for understanding.

He didn't get it.

My anger level was high, Mick Murphy being a friend or not, he had to follow rules. I pushed him against an adobe wall. "You need to listen," I snarled into his face. "We're here because of you, because you need us, so you're gonna follow the ground rules and like 'em."

He stared at me. "Or what? We're all stuck here 'till Jorge comes."

"Something's going on down there." I pointed toward the compound. "It's afternoon and the plane hasn't flown. Why? We don't know and not knowing is dangerous. As you said, we're stuck here, maybe trapped. If Jorge's been compromised, we're up shit's creek."

"Norm, I was taking a piss for chrissake," he said back into my face.

I don't know what I did that made his facial expression change from anger to realization, maybe I snorted like a pig or hawed like a mule, but I got something across to Mick Murphy, finally, and I could see it in his eyes.

He pushed me away. "You thought I left!" He turned to Pauly. "You too?" His words challenged us.

Neither of us replied. "Do you really think I'd go down there?" It was his turn to point toward the compound. "I know what would happen. I wouldn't do that to you. I wouldn't." He walked toward the food and made himself a taco, his back to us, mumbling.

"Movement around the motorhomes," Pauly called. "Something's going on."

I walked over to him, still angry with Mick Murphy, and

looked below. Even with the binoculars, it was difficult to see faces clearly. Men came out of the motorhomes. Only one man came out of the motorhome in the middle.

"The one in the middle," I said. "Could it be Alexei?"

"A good chance," Pauly said. "Tall and the other three are walking to him."

"So's Jorge."

"Let me see," Mick Murphy said with food in his mouth.

I handed him the binoculars.

"Where?" he asked.

"Center motorhome," Pauly said.

Without the binoculars, I could see the cluster of men meeting. I became alarmed when I saw two pickup trucks drive from around one building, both with mounted, heavy caliber machine guns on tripods and two men in the truck bed. I didn't need binoculars to see them. I slapped Pauly's back and pointed toward the pickups.

"This can't be good." Pauly offered me his binoculars. I declined.

"They're going to the plane," Mick Murphy yelled.

I grabbed the binoculars from him and focused on the plane. It looked like Jorge escorted the eight men. They boarded the plane, the engines started and one man came out and talked with Jorge. They walked back toward the buildings.

"You think it's another cartel coming or soldiers?" I asked.

"Hard to say," Pauly said. "Whoever it is, these guys are going head to head with them."

"Maybe running away?" I kept focused on the plane. It had begun to taxi.

"Unlikely, more like circling the wagons," Pauly said. "There's Jorge."

I turned to look toward the building Jorge had entered. He walked out alone, a satchel hanging from his shoulder. He went right to his pickup, got in and drove out the gate, leaving the turmoil behind.

"What's happening?" I looked toward Pauly.

He shook his head.

From somewhere off in the distance I heard the swish, swish, swish of rotor blades. Did the cartels have choppers?

I loved that sound when they were coming to pull my sorry ass out of trouble, but this time the choppers would be carrying Mexican Special Forces and they didn't care one way or another about my ass. Air assault, ground assault and take the high ground, that's what they'd do. We were sitting on the high ground and had nowhere to run and little defense. They were merciless adversaries and we didn't stand a chance against them, a smuggler, a journalist and a guy his own government would deny existed.

"Sorry," Mick Murphy said. "Didn't mean for it to come to this."

Pauly pointed toward the sky. Four troop-carrying, black helicopters headed toward the compound. The ground assault could only be moments behind.

"Plane's takin' off," Pauly yelled and pointed toward the twin-engine plane that probably had Alexei on 1board. We might never know for sure.

Chapter Twenty-Two

We didn't have much time, maybe five minutes, as we headed down the hill, away from the drug cartel's fortified camp. The idea, our Hail Mary pass, was to put as much distance between us and the hill as possible and maybe, just maybe, the Mexican Special Forces would concentrate their attention on the secured compound. If the smugglers put up a fight, as Pauly thought they would, it could give us a few minutes before the elite soldiers focused on the surrounding area. No matter what, they'd be on the hill swiftly, it's the high ground and that gave them an advantage.

Each of us took a bottle of water and as many ammo magazines as we could stuff in our pockets. Every so often, I turned to see if we were alone. We were. Helicopters hovered over the compound and men scurried down long black ropes like drops of water off a mooring line. *Fast Roping*, it's called. Probably the Mexicans called it that too, since it's likely they learned to descend from hovering choppers at American military schools. The English first used the technique when they attacked the Falkland Islands and we've turned it into a well-practiced maneuver.

It sounded as if the soldiers met with small arms resistance and a lot of heavy automatic fire, and then support helicopters returned salvos of heavier fire to protect them. It didn't take long before we heard explosions. The soldiers were breaching the front gate and maybe other areas of the fenced-in compound. I've been in major altercations with less action. A full-scale battle took place on the other side of the hill. We could hear it, we began to smell it as burnt-powder and fetid smoke wafted in the air.

The sun was large and low to the horizon and I sweated like the proverbial stuffed pig. All our shirts were soaked through when we finally reached the dirt road at the bottom of the hill.

Pauly's cell phone chirped. We stopped. He looked at us and then answered.

"We're on the dirt road," he said, almost out of breath. "Hurry." He hung up. "Jorge's coming."

Along the dirt road, there were bumps and dips, but nothing that offered a safe hiding place or protection if either side attacked. No gully, no wash, only scrub plants and shallow furrows. Pauly trusted Jorge, and I wanted to, but I didn't trust on secondhand advice. People earned my trust. There was no other way.

"Mick, get behind that shrubbery," I said and pointed toward a cluster of bushes. "Pauly, if it's not a yellow Hummer, head there." I pointed to a small mound in front of a shallow gorge. "Got it, Pauly?" He nodded.

Mick Murphy and Pauly were on the move before I headed to the other side of the road and hid, as best I could, behind a clump of thorny bushes. I wondered why Pauly decided to hide and not stand in the road waiting for Jorge. Trust can be precarious.

"Norm, you gotta learn to trust others," Pauly called but I couldn't see him.

"If you trust so much, wait in the road." I'm not sure he heard me.

Explosions and rapid gunfire still came from the compound. A helicopter circled the hillside now while other helicopters kept up the attack below, machine guns firing, the loud pandemonium vibrating the ground beneath us. We needed to distance ourselves and fast.

The well-armed smugglers fought, using their military training. *Los Zetas* had deserted from the Mexican military and knew how to fight. In Mexico, it really is a drug war, unlike the American propaganda drug war. Americans would overreact if this happened on our side of the border and that's part of my job, to keep this away from Hometown USA.

I saw the dust cloud coming from the east. You spend enough time is shitholes with dirt roads, you get to read dust clouds, like an Apache reads smoke signals. I knew one vehicle headed our way, a heavy vehicle. As good as I was, I couldn't tell who drove, so I sat with the M-4 pointed toward the east and gave a quick scan to the west, hoping I didn't see another cloud.

The yellow Hummer scurried into view, sending dirt and

rocks flying as its tires tore through the dust, leaving a cloud behind. Pauly stood and walked toward the road, ignoring the heavily tinted windshield. Anyone could've been driving.

The Hummer stopped, the passenger window came down, and Pauly said something as he opened the door.

"Let's get the hell outa here!" Pauly hollered, over the attack noise.

Mick Murphy got up and headed to the vehicle. I stood, my M-4 pointed in their direction, and walked through the underbrush. I still couldn't see Jorge behind the wheel.

"Move your ass," Mick Murphy yelled as he got in the back seat.

"What the hell's going on?" When I closed the door, Jorge took off, turning the Hummer around so he headed back the way he came.

"Problems," Jorge said driving into the dust storm he'd created. "Got little notice that the attack was coming."

"You weren't expecting the soldiers? No hint?" I wondered how good *Los Zetas'* intelligence was.

Jorge answered with a gruff laugh as he drove onto the paved road. "We are always expecting the soldiers. No, our warning came from *el espía*, our contact in the Sinaloa cartel."

"Your spy says the cartels got choppers now?"

Jorge didn't understand, so Pauly translated *choppers*, and it got me another gruff laugh.

"No, the government has what you call choppers," Jorge said, his hands holding tightly to the steering wheel as he entered the paved road. "The Sinaloa cartel, our rival, led them to us. *Los Zetas* are the government's priority. The government attacks us and the Sinaloa *putas* block our escape routes." The Hummer picked up speed.

"So, where are we headed?" I wanted to know his plan of escape.

"We are going to Tampico, so we can all fly to America," he said. He sped along the two-lane highway.

"What about that roadblock?" Ahead of us, less than a

mile, I could see three pickup trucks blocking the road. I held tightly to my M-4.

"Putas!" Jorge cussed.

"Do you have a way around them?"

"No, *señor*."

Pauly raised his M-4. Mick Murphy shook my shoulder.

"What's the plan?" I moved as close to Jorge as I could get from the back seat, wanting to hear his response.

"Forward to the airport," he said without taking his eyes of the roadblock. "Oh, I forgot …"

"Forgot what?" Pauly said.

One pickup truck had half a dozen men in its bed and they took aim at us with rifles. Others lined up behind the pickups, their weapons leveled toward us.

"Forgot what?" I repeated and wondered why Jorge wasn't as nervous as the rest of us.

"I will miss this ride," Jorge said and smiled into the rear-view mirror for me to see. "The Hummer is armored, even the windows. I am surprised you did not notice how thick the glass is." He tapped the tinted side window. "Bullets, *mierda! Agarrarse!*"

"Shit, Jorge," Pauly cussed and hit his friend on the shoulder. "Hold on!"

Jorge laughed at his joke, or maybe at three nervous *gringos*, as he rapidly approached the pickup trucks. I tightened my seatbelt.

Chapter Twenty-Three

The first barrage of bullets hit the hood and windows of the Hummer like a downpour of hail, leaving small scrapes and dents but not penetrating the vehicle. Jorge laughed, enjoying himself, as the Hummer sped toward the roadblock, swerving left to right. I didn't put a lot of faith in this car because I've seen large caliber bullets penetrate drug lords' supposedly armored vehicles in other parts of Mexico. When Mick Murphy and Pauly flinched as the bullets hit, I knew I wasn't alone in my concern. I wanted to be wrong.

The shots kept coming as we recoiled helplessly, hearing the pinging of the bullets' impact. I noticed Jorge kept veering the Hummer away from the center of the road.

Ahead, two pickup trucks were nose to nose across the road and behind them, the third one had backed up so the men standing in its bed could have clear shots at us. The trucks' engine blocks gave strength to the center of the roadblock.

If you looked at the charging Hummer, you might not have paid attention to its erratic movement, or blamed it on the bullets bouncing off the vehicle, if you did notice.

I moved up behind Jorge. "You going left?"

Jorge nodded. "No trees," he said into the mirror. "A lot of dust and dirt. Confuse them, cover us."

"Good move." I grinned back.

He was going to hit the bed of the pickup truck where there was less support, the weakest point, and jolt the blockade, causing the shooters to lose balance during the collision. Confuse them with the added dust and dirt, long enough for us to pass. Hopefully.

"More *putas* ahead?" I touched his shoulder and then sat back, prepared for the impact.

"*Quién sabe*?" Jorge said as we swerved left.

The Hummer hit the backside of the pickup and slid off the road onto the dirt. The impact was loud and slowed the fast moving vehicle, but didn't stop it, as the force of the collision and weight of the Hummer pushed the pickup away, rubber burning as its tires smeared the pavement. The Hummer moved quickly across the dirt, sending up dust and rocks. Our seatbelts kept us from tossing around, but our bodies absorbed the rear-ender shock and the screeching sound of metal-on-metal filled the cab. I shook my head, trying to clear my ears.

Jorge and Pauly let out whooping cries of excitement as we cleared the blockade.

Mick Murphy and I turned to look out the back window. Men picked themselves up from the roadway while others kept shooting. We moved back onto the paved road, and out of range.

"They will follow." Jorge looked at his wristwatch. "We should be at the airport in half an hour."

"Is it safe?" Mick Murphy said. "I mean, won't the authorities know all about this shit?"

"*Sí,* all Tampico knows by now," Jorge said, no urgency in his tone. "*La policia*, the Tampico police will take care of us. *Mi familia, mi tio y primo*."

Smuggling is a family affair in Tampico, I assumed, since Jorge's family were the airport police.

"Will your family fight?" I moved in close to hear because the screeching sound still vibrated in my ears.

"A little," Jorge answered. At least it promised something.

"How much time to get in the air?" I stretched out and touched Pauly.

"Fifteen minutes." Pauly turned to me. "Less if we don't check everything and . . ."

"And what?" I said.

"We didn't land with much fuel."

"*No hay problema*!" Jorge yelled. His ears had to be ringing too.

"You sure?" Pauly said.

"Paid for. It is done." Jorge rhythmically slapped the steering wheel, happy and proud of himself.

"Let's hope so." Pauly didn't sound convinced.

Jorge pointed to the floor, Pauly reached down and lifted

out the satchel we'd seen him leave with from the compound.

"For you." He looked into the mirror at me.

"What is it?" Pauly opened it, handed me a notebook. He left the loose papers in the satchel.

"*El ruso* had it. Sent us to get it. I thought it is important and you would want it. Maybe help you?" Jorge scanned the rear-view mirror to see if anyone followed. "Payment for my flight?"

"He gave it to you?" I took the notebook, looked at the writing and knew I wouldn't understand anything in it.

"He died in the battle, so I rescued the documents," Jorge laughed. "Good papers?"

Jorge had killed the Russian for this bounty and had no idea if it was useful or not. He wasn't a guy I'd want to turn my back on.

Mick Murphy pulled the notebook from me. "Russian!" He was excited. He flipped through the pages. "We need to get it translated. It'll tell us something about Alexei."

"Where do we go?" I took the notebook back. "The Russian embassy is out." My sarcasm went without comment.

Pauly turned to face us from the front seat. "Isn't Burt's lady friend Russian?"

"She's in Key West," Mick Murphy mumbled. "Nadja."

"*Putas!* We have company," Jorge said.

"How much longer?" I saw one pickup speeding to catch up with us.

"Ten minutes," Jorge said.

I looked forward and there wasn't any traffic. "Jorge, where's the traffic?"

"*No sé. Policia?*"

"Another roadblock?" I didn't like the thought or our chances of running successfully through one a second time.

"*Policia*, they will let us pass," he said. "Airport, *no hay problema.*"

"Pauly? Say something." I moved close to hear his reply.

"We should be able to get to Texas." He turned to me. "Get on board and we'll be in the air in ten. We have fuel, we're on our way home."

"We need to find out where Alexei went!" Mick Murphy said. "There could be a lot of information in there." He pointed at the notebook.

"Unless you read Russian . . ." I didn't bother to finish because I saw a helicopter in the air, far ahead of us. "Jorge!" I pointed over his shoulder.

"I see it," he said. "Airport security."

"That can't be good."

"*No hay problema*," he said, again. "They do not know who we are, but they see the men behind us with guns. They are for observation and maybe," he smiled into the mirror at me, "the radioman is on my payroll, or *los Zetas'* or Sinaloa's, so they will not report us right away."

No hay problema seemed to be his favorite expression. I hoped it was more than that. That it was fact and he really had a handle on what was happening.

"There," Jorge pointed ahead at the airport fence. It was open, but no one manned it. No one I could see, anyway. "Soon we are on our way."

Bullets slapped against the Hummer's back window as Jorge sped through the gate toward Pauly's plane. The pickup was only yards behind and no Tampico police were there to stop them. No one to put up a fight to give us those ten minutes we needed to get airborne.

Chapter Twenty-Four

Behind us, men kept shooting. Above, a helicopter hovered. I thought things couldn't get worse, and then I saw three police cars, lights flashing, sirens wailing, headed our way. I leaned forward and shook Jorge's shoulder.

"Whose side are they on?" I looked out the window, hoping to find something useable as cover, if we ended up in a firefight with cops or the shooters in the pickup. Other than airplanes, there wasn't anything else to use for shelter. It didn't leave me with a good feeling.

Jorge kept driving toward Pauly's plane, making a head-on collision inevitable with the police cars. "*Mi primo*," he said and slowed as two cop cars flew past, one on either side.

I followed the cars from the back window and watched the pickup truck stop and direct gunfire toward them, away from us. I turned forward when Jorge stopped the Hummer. The driver's side window came down and he talked rapidly to his cousin in the third police car; of course, I was only guessing it was his cousin.

Two cops sat in backseat, holding large, nasty looking rifles. Maybe thirty-caliber. A brief conversation, a thank-you and we headed toward the plane. The cops went to join the battle.

"Your cousin?" I said, my ears still ringing.

"On my mother's side," Jorge said. "Fuel has been delivered."

"I heard," Pauly said.

Behind us, the three police cars separated, half-circled, stopped, and fired on the shooters. The heavy thirty-caliber bullets ripped holes in the pickup's body. It looked as if we'd have the ten or fifteen minutes we needed to get into the air. The helicopter circled above the shootout.

Jorge stopped two planes away so there'd be clear access to the runway, and we rushed to Pauly's Beechcraft Starship. It still looked strange with the two turboprop engines in back, but it was our savior.

Jorge kept turning toward the shootout, its loud reports

"I'm lucky I read English," Mick Murphy said. I thought it a strange comment from a guy who made his living as a journalist.

Pauly had two bottles of Abbey Ale open on the desk and one pressed against his lips as we came into the office.

"Help yourself." He finished his beer and took another from the small refrigerator.

"Where's Jorge?" I took a long swallow of the cold brew. Pauly knew his beers.

"Jorge who?"

"Jorge no one," I said and guessed someone met the drug lord and whisked him away.

We both turned to Mick Murphy. He gave us another forced grin and put the satchel on the desk.

"I think I know where Alexei's going." He removed the notebook. Mick Murphy knew what page he wanted and opened right to it.

"You figured out the Russian?" Pauly said.

"No. But there's an address in here that I recognize."

Pauly and I came around to his side of the desk. My curiosity piqued, wondering how he understood an address in Russian.

"Right here." His finger rested on 24.5553° N, 81.7828° W.

"Latitude and longitude," Pauly said and then his frown turned into a grin.

"Okay, what do you two know that I don't?" I said.

"Norm, this is the nautical location of Key West Harbor," Mick Murphy said. "Alexei's going back to Key West."

I heard more concern in his tone than excitement.

"And you know this how?" I said.

"When I'm off in the Stream and ready to sail home, those coordinates are a waypoint in my autopilot, so I hit the button and go." Mick Murphy took his hand away from the book. "It brings me to Key West Harbor. I know 'em by heart."

"What would Alexei want in Key West Harbor?"

"You're asking the wrong question," Mick Murphy said. "What would Arabs, trained by Alexei to fly, want in Key West

Harbor with an airplane?"

"Shit!" I understood what he was getting at.

Chapter Twenty-Eight

"Let's not go off half-cocked," I said. The three of us stared at the handwritten longitude and latitude numbers in the Russian notebook. "We could be reading something into this that ain't there."

"Norm's got a point," Pauly said. "No towers in Key West. Nothing worth crashing a plane into."

"But you both thought it," Mick Murphy said. "So did I. The worst-case scenario makes sense because we don't know what else is written in here, but we do know history." He shook the notebook.

"We need to get it translated," Pauly said. "Norm, your people . . ."

"You give this to Joint Special Operations Command and we'll never know what's in it," I said. "Mick, it's Nadja and it means going to Key West."

"You have to call," Pauly said.

"Yeah." Mick Murphy garbled his response. "Couldn't she come here?"

"No direct flights, Mick," Pauly said. "We'd be wasting a day, at least, maybe two."

"Depending on what's in the papers we might have twenty-four hours or we could be wrong on all counts," I said. "One way to find out. Have 'em translated."

Pauly and I watched Mick Murphy. The devil tugged on his shirttails, making Key West the gates to hell. The translation might get him closer to Alexei but it meant going back, relive the horror and loss, something he'd spent the past year avoiding. We all mourn differently. Mick Murphy chose vengeance-filled hatred and avoidance. It had worked up until now. It was time to make a choice.

"I'll call Burt," Mick Murphy said. "I don't have Nadja's number. What do I tell them?"

"The truth," I said. "But the truth the way you tell it, leaving things out."

"What's that supposed to mean?" Mick Murphy snapped.

"You need her to translate some Russian writing," I said. "Don't tell her more than that."

"She's curious, she'll want to know about the papers."

"You could be wrong." Pauly handed us new Abbey Ales. "No one's seen or heard from you in a year, so Burt's gonna be more interested in what happened to you. He's curious too."

"Tell 'em you'll explain everything when we meet," I said. "You sure she's fluent in Russian?"

"She grew up there, left for Paris as a teenager," Mick Murphy said. "She asked about my accent once, so I asked about hers."

"Call Burt."

Mick Murphy looked at his watch. "It's late."

"So maybe he'll be home and not in some downtown watering hole." I had some of the ale.

Mick Murphy nodded and walked out of the office, reaching for his cell phone. Pauly and I watched through the office window as he stopped and looked at the airplane. Mick Murphy turned toward us and raised the phone high so we'd see it. If he made the call, he'd beaten his devils, for a while, anyway. The final decision seemed to take time, but then he hit speed dial and raised the phone to his ear. He'd kept his Key West phone number and all his contacts, while with me in California. If he ever started to erase them, I'd begin to worry about his intentions.

"I don't see another plane." I looked around the large hangar.

Pauly laughed. "Norm, I'm surprised at you! Keeping two planes together would reduce my chances of escape. Right?"

"Yeah, sorry. Don't know what I was thinkin,'" I said. "What will we be flying back in?"

"A Cessna Conquest."

"You like your toys."

"You don't?"

I nodded my understanding and focused back on Mick Murphy, leaving Pauly to his lifestyle plans and preparations.

Neither Pauly nor I thought to time the call, but we

watched Mick Murphy talk as he circled the Beech Starship, moving out of our sight briefly. He walked back to the office pocketing the cell phone.

"Great planners, guys," Mick Murphy said. He took an Abbey Ale from the refrigerator. "Burt asked where he and Nadja should meet us, after I told him not to tell people about my coming back."

"What did you say?" I realized I hadn't thought it through and that wasn't a good sign.

"What I always do, Norm," he growled. "I made it up as I went. Told him I'd be in touch tomorrow afternoon." He turned to Pauly. "We'll be there in the afternoon?"

"Fly into Marathon, call them, and drive to Key West before happy hour," he answered. "Leave after breakfast and flight inspection."

Mick Murphy turned to me. "You happy now?"

Did he want an argument? "Happy as a pig in slop. You?"

"This doesn't change anything. I'm still going after Alexei. If he's in Key West, that's fine, but if not, wherever the notes indicate he's gone."

"No one's disagreeing with you," I said.

"Do you have a land map of Key West?" He turned to Pauly.

"Somewhere." Pauly opened and closed drawers until he pulled out a folded up map. He opened it on the desk. "Best I got."

Mick Murphy moved the map until Key West Harbor showed closest to him. "What's here worth attacking?" He focused on the map.

"A couple of large hotels, Mallory Square and Sunset Key." Pauly pointed at a section of the map.

"What if they've got more than one plane? They only needed one to train on," I said.

"What's the point of hitting two hotels?" Mick Murphy grumbled, more to himself than us. "What kind of damage could a small, twin-engine plane cause?"

"Enough, if it's turned into a bomb," I said. "Didn't Jorge

call the Iranian Arabs?"

"Yeah, said they're all Arabs to him." Pauly looked at me. "What?"

"I told you, the Iranians aren't Arabs, but they use Palestinians and the Lebanese Hezbollah for dirty work. I can't remember an Iranian suicide bomber, can you?" I said. "Jorge said there were four Iranians. What if he was wrong? What if there were two Iranians and two from Hezbollah? Or only one Iranian handler."

"What *do* we know?" Mick Murphy said. "What do we actually know that we're not speculating about?"

"We had four Russians in a Mexican drug cartel camp training two or three Arabs to fly," Pauly said. "That much we got from Jorge."

"Why? Why use Russians to train Hezbollah, if Norm's right? Why are the Russians involved at all?" Mick Murphy was thinking aloud again. "What's Alexei get from it?"

"A lot of good questions," I said and pulled the notebook from under the map. "The answers are in here and to get them, we need to go to Key West."

"Tomorrow." Mick Murphy looked at Pauly. "What's the plan?"

"Register at the hotel, now," Pauly said. "Then go to Landry's for oysters and steak. Get a good night's sleep. We've been up a long time and I need sleep. We'll be back here before nine. In the air at ten and less than three-hours to Marathon. If we run into headwinds, it might take four."

Mick Murphy took the notebook from me and put it back in the satchel. "Okay, let's do it," he said.

He'd have to work on his presentation more if he expected to convince me he was ready to go back to Key West.

. . . is a friend indeed

PART TWO

Mick Murphy's Story

The world breaks everyone, and afterward, some are strong at the broken places.

Ernest Hemingway, 1899-1961

Chapter Twenty-Nine

I sat in the main cabin of Pauly's Cessna Conquest on the flight to the Keys. Norm took the co-pilot's seat and talked to Pauly, leaving me alone in the cabin. I kept Alexei's satchel and knew it held *his* journal. When I came across the longitude and latitude for Key West Harbor in the book, I also knew I had to go back to Key West.

Strange how a place I called home for almost twenty years, and I once held fond memories of, turned so quickly into a black-ass evil that brought on a severe depression. When Alexei's men sent the 20-millimeter shells into the *Fenian Bastard*, killing Tita and sinking the boat, I should've died too. Pauly's retired-Marine sniper killed the Russian shooter before he got a third shot off and that saved me. If I had died all this hatred inside me, a cancer, eating me away a little at a time, wouldn't be and I'd be wherever the dead go. Maybe I'd finally be talking to Padre Thomas' angels.

I used to be scared to death of dying. Now I'm scared to death of living. I have no thought of an existence beyond putting a bullet into Alexei's head. I need him to know I'm pulling the trigger. I need him to realize what a mistake it was to fuck with me; to take the life of the woman I loved, to end the lifestyle I enjoyed and for that split second after the bullet tears into his skull, I want to see the horror and fear in his eyes, especially as they turn lifeless.

The JSOC shrink Norm had me talk to while I recovered from my injuries at his compound, Dr. Arianna Carpino, told me that killing Alexei wouldn't bring Tita back or change the past. Norm told me that, too. They didn't understand I had no future, nothing to care about, if I didn't seek vengeance.

Norm thought I was suicidal. He didn't say it outright, but he moved his arsenal to a lock up somewhere, we never made it to the indoor shooting range at his compound.

On the road, we shared a room. We'd never done that in all our travels together, not in the states, not in Central America.

He didn't want to leave me by myself. I caught other, more subtle things as my physical condition improved and we went outside the compound. At first, he wouldn't let me drive and had a million excuses why. We'd go to the movies, but it was always a comedy. The same with TV programing. He may believe laughter cures all ills. I don't.

The shrink thought I was suicidal too, but she told me straightforward. They're wrong. I'm not going to kill myself. I'm gonna kill Alexei and if I have to die doing it, that's something I'll deal with. The only worry I have about dying is that I will do it before killing Alexei.

I sat, listening to the drone of the twin engines and realized that Norm was right about my being fixated on Alexei. I am, but it kept me on this side of the sanity line.

Going to Key West and seeing Burt and Nadja after all this time caused a panic attack, but I overcame it. For the first time in a year, I realized I missed my island friends. Guilt ate at my nervous stomach because I owed Bob, Burt, Doug, Texas Rich and for sure Padre Thomas an explanation. I assumed Norm kept Richard Dowley, the chief of police, another friend, up to date. He denied it. Norm can do many things, but for some reason his ability to lie falters when it comes to me.

The plane began a slow descent and I could see a small cluster of mangrove islands out the window. Marathon airport couldn't be far. Anxiety made me sweat like a fat man walking Duval Street at noon in August.

How things had changed about me in just one year.

I was afraid of everything, especially the memories of what once brought happiness to my life. The people, the bars, the water, the weather of Key West, it all scared me. A fine mess to find myself in.

I clutched the satchel like Linus holds his security blanket. I could do this, I thought as my hands trembled. I could do this because it would bring me one-step closer to killing Alexei.

Chapter Thirty

A breeze carrying the smell of spilt fuel and exhaust, with traces of salt water and humidity, greeted me as I exited the plane at the Marathon Municipal Airport. Almost sheer, white clouds moved gently across the bright-blue sky and traffic hummed along U.S. 1. A private jet prepared to take off, its engine noise vibrated the air.

We arrived with time to spare, even though Pauly said we were not flying at full speed. There was plenty of time for us to make happy hour in Key West. But I wasn't interested in happy hour. Norm walked out of the Cessna, talking on his cell phone. Pauly followed.

"I've got to check in at the office." Pauly shut the plane's door. "They haven't seen this bird before."

Norm closed his cell. "We'll meet you in the parking lot."

"Give me five minutes." Pauly headed toward the office.

"I need to call Burt." Norm and I walked toward the parking lot.

"Yeah," Norm said. "Where do you want to meet them?"

"You tell me."

"I got us a room at the Mango Tree Inn."

"Get us two rooms," I said. "I need some privacy."

Norm made the call. No argument from him surprised me. Maybe it was a step forward.

"Two rooms," he said after the call. "You get poolside. I get the Simonton Street room."

"First floor?" Poolside was a nice room but it kept me in the gated yard.

"Yeah, hoss." He laughed as he unlocked the SUV. "Last time we were upstairs, there was a major fire."

The memory flashed me back a few years to when a city commissioner, a dirty DEA agent and a Brit mercenary, all working for a Mexican cartel, tried to smuggle drugs into the Keys. The commissioner killed the DEA agent and was about to kill me when Padre Thomas violated everything he believed in, shot the commissioner using my gun, saved my life, and vanished for almost a year.

The Brit got away with most of the drug shipment.

Padre Thomas got the worst of the deal and when he returned to Key West, Norm and his spook buddies claimed the real Padre Thomas Collins lay in a mass grave in Guatemala. I believed differently, even though I'm not sure of what the truth is.

It all gave support to the old theory that Key West is a free-range institution, an open-air asylum, at its best.

"So, where do you wanna meet them?" Norm started the engine and turned on the air-conditioning.

It shouldn't have been a hard question to answer, but it caused me more anxiety. I patted the satchel. "Some place Nadja can read through this without being disturbed."

"The inn?"

"Not sure I want them to know where we're staying."

Norm leaned against the front seat, the SUV's door open, letting the cold air escape. "You need to get your shit together, hoss." His body tensed and his face tightened, losing any trace of a grin. "We could've stayed at the house, but I knew how hard that would've been on you. Okay, I gave you that, but you can't keep your fuckin' head buried in the sand. Man up. You know every place on this island where you can drink and party or you can have privacy. I don't give a rat's fuck about people recognizing you. I want to know what's in that book, so we can move on."

By *the house*, Norm meant Tita's house that she'd left to me. I lived off-and-on with her there, but mostly I lived on the *Fenian Bastard*. Both Tita and the boat were now gone and the memory haunted me. This was the first time Norm reverted to his old, no nonsense self in dealing with me. I took it as a sign of progress on both our parts.

"I appreciate that," I said and felt the humidity for the first time. "It's not easy. Coming back here." I couldn't bring myself to tell him to fuck off and mind his own business, so I tried sincerity.

"We're here, Mick. I'm not interested in a sob story. I wanna finish what we started and we can't do that until the book is translated," Norm said. "Everything else, your feelings, your dread, my wanting to get this over with, means nothing until we know what's in the damn book. Hell, he might be writing a new fuckin' Communist Manifesto or remembering quotes from Chairman Mao!"

Pauly walked over and could see we were arguing. "Everything okay?" He unlocked his car.

"We're trying to figure out where to meet Nadja, before Mick calls."

"There's my place on Key Haven."

"Mick?" Norm turned to me.

"What about Higg's Beach? There are tables and shade," I said. "We can get a Styrofoam cooler, ice and cold drinks."

"No liquor allowed on the county beach," Pauly said.

"Sodas are fine. Look like we're tourists enjoying the view," I said. "Pauly, you shouldn't come."

"Why?" Pauly looked surprised.

"Right now, there's no reason anyone has to know I'm back or that anyone other than Norm and I are involved. Let's find out what's in the book and work from there."

Norm looked more frustrated. "You want to know what's in the damn book? I'll tell you! Alexei is an old-line commie. Everyone worked in the Soviet Union, or at least they were supposed to. When the Wall came down and we got into East German security, the Stasi files were amazing. Know why? The Soviets taught them to keep reports. Stasi agents wrote daily reports and then another agent wrote a report of that report. Everything, from taking a crap to who you were screwin' showed up in someone's report and then that received a report. My guess is that Alexei's doing what comes natural to him. He's accounting for his daily routine by writing it down. That will be good for us. This could be a treasure trove." He tapped the satchel.

"Or what?" I said.

"Or nothing," Norm barked. "If it's Alexei's, it's a daily journal. Maybe even a detailed daily report. But he knows it's gone. He doesn't know who has it. He might think the Mexicans have it. But he'll be careful and change whatever plans are mentioned in this. So, you see, Mick, we need get it translated *now,* if it's gonna do us any good."

I nodded and dialed my cell. I told Burt we'd meet at Higg's Beach at six.

Chapter Thirty-One

Pauly leaned against his Jeep Wrangler in the parking lot across from Higgs Beach, on the south side of Key West, as far away from the business of Duval Street bars and T-shirt shops as I could get. The white sandy beach and blue-green water offered sanctuary to locals and tourists. Saluté Restaurant borders on the edges of the beach and Atlantic Boulevard. Between the restaurant and an old redbrick Civil War fort, concrete roofed picnic shelters line up on the sand's edge like dominos ready to topple. A large building houses the public restrooms where the shelters end.

Norm stopped the SUV next to Pauly. A little after six, Burt Carroll parked his pickup truck close to the Jeep. As he and Nadja Petrowa got out, it surprised me how little they changed. Burt was close to six foot and lanky, with bushy blonde hair and a walrus mustache. Nadja had kept her dark hair short, and hadn't aged a day. Her petite figure still held its shapeliness.

Burt greeted me with rapidly asked questions and I assured him we'd talk after Nadja translated the documents I had. He looked toward Norm and Pauly for help, but didn't get any.

Nadja and I crossed the street and sat in the shade of one concrete shelter, cooled by an early evening breeze coming from the water. She focused on the Russian journal, jotting down information in a notebook. I asked her to start translating close to the latitude numbers because they indicated Key West Harbor. She went back three days and worked forward, sometimes going further back, past the three-day mark, when she read something that referred to an earlier date.

She kept a grim expression and sighed as she read and wrote notes, often shaking her head and glancing at me.

"Do you know who wrote this, Mick?" Nadja looked up, placed her notebook between the pages and closed the journal.

"I've met him."

"Is this real? I mean, does it contain true events?"

"Yes."

"He's without a soul. He's a psychopath." Her words

came between deep breaths. "It reads like a KGB report." She stared at me, waiting for my reply.

"Yes, he's old KGB." How'd she know what a KGB report read like?

"But this was written recently," she said. "What is he now?"

"A gangster," I said. "What does he say in it?"

"He's involved in illegal activities here and abroad."

"Why the latitude? It's Key West harbor." I didn't care about his corruptness here or overseas. I cared about what he was doing in Key West.

"I know that, Mick." I knew she did, we were both sailors.

"Why does he mention the harbor?"

The sun began to descend over the homes of the Casa Marina neighborhood, behind us. Only a few people were in the water and the boisterous happy hour crowd at Saluté slowly changed to a quieter group of couples and foursomes in for dinner, as we sat there. Choppy, wind-driven waves washed up on the beach, rolling along the sand, the splash scratching the air with each recurrence.

"It's complicated. He . . . does *he* have a name?" she said.

"Alexei."

"Alexei doesn't want anything in the harbor."

"What?"

"That's why I have to go to the beginning of the journal, Mick," she said. "The harbor involves others. He refers to them, but they aren't Russians."

"Iranians? Arabs?"

"He mentioned Spanish names, Mexicans he calls them," she said, opening the book and removing her notebook. "*Los Zetas*. More psychopaths, Mick. Drugs. Let me take this home and translate it."

"I need the information."

"And *I need time* to search from the beginning, to see how the Mexicans are connected to Alexei." Nadja closed the journal. "I need to do this at home. Begin at the beginning and see if I can find the Iranians too."

I turned toward the Atlantic Boulevard parking lot where Norm and Pauly waited with Burt, giving Nadja my back.

Making a decision, any decision seemed to be difficult these days. I used to make harder decisions on the run, some of them life or death decisions. I trusted Nadja but letting the book out of my hands terrified me. It was my only link to Alexei and if I lost it . . . I made myself sick, thinking it. Her knowing what KGB reports read like surprised me. What else didn't I know about her?

With my back still turned, I said, "When can I get it back?"

"Late morning," Nadja said. "I'll work all night, if I have to. Probably couldn't sleep after this, anyway. What have you got yourself into?"

I turned and faced her. Could the KGB have sent her to Paris as a teenager? Paranoia worsened my anxiety. I forced myself to remember that Nadja and Burt had been my friends for a long time, that we'd shared sailing adventures, barbecues and hurricanes. Before I could answer, Nadja's stare toward the cars made me turn to look. Bob Lynds had parked his pickup next to Norm's SUV.

"Burt wasn't supposed to tell anyone," I said, feeling a jolt of excitement at seeing my friend.

"Bob isn't anyone." Nadja stood and put the journal in her large purse. "He's *someone*. He's a friend who cares."

We crossed the street, the sun low in the sky, and watched as traffic stopped at the White Street intersection. The road construction on North Roosevelt Boulevard turned the street into the congested, major route off the island.

Bob stood a lean six-foot and wore his silver-blonde hair in a ponytail. A couple of years before my life turned to a living hell, I discovered he'd been a Navy SEAL. You wouldn't know it from his quiet demeanor. He'd walk away from a troublemaker, that's how tough he really was.

"I thought you were dead." His deadpan voice greeted me. "Glad I was wrong."

"Me too," I said.

"Where the hell you been? You missed Richard Collins' funeral. Man, we all thought you'd get your sorry ass to that."

"I didn't know," I said. "Richard was a good friend. I would've come back."

Bob stood there and stared. "It must be something, for you to be gone a year without a word and not to keep track of what was happening on the island."

"Most of it I spent recovering." He knew that, but I had to say something.

"Weren't allowed to pick up a phone?"

"Had nothing to say."

"You coming or going?"

I looked toward Nadja. "Ask me tomorrow."

"What are you doing here with Russian documents? Alexei?" Bob asked questions, but his tone was confident. They were really statements.

Norm made a slight head movement that told me he hadn't said anything. I doubt Pauly had. Bob and Burt went through the calamity with me the night that took Tita and were able to guess what this was all about without my saying a word. These were my friends and they had avoided mentioning anything about that fatal night.

"I've got to go," Nadja said to me. "Okay?"

Granting permission to Nadja to take Alexei's journal left me hesitant, but I didn't see another choice. I was out of Russian speaking friends, even if I had my paranoid doubts about her.

"What time tomorrow?" I said. "Not too late."

"Burt and I will meet you for breakfast. Say ten o'clock, at Harpoon Harry's," she said.

"Too busy, too crowded."

"You name a place."

I couldn't think of any. I was sweating and it wasn't from the humidity. I felt dizzy and losing control. It scared me.

"Harpoon's, 10 o'clock," I said. "Don't be late."

"Mick, when did you last eat?" Nadja said. "Go eat something and rest tonight. You might not be as fully recovered as you think." She spoke to me but looked at Norm.

Chapter Thirty-Two

I waited for a panic attack to kick in as Burt drove away with Nadja and Alexei's journal. My nerves rumbled like an out-of-control roller coaster speeding toward the deepest, scariest drop. I fought nausea. When I turned Bob, Pauly and Norm stared at me. I wondered if I wore my anxiety openly or kept it hidden.

The moon appeared in the sky and the sun hadn't set yet. On our side of Atlantic Boulevard, the parking lot was empty while the beachside had only a few spots left as people arrived at Saluté. No one spoke. Bob took a cigar from his pocket and prepared to light it.

There's a ritual to preparing a good cigar. I remembered the whole process, even though it had been almost a year since I'd last smoked. Bob breathed in the tobacco aroma, while rolling what I knew to be a dark, maduro-wrapped, Churchill-sized cigar between his thumb and fingers. A small piece of tobacco, the cap, is placed over the end of a freshly hand rolled cigar. You want to cut the end where the cap meets the outer wrapper leaf. Bob was able to do that perfectly with only a glance before he made the cut. He exchanged the cutter for his lighter. Rolling the cigar again, Bob put the lighter's flame to its end, making sure it lighted evenly before putting it in his mouth. He puffed on the cigar, while the lighter's flame grew, and the tip glowed red. Satisfied, he put away the lighter.

My turning stomach relaxed and I wanted a cigar. Bob blew thick, white smoke into the air and offered me one. I took it and performed the ritual. How could such a small act relax me? The peppery taste of tobacco lingered as I drew smoke in.

"So, nothing to say?" Bob stood across from me, his words heavy with accusation. "But you had something to say to a black-bag guy and ex-drug smuggler." He turned to Norm and Pauly. "No offense meant guys."

"None taken," Norm mumbled.

"We've been through a lot together, Mick, or don't you remember?" Bob stood tall, using the cigar to point at me. "Burt and I, we've had your back more times than I like to remember. What about these two? You had something to say to them, but not to me? Norm ever been here before the shit hit the fan?" He looked at Norm who raised his hands, palms out in surrender, and nodded. "What were we supposed to think? What were you thinking? We all felt your loss. Tita was my friend too."

I chomped down on the cigar when Bob said Tita. I couldn't remember anyone other than the government's shrink, Arianna Carpino, speaking her name. I thought of Tita constantly, but never said her name aloud. I waited to explode, but nothing happened. Bob continued his rant.

"We worried about you. We didn't know if you were alive or dead, a vegetable or in a wheelchair. Your buddy the priest assured us you were okay. I listened to the guy, can you believe that?"

I believed Padre Thomas had certain gifts, one of them being the ability to see and talk to angels. What Bob and Norm thought of him didn't concern me.

"And you had nothing to say, so you didn't call!" Bob stabbed the air with the burning cigar. "You didn't think about what we might have to say. Kind of selfish, Mick."

I heard Bob as I escaped into the taste and smoke of the cigar. At that moment, if I could've disappeared, I would have. His words weren't said angrily, something they could have been, but there wasn't any sympathy in them either. What they were, were accurate. My emotions became a mixture of denial and belief, but I didn't lose control. I held the cigar, took a deep breath and looked toward Norm for help. He didn't offer any. I was on my own.

"I don't have an excuse," I said, feeling the texture of the tobacco as I turned the cigar in circles with my fingers. "I'm here now."

"Wow! The great Mick Murphy has graced us with an appearance." Bob laughed. He spread his arms wide. "In what, twenty years? We've never been here. Never been to Saluté. What are we doing here now?"

"I needed to talk to Nadja."

"On a public beach, away from your friends and any place that people might recognize you, right?" Bob blew smoke toward me. "Why? Why are you hiding from us, from me?"

It was a good, honest question. I detected hurt in his voice and heard the anger. No matter what I said, the truth or something I made up, it wouldn't matter. I was after Alexei and Bob would be there for me, as I knew Pauly would, if I asked. I had only wanted Norm's help but I didn't have control of the situation and found myself in need of others and chose Pauly. I knew Pauly would walk away when I said to. I knew Bob wouldn't. Bob didn't believe in leaving anyone behind, it was in his SEAL training and he wouldn't let me go after Alexei alone, knowing it was going to be a one-way trip.

I turned to Norm and Pauly. "Say something!"

"I'm hungry." Norm looked at his wristwatch.

I couldn't believe that was Norm's reply, his effort to help.

"Let me put some reality into your world, Mick." Bob dropped his cigar and crushed it under his tennis shoe. "You walk into any of your old hangouts right now and I bet most everyone won't recognize you. Maybe the red hair will get stares, but, hell, it's too long and the beard is shabby. You don't look like your old self. You've been gone a year. You know how many others have packed up and left in that time? Hell, this island has a transient population. People remember you when they see you, forget you when they don't."

"Good to know." I couldn't think of anything else to say.

"I'm telling you this so you can go eat," Bob said. "And you don't have to worry about people recognizing you. Take a walk along Duval. The only thing that's changed is you."

Chapter Thirty-Three

Pauly drove home, promising to see us for breakfast. His curiosity about the Russian journal was piqued when he noticed Nadja's apprehension after reading it. Norm and I went to the Mango Tree Inn. We didn't talk until he'd parked on Southard Street, outside the inn.

"You hungry?" Norm said standing in the street.

"Yeah. Pizza?"

"And beer."

"I'll get the pizza you get the beer at Fausto's and don't forget to buy some salt."

"Large, pepperoni and onion."

"And jalapeños." Food wasn't food to me unless it had a kick.

I walked to Upper Crust for a pizza, Norm to Fausto's for beer. The nice thing about Old Town, you could walk everywhere.

Norm surprised me leaving me on my own. On the way to get the pizza, I realized I hadn't given any thought to the fact that we went everywhere together. He was there when I was ill and needed help during my recovery. His presence had become routine and I hadn't questioned it.

"Took you long enough." Norm sat by the inn's pool, a small table pulled between two lounge chairs. "Jimmy at Fausto's said to say hi and I thanked him for having Harp."

"No Guinness?" I put the pizza box on the table and opened it. "Did you remember napkins?"

Norm pulled a small paper bag from the ground and handed me the salt and a package of napkins.

"Salt's gonna kill you, hoss, you know that, right?" He took a slice of pizza and began to eat. "Your blood pressure ain't too great as it is."

"Do you have a license to practice medicine?" I sprinkled salt on the pizza slice, sat down and ate.

When we'd almost drained our second beer, the pizza was gone. The scent of night jasmine filled the pool area, carried on a soft breeze. Traffic hummed along Simonton Street. The June night cooled off and the temperature had dropped to the mid-70s. Scents I hadn't known since leaving Key West filled the air with everything but smog. Key West wasn't Los Angeles.

"We need to talk." I closed the pizza box and carried it and our empty beer bottles to the trash.

"I'm listening." Norm stretched out, still wearing his old cowboy boots.

I took the extra cigar Bob gave as his parting gift, along with a lighter and cheap cutter, and prepared it. "Whatever we learn from the journal, we leave together."

"Of course."

"Without Pauly or Bob."

Norm sat up a little and rotated his shoulders. "What if we need 'em?"

I shook my head.

"We needed Pauly in South Beach and really needed him in Mexico," Norm said. "There wouldn't be a journal if he didn't have his Mexican connections."

"We needed him when we needed him, now we don't. At least wait until we survey the situation." I wanted as few of my friends involved as possible and Norm knew that.

"Mick, you need to prepare yourself for disappointment," he said. "Your hopes are too high that something important is in that book. No one, Jorge especially, ever mentioned Alexei by name."

"You think it's some other Russian?" It came out as a challenge. I didn't mean it to, but that's the way it sounded.

"I think it could be him." Norm took a long swallow of beer. I lit my cigar. "I also know the Russian Mafia has businesses in Houston, Dallas and San Antonio, so it could be someone from there. I'm just saying, be prepared for that."

"We got the information about Mexico from one of his lieutenants," I said. "Isn't that why we had the warehouse in Fort Lauderdale, to get Alexei's whereabouts from these guys?"

"A man who knew he was going to die." Norm sat up.

"Torture gets you what you want, not necessarily the truth."

I knew that. I learned it while reporting from Central America, where imprisonment meant torture if the military thought you might be a supporter of the insurgents. That usually involved college students, union leaders and Jesuits. I had interviewed a few that weren't disappeared by the military and their stories made it difficult for me to write because of the horrors. Not reporting the truth would've been an added insult to them and writing the truth wouldn't pass the editors' red pencil. The result was always the same, they told the torturers what they wanted to hear.

True or not, I didn't want to hear it. I needed the journal to lead me to Alexei.

"It's all I've got Norm," I said. "I need it be Alexei's."

"You know my philosophy, Mick, hope for the best, prepare for the worst. Just be prepared."

"Yeah, I know."

Norm sat back and finished his beer. I smoked and enjoyed the seclusion of the garden. The breeze caused the pool surface to ripple and the colored underwater lights splashed wavy patterns onto the plants.

"You still want to leave right away?" Norm looked at the pool.

"Yes! As soon as we know anything," I said. "Alexei has to be wondering who has the journal. You said so yourself."

"Whatever plans he made, he'll change 'em. He might give it twenty-four hours, maybe a little longer because it's Mexico and he doesn't have his usual contacts right there to search for it. But he'll think it's compromised and that means the information won't be good."

"Tomorrow, we've got to act as soon as we know."

"If it leads us to Miami, sure. If it's New York, we might be out of luck."

I leaned back and tried to enjoy the cigar.

"You think you'll come back here, settle up things?" Norm threw his empty beer into the trash.

"I don't know." I had spent a year avoiding that decision.

"Tita left you the house." He stood over me. "She wanted you to have it."

"I'm not ready to go there."

"You need to make yourself ready," he said. "It won't go away. Confront your devils. It's the only way to beat them. Go there and give her personal items to the family. They deserve that much. Think of what Tita would want you to do. Fuck your emotions. You know it's the right thing to do."

"I wish it was that easy," I said. "I don't know what will happen when I walk through that door. I could lose it. I mean, really lose it."

"You don't exactly have it all together now, hoss."

Chapter Thirty-Four

Norm went to his room, after I'd promised not to leave and walk Duval Street alone. If I had such an urge, which I assured him I didn't, he wanted to go with me. What happened to trusting me on my own? I kept the thought to myself, while I sat back on the lounge, rolled the cigar between my fingers, looked at the star-filled sky and breathed in the scents of night jasmine.

Sadness overcame me as I realized Key West no longer offered the phenomenon it once did. The fun-filled days and nights of loving Tita, enjoying how quickly she turned into a sailor, how she tagged along on my Sunday bar stroll, meeting and greeting friends; our quiet moments alone, the aroma of her *arroz con pollo* simmering on the stove, her brewing *café con leches* – Puerto Rican coffee she'd always correct Norm when he called it Cuban coffee – these were gone forever. Forever was a long time.

I wanted vengeance. Vengeance against the man responsible for killing Tita, for making me face forever alone. I had no idea where I'd go after I killed Alexei.

Maybe Norm was right and I had to be responsible. I needed to close up Tita's house, send her things to a family that no longer talked to me. I couldn't blame them. There was no trace of Tita to bury after the 20mm shell made its direct hit, no body to grieve over, no casket to inter, and even her brother Paco, my college roommate, held me responsible.

I could sell the house, send her family the money and ship her belongings. That would be the honorable thing to do.

I blew cigar smoke toward the pool and wondered, half-dozing, if I had ever been an honorable man.

"Mick." The soft dream-like voice pulled me from sleep. "You shouldn't fall asleep smoking."

I rubbed sleep from my eyes and looked up to see Padre Thomas Collins, my Jesuit friend and seer of angels, standing over me, holding my half-smoked cigar. At first, I thought I was dreaming because he hadn't changed in the year I'd been gone. Padre Thomas stood about five-eight, thin as an anorexic model, a long, narrow nose too large for his bony face and dressed in the usual sleeveless, buttoned-down Oxford shirt that looked a size larger than he needed, with two packages of Camel cigarettes in the shirt's pocket.

"Cat got your tongue?" He sat across from me.

I took the cigar, it had gone out.

"Padre Thomas," I muttered, trying to decide if he was a dream or real. "What are you doing here?"

"I should ask you that." His pale blue eyes shined in the shadowy patio. "Are you okay?"

I sat up, lit the cigar and wondered how he knew I was at the inn. It had to be the angels and when I thought that, I think I might have smiled.

"I wonder if you're okay . . ." he tapped his chest. "Is your heart in the right place?"

"Not sure, Padre," I said.

He grinned at me even though I could see disappointment in his expression. "Do you want to talk about it?"

"Not really."

"It's not good to let it eat away at you."

"What's *it*?"

"Your hate." He lit a cigarette. "It's directing your life. Once you've got your revenge, nothing will have changed. "

"Some debts have to be collected." I stubbed out the cigar and handed him a Harps, it had almost lost its chill. I took the last one.

"Thank you." He was a Bud drinker. After reading the label, he took a sip. "Not as good as the real Irish beer."

It felt good to see Padre Thomas. He didn't talk too often about his ability to communicate with angels, but he had no problem discussing them with me, as if he thought I was a believer. Sometimes I had to believe because it was the only explanation of how he knew what he knew, like to come to the inn. Other times I think that maybe we were both a little crazy. He'd saved my life a few times and there's no explanation for that, except his angels.

He finished the beer before he spoke. "You think your revenge will be a debt collected?"

"In a way."

"For Tita?" He put the empty bottle down. "There's nothing you can do for her now."

"Because of me, she was murdered." I let out a deep breath. "Alexei's men were after me. That leaves me with a debt to collect and Alexei to pay."

"No good can come from it." He crushed out his cigarette.

"I'm not looking for anything good," I said. "I don't deserve it."

"You deserve better than how you're treating yourself, Mick," he said, shaking his head. "You should realize that."

"I have another opinion."

"You have a decision to make and I pray that you'll make the right one."

"Don't waste your prayers, Padre. I'm going after Alexei."

"Prayers are never wasted," he said. "Your decision will be to stay or go."

"I'm going after Alexei. No prayers will stop me."

"But you don't know what's in the Russian journal. It may change your mind."

"And you do?"

"No," he said. "I know that tomorrow you will be forced to choose between your selfishness and the lives of others. Before all this happened last year, the Mick Murphy I knew wasn't selfish, so he'd choose others."

"But now it requires you to pray I make the right decision?"

"Yes Mick, because you've changed, changed what you believed in and you've changed from the man Tita loved into someone she wouldn't recognize."

Chapter Thirty-Five

Padre Thomas left and I went to my room. I couldn't sleep. I lay on top of the covers, watched lights from the garden come through the window and reflect onto the ceiling. The air-conditioner hummed and I heard cars as they drove past on Simonton Street.

Eventually I got up, walked to the bathroom and stared into the mirror. I looked like warmed-over shit in a cow pasture. My hair was too long, hanging over my collar, and my beard looked like Santa's but it was a dull red, not white. I threw cold water on my face. It did nothing for me. I still looked scruffy as hell.

I opened the door and it was quiet outside. The sky, black as my soul, but pierced with starlight, remained cloudless. Carefully, so I wouldn't wake Norm, I left the side yard of the inn, walked to the all-night drug store on Duval, and bought an Oster electric hair clipper set. At the last minute, I added a throwaway razor and a can of shaving cream.

Unless I wanted to shave my head, it would be impossible to cut my hair evenly, but I could trim my beard.

I looked into the bathroom mirror and remembered when I grew my first beard in the mountains of El Salvador. Bathing wasn't an option and shaving was out of the question, during the civil war. When I got back into San Salvador, I had a three-week beard growth. An Irish AP photographer, named Seánan, had been cutting my hair for months, but when she saw my beard, she laughed. She only had scissors, so she trimmed the beard as close as possible and then trimmed my hair. That was a long time ago and I've had the beard since.

When I figured out which blade guide was the shortest – a half inch – I started trimming my beard. I did it slowly and had to clean hair from the guide and blade a number of times. I lathered up and used the razor to clear away the hair stubble on my neck.

The person looking back at me seemed more human than he did earlier. I cleaned up and fell onto the bed fully clothed, feeling a few pounds lighter.

Norm woke me by banging on the door. The clock showed

it to be a little before eight. I hadn't slept until eight for a long time.

"Coming," I yelled.

Norm looked at me and frowned.

"What?" I said as I closed the door.

"Where'd you get the clippers?" He commented about my beard as he came into the room. "You been to bed?" He looked at the wrinkled comforter.

"I feel asleep on top of the covers. Padre Thomas came by."

He looked at me strangely and sat in a chair. "Really? What time was that?"

"After you went to bed."

The look didn't change with my explanation. "I was in my room on the phone," he said. "I had a good view of the pool and never saw the priest."

"He was here, we talked."

"Before or after you went to Duval Street, hoss?"

"Why didn't you come with me?"

"Before or after?" He asked again.

"Before. Why didn't you come with me?"

"You're a big boy, this is your town. Why would I go where I wasn't invited?"

"It was a spur-of-the-moment decision." All of a sudden, I felt guilty for not telling Norm I went to Duval, as I promised earlier. "Everyone's been saying how scraggly the beard looked, I saw myself in the mirror . . ."

"You don't have to explain yourself," he said. "The beard looks better, but you still need a haircut."

"When we get to Miami."

"If we have time," Norm said. "Back to the priest. Did he have anything to say, I mean besides his usual mumbo jumbo?"

"No." I didn't want to share our conversation and listen to his ridicule.

"No insight into what's in the journal?"

"No." The question surprised me. "I thought you weren't a

believer in things he said."

"I ain't. What I think is you had a dream. No one knows we're here, not even the angels. I'm not a shrink, Mick, but I've been around bad situations enough to know when someone's subconscious is kicking in. You should listen. Maybe it's your conscience speaking."

"I didn't dream him," I said. "And my conscience is fine."

"Mick, I watched you. You drank the last two beers, dropped your cigar and fell asleep on the lounge, woke and found the cigar, relit it and walked to your room. You dreamt him."

"I know reality from a dream."

"Do you? Padre Thomas has shown up at some unusual places in the past and he's never been shy of the people around you. Why'd he show up so late?"

I shook my head and even though I believed Padre Thomas had been there, Norm's words caused me to have doubt. I didn't like second-guessing myself. My cell chirped and the doubt took a backseat when I saw Burt's name on the cell screen.

"Answer it."

"Morning Burt." I checked the time, eight-thirty. I had a bad feeling about the call.

"It's not Burt," Nadja said. "I didn't have your cell so I had Burt call."

The bad feeling got worse. "There a problem, Nadja?"

Norm gave me his full attention when I said her name.

"I wanted you to know I finished translating the journal," she said. "Burt's making copies."

"We don't need copies," I said. "I need the original and one translation."

"I think after you read this, you'll see the need for copies."

"How many is he making?"

"Six."

"I want them all, all the copies." I didn't want the journal distributed around Key West, or anywhere. I regretted my decision to let her take the journal and shook my head, disgusted at myself for giving in to her demand.

"Mick, I wouldn't keep a copy if you asked me to."

"You want to meet earlier?" I hoped that was the reason behind the call.

"Sure," she said and hesitated. "I'd like to change the location too."

I closed my eyes and cringed. "What's wrong with Harpoon Harry's?"

"You have to read this, Mick, and Norm too," she said. "Believe me, you'll both want more privacy than Harpoon's gives."

"Does it tell me where Alexei is?"

"As I said before, the writer's name is never mentioned." She breathed heavily. "He does record where he'll wait."

"Wait for what?" Her cryptic conversation bothered me.

"I'm not comfortable talking about this on the phone, Mick."

"Meet you at Harpoon's in half an hour," I said.

"It's not the right place to do this."

"It's the only place, and you chose it," I said. "Be there with all the copies and the original, Nadja." I disconnected the call.

"Why is it the only place?" Norm had a puzzled look. "We might need privacy."

"A few reasons," I answered. "She chose it and now she's backing out. It's a public place and she can't set us up, if that's her plan."

"Set us up for what?"

"I don't know. I don't trust her."

"You trust Burt."

"She wouldn't be the first woman keeping secrets."

"What other reasons, Mick?"

"If she does anything, makes a scene, leads Alexei to us . . ."

"Hold on, hoss." Norm used his hands to make a timeout T. "You're moving too fast. Slow down."

"Okay, answer me this, why couldn't she just drop off the

translation and original and leave it at that?"

"I don't know, why didn't you ask?"

"If I don't trust her, why would I expect the truth?"

Chapter Thirty-Six

I washed up quickly in the bathroom, while Norm blamed Nadja's behavior on her being an amateur.

"I don't buy it." I dried my face. "She said the journal read like a KGB report. How the hell did she know what their reports read like?"

"You think Nadja's Russian mafia?" He almost laughed. "East German documents were leaked all over Europe after the Wall came down. She could have read a newspaper account. The Stasi made for great TV coverage, too."

"We know the Russian mafia's in South Florida," I said. "You're the one that said they recruit Eastern Europeans for their network, forcibly if need be. Why wouldn't they be in Key West? Where do you think most of the girls in the local strip clubs come from?"

"Mick, the possibility is slim to none." He stood by the open door, putting an end to the conversation. "Call Pauly."

"No!" I snapped my answer. "We get the info on Alexei and go."

"You might want to know why Alexei's waiting around."

"I don't care. He can be waiting for hell to freeze over, I don't care. I'm going wherever Alexei is."

"What if we need Pauly or Bob?"

"When that time comes I can call them."

"I'd be pissed if I showed up for breakfast and found out you'd come and gone without calling."

"You'd get over it. So will Pauly," I said. We walked to the car.

The city parking lot, across from Harpoon Harry's, was early-morning empty and Norm put the SUV there.

The restaurant's wall of glass doors was open, catching the ocean breeze. I had mixed emotions as I stared at the occupied booths. Harpoon's had been where I had breakfast for years, as well as a place that had been shot up because of me, more than once. Ron, the owner, even commented on how his insurance company insisted on bullet-resistant Plexi glass in all the doors after the second shooting.

"What are you smiling about?" Norm said as we waited for cars and scooters to pass before we crossed the street.

"If there's any place on the island I should be 86ed from it's here," I said. "Ron's one of a kind."

"Lucky for you."

Nine o'clock on a Saturday morning and the restaurant was busy with a mixture of locals and tourists. Mostly boaters sat at the counter, sipping their morning coffee and eating. Two or more people sat in the booths in the front, taking advantage of the breeze. The aroma of bacon sizzling on the grill, brewing coffee, fried eggs and potatoes eddied about, mixed with the noisy conversations. The interior seemed like a welcoming kitchen, full of family and friends. The emotion startled me and I didn't mention it to Norm. I had no need for the island to be my home again.

"Mick?" Ron called my name, came from around the counter and stopped in front of me. "Mick! Jesus, it's good to see you. You okay?"

"Just got back, Ron." We shook hands and I was surprised at the sincerity of his handshake and smile.

"Booth for two?"

"Maybe four." We followed him toward the back and he sat us at the large, end booth.

"Still drinking *café con leche*?"

"Yes." I hadn't had a *con leche* since leaving Key West and wondered why I now had a craving for the strong espresso and hot milk.

"Be right back. Good to see you, Mick. I was worried about you." He slapped my shoulder and walked away. "Good to see you too, Norm."

"I guess he's not gonna 86 us," Norm said and sat next to me, our backs against the wall. We had a good view of the street and watched for Nadja and Burt.

Ron brought us the coffee and excused himself to seat new arrivals.

"You know there are Cuban restaurants in Los Angeles." Norm stirred sugar into his cup.

"Meaning what?" I added three sugars and sipped the creamy mixture. It woke up my taste buds.

"You wanted *con leches* they weren't far away."

"Wouldn't have been the same."

"I've had 'em downtown and they tasted the same to me."

"Yeah, well, you've got an LA state of mind, so I wouldn't think of you as an authority on *café con leches*."

Norm nodded his head forward. Nadja walked toward us, carrying the Russian satchel. Burt followed holding a Winn-Dixie bag.

"Here!" Nadja placed the satchel on the table in front of me. "The original and my translation, with a summary."

Burt placed the shopping bag next to the satchel.

"Six copies." Her words came out abruptly.

"Sit down," I said.

"We're going to Schooner for mimosas. You might want to join us after you read my summary." Nadja turned and walked away.

Burt sat on the edge of the seat facing us and leaned forward, his voice low. "She's mad Mick, because she wanted to pass this onto the authorities."

"Why didn't she?" Or did she pass it on to the Russians and didn't say anything, I thought.

"I assured her you'd do whatever it took to see it didn't happen," Burt said looking at me. "I'm countin' on you, Mick. Nadja's countin' on you too." He stood up and fingered his bushy mustache. "Don't let us down. She'll get even with me, if you do." Burt smiled and left the busy restaurant.

I took Nadja's translation from the satchel and opened it. The first page began with her summary, three double-spaced, typed pages.

Norm took a copy from the shopping bag.

The server came and we ordered breakfast, finished our *con leches* and began reading.

Norm turned to the second page. “Shit, can it get worse? We need to do something, Mick.”

I folded the page and looked up. I wanted to scream. Hell was about to freeze over.

Chapter Thirty-Seven

Bob met us as Norm and I hurried out of Harpoon Harry's.

"You leaving?" he said.

I hesitated before I answered. "Yeah. I've got the translation."

"Must be some news if you're in such a rush." He looked at Norm who carried the plastic bag of document copies. "Can I do anything?"

"We have to go to Miami," I said. "If we need help, I'll call."

"We ain't going to Miami, Mick," Norm said. "Not right now."

I turned to him, surprised at his comment. "I'm going!"

"Then you're going by yourself," Norm said. "Someone has to handle this." He shook the bag. "It might take a day or two. You can wait."

"Bullshit! We talked about this."

"Not *this*, Mick," Norm said. "Alexei is waiting for results, so he'll sit still. He wants the Mexican deal and that'll keep him close."

Bob tagged along as we crossed the street to the parking lot.

"This could be my best chance to get him," I said. "We know his clubs, his crew."

"And that won't change in a day or two." Norm stopped next to the SUV. "Your opinion might be helpful," he said to Bob.

"Anything I can do," Bob said. "Mick?"

"I'm going to Miami," I said. "You two do what you have to. I can do this on my own."

"I'll drive with Bob, you take the SUV."

I didn't know what to say. My best friend was deserting me when we both knew I was getting close to Alexei. I needed to move, now. "What are you gonna do?"

"Read the whole damn translation and try to get an idea of the bigger picture." Norm tossed me the keys to the SUV. "See who I can pass this off to. It's an act of terrorism, so it goes to the FBI." He didn't seem happy about that and I knew why.

"Yeah, as if you've got a good history with them." I took the keys. "We've not been on their best-friend's list for a while."

Boston FBI agents and U.S. Marshals chased me down last year because they thought I knew the whereabouts of an old Whitey Bulger hit man who walked away from witness protection. A few other retired FBI agents also found me, and were looking for Whitey's hidden money and were willing to kill for it. They failed, thanks to Norm and some others, and won't be able to try again.

"We need someone who can pass the information along," Norm said. "A credible someone."

"You coming to Miami afterward?"

"Mick, as soon as this is taken care of I'll come, but no sooner," Norm said. "This will be a major catastrophe if it happens. Sorry, but Alexei's a coyote and right now I'm looking at a grizzly bear."

"What the hell is this all about?" Bob said, dismissing me.

"We need charts of the harbor, a notebook . . . I've got to work through a list of people I know who might help us with the FBI." Norm handed Bob a copy of the document. "Read it, you'll understand."

Bob opened it to the summary and frowned as he read. "Some of Mick's old charts are at the house." He looked at me. He had avoided mentioning Tita's name, but I knew it was her house. "I'm sure there's a notebook or two."

"You're going to Tita's house?" I said, banging my hand on the hood of the SUV. "Christ! I'm out of here!"

I drove back to the Mango Tree Inn, angry and hurt, feeling betrayed. Panic engulfed me, knowing Norm and Bob would enter *the house*. My resolve sapped while I packed and guessed they had probably stopped at Schooner so Nadja and Burt could join them. Norm would want Nadja there to explain how she translated passages he had questions about.

I feared the floodgates of memories entering *the house*

would open but knew Norm's opinion that Alexei would wait was accurate.

My doubts about Nadja continued and I wondered why Norm wasn't concerned. Usually, he was most suspicious of people who spoke of things they shouldn't have knowledge of. I still wondered how Nadja knew about KGB reports.

Because Southard was a one-way street, I had to circle around to get to Frances Street, where *the house* sat across from the Key West Cemetery. Bob had found a spot close by. Burt wasn't as lucky. He parked up the street. I stared at *the house*, not knowing what to expect. I had dreaded this moment for the last year.

Pauly pulled his white Jeep next to the SUV. "If you're just getting here, I'm not late." He parked half on, half off the sidewalk, on the cemetery side of the street.

I parked behind him and sat with the passenger window open.

"You okay?" Pauly leaned in the open window.

I shook my head. "Not sure I wanna go in."

Pauly feigned a smile. "Sure. I guess the first time back would be hard. You want me to wait here with you?"

The last thing I wanted to do was look like a whining asshole, but the gates to hell were more inviting than the front door I stared at.

Chapter Thirty-Eight

Pauly waited for an answer and I wasn't sure I had one. He turned to look at the house and then back at me.

"It's just a house, Mick," he said. "It won't bite."

"It might." I got out of the SUV. "Who called you?"

"Norm," he said. "Told me you might not be here."

Might not? I thought to myself. Damn Norm, he was playing me, giving me the SUV so I could go on my own. What made him know I wouldn't? Did he think I needed him that badly? "You should go in and read the summary."

"Come with me."

"Why's it so hard? Why can't I let the past go?"

"You're asking the wrong guy, Mick." He slapped my shoulder. "My past hasn't begun yet."

"Wish I felt that way."

"Look it, I've never had a relationship like you and Tita did," he said. "My real friends I can count on one hand and if Alexei, or anyone, did to a friend what he did to you, I'd be after him too. I understand that. But that house," he turned and pointed, "it holds a lot of fond memories for me because of both of you. Don't let Alexei take that away, too. Don't let him steal the good memories."

"Pauly the philosopher," I said. "You missed your true calling."

"No I didn't," he said. "I am what I am. Or, I guess what I was."

"I hope I'm one of those friends."

"You know you are." He walked away, leaving me to make my decision. "See you inside."

Nadja opened the door as Pauly approached. She looked at me. They spoke briefly before he went in. Then she walked toward me.

"You read the document?" Nadja leaned against the SUV.

"The summary."

"The writer, whoever he is, is in Miami, waiting."

"Yeah. I know." Was she telling me to go to Miami?

"You coming in or just looking?"

Nadja was either very good at deception or I was wrong about her. Neither answer pleased me. "Not sure."

"Mick, there's nothing inside."

I didn't understand. Of course, there was something inside.

"Burt and Bob have kept up the payments on the mortgage, electric and water," she said. "When we hadn't heard from you for months, we came to the house and went through everything."

"How'd you get in?"

"Tita told us a long time ago where she kept the extra key in the backyard."

"She would. Why'd she bother to lock the door?"

"We found her address book and Richard called her brother. We thought as chief of police, he was the right one to call."

I nodded. So Richard Dowley had kept up. Where was Nadja leading me?

"That's how we found out Tita left you the house," she said. "Her brother told us. Anyway, he wanted her personal things. Photos, jewelry, things like that. We said our good-byes to her in our own way, by having a packing party. What we didn't ship to her family, we gave to the women's charity at Samuel's House. Tita always supported its fundraisers. The women there appreciated the clothing and other items. We kept the TV, a radio and the kitchen items because they helped entertain us when we came here and did yard work, checked on the house, put up the hurricane shutters and took them down."

"Thanks." It was all I could say.

"What I'm telling you is all that's left inside are your memories." She put her arm in mine and pulled me toward the house. "Those are good memories and you don't want to lose them. But memories are for later, when you're alone. Right now, your friends are inside trying to save Key West from a tragedy. Be part of the solution, Mick."

We walked slowly toward the porch stairway and I hesitated as I heard Tita's laugh. *A memory or a ghost*, I wondered and then followed Nadja up the stairs. Norm opened the door.

Chapter Thirty-Nine

I didn't know what to expect, what horror might be creeping inside to attack me, mentally or physically, if ghosts would scream and float through the interior, or if I would fall apart when I entered the living room full of memories. I felt my body tighten, preparing for the unknown, and I took that final step.

Norm closed the door behind me. "Thanks," he whispered as I walked past.

I knew that he fought not to smile and his *thanks* was for my not leaving for Miami. If he hadn't been my friend, his whispered word would have bothered me more than it did, but I had bigger concerns.

There were no devils in the room. No ghosts. No memories overwhelming me. It was just a room and, as Nadja said, all traces of Tita were gone. I took a deep breath and relaxed a little. With the exception of the furnishings, Tita's personal touches no longer existed. I thought I smelled a faint trace of her perfume and found the scent made me smile not cringe. *My imagination*, I told myself.

I once read that the anticipation of encountering your fears is actually worse than when you face them. Had I anticipated too much? Had my fears taken control of my judgment? *Maybe*, I admitted. But I couldn't help thinking that it was too early to disregard my agenda, to toss aside revenge and to question my choices. I would play this through for a little while and see what happened.

Bob and Pauly nodded at me from the sofa, while they read from Nadja's translation. I saw Burt in the kitchen, sitting down, drinking coffee. The radio and TV were off. Norm had turned my friends into his own personal Key West think tank and I knew he planned to use them on whatever he came up with. It made me uneasy.

Norm handed me the Russian satchel. "You left this in the parking lot."

I'd left in an anger-driven haste and forgot it. "Thanks." I mimicked his whisper.

"Coffee?" Nadja asked. Maybe she felt the tension between Norm and me and needed to say something.

I shook my head. I still harbored fears that something small would trigger my panic, my uncertainties. I wasn't sure I could sit on the furniture. I was suspicious of my surroundings and waited for a crack in my reality to rupture.

"You think you're up to date from reading the summary?" Norm said, standing beside me.

"The summary pointed out the important things." I took her original translation out of the satchel. "You think you know me, don't you?" I kept my voice low and looked him in the eyes.

Norm grinned like the gorilla he is, minus the pounding on his chest and the grunting.

"I'm still going," I said. "Alexei is close and I'm not letting him get away."

"Priority, hoss, you gotta set priorities." He continued to whisper.

"I have." I knew our priorities differed now.

"Your flexibility impresses me." Norm grabbed my shoulder. "We'll get Alexei, but let's figure out what we can do to stop this."

I nodded in reply.

"Hey!" Bob called across the room. "This reads like a terrorist meeting. Mexican cartels, Palestinian suicide bombers, Iranians intelligence, Russians gangsters, and Hezbollah. What the fuck? All we need now is the Mossad."

"Those names aren't important." Norm took his hand away from my shoulder and walked to Bob, ignoring the Mossad comment. "Let's have Nadja explain her summary."

I remained standing. Nadja looked uncomfortable as she picked up a copy of her translation.

"The original document is written in Russian and kept as a journal, so many of the things in it are informative, but not important to us, at this point," she said leaning against a windowsill. "What is important is the information pertaining to Key West. I read over the Key West details a few times to make sure I understood what the writer had written and what it meant."

"Russian is your first language, right?" Norm held his copy of the document.

"Yes," Nadja said. "I grew up outside Moscow and moved to Paris with my parents as a teenager. But it has been a while since I talked or read the language." She held the document pressed against her chest. "That's why I went over this a number of times, to satisfy myself that I understood.

"I kept the summary as brief as possible and only pointed out the atrocity that it mentions for Key West." Nadja looked toward Norm. "I think you'd be better explaining the rest. I can't."

"Okay." Norm nodded to her. "Thank you for this."

Nadja looked uneasy and offered Norm a tired smile. Was she playing a game? Did she translate the Russian journal correctly or did she give us a fictitious document to keep Alexei safe? I couldn't stop the negative thoughts and all because earlier she had mentioned the journal read like a KGB report. A small thing, I admit, and Norm thought I blew it out of proportion.

"We're assuming Alexei is the writer." Norm held up the document. "He wants exclusive distribution rights from the Mexicans for their cocaine and barbiturates in Eastern Europe. The cartel wants money and the Iranian Intelligence offered the cartel millions to train two Palestinians to fly."

"VEVAK, the Iranian intelligence service," Bob said. He must have been drawing from his SEAL experiences. "Smart, well trained and financed, and ruthless."

"Yes," Norm said. "You don't hear of Iranian suicide bombers. They want dirty work done, they use Hezbollah's soldiers. That's why Alexei's men trained two Palestinians, while an Iranian watcher stood close by, probably VEVAK like Bob said."

"The *Arabs* Jorge mentioned?" I said, still standing away from the others.

"Yes. He was half-right. The Iranians are Persian, not Arabic." Norm looked at his copy. "Alexei supplied the plane and training. He was expected to get the plane and pilots into the U.S. and eventually to Key West."

"Says he only had to teach them to fly," Pauly said, leaning forward on the couch. "Not land."

"And we all know when we last heard that scenario," Norm said. "The plane and the terrorists, as well as the Russians, left Tampico in a hurry. We witnessed that. If you look at the deadline, Thursday, less than a week from tomorrow . . ."

"Why wouldn't the Iranians train the pilots?" Bob said, stretching his legs straight out and then back, to make himself comfortable on the sofa. "It should have been easy for them."

"Have the Mexicans do it," Norm said. "Close to the U.S. border, easier to get the plane and pilots across, and if something goes wrong, the Iranian government has distanced itself."

"Why'd the cartel go to the Russians?" Pauly said, leaning back and looking at Bob. "Seems like a stretch of the imagination."

Bob nodded his agreement.

"Timing, Pauly. It's was all timing. My guess is that the Russians approached them about distribution rights in Eastern Europe about the time the Iranians offered the big bucks to the cartel. Pass it off to the Russians, who are already well established in Miami, which is closer to Key West than Tampico, and if something goes wrong, they've distanced themselves, too."

"A win/win for everyone but the pilots," Pauly said.

"Until we found them training in Tampico," Norm said and began pacing the small room. "I have no idea where they've gone, but eventually they're headed here. As I said, the deadline is a week from this Thursday. Early morning."

"Why Key West? Why a cruise ship?" Pauly stood, leaving the document on the sofa. "There are so many populated places in Florida, like Miami, with tall buildings."

"A good question," Norm said, moving toward me. "I'm only guessing, but the plane we saw in Tampico is a small twin-engine. Load it with explosives and it could do real damage to a cruise ship."

"It's too small to do much unless it's got a nuke," I said and felt concern for Key West.

"No nuke." Norm held up his hands to quiet the mumbling. "A nuke would fit inside a suitcase and Miami would be a more likely target."

"How can they hit a cruise ship?" I said and moved away from Norm. "The Coast Guard is here, the Naval Air Station is here. Christ, they'd be shot down in a minute." I wanted this over with.

"An attack on an American cruise ship in a U.S. port would get them all the press they want," Norm said and began pacing again. "Why do you think there's been no cruise ship attack on the open ocean? No wreckage, no press coverage! Al Qaeda wants to hit us at home again and make sure the aftermath, death and destruction, is on the TV for the world to see. It might be payback for bin Laden's death. "

"So it is a cruise ship," Bob said. "Which one?"

"Using Nadja's laptop, I went to the city's cruise ship arrival page and there's only one ship due in next Thursday. The Family Adventure. It's the inaugural cruise and designed for families, with most of the ship themed out to entertain kids," Norm said, taking a moment to look at each of us.

"What about the Coast Guard?" I said again. "Aren't they supposed to protect our borders?"

"Yeah and they do a hell of a job, if the attack comes on the water." Norm stopped pacing and looked out the window. "TSA is a Homeland Security smoke screen and with other agencies' cooperation, it's worked well. But if you think airport screeners have kept Al Qaeda or homegrown terrorists from taking over commercial airlines, you're wrong. The screeners are there to make you feel safe."

"Wait a minute," Nadja said. "I'm flying all the time and the screeners are a pain in the ass. They go through everything. The X-ray, the body scanner. They do their job."

"Yeah, I agree and their job is to make you feel safe," Norm said. "Journalists and internal security have gotten items past screeners whenever they've tested. I give you that it discourages, but think about it. Most TSA employees are paid low wages.

Who's gonna take the job? Not professionals in the security field. Put all of it together and see what you come up with."

"We're not talking about screeners," I said. "We're talking about cruise ships and about a plane attacking one in Key West Harbor. There has to be safety measures in place. Things we don't know. No fly zones."

"You'd think so, wouldn't you?" Norm began pacing again. "But you'd be wrong. And I know that from experience."

"How many people on the cruise ship?" I knew I wouldn't like the answer.

"It can handle two thousand passengers and being the inaugural it's probably full," Norm said. "At least a crew half that number. Could be three thousand people on that ship."

For a moment, the room was as quiet as the cemetery across the street.

A soft knock on the door interrupted the silence.

Chapter Forty

All heads turned toward the door. Norm's right hand went to his concealed semiautomatic. Hell, he seemed ready to shoot Jehovah Witnesses or teenage Mormons. What was I missing? He opened it a crack and looked out. His hand remained at his back, under the shirt, gripping his weapon. He had everyone's attention.

"What do you want?" Norm kept his voice low but we all heard the malice in his words.

"To help." The murmur barely overheard.

"Do you know where the men are?"

"No."

"Do you have a solution?"

"No." I recognized Padre Thomas' voice. "But neither do you," he said without it sounding like criticism.

I walked to Norm and opened the door wider. "Come in, Padre."

Norm's hard look came close to threatening, as Padre Thomas walked in. He brought his hand away from his gun but didn't seem comfortable in doing it.

"He can't help!" Norm said and closed the door.

"He's not the enemy," I said, not understanding his sudden bizarre attitude.

Padre Thomas nodded at everyone, fumbled with a package of cigarettes, and then left it in his pocket. Tita wouldn't let anyone smoke in her house, and maybe he remembered that.

"I knew you'd make the right decision," he said to me and seemed impervious to Norm's hostility.

Those were close to the words he said by the inn's pool last night, the night Norm said Padre Thomas hadn't been there, that I'd dreamt him. I wanted to get the good padre alone and ask about that.

"Decisions can be unmade," I said.

"If we can get back to the subject." Norm stared at me." What we have is a terrorist threat made by an unknown party. Without ironclad proof, I'm not sure anyone will give us the time to explain."

"We know it's more than a threat," I said. "We know Alexei . . ."

"We do not *know*. And we're not credible. Do I need to remind you of that?" Norm began his nervous pacing again. "I'm going to JIATF to see Captain Ashe. Maybe the FBI agent assigned to there, Shane Papps, can find out if this operation is already on the radar. Anyway, Ashe can get me to meet him."

I knew Captain Jim Ashe from a couple of Norm's earlier visits to Key West. Navy officer, military intelligence, assigned to the Joint Inter-Agency Task Force South, in Key West. JIATF is made up of agents from all U.S. intelligence agencies and a few from foreign countries. Originally, JIATF dealt with drug interdiction and related crimes, it now included anyone south of our border who meant us harm, including cartels, migrant smugglers and terrorists.

"Do you think the agent is going to help?" I said.

"He ain't a bad guy, as far as FBI agents go. Papps can be sensible. I've worked with him before so maybe he'll listen," Norm said, pacing across the room. "There's every chance the bureau is aware of this. If so, he'll believe me."

"If he won't?" I said.

"Well, there's always prayer, right Padre?" Norm stopped by Bob and Pauly.

"Yes, Norm," Padre Thomas said as if he believed Norm would try prayer. "There's always prayer. Unfortunately, people use it as a last resort." He didn't even crack a smile.

Norm ignored Padre Thomas. "Mick, you need to go to the Coast Guard. Do you think Captain Santos, will talk to you?"

"We were friendly a year ago. Layout the scenario?"

"Yes and like I said, the Coast Guard maybe involved in stopping this already. It might be nothing to concern ourselves with." His tone didn't convince me he believed that.

Norm looked toward Nadja, who'd moved into the kitchen with Burt, then at me. "I think we'd better take a copy of the document with us."

"Give it to them?" I couldn't hide my surprise. I didn't want copies floating around because I didn't want anyone, especially the government, connecting Alexei to this. Alexei was mine.

"Yeah," Norm grumbled. "I know you don't want to, but maybe if they read the whole document they'd at least send it up the chain of command."

"I don't know," I said. "Isn't there another way?"

"There's no time to find another way," he said. "If I gave JIATF or the FBI the original document, it would take weeks to get it translated. We offer them the translation . . . They'll want the original."

"No way!" I said.

"It may be the only way."

Padre Thomas reached out and touched me. "You should trust Norm, you're in his world now and you've told all of us here, how good he is."

My bravado came back to bite me on the ass, but Padre Thomas spoke the truth. In all the years I've known Norm, or crossed paths with him in Central America, he was always at the top of his game, in command of the situation, and got the job done.

Of course, people always died around him and, as I looked at my friends, that fact alone weighed heavy on me.

Chapter Forty-One

Norm left to meet with Jim Ashe and FBI agent Shane Papps. At three o'clock, I called Captain Santos. He answered on the fourth ring and I could hear music and loud talking in the background. I'd forgotten it was Saturday.

Captain Francisco Santos is the Coast Guard Commander for Sector Key West. He's Mexican-Italian. Pancho, as we called Francisco, grew up speaking three languages, adding French and a few others between high school and college. He's bright and a linguist, all of which helped him advance in the Coast Guard.

"Hold on," he said. He must have walked outside from wherever he was. "Captain Santos," he said in his official tone. "Who is this, please?"

"Pancho, it's Mick Murphy. Where the hell are you?"

"Me?" he said. "Where the hell you been, *chico*?"

"Long story, I'll tell you one day. Right now, I need to talk to you about something important. Important for you, too."

He didn't answer right away. "Mick, can it wait until Monday? The wife and I are with some friends from D.C."

"Give me ten minutes and you'll be glad we didn't wait until Monday."

A few more moments of silence greeted my comment, while the loud background music played in my ear. I couldn't blame him for his hesitation. I'd been gone a year and I call unexpectedly, interrupting his weekend.

"We're at Schooner," he finally said. "As soon as McCloud finishes this set we're walking to Duval. Be here and you can walk with us. Okay?"

"I'm on my way," I said. "Thanks, Pancho. You won't be sorry."

"Don't worry about me," he said, his tone warming. "Worry about my wife, she's been looking forward to a quiet weekend with our friends for months." He hung up.

"Pancho's gonna see you?" Pauly stood in the doorway, ready to leave.

"Yeah, but I need to hurry."

"I might be a pessimist, Mick, but I don't think either you or Norm are gonna get a lot of help from the government," Pauly said. "Maybe Norm can pull some strings and rattle a cage or two when he's in a jam, but this is different."

"We have to do something, Pauly."

"I was thinking as Norm talked, these Iranians or Hezbollah, or whatever, went to the Mexicans for a couple of reasons," he said. "The Mexicans are smugglers and that's what the Iranians needed. Fuck the terrorist angle. You wanna find them, think smugglers. They got across the border, now they need to find a safe place close to Key West for the plane."

"Pauly," I said. "I need to run."

"Listen for a minute," he said. "They haven't flown into Miami or Fort Lauderdale. Too big. But they don't need small, they'd stand out. They'll be working on the plane in a hangar. Take out the seats, make room for the bomb."

"If it's not a nuke."

"It's not," he said. "Norm's right, that would happen if the target was Miami. So, what makes Key West attractive to these assholes? They want news coverage for the bombing and this ain't the place for news crews, unless there's something going on we don't know about."

I looked at Bob. "Any event you can think of?"

Bob shook his head.

"Me either," Pauly said. "You and Norm chase down your government contacts. Maybe, like he said, the feds are onto this plan and we can all go listen to some music and drink a few beers."

"You think so?" His comment surprised me.

"I hope so, but hope's a bottomless pit," Pauly said. "I'm gonna follow the smuggling trail and bet it leads us to these guys. They're off the radar, illegally here. Someone's hiding 'em and I think that someone is a smuggler." He looked at his watch. "Meet you back here in a few."

"I'm going with Pauly," Bob said as they left.

Nadja and Burt walked out of the kitchen. "We're going too. If you need me, just call," Burt said.

Nadja kissed me on the cheek. "I'm glad you're in the house," she said. "Do some shopping, there's not much to eat. Make it your home." Nadja hesitated. "Let Norm do his job."

Padre Thomas stood beside me and we watched Burt and Nadja walk away.

"Are you going to stay, Padre?" I walked to the porch.

"I'll wait," he said. "Is there anything you need me to do?"

"I wouldn't wait until the last minute to pray, Padre." I closed the door and decided I'd walk the few blocks to meet Pancho.

Chapter Forty-Two

As I came down the stairs, I realized walking was the only choice I had. Norm took the SUV I parked behind Pauly's Jeep on the sidewalk.

I felt the ghosts from the city cemetery watch as I left the house. Tita once told me they were friendly and her protectors. I wondered if they held me responsible for her death. Did I even believe in ghosts or, for that matter, did I believe in Padre Thomas' angels? For the time being, I'd ceased believing in anything but revenge.

The sky was clear and the scent of jasmine and gardenias filled the afternoon. As I got closer to the waterfront it turned humid and the thickness of salt air overrode the tropical scents. It confused me why the streets and old Conch houses looked the same as they did a year ago. Didn't they feel the loss of Tita? How could the island continue as if all was normal? The trees grew, the bushes bloomed and the birds flew. I walked onto Caroline Street, shaking my head, hoping to clear it of my thoughts. I needed Pancho to put an end to this crusade, so I could go on and find Alexei before he left Miami.

I inhaled the aroma of B.O.'s Fish Wagon before I saw the rustic open-air restaurant. Customers sat at the old spool-tables, eating fish sandwiches. If I could've stopped, I would have joined them.

Turning on William Street, the masts of the sailing schooners greeted me and I heard the music from Schooner Wharf Bar. Tourists gawked at the large underwater mural by Wyland on the side of the old market building. Others stopped and admired the boats docked at the seawall. Bicycles and scooters parked on the dirt area along Lazy Way Lane, the one-way alley behind Schooner.

Late Saturday afternoon and all the tables were taken in the patio. I turned and walked around the building to the waterfront entrance. I looked down and large tarpon swam through the dark blue water. Spectators yelped with excitement, some screaming that the fish were sharks. Things refused to change.

"You've never seen a tarpon before?" Pancho grabbed my shoulder, smiled as I turned and shook my hand. "The rumors," he said, leading me toward the bar's T-shirt shop. He stopped when we stood in shade. "You'll have to tell me which are true, but I guess I can scrap the one that said you're dead."

He stood six foot, short military haircut, deep, dark brown eyes and in civvies. He didn't look like a man that would be in charge of the local Coast Guard base. A lot of people mistook him for a Cuban.

"They're all true, Pancho," I said and handed him a copy of the Russian journal. "The original is written in Russian."

He took the document. "What is it?" He hadn't even looked at the title page.

"I've put paperclips on the three pages you should read first," I said. "There's going to be an attack on a cruise ship this coming Thursday."

After I said it, his expression changed and he quickly turned to the pages I'd marked for him. He read the three pages, then went back, and read them a second time.

"Where'd you get this?" All friendliness had gone from his tone and he looked worried. "Mick, this isn't a god damn game, where'd you get it?"

I held back a lot of the truth, but gave him most of the facts. The truth would only cloud the situation, I told myself.

"I need the original," he said, keeping his voice low. "It will have to be examined for authenticity." He motioned me to follow him and we walked toward William Street and stopped by the bar's ice machine. It offered us about as much privacy as we were going to get, set away from the street.

"I can get a photocopy," I lied. "I can't get the original. Something you want to tell me?"

"No."

"Pancho, you're a lousy poker player."

He rolled up the document and slapped it against his palm a few times. "Nothing I can talk about."

"But something is happening that you can't talk about," I said.

He ignored me. "Where can I reach you?"

"You've got my number."

"Where are you staying?"

"Call me, I'll meet you."

"It won't be me." Pancho's expression turned grim.

"Men in black suits, dark glasses and sedans?"

"I'm afraid so. Homeland Security, not FBI," he said and it sounded more like a warning than a statement.

"Pancho, what the fuck's going on? I'm bringing this to you. I'm one of the good guys."

"It's out of my hands, Mick," Pancho said. "I have to pass this up the chain of command."

"I want you to, for chrissake. What's going on? Talk to me!"

"Mick, take this from a friend, you've got yourself in way over your head."

"Pancho, I'm telling you, I want to be done with this. I've got better things to do. I need to know you can stop this and then I'm gone."

"If this is real," he slapped the document against his palm again, "a lot of people are going to want to stop it."

"It's real. Read the whole damn thing, it'll make sense," I said.

"Time, Mick. You're not leaving me much time to do anything."

"Damn it, you've almost five days. What more do you want?"

"If I was the guy looking into this, I'd want to know where the plane is. Where the bombers are. And a lot more. That's why they'll be getting in touch."

"Who they hell are they?"

"I've already said too much, Mick," he said. "I have to put this above our friendship. It's my duty."

"Pancho, I understand. What I don't understand is what

you're not telling me."

"I can tell you one thing." He slapped the document against the top of my head. "You'd better get out of here before I tell my wife duty calls. She'll kill you for sure."

"Pancho," I said wondering why he masked his concern behind a playful slap and mention of his wife.

"Mick, I can't tell you anything." He walked away.

Chapter Forty-Three

I followed Pancho onto the boardwalk and watched as he walked into Schooner Wharf Bar. I wanted to grab him and ask, *what the hell is going on? Why the sudden attitude change?* He turned, just before entering, and looked in my direction. He wasn't smiling.

I left without answers and took the same route back to the house, wondering why the date of the attack caught Pancho's attention more than the attack itself did. His concern didn't peak until I mentioned it would happen Thursday. There was something brewing. No matter what scenario I ran through as I walked, nothing was more important to me than an attack that would kill or maim thousands. Nothing! So, what was it about that Thursday?

Norm would have an answer when he returned and all this would go away, I told myself. He was the government's man. They'd be straight with him, and I could move on.

Alexei waited in Miami for the results of the attack and while he waited, I waited. I would bring an end to my life of tumult by putting a bullet into his head.

I approached Tita's house cautiously. Were the cemetery's ghosts planning an attack on me? I began to sweat but knew it had to be due to the long walk back from the waterfront. Padre Thomas was inside, alone. I didn't recognize any car parked along the street. When had I turned into such a sniveling jerk? The house couldn't hurt me. I took a deep breath, repeated that about the house, walked up the stairs like a man on the way to the gallows, and went in.

Spicy aromas attacked me, not ghosts. Padre Thomas sat at the kitchen table, a Budweiser in front of him as he ate.

"You're back," he said with a mouthful of food.

"Where'd you get the food?"

"At the corner store, Angela and Windsor Lane. Indians own it and the curry is good." He took a long swallow of beer. "Spicy too."

"Budweiser?" He liked Bud. I preferred Irish or Mexican beer.

"Nothing you would've liked, so I bought what I liked," he said. "I bought enough chicken curry and rice for everyone. Like Nadja said, there's nothing to eat here."

"Now there is, Padre." I walked into the kitchen and half a dozen to-go boxes were on the counter. I sat down next to him.

"Something wrong?" He stopped eating and stared at me.

"Yeah." I needed a deep breath to think where to begin. "I have to talk to Norm."

"Call him."

"He isn't answering his cell," I said. "I called him on the way here. Twice."

"Can I help?"

"Yeah," I said, but it was a joke. "Tell me what's so special about Thursday. Ask the angels." I added as sarcasm.

"They don't come as often, since you've been gone." He finished the beer and looked at his plate. "I tell you, Mick, sometimes I think they were your angels and used me to reach you."

I stared at him, and wondered if he answered my sarcasm with his own. What would angels want with the likes of me?

My cell chirped, so I didn't ask, I answered.

"Where are you?" Norm asked.

"Waiting for you," I said.

"Ten minutes away." He hung up.

"Norm?" Padre Thomas said.

"Yeah. He sounded upset."

"Maybe he is."

More sarcasm?

Chapter Forty-Four

Norm wasn't carrying the document as he entered the house. Like me, I guessed, his contacts kept it. He seemed upset, too. I took it as a sign that not everything had gone as I'd hoped.

He looked at us, Padre Thomas, with a beer and a plate of half-eaten food, me sitting next to him. When he opened the fridge, Norm took a beer and checked out a few of the to-go containers, but left them untouched.

"How'd you do?" He sat down across from me.

"About as well as you," I said.

He tilted the beer bottle back and took a long swallow. "Pandora's Box, Mick." Norm put the bottle on the table and looked toward Padre Thomas. "You tell him?"

I nodded.

"Padre, do I have to remind you that you don't repeat any of this?"

Padre Thomas shook his head. He understood. It was close to confessional.

"I met Jim Ashe, let him look at the document. He read the three pages that you marked a couple of times and lost the nice guy attitude," Norm said. "Damn it, he left me outside the JIATF office, in a hallway, for chrissake. I'm part of the team and he treated me like a civilian."

I knew the feeling. "He take it to the FBI?"

"Yeah. Next thing, about ten minutes later, here come Ashe and Shane Papps. They move me to a small conference room." He banged his hands on the table. "I know the room's used for interrogation. We're playin' fifty questions, like I'm a perp! They won't tell me shit. Papps wants answers. How'd I get the copy, where's the original? Where's the plane?"

"Where are the men?" I added and Norm stared at me.

"Preaching to the choir, am I?"

I told him about meeting Pancho outside Schooner on the boardwalk and moving to the ice machine.

"Norm, he seemed more interested in the date than anything. It doesn't make sense. Attacking a cruise ship in the harbor should've been the important thing."

"I got the same feeling," Norm said, hands on the table. "The only thing Papps would tell me is he wasn't aware of the planned attack. And who knows if that's the truth? But the main question, the one they kept repeating was how'd the terrorists choose the date? How the hell was I supposed to know?"

"Pancho said Homeland Security would want to talk to me," I said. "It sounded like a threat."

"Probably his way of warning you of the threat," Norm said. "So what have we got here, Mick? The FBI and Homeland Security. One's thrown away the rulebook and the other never had one. Terrorism gives 'em a green light, full speed ahead. Hello Gitmo!"

"Maybe they'll follow up on the information and stop the attack."

"You think so, Dick Tracy?" Norm murmured. "Every desk the document gets to will want to talk to us. That's the back-ass way they work."

"What choices do we have?" I wondered that myself, and wanted Norm to have an idea. I didn't even want to think about Gitmo.

Norm got up and Padre Thomas and I followed him into the living room. He stopped at the window. "The house is still in Tita's name?"

"Yeah." I said.

"The Feds shouldn't know about it," Norm said. "We need a safe house and this could be it."

"Jim Ashe has been here before." I reminded him. "Richard too. The Feds will go to the cops."

Norm laughed. "No they won't. Homeland Security deals with the FBI 'cause they have to. No one will deal with the local cops. Local yokels, that's the cops. Homeland's got a superior attitude. We can use it against them."

"That still leaves Ashe," I said. "He knows."

"Ashe is military." Norm's window reflection showed him

grinning. "I might be able to get him to change sides, or at least keep his mouth shut."

"How?" Padre Thomas said.

"JSOC, Padre." Norm opened his cell and walked out onto the porch.

"Jay sock?" Padre Thomas looked at me.

"Joint Special Operations Command," I said.

"Is Norm part of it?"

"I don't know, Padre, but over the years I've found he's part of most everything covert."

Padre Thomas grinned. "Maybe this time, that's good."

"Maybe," I said and wondered if Pauly had been right about Norm not getting help this time.

Chapter Forty-Five

Norm paced along the wraparound porch, talking on the cell phone and at times I could hear him shouting. Twice he disconnected the call, or had he been disconnected? Whatever happened, he dialed again and talked to whoever answered. Had he made the same call three times or three different calls? Had his request been rejected? Or had he been told to go up the chain of command? I couldn't focus on any good reason for three calls. Uncertainty made me jumpy.

Tired of watching the angry man on the porch walk in circles, Padre Thomas left to finish his dinner.

Night blanketed the sky, faraway planets and stars flickered in blackness, and the old cemetery dispatched eerie images. The dim streetlights did little to penetrate the shadows.

"Do you want me to heat the curry?" Padre Thomas called from the kitchen.

"Not right now, padre. Thanks." I kept watching Norm. Was it anger or angst that made him pace and shout? Both possibilities concerned me. It took a lot for Norm to show his anger and it was usually followed with a violent explosion. When he worried, it meant he'd lost control of the situation. When that happened, all his energy went into getting it back.

Norm looked at me through the window. He didn't smile, but he nodded. I had no idea what the nod meant. I decided to go outside when my cell chirped and Pauly's name came onto the phone's screen.

"Pauly," I said, glad to have a distraction. "You and Bob coming back?"

"You or Norm have any luck?"

I could hear airplane noise in the background. "None. Norm's on the phone now, but from the sound of it, I think he's running into a brick wall."

"What did you expect from government bureaucrats?"

"Where are you?"

"I made some calls." Pauly continued to ignore my questions. “You got a minute?”

“Waiting on Norm to finish the call.”

“Okay, hang up if you need to. But listen,” he said. “I made a few calls, asking about a twin-engine plane, foreigners, questionable activities.”

“I get the point, Pauly. Did you get any feedback?”

“Of course,” he said. I heard the smile in his voice. “I know a guy, who knows a guy …”

“Pauly!”

“You’re losing your sense of humor, Mick,” he said. “Yeah, I talked with someone and I’m meeting him in the morning at the Opa-Locka Airport.”

“Who is it?”

“You don’t know him and he doesn’t wanna know you.”

“Probably for the best,” I said. “Are you flying up there?”

“I’m here,” he said. “I checked out the hangar situation and only one’s tight as a drum.”

“You think they’re there?”

If he was right, this could be over tomorrow. The Feds would end it. All they needed was the locale. For whatever the reason, everyone seemed to want to know how these guys chose that date. I was beginning to want to know, too.

What was so special about a week from tomorrow?

“Not sure who’s here, but my guy said there were some strange happenings a few nights ago,” Pauly said. “Reminded him of the good old days, night landings, locked hangars, people coming and going at weird hours.”

“What time are you meeting him?” I needed results not remembrances.

“He’s due in at sunrise, has to do what he does and then he’ll meet me for breakfast.”

“Bob’s there, right?”

“Yeah. Everything okay down there, considering?”

“Nothing’s falling in our lap,” I said. “Maybe you can change that.”

“I’ll get answers, but I don’t know if they’ll be the ones

you want."

"Norm's off the phone," I said, and wondered what Pauly meant, but it would have to wait. "Call me first thing tomorrow."

"As soon as I've had my talk." Pauly hung up.

"Food smells good," Norm said as he walked in and closed the door. "Let's eat." His mood seemed better than I expected.

I followed him to the kitchen where Padre Thomas had already put our plates in the microwave.

"What happened?" I sat down and Norm took three beers from the fridge.

"Jim Ashe has received orders to work with us." Norm took a plate of curry and rice from Padre Thomas, gave us each a beer, and began to eat.

"What's that mean?" I tasted the curry. I opened the beer as Padre Thomas removed his plate and went to the sink.

"It means he can't talk about us to anyone," Norm said. "Including Homeland Security."

"JSOC has that much pull?"

"It's outside of Homeland Security's authority." He smiled and ate two forkfuls of curry. "I love stickin' it to those pompous asses. Tellin' them to fuck off is better than cold beer and a Dodger dog at the ballgame."

Chapter Forty-Six

I told Norm about Pauly's phone call. He didn't seem impressed. That didn't surprise me, since they're usually on different sides of the equation.

"You need to call Richard," Norm said. "We get the chief of police taken care of and this is our safe house."

It was a little past eight and I knew Richard would be home. "First thing in the morning." Richard was one more contact to my past and I wanted to avoid him for as long as I could.

"Now!" Norm said. "You can't let loose ends flop around overnight. You think he's home?"

"Yeah. He's gone by six, unless something official keeps him at the station."

"Call." Norm took my plate to the sink.

I nodded and dialed Richard as I walked to the living room.

"I don't believe it, there's phone service in hell! You gotta be shitting me," Richard said as a greeting. "This really you, Mick?"

"Nice to hear your voice too, Richard."

"Depends," he said. "Where are you? And God only knows how I hope it's a million miles away."

"That's a nice greeting," I said, surprised at his hostile attitude.

"For the last year, the year you've been gone, the worst things on the island were the drunks during Fantasy Fest, the noise of powerboat races and a few nights when the temperature went to the low sixties in January," he said. "No dead bodies, no FBI or U.S. Marshals, no Mexican drug cartel members shooting up the waterfront . . ."

"Richard, can we get serious?"

"One more thing, Jimmy Buffett's Parrotheads were in town," he said. "They're growing on me, but I'm still not comfortable with the hats they wear."

"You done?"

"When I'm done, I'll hang up."

"We need to talk."

"I thought that's what we were doing."

"In person." I listened to silence.

"You're here," Richard said and it wasn't a question.

"Yeah, I'm here. Now, can you give me a half-hour?"

"You know Murphy, you're in town less than forty-eight hours and already I can feel the shit coming through the fan," he griped louder than necessary. "Where?"

"You're in such a good mood, you choose a place." How did he know I'd been in Key West for two days?

"I'll call you back in half an hour."

It sounded like a delay action and concerned me. "Richard."

"Yeah Mick."

"Don't tell anyone we're meeting."

"Your shit pile keeps getting bigger," he said. "I'll call you back. Mick, if you don't trust me, don't show up and get off my island." He hung up.

Chapter Forty-Seven

Since I'd been gone the biggest change at Sandy's, a *café con leche* kiosk on White Street, was that it now stayed open 24/7. The Laundromat attached to it closed at eight, but the kiosk kept busy with a steady line of customers needing their *bucci*, a single shot of espresso with a lot of sugar, no matter the hour.

Sandy's had always been neutral ground in Key West, with its mix of cops, lawyers, city and county employees, laborers, tradesmen and the island's miscreants stopping at all hours for a quick energy boost. You came, you ordered and you left. You didn't cause problems and the unwritten rule applied to everyone.

Richard chose the location. An hour after our first conversation in a year, I arrived and ordered a large *café con leche* with four sugars. Tita made them better, but she always referred to it as Puerto Rican coffee. I smiled at the thought and took a sip from the steaming cup.

"I would've bought." Richard's words caught me by surprise.

"Next one." I turned to him, his city car in the red zone. The chief of police parks where he wants.

Richard ordered a small *café con leche*. I wondered if that meant he didn't plan to spend much time or had his wife Peggy put him on a caffeine-free regimen that he only cheated on a little. I followed him to the steps that went to second-story apartments above the Laundromat. It took us a few extra steps away from the order window so whatever we said would be lost in the din of other conversations and traffic noise.

"You look the same," he said. "A little weathered, but the same."

"You too. How's Peggy?"

"Visiting the kids at college." That explained his willingness to meet me. "Are you back?"

"Possibly," I said without thinking and wondered if it was true.

"Think hard before deciding." He blew on the hot drink.

"You alone?"

"Why?"

"Looks a lot like your buddy Norm parked up the street in the Lower Keys Plumbing driveway." Richard sipped from the cup.

I looked up past the two houses to the plumbing company and didn't see the SUV. "Where?"

"In the driveway."

I had told Norm I needed to meet Richard alone. He didn't like it, but dropped me off, saying he wanted to go to Winn-Dixie and would wait there for my call. He lied. But he often did.

"Let's cut the bullshit, before my coffee gets cold," Richard said. "What do you want or should I ask what fuckups are you bringing to my island?" His words lacked any illusion of kindness.

My cup was half-empty. I didn't realize I'd drunk that much so quickly. "I'm trying to stop something from happening on *your island*."

"Of course you are." Meanness crept into his tone. "You're always trying to stop something that you began and lost control of."

"That's not fair, Richard." I tried to keep control of my voice because we were not that far from others gathered at Sandy's window. "I haven't done anything that deserves your attitude."

"Oh no, not Saint Murphy," he said. "Your whole fucking life full of disasters has followed you wherever you go and you can't deny that. Being here is what *you've done*. Just being here has brought trouble that's mushroomed into disasters. Need I remind you?"

I began to realize our friendship of so many years had been lost.

"I need your help," I said.

"So, what's new?" He finished his coffee.

We both remained silent. Cars passed, rushing to beat the yellow light before it turned red at White and Virginia streets. People kept arriving, walking past us to Sandy's or from the kiosk with cups of the strong Cuban coffee. The nighttime had its own sounds.

Richard pointed and I turned to see Norm headed toward us.

"I guess I was right," Richard almost growled. "You used to be better at lying."

No matter what I said, he wouldn't believe me, so I kept quiet.

"You boys talking or is this a quiet war?" Norm said before he stopped at the order window. People turned to look at us. They knew Richard was the top cop.

Norm brought us each a *café con leche*. We tossed our empties in the trash.

"Three sugars," he said, meaning for us to take it or leave it, as we accepted the cups. "How you doing, Chief?"

"I've had better nights." Richard sipped from his cup.

"Haven't we all," Norm said.

"Thanks," Richard said.

"Always glad to buy you coffee." Norm raised his cup in a beer bottle salute.

"Not for this," Richard said. "For letting me know this asshole was above ground."

I looked at Norm. He grinned at me. "Someone had to, you weren't talking to anyone," he said to me and lost the grin.

It wasn't the time or place to argue, so I let it go. And maybe Norm had been right to keep in touch with Richard. The past shit storms had affected his officers, as well as many others and I had been ultimately responsible.

"What has he told you?" Norm turned to Richard.

Strange bedfellows, I thought as they ignored me.

"Nothing," Richard said.

"Took him a long time to say nothing." Norm sipped his coffee then handed Richard a rolled up copy of the translated document. "This is why we're here."

Richard put his cup on the steps, opened the document and began reading. I looked hard at Norm. We hadn't talked about giving Richard anything. We were supposed to warn him about the possibility of either the FBI or Homeland Security approaching him about my whereabouts and see what happened.

After reading a page, Richard looked at me and then read another page. He only got as far as Nadja's synopsis of the document. When he'd finished the three pages, he turned to Norm. "You need to go to the FBI with this. It's out of my jurisdiction."

"Been there," Norm said. "Mick's been to the Coast Guard."

"And?" Richard waited for an answer.

"Let me ask you a question," Norm said. "What the hell's happening next Thursday?"

"The day this says the attack will happen?"

"Yes. We know a cruise ship stops here on its maiden voyage," Norm said. "But what else?"

"Nothing I know about." Richard held the document as if it might burn his hands. "Why?"

"Because both the Feebs and the Coasties were more interested in why the terrorist chose that date than they were in an attack on a cruise ship," Norm said.

"Why Richard?" I finally spoke up. "It's *your island*, what's so important about the date?"

"Nothing." He looked at the document, rolled it up and slapped it into his palm. "Nothing, but I think you're telling me something is."

"Yeah, we are," I said.

"But we don't know what," Norm added. "Wanna come with us?"

"For chrissake, Mick, couldn't you just once show up and buy me dinner so we could laugh at your past? Even a beer would be appreciated."

"Nothing to laugh about, Chief," Norm answered for me. "His life's a tragedy, not a comedy."

"Where are we headed?" Richard looked at the document. "Can I read the whole thing?"

"When we get where we're going," Norm said and took

the document. "Mick will ride with you."

No trust, you gotta love that about Norm.

"You know the car," Richard said, trashed his unfinished coffee. "Don't expect me to hold the door open for you." He walked away.

Chapter Forty-Eight

Richard turned right onto Virginia Street without saying a word. Virginia used to be a quick ride to the Basilica of Saint Mary, on Windsor Lane, and onto the cemetery, but now each cross street had a four-way stop to slow traffic.

"You're an asshole, Mick Murphy," Richard said, looking into the shadows of the poorly- lit street. "You're selfish. Do you think you're the only one that felt loss? Tita's death affected a lot of people and most of 'em thought they were your friends." Richard drove a block, stopped, drove another block and stopped again. "I lost a friend I cared about and you were knocking on death's door . . ." Richard hesitated midsentence, as his voice got louder.

He pulled over to the side of the road. "I lost a friend in Tita and then you were in the hospital beat to shit and, like Houdini, you were gone." His voice lowered. "I didn't know how or where. Bob and Burt asked, thinking I'd know. No one knew if you were alive or dead, but we cared. No one could reach you." Richard turned to me. "Five months later Norm, of all people, called me and that's how I found out you were alive. Is that the way you treat friends?"

I didn't answer.

"Five months," he repeated. "Those months gave me time to think. I got angry, not knowing anything or hearing from you, and I started to focus on your fuckups. That gave me a lot to think about. I came to realize that the only real crime I've had to deal with on this island somehow involved you and eventually I was glad you were gone."

"What do you want me to say?" I turned to him, tired of other people's frustrations. "Those first months I didn't wanna live. When I knew I would, I had only one objective and it wasn't friendship."

"Revenge thrives while friendships die?" Richard shook his head. "As usual, you got it ass backward." He pulled back onto Virginia Street. "Who else is at Tita's?"

He surprised me because I didn't think anyone would have

considered I'd go there. Richard knew me better than I knew myself and he saw the surprise on my face.

"Yeah, I figured you'd go there," he said as a response to my look. "No boat, no friends. Where else would you slither off to?" Richard's words came callously and they hurt, which confused me.

"Padre Thomas is there." The words came without my usual bravado.

"I have a lot of questions," he said. "About that document, but I'll wait to ask Norm, that way you won't have to lie."

"Thanks," I said to be sarcastic and then shut up.

A quick turn onto Windsor Lane to the cemetery and then Tita's house. A short distance but the silent ride seemed to take forever. Richard parked by the hydrant, got out and looked around. Did he see Tita's friendly ghosts? He didn't say. Ignoring me, he walked to the house and Norm met him on the porch. I followed close behind, lost in doubt about what I'd been doing the past few months and wondered why I was so self-consumed that I hadn't considered others.

When I walked into the house, Richard sat in what had been my reading chair, pole lamp glowing, going over the document. He didn't look up as I closed the door. Norm pointed toward the kitchen. I followed.

"You two okay?"

"You tell me," I said. "He's pissed."

"Everyone's pissed at you."

"I'm not," Padre Thomas said.

"Thank you," I said.

Norm ignored Padre Thomas. "Will he keep the house location to himself?"

I gagged on a laugh. "You're the one that's been talking to him, what do you think?"

"Let's live in the present, Mick."

"Okay," I said. "Presently, why's Richard got the document? If you don't trust him, why give it to him?"

"The truth, Mick, he needs the truth," Norm said. "If

Richard believes we went to the FBI and Coasties, and they brushed us off, and he believes what's in the document, he'll want to do something. He isn't gonna like it, but he knows the Feebs won't deal with him, keep him in the dark if they can."

"And then?"

"He'll realize we're a few steps ahead of everyone else." Norm grinned. "Like he said, it's his island and he stands a better chance of working with us than fighting with the government."

"If you're wrong?"

"We'll get the hell out of Dodge before anyone can find us," Norm said. "We'll go to Miami, find Alexei."

His comments tempted me but for reasons I couldn't, or wouldn't explain to myself, I wanted to see this through and mend the friendships I'd ignored. I wanted Alexei, I knew that, but I wanted to keep the few friends I had, too. They were all that I had left that were worth a damn. I needed to see if I could fix what I'd broken.

"You can't go!" Padre Thomas said. "You can't leave this unsettled."

"Don't plan to, Padre," I said.

"Where'd you get this?" Richard stood in the kitchen doorway, the rolled up document in his hand. "And without the bullshit."

"Sit down." I pulled out a chair at the kitchen table. Norm and I sat, Padre Thomas stood by the sink. "It's a long story."

Richard sat and listened as I told him a cleaned-up version of chasing Alexei to Tampico. I mentioned the clubs in Miami, but left out the shootings and avoided the Mexican Navy's attack on the cartel's base.

"It's not your doing," Richard said. "This time."

"I chased Alexei and found this by accident. I had nothing to do with what's written in that." I pointed at the document.

Norm nodded, showing his agreement.

"What's that mean? *You found this*?" Richard still hadn't decided if he'd been told the truth. He should've known better than to expect the whole truth.

I mentioned Jorge and Richard groaned at the cartel leader's name and involvement.

"You have the original?" Richard banged the document against the table. "In Russian?"

"Yes," I said.

"Who translated . . ." Richard shook his head. "Never mind. Burt's lady friend, the Russian Frenchy, right?"

"Yes. Gave us the translation, said the guy that wrote it is crazy and dangerous and that's the last I've seen or heard from her or Burt," I said.

Richard looked at Norm. "I don't know what you are," he said, "but you're telling me that the agency taking responsibility for you can't put a stop to this?"

"Time's not our friend," Norm said. "Making decisions in the field is one thing, I can do that at a moment's notice. I can get what I need to do the job. But making official requests requires forms and procedures to follow. All these things eat up time. Time we don't have."

"Is that a yes or no?"

"Officially, the information and request are in the pipeline."

"Unofficially?" Richard asked.

"Unofficially, if the shit spreads too thin, I'm left swinging," Norm said. "I have people looking."

"What aren't you telling me?"

"Peripheral stuff that happened but doesn't involve the document," Norm said. "Things that it took to get where we needed to go."

"Things I don't want to know, right?"

"Yeah, doesn't add to or change what you've got in your hand."

Richard took a deep breath. He looked around at the three of us and we must have appeared like a collection of mismatched reprobates, frail Padre Thomas, forceful Norm and me, an unkempt Mick Murphy. All of us possibly crazy and lying. Richard had a career decision to make. A decision that also affected me.

"I can't afford not to believe you," he said. "I'm going to do what I can. Not for you," he stared at me. "I don't want this to happen on my island . . . but remember, I'm still the law and I might walk a fine line to get things done, but don't expect me to cross over it."

Chapter Forty-Nine

Jasmine and camellia scents carried on a light breeze that made sitting on the back porch comfortable. Light from the kitchen spread across the deck, chasing shadows into the yard. My weathered white Jeep, its bikini top sagging, rested in the pea rock driveway, and like an old family portrait found in a shoebox, it brought back memories. I tried to push them aside.

"I thought that would've been towed," I said. "Is it running?"

"Not sure who put it there," Richard said.

"We won't ask you to do anything that can come back on you." Norm leaned against the railing returning the conversation to our purpose.

"We need to find the plane." Richard disregarded Norm's comment. He didn't plan to do anything that would come back on him either. "Could it be here?"

"No," Norm said. "We lost it in Mexico. Could've gone north or south, but it has to come this way. And soon."

"We have someone looking for it on the mainland," I said.

"Who else is involved?"

Norm looked at me, knowing Richard wouldn't like the answer.

"Pauly," I said and waited for Richard's response.

He closed his eyes and shook his head as if wishing we'd be gone when he opened them. Maybe he did wish it.

"You kept in contact with him?" Richard snarled.

"I didn't keep in touch," I said and heard apology in my tone. "When we were in Miami we needed . . . someone with his background." I didn't want to explain too much about Miami.

"Anyone else I should be concerned about?" Richard said.

"Bob is with Pauly," I said. "We're looking at these guys as terrorists."

"Crashing a plane into a cruise ship," Richard said. "Yeah, I'd say terrorists."

"You read the document. Pauly thought we should think

like smugglers. That's why the Iranians went to the cartel. The Russians taught them to fly, but they needed to be smuggled into the country. Smugglers have trusted routes, be it people or drugs."

"What do you need me for?" Richard sat on an old wicker chair and finally asked what was really on his mind.

"When Homeland or the FBI contacts you about Mick, we need you to put 'em off," Norm said. "We need this to be a safe house so we can solve the problem without the door being kicked in."

"Last time I looked, lying to those guys is a crime." Richard didn't sound angry or concerned about lying, he seemed to accept the issue. "They also are not the most sharing agencies I deal with."

"Mick's gone to the Coasties and I've dealt with the FBI, so the info is moving up channels," Norm said. "Trust me, the next thing is, they're gonna want to pull Mick and me in. Especially if they cross-reference and find we both presented the same info. Together or separately, they'll come looking for us."

"Why would they come to me?"

"Because we approached them in Key West and you know Mick," Norm said. "Homeland has the new complex here. You ever wonder why? With the FBI, the Coasties, JIATF, ICE, all in Key West, why a whole complex exclusively for Homeland Security? You should think about it. Think about whose island this really is."

"I've thought about it." Richard grumbled. "Hell, they leave me alone and I'm not sure I want to know why they're here."

"In other words, you don't know what they're doing on *your island*," Norm said.

"I have my contacts there," Richard said.

"And they have their *contacts* in your department." Norm sat across from Richard. "It's best you keep this between us."

"I suppose you're right." Richard sulked, realizing his troops weren't as loyal as he wished. "Promises to hire them. It happens everywhere the federal agencies go."

"Everywhere," Norm said in agreement. "And it's usually

false promises."

"I know those agencies have lied to me," Richard said and a small grin came to his mouth. "Maybe I can lie like Mick, by omission. You got any tips for me?" He turned to me. "Is anyone checking the airport?"

"No," I said. "We don't think they'd be this close, so soon."

"Your not thinking is one of your weak points." Richard stood. "I've got a couple of officers with planes out there. I could ask them to look . . ."

"I don't want to draw too many into this, just yet," Norm said. "We should wait to hear from Pauly and Bob before we do anything."

"Is it being whatever you are that makes you so cynical, Norm? Mick your only cohort or is even that trust questionable?" Richard stood in the doorway, not expecting an answer. "I'll wait to hear from you. Remember what you said about time, Norm. You don't have that luxury and neither do I. I've got to do something about this." He shook the document at us. " This isn't going to happen on my island. I won't let it. Call me by noon, Mick, the clock is ticking."

We watched Richard walk into the house. Padre Thomas came to the doorway, looked at us and then followed Richard.

"Is he playing us?" Norm stood up.

"We'll know tomorrow at noon," I said.

Chapter Fifty

My chirping cell phone woke me a little after six in the morning. I'd slept on the couch, in my clothes. Norm bunked in the guest bedroom. I wasn't ready to sleep in the bed Tita and I had shared. Using a sheet or blanket from her bedroom was out of the question. The scent on the pillows, and the memories hiding there, would push me over the edge and I'd already spent too much time on the rim, looking down.

"Hello," I said, trying to chase the drowsiness away. The dream I'd had evaporated and I couldn't recall what it was about so I considered that good. My first night in the house and I expected nightmares.

"Liam?" A voice I didn't recognize said my given name.

"Who is this?" No one called me Liam.

"This is Michael Shields from Key West Police dispatch," he said. "I'm sorry for the early hour."

"What is it?" All I could think of was something happened to the Chief, but why call me?

"Ah, I just got to work and ran into Chief Dowley in the hall," Michael said. "He gave me a note with your name and number and said to call you right away."

I sat up, awake now. Defused sunlight seeped through the blinds. "What's in the note?"

"He said to read it to you."

"Okay. Read it."

"The Chief wrote 'As soon as you have your new phone, call me.' That's it," he said. "I don't know what he meant. Do you understand it?"

"Yes," I lied. "Why didn't the Chief call me?"

"He's in a meeting. I just came on, and he walked out of the men's room and handed me the note."

"Thank you." I hung up.

I stood, stretched. What new phone? What meeting?

"Who the hell calls at six in the morning?" Norm bellowed from the guestroom doorway, rubbing sleep from his eyes.

"Richard had one of the dispatchers call me. Gave him my phone number and a note."

I told Norm what the dispatcher had said.

"He gave the guy a note, had time to write it but not time to call you?" Norm hummed to himself. "Do you know who he was meeting with?"

"Forgot to ask."

"The Feebs got to him damn quick," Norm said biting his lower lip, guessing at the answer to his own question. "Not good."

"Do you think?" I stared at Norm and doubt I hid my concern.

"Shut your phone off and take the battery out," Norm said. "Now!"

I began to dismantle the phone. "Why? What's going on?"

"Sounds like he's saying they'll track your location through the phone signal," Norm said. He took his phone apart too. "Better to be safe."

"We need phones," I said and tossed the pieces of mine onto the couch. "Pauly's calling later about the plane."

"There's gotta be somewhere on the island we can buy pre-paid phones. Get the phones and call Pauly with the new number."

"There's a couple of rental mailbox places, I think. Maybe Radio Shack?"

"We're in trouble," he grumbled. "They're looking for you and maybe me or will be shortly." Norm paced the room, looked out both front windows and then checked his wristwatch. "The mailbox places open before nine?"

"No idea." Seeing Norm nervous made me nervous. "What are we doing?"

"Maybe the FBI had a handle on these guys," he said. "They could think we're a problem for their operation and wanna get us off the street. Find out how we know what we know. How'd we get the document? That's gotta be drivin' 'em crazy!"

"Us? A problem? For chrissake, we brought the information to them asking for help!" I said. "Wouldn't they know who you are?"

"You're thinking like a civilian, Mick." Norm looked out the window, again. "They'll want both of us."

"What are you looking for? Richard won't tell them we're here."

"You sure?"

"He sent the message."

"It buys us time. Maybe he's telling us to scram because he'll have to tell them, eventually."

"Okay, to be safe, we bug out, for now," I said. "We don't know who he's meeting. We might be overreacting."

"Overreacting is very underrated," he said. "It's also saved our asses a few times, hoss."

"Yeah," I said but didn't want to dwell on the past. The future had begun to look gloomy enough. "We need to drive by the mailbox stores to see what time they open."

"Yeah, and if they sell prepaid phones." He eyed me and shook his head. "Your fuckin' red hair! Stands out like a guy wearing a jockstrap at a nudist camp."

"I can wear a hat."

"Let's hope we've got some time." Norm frowned as he walked to the guestroom. "Get dressed."

"What's your plan?" Norm always had a plan and I always counted on it.

"Get to that twenty-four-hour drug store and buy hair dye." He turned at the doorway. "It's that or shave your head and beard, but make up your mind, every minute puts them closer."

"I got a better idea," I said. "Sissy used to cut my hair at the marina. I'll call her, trim it short, the beard too."

"I like dye." He stood at the doorway.

"Neither of us knows how to do it right," I said. "Short hair and a trimmed beard, like a two-day growth. With a hat, it should work. I'll call her at home."

"Maybe she can dye it right?"

"Do we want one more person involved? Dying it would raise questions."

"You ain't gonna like prison food," Norm said. "I know I won't."

"Hell, Norm," I moaned.

"What?"

"Who isn't after us? Now it's our own government." I pulled my bag from the floor and walked toward the bathroom.

"We don't know that for sure." His grin wasn't successful. "If it is the Feebs, the upside is they don't want to kill us."

"Says you." I closed the bathroom door.

Chapter Fifty-One

I called Sissy and she agreed to meet me at Hot Cuts on Flagler, after I promised her coffee and an explanation of where I'd been. Norm and I met her at eight, before the shop opened, so we'd have the privacy I requested. I wondered if I'd made her shit list too. Norm stopped at Sandy's and picked up three *café con leches.* Sissy liked hers with extra milk and four sugars. Norm wondered how I remembered that. I just did.

By eight-thirty, my shaggy red hair had been cropped to within an inch of military style. Norm insisted. I argued. We compromised. Sissy thinned the beard until its length appeared as a two- or three-day growth, the look celebrities go for these days, hinting they were too busy to shave every day. The redness of my beard lessened thanks to short, bristly white hairs that mixed with the ginger stubble. I felt naked but looked human. It had been a while since I'd looked ordinary and I wasn't sure I recognized myself in the shop's large mirror, or liked what I saw.

Norm laughed as we walked to the SUV. "It's certainly a different look for you. Should've dyed it."

"Sissy's fifty questions would've been different if I'd asked her to dye it," I said. "She is curious, but like most boat people, she doesn't pry."

"Not too much, anyway." Norm got into the SUV. "She certainly wants you back at the marina."

"Won't happen." I got in and closed the door.

"Where are we heading?"

"Go to Kennedy and make a right," I said. "Shopping center on the left, at the light."

Traffic seemed heavier than I remembered, but with road construction on North Roosevelt Boulevard, it might have been the standard these days.

"Stay in the car." Norm parked in front of the mailbox rental store. He walked to the entrance, took a step back so he could read the window signs, checked his wristwatch and opened the door. Before closing it, he turned to me and shook his head.

The back of the SUV held the duffel bag with our guns from Miami and I wished my Sig Sauer rested against my back. I promised myself to get it, before we got to wherever we were going.

Norm walked out of the store with a shopping bag. He handed it to me and drove to another section of the large parking lot where we had a few spaces between us and other cars.

"Six phones?" I opened the bag and took two out.

"That's my count." Norm picked up a phone and read the directions. "I paid for two hundred minutes on each phone."

I unpacked a phone. "Isn't that a lot?"

"We won't be buying more time, so keep calls short. It has to be enough, it's almost four hours of use."

"Okay." What else was there to say?

"Turn the phone on. The number comes up on the screen, so memorize it. Now you've got an untraceable phone." He looked at the number on my phone screen and dialed. "And we have each other's number." He hung up before I answered. "Save it to memory."

I looked at the time displayed on the phone. It was a little past nine. "I should call Pauly. If he's been trying to reach me, who knows what he's thinking."

"We need to remain cautious, Mick," Norm said. "Tell Pauly we have burner phones for him and Bob. We have no idea how deep the government will dig, so it's better they're untraceable, too."

I nodded and realized I had to dial Pauly's number not just punch speed dial.

"What's the matter?" Norm stared at me. "Call him."

"I'm trying to remember the number," I said. "Been a long time since I dialed anyone's number from memory."

The first number I called wasn't Pauly, the second number got me an outraged husband. I reached Pauly on the third try.

"I've been leaving messages for you since seven," Pauly said. "Good and bad news, Mick."

"Of course," I said. "Give me the bad news first."

Norm reached over and hit the speakerphone button.

"I'm at the Tamiami airport," he said. "Going to Homestead next."

"You've been to Opa-Locka?" Norm said.

"Yeah, that's where the bad news comes in." Pauly stopped talking and I could hear airport noise in the background. "Opa-Locka is crawling with Russians."

"Why's that bad news?" I said.

"Because I recognized some from Miami," Pauly said. "They're big fuckers and aren't smiling. I don't wanna be around when they're enjoying themselves. Thinking about it scares me."

Norm and I looked at each other. I could tell he was considering what Pauly said and his concern worried me.

"Muscles, not brains," Norm said. "What's the good news?"

"We know where the Russians are, so the plane can't be far behind."

"Can you tell what they've got in the hangars? Is one empty?" I said.

"A couple are empty, but I'm keepin' a low profile. Don't need one of 'em to recognize me."

I told him about Richard's cryptic message and the Feebs tracking us by cell phone usage. Norm and I were breaking down our phones and Bob and he should do the same. He didn't argue after I assured him Norm had burner phones for them.

"I got someone that wants to meet with you," Pauly said. "He's flying into Key West this afternoon. I'm going back to Marathon now, and none too soon. He wants oysters at the Smokin' Tuna. You good with that?"

"Why does he want to meet us?" Norm said.

"Why do we want to meet him, in the middle of all this?" I said.

"Because he's a man with many talents. He's fluent in Russian and he deals with them. He also owes me one." Pauly has the ability to put a grin into the tone of his words. I could hear it then. He was proud of himself. It also meant the meeting had more to do with the man, than eating oysters. "He hasn't been in Key West for a while, so he's coming to you."

"What time?" Norm said before I could answer.

"I'll call from the Marathon airport office. My phone is down once I hang up."

"Good-bye," Norm said and hit the off button on my phone.

Chapter Fifty-Two

Norm stared at the Kmart across the parking lot. He got out of the SUV and began walking. I followed him into the store and we bought baseball caps, some touristy Hawaiian shirts and sunglasses. A change of look required a change of clothing, I guess.

When we loaded our packages into the SUV, I grabbed my Sig and extra magazines.

"You not telling me something, hoss?" Norm drawled as he closed the back door, holding two baseball caps and large sunglasses. He handed me mine and he put on his. I put on mine.

"I felt uneasy when you were in the mailbox store." I got into the SUV, pulling the ball cap down low.

"You worried?" Norm sat but didn't start the engine. "Or are you pulling a Padre Thomas on me?"

"I'm always worried." I tried to make light of my feelings and ignored his comment on Padre Thomas. We both knew I didn't deal with angels. "I don't know, when I was alone, I felt vulnerable. Maybe I'm getting paranoid?"

"Difference between cautious and paranoid is a blurry crevasse," he said. "You need to know how close you are."

"How close am I?" I knew Norm wouldn't lie to me.

"Crazy people don't know they're crazy." He grinned into the rearview mirror. "Same goes for paranoids."

"Thanks."

"We've got a lot of time to kill, Mick." He started the engine. "Any ideas?"

"We can't go back to the house and should probably stay away from the Mango Tree Inn until we have a better handle on this," I said.

"What's that leave us? Change and blend in with the crowds?"

"Call me paranoid." I tried to laugh but it didn't come off. "I think we lay low until Pauly calls. I know the women who own *La Pensione* guesthouse. It's Sunday, so they might be able to give us a room."

"Two rooms," Norm said and drove back to Kennedy Drive. "Where to?"

"Left on Roosevelt and it'll turn into Truman Avenue. I'll tell you when we get to the guesthouse."

* * *

Monica and Janie, owners of *La Pensione* were in the front room of the guesthouse with their morning coffee. If I was going to continue showing up at my old Key West haunts, I needed to remember people hadn't seen or heard from me in a year. I didn't know how to lessen the surprise or if I would be welcomed or not. I figured the coconut telegraph would eventually announce my return, but with any luck, not for a few more days. The women looked at me as if I was a ghost and that's not an expression of joy.

"Mick?" Monica said, her voice low, a surprised look as she almost dropped her cup.

Janie looked up and her expression wasn't much different. She looked at Norm and then back at me. "Nice you're back, Mick."

We shared a moment of polite talk. The women masked their curiosity with smiles and well-mannered questions before showing us to two connecting rooms on the second floor that overlooked the backyard.

We took everything from the SUV, including the duffel bag of weapons and our new clothes.

"Do I remind you of Magnum?" Norm stood in the doorway that connected our rooms, wearing a flowery Hawaiian shirt and Key West baseball cap.

"Magnum in cowboy boots," I said.

"You shave your head, I'll wear flip-flops." He grinned. "You gonna call Burt?"

I hesitated in answering, still wondering about Nadja and her Russian contacts. "Maybe later."

"The priest?"

Now I had to laugh. Even though Norm had misgivings

about Padre Thomas and his claim to communicate with angels, he still bought him a burner phone. "You think we need him?" I said it as a tease.

"I doubt it, but he's in your circle of friends and he's persistent," Norm said. "You don't understand how the government digs, Mick. In your case, they get to him and who knows what crazy things he'll say. They'll go to every bartender on the island and then to anyone the bartenders say they've seen you talk to. They'll go to every boat at the marina and the staff, asking who you know. They want to find someone, they don't stop digging."

"Good to know they're thorough," I mumbled, feeling anxious.

"Oh, that's only the beginning."

"What about you?"

"Don't even want to go there."

"Thanks for stoking my paranoia." I forced myself to remember Padre Thomas' cell number and dialed. I got the number right first try because I recognized his voice message. "Call me," I said and repeated the new number.

"Voice mail?" Norm slipped his hoister under the shirt.

"Yeah."

"Why do you have a problem with that? He didn't recognize the number. He'll call you back," Norm said.

I waited. He didn't call back.

Chapter Fifty-Three

The morning turned into afternoon and Padre Thomas hadn't called. In the past, in the rare instance he didn't answer his phone, he always called back. Padre Thomas wasn't the kind of person who could let a ringing phone go unanswered. It shouldn't have taken this long for his call and I said so to Norm.

We sat on the back porch of *La Pensione* with Cuban cigars Janie had given us. New guests checked in, but like most tourists, they unpacked and headed to Duval Street. To complement the cigars, Monica made fresh *mojitos*. They were busy with arriving guests and housekeeping, so we were on our own once the pleasantries ended.

"You haven't had contact with him for a year, hoss," Norm mumbled between sips of his drink. Holding the freshly-lit cigar, he pointed it at me. "You don't know what's changed in his life or his routines. Hell, maybe the phone battery's dead. The old man might not have remembered to charge it."

"Did he seem senile to you?" Sipping the mojito brought back fond memories of Key West and Havana that I pushed away. "And don't be a smart ass," I said.

"If he's not in jail, he's probably out buying cigarettes at a bar and can't hear the phone."

Norm had a point, but I didn't say so. I found a phone book and called my old haunts asking if Padre Thomas was there or had been in. Without exception, the answers were the same, *no*. The numbers were on my personal phone's speed dial, but that did me little good now, I needed the directory.

"Does he live far from here?" Norm said.

"A few blocks up, by the cemetery."

"Of course," he griped. "I can never get enough of the Key West cemetery!"

We had a history of mishaps at the cemetery, usually in the rain, and Norm never let me forget it.

"On the other side of the cemetery," I said. "Not Tita's side." I surprised myself by mentioning Tita's name so easily. I hadn't meant to. It just came out. And it came without torment, but carried a tinge of sadness as excess baggage.

"An afternoon stroll?" Norm stood. He didn't wait for an answer. "Give us a chance to try out our disguises." He laughed, finished the mojito, reset his baseball cap and walked away.

I touched my Sig. I knew it was against my back, hidden by the gaudy Hawaiian shirt, as Norm's forty-five was, but the feel of the cold, lethal weapon was reassuring.

Traffic on Truman Avenue snaked along, busy for a Sunday afternoon in June. The sun shined high in the sky, keeping temperatures warm, and a few threads of clouds floated by like wisps of ghosts spying from above. Basilica of Saint Mary had its side doors open, but Masses were over and the bells had stopped ringing. We turned right onto Windsor Lane.

Padre Thomas lived in a cottage left to him by an old seahorse everyone called Captain Maybe. He got the name because he answered questions by saying, "Maybe, maybe." He left Key West a year or so ago because he was dying of cancer and wanted to die on the water. The Cuban Coast Guard towed his boat into Havana and the old captain died alone in a Cuban hospital.

When we got to the corner of Windsor and Williams streets Norm stopped, took a last puff on his cigar and crushed it under his foot. "We walk by. Don't look at the house, babble to me, if you want, but just keep walking. Got it?"

"Yeah." I blew cigar smoke in his face. "Ain't my first rodeo."

Nothing seemed out of sorts on the street. A few scooters, some Conch cruisers, a handful of SUVs, two vans and parked cars stood empty within the long block of homes. Halfway to Southard Street, Norm stopped.

"I think you might be overly concerned for the priest," Norm said.

I flipped my cigar into the gutter. "And maybe I'm not."

"Let's go knock on the door and find out." Norm turned and we went to Padre Thomas' cottage.

The gate squeaked as I pushed it open. Norm looked at

me, then around the street.

"I've poured a ton of WD40 on the hinges," I said. "The gate always squeaks."

"Go knock on the door."

I didn't need to. The front door stood wide open. The rickety-screened door kept mosquitoes and other insects out.

"Padre Thomas," I called into the dim living room. "Are you there?"

He didn't answer. I put my face against the screen. The room appeared empty. I opened
the screened door. Norm stood next to me, his forty-five semi-automatic in his hand.

"He got a backyard?" Norm's voice low.

"A small one. He could be back there."

"Let's see." Norm walked ahead of me.

I held my Sig to my side.

The ceiling fan spun on high. No lights anywhere. We stopped and listened. Norm pointed at me and then toward the kitchen. The back door stood open. He pointed to himself and then at the hallway off to our left. I nodded and walked to the kitchen. Norm went to the hallway.

I only had to take a few steps. A man I assumed was Padre Thomas because of his frail build sat at the kitchen table with a black hood draped over his head, his arms tied behind him. I turned to my right, quickly, and saw a man, leaning against the kitchen wall. I couldn't see a weapon. I aimed my Sig at him and removed the hood from Padre Thomas.

"It took you long enough, Mr. Murphy," the man said.

I removed the tape from Padre Thomas' mouth. "Are you okay, Padre?"

He nodded and rattled the chair. His hands were tied behind him. I looked at the man. He hadn't moved. He smiled. I kept my gun pointed at him.

"Norm!" I yelled. "In the kitchen."

"Would you mind pointing the gun somewhere else?" The man remained leaning against the wall. "Thomas is unhurt and if you weren't so damn hard to find, I wouldn't have needed to do this."

"Shut up," I said and tried to untie Padre Thomas. "Norm!" I yelled again.

"My knife is on the sink counter," the man said. "You can use it to cut the ropes, but be careful, it's sharp."

"You move, you're dead." I kept the Sig pointed at him, and took the folding knife from the counter. It cut cleanly through the ropes on Padre Thomas's wrists. "Now who the hell are you and what's going on?"

Padre Thomas rubbed his wrists but didn't say a word.

"Norm!" I yelled again and his not replying made me nervous.

"All in due time, Mr. Murphy. First I have some questions." The man stood away from the wall and looked at the doorway. Why wasn't he nervous?

I turned to see Norm standing there. Then I saw the three black-clad men behind him. Each pointed a menacing looking rifle at Norm's back. We had the same rifles in the duffel bag.

"Been a long time, Norm," the man said.

"Not long enough, Colonel," Norm said.

Chapter Fifty-Four

Norm stayed in the doorway and never lost his *not-glad-to-see-you* scowl.

"Norm, you shouldn't be so negative," the colonel said. "My being here might be a good thing." He pointed toward the countertop. "Would you mind putting your weapons down?"

I looked at Norm, he nodded and placed his forty-five on the counter. I put my Sig next to his.

"What are you doing here, Colonel?" Norm took a bottled water from the fridge and gave it to Padre Thomas, who gulped from it.

"Still a get-to-the-point kind of guy, huh Norm?"

"I've got things to do. So if you don't mind, lose the muscle and say what you came to say," Norm said.

The colonel signaled the three men with rifles and they walked back into the living room. I heard the front door close and the lock slide into place. The colonel didn't want uninvited guests, but kept the backup close. I wondered if he was afraid of Norm.

"The diary," the colonel said. "I need the original copy. The Russian copy."

"You read Russian?" Norm said.

"I need to see how accurate the translation is. I trust my translators."

"It's a good translation."

"I need to see for myself, Norm."

"I don't have the original."

"Do you Mr. Murphy?" The colonel turned to me.

"No."

"Who does?" The colonel stood next to Padre Thomas. "Do you want more water?" He touched Padre Thomas' shoulder, an unspoken threat.

Padre Thomas shook his head and looked more nervous than usual. I'd been through the hood ordeal, so I understood his edginess. The colonel standing next to him, the man responsible for the hood, frightened him. Our being there didn't offer any solace.

"So, who has the original copy?" The colonel looked at us.

"Not sure at this point," I said. "I don't read Russian. I only wanted the translation," I lied.

"Who translated it?"

"What's so important about next Thursday?" Norm said.

"Ah, negotiation." The colonel's cold grin broadened. "Still got the touch, don't you, Norm?"

"Who are you?" My curiosity about his and Norm's relationship piqued. I'd known and worked alongside Norm for almost twenty years and never heard mention of the colonel.

"I'm the man that's going to stop the plane from crashing into the cruise ship."

"And how are you going to do that?" I said.

"I'm going to find the terrorists and kill them," the colonel said. "My team doesn't take prisoners. Do we, Norm?"

"No," Norm said.

"What's so important about Thursday?" I repeated Norm's question.

"That's the day, according to your translation of the diary, that the terrorists are attacking the cruise ship."

"You're lying, Colonel," I said. "The Coast Guard and the FBI showed more concern about the day than the attack. Where do you fit in?"

"You were right, Norm, he is an inquisitive son of a bitch."

"Cut the bullshit," I yelled. "You want me to know you and Norm have a history. Who gives a fuck? Not me! You have an alphabet soup of IDs up your sleeve, it doesn't impress me. You some gran-poo-pa of spooks, I don't give a rat's ass."

"Being inquisitive is not always a bad thing," Norm said to the colonel and turned to me. "What you have here, Mick, is a guy with an agency that can't do its job in the states. Right, Colonel?"

The colonel remained silent.

"Colonel, you should know that we're chasing the Russians, not the Palestinians or Iranians. We're not in your way."

"Never said you were, Norm." The colonel finally spoke.

"My guess is you could care less about the Russians," Norm said. "You're after the Iranians. You want . . . no, you *need* to put them next to the Palestinians and Hezbollah. Maybe after the suicide attack would be perfect. Something concrete against the Iranians. You'll leave the Russians to the FBI and Homeland Security. Am I warm, Colonel?"

"As a Mexican tortilla," the colonel said. "I can't use a Photostat copy of a translated document as evidence. I need the original. It's proof, if this is a good translation."

"How close are your colleagues?" Norm said.

The colonel laughed. "They have a playbook, Norm. They follow it. Copies of your document are still being gone over."

"Will they stop the attack?" I said.

The colonel looked at Norm, who nodded. "If they get off their asses and out of their own way, it's possible, but probably not."

"What's that mean?" I wanted him to explain.

"First, they've got to believe what's in the report."

"Do you?"

"Yes, Mr. Murphy," the colonel said. "I believe it but it's not my job to stop it."

"What the hell is your job?"

"My job is to connect the Iranians to the terrorists."

"Before or after the attack?" I yelled.

"Before, if I can. After if that's the case." The colonel made the comment without emotion. He believed an attack was imminent but had another agenda to follow.

I couldn't understand how a man, any man, could live with knowing his failure to act was responsible for the loss of innocent lives. I couldn't imagine it, but I could imagine this man before me was a monster because of his treatment of Padre Thomas.

"What else do you need?" Norm cut off my verbal assault.

"The original document," the colonel said. "And I need to

know where the terrorists are. Where's the plane, where's the crew and who's making the bomb?"

"You think we've done your job for you, don't you?"

"Part of it, if I'm lucky, Norm."

"We're in the same boat, Colonel," Norm said.

"Yeah. We thought the FBI or Homeland Security would take the reins." Seeing Norm relax made me curious. How did you relax your guard in front of a man like this? I glanced at my Sig, but Norm kept focused on the colonel. "That's why we went to them. This shit isn't what I signed up for."

"You've been drafted, Mr. Murphy," the colonel said. "I'm limited in what I can do, as Norm mentioned. Officially, I'm waiting for reports from D.C. I'll die an old man first."

"We've no idea where they are," Norm said. "We're waiting here and counting on luck."

"You've always made your own luck, Norm." The colonel walked away from Padre Thomas and draped his arm over Norm's shoulder. "You're hiding instead of running, so you've got something you're waiting on. Your sidekick here, he knows this island inside out, so if the plane shows up, you're gonna know. Right?"

"What we wanted was an agency with clout to get to the terrorists before the plane arrived here." Norm removed the colonel's arm.

"Not happening, Norm." The colonel walked to the counter and looked at the semi-automatics. "You and whatever gang of thieves and drunkards you hang around with," he spoke to me, "stand a better chance than the authorities. You hide from me, I'll find Thomas or someone else. Clear?"

"Let me tell you something, asshole," I said between clinched teeth. "If you go near this man again, I'll kill you. You, a big, brave savior of the free world and you go after the most vulnerable prey. I'd just as soon shoot you, as I would step on a roach. If there's a next time, you come after *me* and leave your boyfriends home." I felt my blood pressure rise.

"Get me what I want and this is over," the colonel said, smirking at my rant.

"I wouldn't piss on you if you were on fire and my bladder was bursting," I said.

The colonel laughed. "You're a piece of work. Norm, straighten him out, so I don't have to kill him."

Norm didn't say anything.

The colonel picked up the forty-five and handed it to Norm. He held my Sig a moment before handing it to me. "We're on the same side, boys. So, don't let me down."

Chapter Fifty-Five

Norm, Padre Thomas and I stayed in the kitchen as the colonel walked away, a *know-it-all* smirk telling me he thought he'd won whatever game he had involved us in.

"Bullshit," I mumbled under my breath and turned to say something when Norm grabbed me by the shoulder. He spun me toward Padre Thomas, still sitting or maybe frozen to the kitchen chair.

"How'd this happen?" I sat down and tried to block out thoughts of the colonel.

"He knocked on the door and I answered it," Padre Thomas said. He brought his hands together on the table, making it sound so simple. Bad experiences often are. "The others must have come in the back door. I didn't see them. I was saying I didn't know where you were when someone taped my mouth and the hood came instantly. Then they took me to the chair and tied my hands behind me. No one talked to me. They whispered between themselves, but I recognized your name. They wanted you."

"I'm sorry Padre." I knew from my own encounters with fear that my words meant little. "Who is he?" I turned to Norm and couldn't keep anger out of my tone. Anger toward whom, I wasn't sure.

Norm closed the back door and locked it. He paced between the table and living room doorway. "He's your worst nightmare," Norm said. "He doesn't belong here. I don't mean Key West, I mean in the country."

"So, what's he doing here?"

"He's not gone rogue, I can tell you that," Norm said. "He's here because of whatever is happening next week. I would think seriously about giving him the Russian document."

"You're afraid of him?" Norm surprised me by his quick willingness to give in to this guy.

"I'm afraid of what he's capable of and you should be, too." His eyes moved toward Padre Thomas and then came back to me. Norm wasn't a fan of Padre Thomas and his sudden unease for his safety concerned me "He has only one rule and that's to get the job done. Laws that protect us in this country, don't mean shit to him."

"Screw him," I said. "Padre, you've gotta come with us. You can't stay here. It's not going to be safe."

"I'm not leaving my home." Padre Thomas finished the water from the bottle Norm had given him. "I'm not afraid of him. At first, the darkness of the hood scared me. But I prayed and then the darkness became nothing and I saw things. I saw the fear of the Guatemalan men, women and children from my village as the dictator's men slaughtered them with machetes. Among the fear, there were brave acts from these simple people, failed attempts to protect others, but courageous. This man can do nothing to me but take my life. It should have been taken years ago."

"I can't leave you here, Padre," I said.

"You can't make me go, Mick. I will not give him that kind of power over me." Padre Thomas got up and took a bottled water from the fridge. "You can't give him what he wants and I won't give him my dignity."

I turned to Norm who nervously moved around the small kitchen. "If he had the document, would he go?"

"I don't want you to give him the document for me," Padre Thomas said. "I won't let you."

"It's all relative, Padre," Norm said. "His word is good, unless he's lying. He makes your lies look minuscule." Norm stared at me.

"How do you know when he's lying?"

"Same way I know when you're lying."

"How?" I shouted.

"His lips are movin'." Norm smiled and he broke the tension that had filled the room. "He's gonna say whatever he has to, to accomplish his assignment."

"And what's his assignment?"

"We find out what's going down Thursday and we'll know." Norm spoke to me but his eyes darted toward Padre Thomas. Neither of us knew what to do with the defiant priest.

Chapter Fifty-Six

I knew that arguing with Padre Thomas was useless but to relieve my conscience, I did anyway. Padre Thomas became resolute. The futility of it all ended when my cell phone chirped. Only Pauly, Padre Thomas and Norm had the new number and two stood in front of me.

"You in Marathon?" I walked into the living room. The colonel didn't bother about our security and left the front door opened.

"Yeah," Pauly said. "Five o'clock at the Tuna, work for you?"

It was three, which gave us two hours to get to the Tuna without running into the Feebs. "Yeah, five works."

"You okay?" Pauly said. "Sound tired."

"Tired and anxious. See you at the Tuna." I closed the connection.

"Two hours?" Norm said from the doorway.

"We could walk and still be there on time."

Norm scratched his ear. "I wish I knew who Pauly's guy was."

"Pauly thinks he can help us."

"Yeah." Norm frowned. "Last time he had someone help us, we had half the Mexican Special Forces and two cartels shootin' at our asses."

I didn't answer but pointed toward the kitchen.

"Stubborn old . . ." Norm hesitated before cussing. He walked to the front door and looked out. "I'll have Jim Ashe put people on him."

"Speaking of trust," I said. "Whose side are Ashe and JIATF on?"

"Ours, right now. He won't like knowing the colonel's in town." Norm turned to me and nodded toward the kitchen. "Don't tell him he's got baby sitters." He walked outside to call Ashe.

I began to wonder why others, like Ashe, new about the colonel, but I didn't. Why was Norm hiding him from me?

* * *

At the guesthouse, we arranged to rent scooters. Nothing screams tourist more than a scooter driven erratically in traffic, tinny horns echoing, and a rental decal on the back.

The Smokin' Tuna Saloon is off Duval Street, down narrow Charles Street that's not much more than an alley between the saloon and the Red Garter strip club. Any surveillance of the saloon would be noticeable because the backstreet is a one-way alley for delivery and trash trucks. Neither street offered doorways or shops for people to hide in. If you stood around the two alleys, it wouldn't be long before it looked like a stakeout.

Of course, if you wanted a backup crew outside, the vacant locale worked against you.

Norm insisted we circle the deserted area a few times, looking for anything out of place. Deliveries arrived in the morning, trash pickups came in the early hours, after the bars closed, so at five in the afternoon the alleys were empty, as they should be, and only scooters parked in the dirt strips running alongside narrow, cracked and uneven sidewalks. On our third circling, we parked across from the saloon's side entrance.

"What should we be looking for?" I said before we crossed the alley.

"Trouble," he muttered almost to himself. "I'm still bothered by the colonel being here. He's the wrong guy in the wrong place and I can't put my finger on why anyone would set him loose in Key West."

"Shouldn't we be focusing on the plane and finding out where it is?" We walked into the Smokin' Tuna.

"The scary part, Mick, is they're connected somehow."

No band had set up on the stage yet. A poster said Scott Kirby would begin at six. A light crowd gathered around the main bar waiting for the show, leaving only a few empty seats. Norm scanned the area slowly. I recognized bartenders Laura and Steve as they set up the satellite bamboo bar. Five o'clock happy hour would keep them busy.

Norm pointed to a table by the T-shirt shop that allowed

us to see both entrances. Angela, the manager, walked by and was surprised to see us.

"Mick, are you back to stay?" She walked over and we hugged.

"I hope so," I said. It was only a half lie.

"You just missed Charlie."

Charlie was one of the owners and a long-time friend. "I'll catch him later."

"I'll let him know you were in." Angela took the stairs to the second-floor office.

"When this guy arrives, let me do the talking," Norm said. "I wanna see what he knows, if anything, about the plans for next week."

Laura walked by, carrying a large bucket of ice for the bar cooler and stopped. "Mick?"

I smiled as I stood. "In person."

"It's nice to have you back," she said. "Norm, how you doing?"

"Enjoying the weather," he lied.

"Still a Jameson's on the rocks?"

"Why not?" I sat down.

"Same for you, Norm?"

"I'll take a draught," he said. "Surprise me."

Laura nodded and took the ice bucket and our order to the bar.

"You okay?" Norm stared at me.

"She's not the only one I'm gonna run into," I said. "Before this is over, everyone will know I'm here."

"Yeah, but you knew that."

"Thinking about it too much made it worse," I said. "I miss the island life, but I'm not sure I can come back. It won't be the same."

"Change, hoss, you can't stop it, not even in Key West."

Laura delivered our drinks. "First drink is on me." She kissed my cheek. "Happy to see you, Mick. Beer's on me too." She smiled at Norm and left.

"Some things don't change." I took a sip of the whisky. "Jameson's, for example." I hadn't had Irish in a year. Memories of Key West flooded my mind with the first swallow.

The first sip was strong, bit my tongue and at the same time chilled my taste buds. Norm grinned and drank his beer.

We sat quietly, watching the entrances. Pauly entered off Charles Street, saw us, and came over.

"Let me get a beer." Pauly walked to Steve and came back with a bottle of Corona.

"Who is this guy?" Norm said as Pauly sat. "Why should we trust him?"

"He's in the business."

"What business?" Norm said. "Crashing planes into cruise ships?"

"He's a smuggler I knew back in the day," Pauly said as he drank. "We caught up at the Tamiami Airport."

"And he told you all about the Russians?" Norm said unable to hide his distrust.

"No, of course not," Pauly said. "Look it, we hadn't seen each other in years. You don't see someone in that line of work for a while he's either dead or in lockup. So, we caught up on old times."

"Who brought up the Russians?" Norm demanded.

"Cool your pants, Norm," Pauly said and shook his head. "He said he's been flying the Russians' product to the Bahamas for shipment to Europe. Big shipments."

That made sense to me. Cargo containers from certain Central and South America countries came under more scrutiny than containers from the Bahamas and it was all because of drugs.

"What did you tell him about us, about this, the plane?"

"Never came up, Norm," Pauly said. "When he asked what I was doing now that I'd left the life, I told him hanging in Key West. He said he was looking for an excuse to come to the Keys and eat oysters. I told him the Tuna's were the best, so he invited himself. You do it tactfully, you may be able to find out what the Russians are doing at the airports and maybe, just maybe, he'll know something about Alexei's whereabouts."

"Pauly, conch is the local cuisine. Oysters are flown in from the Gulf," Norm said.

"So maybe he likes to eat his oysters in Key West. Maybe he likes the sunsets. Who gives a damn?"

"Maybe you're right." Norm took a drink of beer. "But maybe he likes Key West for other reasons."

Chapter Fifty-Seven

We nursed our drinks and waited. Five o'clock came and went. Locals walked into the saloon to listen to music and for a Sunday evening drink. Scott Kirby worked at his sound check on stage. The bartenders kept asking if we needed fresh drinks. We did, but we didn't order. Not then. It wasn't the right time for an alcohol haze.

I saw him. I knew as soon as he walked in, he was Pauly's guy. He stopped a few steps into the bricked patio, next to the large banyan tree. He looked past us, stared at the side exit for a beat too long. An alternative exit if he had to run. He saw us but gave no acknowledgement as he shook a cigarette from its pack. For a very brief moment, he scanned the bamboo bar and those who sat there and then focused on the crowded oval bar. Lighting the cigarette gave him more time to evaluate his surroundings.

He walked to the crowded bar and seemed to be searching for someone. He didn't trust us. When he made the full circle, he stood in front of the stage, minus the cigarette, nodded to Kirby, and walked to our table.

"He's here." I tapped Pauly's shoulder.

"Yeah." Pauly stood. "I saw him walk in."

The smuggler walked with a swagger. He stood about five-foot-ten, and if he'd lost a few pounds, he would've looked fit. Thick, salt-and-pepper hair and a clean-shaven face, with dark brown eyes, revealed little else about him. Jeans and tennis shoes and an expensive Tommy Bahama shirt filled out his wardrobe. Maybe he carried a weapon under the loose fitting shirt, too. He smiled as he and Pauly shook hands, then turned a cold stare toward us.

"Mick, Norm." Pauly nodded at us. "Larry."

Norm and I remained sitting and we didn't offer to shake hands. We each said his name, "Larry," and nodded our greeting.

Larry's eyes focused briefly on Norm, then me before his lips parted, and the smile returned. Only his eyes, cold and hard looking, didn't brighten. Like so many people who lived within the life-and-death world of drug cartels, he had the survival instincts of a chameleon when it came to dealing with people he didn't know or trust. As a journalist in Central America, I'd met a lot of chameleons. They were all cold-blooded, like the lizard.

Pauly pulled out the fourth chair and he and Larry sat.

Steve took Larry's order, a new round for us and two dozen raw oysters. We waited, almost in silence. Pauly kept trying to get us into a conversation, but Norm would only smile and maybe mumble a word or two. I followed Norm's lead. I guess it was an issue of trust because of past experiences that made me go along. Something bothered Norm.

Laura brought the drinks, while Steve shucked the two-dozen oysters.

"To an old friend and new ones." Larry raised his beer glass.

We all said *"salud,"* touched glasses and drank.

"You I've heard about." Larry looked at me. "You used to meet Pauly in the Dominican Republic."

"A few times," I said.

"Norm, how are you connected to these two?" Larry kept the grin.

"Law enforcement." Norm didn't smile.

Larry looked at Pauly and then laughed. "Running from it?"

"Running with it," Norm said without the laugh. "You know, chasing the bad guys through Central America. Catching them. Killing them."

Larry turned to Pauly. "What's his problem?"

"You're my problem." Norm held his cup and circled it on the table in front him.

"Lighten up, man." Larry fumbled his words. "I came here as a friend."

"You speak Russian?" Norm said.

"Yeah, fluently. Took it in high school because a girl I liked did. Surprised me, I was good at it." His word flowed together, spoken too quickly.

"How long have you been working with the Russians?"

"About five years." Larry kept looking toward Pauly for answers. "Do we have a problem here?"

Pauly stared at Norm and then me. I shook my head and Pauly didn't say a word.

"How long before the Russians get here?" Norm moved his drink to the side.

"What do you mean?" Larry nervously looked around.

"Pauly," Norm said, without taking his stare from Larry. "If you had to make a delivery at five-twenty-two, how long would you wait around?"

"'Til five twenty-seven." Pauly looked from Larry to Norm. "Max, 'till five thirty-two."

"So you expect people to be prompt because you're prompt. It's a requirement of your past life and now it's a habit."

"Yeah, Norm. What are you doin'?"

"Larry here was a half-hour late." Norm never removed his eyes from Larry. "Did the Russians tell you to wait a half hour, to give them time to get here?"

"What the fuck are you talking about?" Larry nervously played with his drink.

"You walked through here, scoping the joint out, making sure we didn't have cops or hired guns waiting around. Routine had you check it out."

"Yeah," Larry said. "I'm cautious."

"What I think, Larry, is you were looking for your Russian backup." Norm pulled out his phone and hit speed dial. "When you saw the alley, you knew they couldn't be outside so you looked for them inside."

"You're crazy." Larry turned to Pauly. "You didn't tell me these guys were crazy."

"Larry, I hope this is all bullshit," Pauly said. "Norm's not known for his sense of humor."

"Christ, Pauly, how long do we go back?"

"A long way, Larry. We've shared a lot."

"So who you gonna believe? Hot shot in his cheap flowery

shirt or your old *amigo*, me?"

"Why were you late, *amigo*?" Pauly said.

Norm spoke into his cell phone. "You can come now. Side entrance." He looked at Larry and disconnected the call. "Tell us, why were you late?"

"Fuck you!" Larry shouted.

"You stand up you're dead." Norm slipped his forty-five from its holster, hid it beneath the table and kept it pointed at Larry. "Hands on the table."

Larry looked toward the crowded bar before he put his hands on the table.

"How much time do we have?" Norm demanded.

Larry turned to Pauly. "Sorry," he stammered. "They're very persuasive. A cigarette?" he said to Norm.

Norm nodded. "Keep your hands above the table."

Larry lit a cigarette and lost the grin, no longer a chameleon.

"How much time?" Pauly said.

"I don't know." Larry took a long drag on the cigarette. "I told them I shouldn't be late," he exhaled smoke. "But you don't tell them anything, they tell you."

"Why?" Pauly said.

"They wanted the shooters from South Beach," Larry stared at Pauly. "They had security camera footage of you inside and grainy shit from the alley. Showed it to everyone on the payroll. Someone remembered you and Mick from Key West last year. That and you killed a couple of their people at the club and others are missing. They don't tolerate that. If they didn't get even, they'd lose face."

"And you ratted me out!" Pauly almost yelled.

"Not at first." Larry crushed out the cigarette. "I had no way of reaching you or knowing where you were. They knew of my history with you, so I told them it looked kind of like you."

"Kind of! That's a death sentence with the Russians."

"You know the life." Larry garbled the words and settled into the chair. "You know the rules. Self-preservation with these assholes." He lit another cigarette without asking.

"No room for friendship in the life, right?" Pauly said.

"Friendship within limits. You know that, too." Larry inhaled and then let the smoke out. "If they thought I lied, they would've killed me! I had to consider that."

"Mick Murphy, you son of a bitch!" A woman yelled as she walked through the side entrance.

I looked up and saw Deb and Ken Armitage, two long-time friends. I stood, nodded to Norm. I knew he wouldn't want them coming to the table because the situation could turn deadly instantly. I met them by the bamboo bar. Deb I hugged. Ken and I shook hands. I kept a wandering eye on the table.

"I have to hear you're home from Laura on the phone!" Deb said and led me to the bar. "We're sorry for your loss, Mick."

"We wanted to do something," Ken said. "But no one knew where you were."

"He's back now," Deb said. "We're glad you're okay. You are okay, right?"

I laughed along with them, hoping it hid my nervousness. "Yeah. I'm adjusting. Right now I'm in the middle of something, but I promise to catch up later on in the week."

"You know where we'll be," Ken said.

"Time for one drink?" Deb said.

"In a day or two and I'll buy." When I turned everyone at the table stood up. Norm kept close to Larry, and Pauly headed toward me. Norm pointed to the side entrance.

"What about the oysters?" Steve called from the bar when he saw us walking away.

"Money's on the table, share them with Mick's friends." Pauly stopped at the gate. "Two four-door Jeeps."

"Jim Ashe's people." Norm pushed Larry out the gate.

"Company at the front," Pauly said.

I turned to see three burly, fire-hydrant-built thugs walking through, wearing poorly-fitting sport coats and slacks. Definitely not locals. When they spotted us, one spoke into his cell phone. They hurried toward the exit. I closed the gate as Norm shoved Larry into the back seat of the Jeep with one of Jim Ashe's men's help, and it sped away. The gate locked. Norm led us into the second Jeep and we got in.

As we drove past Charles Street, more Russians hurried toward the bar. The driver of the Jeep and the other man in front wore civilian clothes but the haircuts shrieked military. They didn't bother to slow down, they'd probably seen Russians before.

"Could you cut it any closer?" I said.

"Pauly, don't take this personal, but we don't want to meet any more of your friends," Norm said.

"Where are they taking him?" Pauly said.

"He's being babysat until we know what's going on," Norm said.

Chapter Fifty-Eight

The front passenger in the Jeep turned to us. "Captain Ashe said to take you wherever you wanted to go."

"First stop is *La Pensione* guesthouse on Truman," Norm said and the driver nodded.

"Then what?" I said. "Everyone's looking for us now."

"But not everywhere." The chase excited Pauly, it was as if he were back in the game. Maybe we all were, but it wasn't a game. Everyone was deadly serious, from the colonel to the Iranians with us caught in between. "We go into the belly of the beast, where no one's expecting us to be."

"Moscow or Washington?" Norm did have a sense of humor, even if Pauly couldn't see it.

"Opa-Locka." Pauly said, missing Norm's jest. "No one's gonna think we'd go there, especially the Russians. Hell, planes and strangers are in and out of there all day and night. We won't stand out."

"How do we get around, with the Russians looking for us?" Norm sounded interested in what I thought was a risky propostion.

"Carefully, Norm. We don't stand out by being curious. We're low profile and we'll be there when the Iranians arrive." Pauly was thinking on the run, something that had kept him out of jail in his smuggling days; that and his daredevil antics to escape the authorities.

"What if the plane doesn't go there?" It wouldn't be the first bait-and -switch scheme I'd seen. Politicians and white color criminals tried it all the time when dealing with journalists.

"You have a better plan, now's the time, hoss," Norm said.

I didn't answer.

The Jeep parked at the guesthouse as we accepted Pauly's idea in silence.

Sunday, early evening, and we found guesthouse owners

Janie and Monica ready to go downtown. As carefully as I could, I told half-truths about reasons people might show up asking questions about us because our rental scooters were parked outside the Smokin' Tuna Saloon and could be traced back to the guesthouse.

"Just tell the truth and you'll be okay," I said as we left.

Jim Ashe's men dropped us at the Marathon Airport. Pauly's concern that the Russians might figure we'd use either Key West or Marathon airports to escape, made him hurry and we were in flight soon after the quasi-instrument check. Norm gave him a burner phone.

It took less than an hour for us to approach Opa-Locka Executive Airport.

The sun was a good hour from setting, but on the mainland that meant dusk. Most workers at the airport had gone home or were preparing to. Private planes came and went at all hours but as night approached, the traffic on the tarmac dwindled.

Pauly's hangar was at the far end of the airfield, away from the main terminal, and I expected the Russians' hangars were too.

Bob waited by the large hangar and as Pauly set his plane inside on its marks, the automated doors began to shut. Overhead light dimly lit the Quonset hut interior. Like Pauly's hangar at the airport outside Baton Rouge, the office was set in the back and well lit.

Bob got his burner phone from Norm and removed the battery from his personal cell. Pauly carried his duffel bag of weapons into the office and emptied it. Norm opened the door in the back of the hangar, looked outside and then closed it.

"Walkway leads to the terminal," Pauly said before Norm could ask. "All the hangars have back doors."

Norm looked up at the dark ceiling. "Skylights too?"

"Yeah." Pauly switched on brighter indoor hangar lights. "They don't open and they're hurricane proof, so you can't break through them too easily. Make a hell of a racket trying to get in that way."

If I've learned anything during my years as a journalist,

especially during Central American civil wars, it's that I spend most of my time waiting. I became accustomed to it, but never comfortable with it. It's no different in Norm's and Pauly's world. The action, or whatever you may want to call it, equals a small percentage of time involved with an operation. In my case, I spent more time on research, waiting for returned phone calls, sitting in bars or coffee shops hoping a contact would show, staking out a location and other such exciting things, than I was involved in a final action. That's the mode we were in, hurry up and wait.

In less than a week's time terrorists planned to crash a small, twin-engine plane, loaded with explosives, into a docking cruise ship in Key West Harbor; Russian gangsters were searching for us; federal government agents were searching for us and we hid a few hundred miles from Key West, waiting.

Norm and Pauly used the time to plan a defense of our position. It might as well have been the Alamo, if the Russians found us. I wasn't sure how Pauly would react if the Feebs found us, but I knew Norm and I would go peacefully. Maybe Bob, too. There was no escape for us unless the Russians were really stupid or we were blessed with the luck of fools. I feared we'd used up most of our luck in Mexico.

Pauly smoked and I think he beat Padre Thomas for chain-smoking awards. Norm found wood blocks and wedges that would keep the large hangar doors and small, built-in, walk-through door from opening when placed correctly. He assumed the Russians would have a remote of some kind that could open the doors. The back door opened in, so he put a heavy rolling toolbox against it, wood wedges against the wheels. If we needed to exit in a hurry, at least the wedges could be kicked away.

We spent close to three hours with small talk and setting up the sleeping cots, before Bob spoke up. We sat at the small picnic-styled table outside the office, drinking coffee or sodas. It was almost midnight and our anxiety had beaten away sleep.

"I have an idea," Bob said. "If you want to hear it."

"Let's hear it." Norm almost sounded interested.

"I've been watching these assholes, day and night, since

Pauly left me here." Bob stood up and began to pace. "I don't know where they go, but by now they've locked everything up and are gone. They leave two guys who walk security. I don't understand what they're saying, but they seem to be laughing a lot. I'm not sure how seriously they take their job. They check the doors, if it's locked they move onto the next hangar."

"Front and back?" Now Norm seemed interested.

"I didn't follow them," Bob said. "But they make the circle from the tarmac and around the hangars, so yeah, I'd say front and back."

Bob stopped at the end of the table. "Only one of the hangars they go into has received deliveries and that's usually late at night."

"What kind of deliveries?" Norm said.

"Paneled van, after ten when there's less traffic around the tarmac. Van goes in, doors open just wide enough for it and then they close. Doors open the van comes out, maybe forty-five minutes later."

"A quick unload." Even Pauly had become interested.

"My guess. What do you suppose they're unloading?"

"How many times have you seen this, Bob?" Norm said.

"A few times, but it doesn't mean I haven't missed a delivery."

"Do you know what's in the hangar?"

"No. The doors open and close for the van. Otherwise they're kept closed."

Norm scratched his chin and looked at each of us. "Could the plane be in there?"

"According to my contacts here, these guys rented three hangars, but no one has seen a plane arrive," Pauly said.

"Let's get back to my plan," Bob said. "You three break into the hangar and I'll take out the two guards. Then we'll know what's in there. Get this shit over with."

Bob surprised us. Norm smiled and nodded, followed by Pauly.

"If it's explosives, we blow the hangar and they don't

have enough time to get more for Thursday." Bob stood tall. "Simple and maybe the answer to our problem."

Chapter Fifty-Nine

None of us was a locksmith. Fortunately, Pauly found bolt cutters and two crowbars to help open the Russians' hangar door. Bob's job was to neutralize the guards. With that taken care of, no one felt it necessary to use stealth to break into the hangar.

We waited. There was still tarmac activity outside. We would wait a while longer.

The Russian mob soldiers hadn't left yet, so that kept us inside too.

Bob went out every half hour to smoke a cigarette, checking the perimeter.

By 1 A.M., most activity at the airport had ceased.

We had no way of knowing if the door had an alarm, but there was no sign of foil connectors and wires on the walk-through door's small window that would have indicated one. The other uncertainty was what waited inside. Explosives were the consensus and that meant the possibility of a booby-trapped door or interior. Booby-trapped explosions were one the Russian mob's calling cards.

Bob signaled that the guards had passed. He followed. With his Navy SEAL training, I doubted he'd need the Kimber semi-automatic forty-five that he carried.

We hugged the shadows on the way to the Russians' hangar, armed with M-4s, flashlights, bolt cutter and crowbars.

A few clouds and a bright moon filled the sky. The tarmac's runway lights were on.

Norm signaled us to the side as he pried the door at its bolt lock location. Two grunting pries and the door opened. He waited a beat and then Norm pushed it inward. Darkness, not an explosion, greeted us as the door creaked open.

We moved inside and closed the door. Using our flashlights, we quickly realized there was little to see. We entered an empty hangar. We walked to the rear office, using our flashlights to check the floor for trip-wires. The office had a desk, chair and window A/C unit. The desk drawers were empty. A nonworking phone sat on top and that was it.

"What the fuck?" Pauly slammed a drawer closed and then switched on the lights. All we saw was a dusty floor. "Were the trucks taking things out?"

Norm searched the office, touching surfaces, pushing the desk aside a few inches, and sat on the chair, rolling it to the wall. He took each desk drawer out, checked the bottom and stacked it on top of the desk. Nothing anywhere. Whatever he hoped to find wasn't there.

"Turn the hangar lights on." Norm stood up.

Pauly found the switch and turned on the upper lights. No trip wires anywhere.

"Walk around," Norm said.

"What are we looking for?" All I could see was an empty hangar.

"Some place there ain't dust because something was there. Maybe they were taking stuff out of here." Norm began slowly walking along the left wall.

Pauly walked the wall to the right and I walked the rear wall.

The backdoor was locked. Dust spread along the lower doorframe. Between the wall and floor, there were traces of dust but no signs of anything having been stored or moved. No tire tracks, no shelving.

I walked to the center of the hangar and met Norm and Pauly at the large doors.

"No pallet scratches, no manual lift for moving heavy items." Norm pointed at the floor. "The van came in and stopped here."

There were smears of tire tracks on the dirty floor.

"What were the trucks doing?" Pauly said what I was thinking.

"This is the hangar Bob said they used, right?" Norm said. Pauly and I nodded.

No one said anything, but I knew we were thinking alike. The whole operation was a ruse to throw off any surveillance the

Russians might have been under.

"The plane's not coming here," I said.

"No shit, Dick Tracy." Norm looked out the door he had forced open. "They didn't go to all this trouble because of us."

"Who are they trying to fool?" Pauly said.

Bob walked into the hangar. "Saw the lights." He looked at the empty hangar with a puzzled expression.

"They were guarding nothing." Norm spread his arms wide. "Joke's on us."

"Joke's on the dead guards," Bob said. "There a problem?"

Norm explained his theory about the ruse.

"So there's a chance someone out there is watching us, right now," Bob said.

"They'd have to have noticed us break in, so yeah, a good chance," Norm said. "If they're following the Russians and leave when they do, we might be okay."

"There'd be someone here watching the hangars," Pauly said. "They have to think there's something in here, too."

"And they would've seen us," Norm muttered. "Fuck!"

"What?" Pauly and I said at the same time.

"They're either government agents or the Russians' competition. Those are the only two that would do surveillance."

"Okay, so how do we handle it?" I said.

"Is the plane ready to go?" Norm turned to Pauly.

"We've got fuel. We can get out of here right now," Pauly said. "But to where?"

"Back to Key West." Norm smiled and that worried me because I'd seen the look before and it warned of his devil-may-care approach to unsolvable circumstances. "We might as well be the ones to put an end to this shit."

We each looked around at each other. When there wasn't an objection we headed toward the hangar exit.

Chapter Sixty

Bob stopped us before we reached the door.

"If there's someone out there, we're being watched." Bob looked out toward the dimness. "For all we know, whoever it is has called in and others are on the way." Bob stared outside.

"So time is of the essence, why are we talking?" Norm turned to look outside. "Did you see something?"

"Nope. But I've got a suggestion."

Our silence gave Bob permission to go on.

"Whoever is out there has to be using one of the hangars across the way." Bob pointed at the window. "There's no second story, no office windows and no one's on the roof. Give me five minutes, I'll go out the back and circle around. Y'all go out front after five, smoke a cigarette, talk, argue, anything to keep the attention on you."

"And you?" Norm nodded as if he knew what was coming.

"I'll neutralize him."

"If it's more than one?" Norm said.

"Let's hope it's not. One to watch the store, would be my guess."

"I'll go with you." Norm handed me his M-4. "Two are better than one."

"Mick and I just wait?" Pauly almost seemed hurt that he hadn't been included.

"In five minutes you go outside for a smoke, do something to keep attention focused on you." Norm looked at Bob, who nodded. "They watch you, we get them."

"Ten past two, go out and do something, point inside so it looks like you're talking about us." Bob checked his wristwatch and then he and Norm headed to the rear door.

"I wish we were on the water." Pauly shook a cigarette from its package. "Escaping is a lot easier on the water. Hell, you've got the whole ocean to run into."

"You can't outrun a Coasties' chopper," I said.

"You've got a chance if there's a few mangrove islands around." He smiled and put the cigarette in his mouth.

We never heard the back door open or close.

"Show time." Pauly offered me a cigarette after the five minutes had passed. "You'd better smoke. Look like we came outside because something inside might go *boom* if we light up in here." He exaggerated boom with opened arms and we walked outside.

The moon had moved west and the clouds hung in the black sky as if they'd gone to sleep. Humidity blanketed the quiet airport. Pauly held his lighter out while I lit my cigarette and then he lit his.

"You think this whole thing here is a stunt?" Pauly pointed inside.

"A big one," I said. "Three hangars, and what, a dozen thugs, security twenty-four/seven and the vans."

"A lot of effort."

"For what?" I said. "We've got one thing on our minds, but those assholes have a lot on their plates."

"I don't know." He lit another cigarette. I crushed mine and refused one more. "If the bombing goes off, the Iranians owe the Mexicans, the Mexicans owe Alexei and give him the distribution rights to their drugs for Central Europe. That's big business."

We turned away from the hangar as we talked, looking across the tarmac. As Pauly fumbled with his cigarette package, thinking of a third smoke, we saw three brief flashes of light in the walk-through door window of the hangar across from us. Muzzle flashes but no noise. Without speaking, we both entered the hangar and grabbed the M-4s.

Waiting again, not sure if Norm and Bob would greet us or some pissed off bad guys.

Chapter Sixty-One

Pauly shut the overhead lights off and the office went dark. He waited by the locked back door, not knowing who might come through it. I stood by the front door, Norm's M-4 against the wall, mine cradled in my arms, and watched the opposite hangar from the window. If whoever they were came from the hangar, I would see them. Pauly took the short end of the stick willingly and stood quietly in back waiting for the door to open suddenly.

Waiting.

Damn waiting.

I had to believe Norm and Bob did the shooting, but not knowing for sure caused anxiety. Three bright flashes, three shots fired. How many people were inside when my friends surprised them? Each minute felt like an hour. I checked my watch and sometimes when I looked, the second hand hadn't made a full circle.

The small door of the hangar opened. No one exited. It took an eternity before Norm looked out. He studied the tarmac and then the other hangars. He walked out, followed by Bob. I yelled to Pauly and he joined me. Norm pointed toward Pauly's hangar and headed that way, meeting up with us out front of it.

"We gotta leave." Norm took an M-4 from me. "Right away."

We went into the hangar and Pauly made a straight shot to his plane. "Ten minutes," he said without turning back. "Open the hangar door."

As we gathered our few belongings, Norm told me what happened.

Two men were inside with expensive surveillance equipment, including a directional mic so they could follow and tape conversations between the Russians. One of the men got a shot off as Norm and Bob entered, and then they fired back. The two men were dead. The two security guys were dead. The numbers were racking up and quickly. Who else is going to be pissed at us now?

"Russians?" It sounded like Feebs with all the equipment.

That would be bad.

"Didn't get to talk to them," Norm mumbled. We shared the same concerns. "But they didn't have government issued weapons."

"Who do you think they were?"

"Ukrainians, if I had to guess." Norm shook his head. "It wasn't set up the way we were taught to do surveillance, but it's been a long time."

Russians, Ukrainians, the whole fucking Eastern European bloc would be after our asses if this didn't end soon.

Bob had the hangar door open when the plane's engines started.

"We don't have a hangar in Key West," Pauly said as we got on the plane.

"Does anyone know about this plane?" Norm sat in the copilot's seat.

"No one down here should, it hasn't left Baton Rouge in a long time."

Bob stored the weapons on the back seat and sat next to them.

"What's the plan?" Norm always had a plan and I expected him to have one now.

"Stop the plane from crashing into the cruise ship." He looked up at me with that damn devil-may-care smile.

"How?" That smile scared me.

"Hell if I know."

Pauly began to taxi to the tarmac for takeoff.

I took my seat and wondered if anyone remained an atheist around Norm for very long.

Chapter Sixty-Two

I stood behind Pauly and Norm after we were in the air. It only took a few minutes before the plane followed the chain of islands that make up the Florida Keys, flying southwest to home. Stars flickered in the sky and some reflected off the dark water, mimicking the lights of cars and homes below. Moving lights on the water were probably fishermen or shrimpers going out early or coming back late. Or, maybe smugglers trying to beat the morning sunrise to a clandestine dock.

"You know Freddy Cabanas," I said to Pauly.

"Yeah. Why?"

"He's got a hangar there."

"Don't really need a hangar," Pauly said. "Just wanted to make sure everyone knew we'd be out in the open and need a place to crash."

"Who's Cabanas?" Norm looked at me.

"A popular local pilot," I said. "When the Blue Angels are on the island for a show, Freddy opens up for them with stunts a jet couldn't get away with."

"The Blue Angels aren't gonna help us." Norm looked out into the darkness and I wondered what he saw. "We've got to work with what we have."

"That ain't much." Pauly banked the plane westerly. He wanted to give himself distance between Boca Chica Naval Air Base and its runway.

"It's almost nothing," I said.

"We know two important things." Norm's damn grin seemed to get bigger.

"When and where," I said.

"Exactly." Norm turned in his seat. "We know they seem to be locked in to hitting the ship as it docks this comin' Thursday morning. How can we use it?"

"What would happen if we warned the cruise ship company?" Pauly said.

"If they believed us, what would they do?" Norm turned

to Pauly.

No one answered. The government didn't believe us, why would the cruise ship company?

"What about this?" Bob said. I hadn't heard him approach.

"This what?" Norm said.

"Couldn't we fly interference? Keep them away until the ship docked and people got off?"

"I'm doing my best to stay alive," Pauly said. "Other than hitting the plane broadside and making them crash, there's no way to divert them. Christ, they're doing this knowing they're gonna die."

"Damn!" Norm yelled. "Could you fly alongside them?"

"And do what?" Pauly looked away from the windscreen and stared at Norm. "The closer we got the more likely the explosion would affect us too."

"We circle out there." Norm didn't seem to care about the aftereffects. "There won't be another twin-engine plane heading toward the ship, so we pick it up as far out as possible and shoot it down ourselves."

"With what?" Pauly checked the instrument panel. "M-4s? We'd have to get too close and again, the explosion would take us down too."

"We need a bigger gun." The excitement hadn't left Norm's voice.

"You need a bigger plane," Pauly said. "One with a door you can open while in the air."

For what it was worth, we'd agreed with Norm that stopping the attack on the cruise ship fell on us. Why the government – the FBI and Homeland Security – didn't believe us or give any credence to our warning puzzled me and kicked my pessimistic journalist's curiosity into gear. None of my conclusions boded well for the government agencies and while that excited my reporter's energies, it also caused major anxiety. Exposing a corrupt official or shady politician was one thing, but questioning a whole government agency's policy was like trying to answer to the old question, which came first, the swamp or the mosquito. Swimming through the bureaucratic sludge of Homeland Security tributaries was an endless upstream battle. And, to date, I knew of no one who had succeeded.

Norm couldn't get a credible answer from any of his government or spook contacts – CIA, FBI and JIATF – and that confused me. The apparent inability of these agencies to coordinate between themselves and inability to accept things were happening that they'd missed baffled me. Everyone seemed to have a separate agenda until it came to us.

Norm's agencies protected us from detention – for the moment, anyway – but other than that, they ignored our warnings, and the information we'd passed on fell on deaf ears.

"Key West." Pauly turned to me. "Take your seat, Mick, we're landing."

He called the Miami Air Traffic Control Tower, since the Key West tower wouldn't be in operation for another hour or so. We descended onto the sleepy island shortly before sunrise and crowing roosters welcomed us as the plane landed.

Chapter Sixty-Three

I watched through the window as the plane descended, its landing lights adding to the spotty glow of runway lights, leaving the surrounding area in eerie shadows of planes stationed like sentries outside a sanctuary. Pauly taxied the Cessna along the passage between parked planes. He stopped not far from Cabanas' Quonset-hut hangar.

Norm and Bob collected the weapons and put them in the duffel bag. It wouldn't be good to have them seen at the airport. Pauly shut down the plane, following the procedural check this time because he was not in a hurry. I was the first one off and saw Padre Thomas sitting at the picnic table outside the hangar, a large cup of coffee in his hands. Where did he find coffee at the airport? His old bike leaned against the parking lot fence. He surprised me and I had to shake my head, close and open my eyes, to make sure I wasn't imagining him. I wasn't.

"Padre Thomas." I looked to see that Norm and the others were still on the plane. "What are you doing here?" What business could he have with Freddy Cabanas this early in the morning?

"They're back, Mick." He stood, placing the cup on the wooden table.

"Who's back?"

His puzzled expression confused me for a moment and then I knew what he meant.

"The angels." He smiled, happy to have the sentinels back in his life. "They told me to be here."

"Why?" I looked to make sure we were still alone.

"Because they want you to stop the terrorists."

Padre Thomas had been involved with us since my return and he knew about the planned attack on the cruise ship from listening to us. His assumption that we'd be back to do something, didn't surprise me, but being at the airport, at this time and at this location, did.

"And did they tell you how we're supposed to do this?" I heard the others coming off the plane.

"Yes." He pointed into the shadows. "With that plane. You have to shoot the terrorists' plane down before it gets to the cruise ship."

I thought he pointed at Pauly's plane and turned to see my friends coming toward us. They looked as surprised as I must have at seeing Padre Thomas.

"Not that plane." He continued to point, shaking his hand. "That one."

I turned and stared into the twilight and recognized a half-dozen planes outside the hangar. Some were Freddy's and others he kept for friends. Most were collector items from the '40s and '50s. His bi-plane was older than that.

"Padre, no souls to save out here," Norm said as he approached.

"Your soul could use saving," Padre Thomas said.

"Amen to that," Pauly said.

I led Padre Thomas to his bike. I wasn't sure what he would say and didn't want to involve the others if he rambled on about the angels. We could be seen but not overheard.

"Padre, what are you talking about? These old planes don't have weapons." I kept my voice low so it wouldn't carry across the tarmac.

"Mick, I don't know how. I'm just telling you what the angels showed me. They came to me in a dream." He was used to people not understanding. "They said you were looking for a way to stop the attack and this was it." He pointed again toward the collection of planes. "I saw the plane flying."

"Did they tell you that to shoot the terrorists down we'd have to get close so if the bomb goes off, we'd go down too?" I fought to keep fear out of my tone but knew I wasn't successful.

"No," he mumbled. "I don't think they'd let you die."

"They let people die all the time," I said. "Even you've told me they can't interfere to help mortals and, Padre, I'm as mortal as they come."

"Mick, I can't make you do anything." Padre Thomas pulled his bike off the fence. "I can tell you what the angels said, but it's your decision. I don't understand why they watch over you through me. I wish I did. I know whatever you decide, it'll be for the best."

"You had the angels long before you knew me, Padre."

"Yes." He sat on the bike. "That was so they could lead me to Key West. I believe that now. I thought a lot about the angels and me and you, while you were gone. I missed them and I missed you. Is it coincidence that you're both back now?" He pedaled off toward the exit gate.

"What was the old man doing here?" Norm held Padre Thomas' coffee. "Where did he get hot coffee?"

"The angels . . ."

"Oh, poor Jesus," Bob moaned. "Him and his damn angels. He knows how to pull your strings."

"What about them?" In the past, Norm swayed from skeptic to believer when Padre Thomas predicted things. He said Padre Thomas' knowledge reminded him of the shamans in third world countries that seemed to have a certain intellect. How and why they did, he didn't know, but he knew it existed. He thought the priest was a phony, but one with a gift.

I told them about how the angels said we should use a plane to shoot the terrorists down. Norm looked at Pauly and Pauly grinned.

"If the old planes were armed, a piece of cake," Pauly said. "But they ain't."

"But they could be!" Norm grabbed Pauly and me. "What plane did he point out?"

The sun started to rise as we walked toward the stationary planes.

Chapter Sixty-Four

Pauly pulled away from Norm and went to a plane with a single prop set in its nose. I recalled seeing the plane in a hundred black-and-white war movies, but had no idea what it was. It didn't look that old. It looked like it had just been painted or maybe scrubbed clean.

We stopped next to it. "You think this is the plane Padre Thomas pointed at?" I wasn't sure, since it had been dark and all the planes were silhouettes on the field then.

"P-51 Mustang, a beauty." I'd never heard reverence in Pauly's voice before. "I know someone in Arizona with one and I've flown it a few times. If the angels didn't point this one out, they ain't real."

"It can't be armed," Norm said, bringing Pauly back to reality. "What engine do you think it has?"

Bob stood back and said nothing. I guess SEALs weren't into fighter planes.

Anyone could tell the plane had been well maintained, but Norm and Pauly talked as if they were discussing a beautiful woman they wanted to know intimately.

"Hard to tell." Pauly reached up and ran his hand along the bottom of the wing. "Doubt it's the Rolls engine, too old. Don't suppose there's anything in these." He pointed at the machine gun's fissures on the outside edge of the wing.

"What are they?" I showed my ignorance.

"The original plane was armed with three machine guns on each wing." Norm touched the bottom prop blade. "But surplus planes sold to civilians had them stripped out."

"That would be too easy, if they were working." Pauly kept stroking the wing.

"Is this your friend's plane?" Norm looked up at the closed cockpit.

"His or a friend's," I said. "I don't see him letting us use it."

"You're thinking of asking?" Norm gave me that devil-may-care smile again.

"And what are you thinking?"

Norm didn't answer.

Pauly climbed onto the wing and looked into the cockpit. "It's been modified."

"How?" Norm walked to the side of the plane.

"Cockpit holds two." Pauly put his face against the clear cover. "Throttle and stick in front."

"Can you fly it or not?"

"Is the pope Catholic?"

Norm turned to me. "The original plane sat one pilot. Some civilians modified the plane to seat two. Usually so they could take a paying guest on a ride." His cell phone rang.

Norm took the phone from his pocket and answered it. The only person who knew the burner phone number who wasn't here was Padre Thomas. Norm walked toward the hangar, leaving Pauly, Bob and me by the plane. I guessed that it was someone other than Padre Thomas calling, but wondered who else he'd given the number to, and why.

"With this, I could've taken out the Russians, Iranians, Palestinians and the damn plane in one quick pass in Mexico." Pauly jumped down off the wing. "And had time and ammo enough to get some of *Los Zetas* too."

"You in love?" I watched Norm walk circles around the picnic table.

"The government gave these away after Korea, for a few grand." Pauly smiled at my comment. "If you can find one today, it'd go for a cool million, easy."

"A good plane in its day?" I kept following Norm as he circled, curious to the identity of the caller.

Pauly laughed. "This is a good plane today."

"Any idea of what he's got in mind?"

"With this?" Pauly pointed at the plane. "Unarmed, I have no idea."

"What if he can get it armed?" Bob finally said something.

"Is that possible?" I turned to Pauly.

"No idea. I don't know if anyone alive knows how to re-work the mechanism for the guns." Pauly reached up and tapped the three machine gun openings. "Are they empty or clogged up so they're useless?"

Norm hung up the cell and came toward us, the grin still in place. "We're kind of free to come and go again."

"Who was that?" My curiosity got the better of me. "It wasn't Padre Thomas, who else has your number?"

"Mick, there are some people that you can't hide from even if you want to," he said. "It was someone from JSOC and they did a lot to get these assholes off our back."

"But?" I knew there was always a *but* with Norm.

"But we have to be off the island by sun up Thursday morning and we stay away from the cruise ship port and the harbor. If we're here after three, Homeland Security will BOLO us."

"What sense does that make?" I said.

"It gives us five days . . . well almost five days, to get the plane ready," Norm said. "It's all we've gotta care about now, getting ready."

"Ready to do what?"

"Stop the terrorists."

"What the fuck you talking about?" Pauly said. "Which plane are we getting ready?"

Norm pointed at the P-51.

"We gonna duct tape the M-4s to the wing?" Pauly laughed. "I fly it and Bob bolts you and Mick to the wings and off we go!"

"If it comes to that," Norm said. "But I don't think it will."

All three of us looked at Norm as if he were a crazy man preaching from a soapbox on a street corner. Norm laughed at us.

"I know a guy . . ."

"Of course you do," I said.

Norm ignored me. "I need to warn you, he's a little odd."

"What's that mean?" Sometimes what Norm says and what he really means are different, so I wanted an explanation.

"He's the CIA's go-to guy, unofficially because he's been retired longer than I've been active," Norm said. "He was in the agency years before all the whiz kids and their toys. He kept things running. When the agency went with technology they had no use for him."

"I feel another but coming," I said.

"But some of the field agents still liked the old equipment and when it broke the agency gave them the new technology." Norm stopped and looked to make sure he had our attention. "The agents kept using him, off the books, and eventually he built up a collection of items from the old systems. Some of the countries the agency works in today haven't caught up with today's technology, so he's been useful, again. He might know how to arm this plane."

"Got a name?" Pauly said.

"Doug Brian."

"Two first names," Bob said. "Don't like guys with two first names."

"He's in his eighties and doesn't like to be asked questions or haggle over price." Norm smiled. "I've seen agency smartasses try to negotiate with him and he walks out of the room or hangs up the phone. No questions, his price is the price. His rules or go somewhere else and there is no somewhere else."

"We can't ask him what he's doing?" That made me suspicious.

"You tell him what you want," Norm said. "He tells you if he can do it and gives you a price. Half down up front and the rest upon completion."

"Where is he?" Pauly said.

"No idea. The agency guy gave me a phone number with a North Texas exchange, but if I know him, he's in Maine."

"So we wait?" I said.

"Yeah. We wait over breakfast because I'm starving and then we go back to one of the guesthouses." Norm called a taxi. "We gotta sleep while we're free men and can."

"When will he call?" How long would Norm wait before coming up with another plan?

"Soon, I hope." Norm yawned. "Maybe never."

Chapter Sixty-Five

I was halfway through breakfast at Harpoon Harry's, my mind raced with unsolvable problems, when it suddenly hit me how natural things were beginning to seem. I hadn't been in the restaurant in a year and now, twice within a few days, I'm back and Kathy brings me a *café_con leche* before she asks for our orders._K.C. called her greetings as we walked in, Annie handed out the menus and then came back to take our orders, joking with us. Judy, Cathy and Gary brought food out of the kitchen, balanced somehow so they didn't need a tray, talking, walking, serving. Kristy bussed the tables, dodging between servers and customers like a cherub out of a Dickens' novel.

Ron sat customers as usual, but when we came in, he told us what table to go to and then greeted a tourist couple, leaving us on our own like every other local. I didn't want to like that I'd fallen so easily back into routine and that people who hadn't seen me for a year assumed I was back and saw no need to spend time smothering me with attention. I didn't want to like it, but as I drank my *con leche*, I realized it made me feel at home.

"You okay?" Norm finished his breakfast. He and Pauly sat across from Bob and me.

"Yeah."

"You look like you know something and don't wanna tell us." Kathy refilled Norm's coffee cup.

"No," I said. "If I knew anything I wouldn't have unanswered questions running around my head."

"It's hurry-up-and-wait time, hoss. We wait. We get some sleep."

"Do you think it's safe for me to go home?" Pauly said.

"It's your call." Norm frowned. "They're still looking for Mick and me. Government guys, I'm talking about. If they find us, they'll follow us. My guess is they want to know where you are too."

"That doesn't mean squat, since the Russians are looking for us too. Government guys ain't the problem, right now." Bob threw his paper napkin onto his plate. "The Russians know about you, maybe about all of us, so I wouldn't go home."

"Where are you going?" Pauly looked to me.

I looked at Norm. "Guesthouse?"

"Ocean Key House, maybe the two-bedroom suite is available." Norm finished his coffee.

Pauly went with Bob to the marina, deciding to stay on Bob's boat. Norm and I walked to the Ocean Key House and got the suite that looked down onto the Sunset Pier bar and the harbor. A breeze blew through the opened patio door.

"You okay?" Norm looked at Sunset Key from the patio.

"Why, don't I look okay?"

"Just asking."

"It's a little strange, though."

"What is?" Norm turned to me.

"I didn't want to come back and now I'm glad I did."

"Good."

"I think I'm gonna stay. Everything I dreaded, all the shit I thought about, it didn't happen." I kept my gaze toward the water. "Tita's ghost is everywhere but it isn't haunting me. I miss her and I have a hole inside, but I'll take that wherever I go."

"You'll keep the house?"

"No," I said. "I'll sell it and send the money to her brother. He isn't speaking to me but I'll let the realtor handle everything. Maybe he won't know I was involved."

"Maybe he won't care."

"Maybe."

"You, ah, staying does it mean . . .?"

"I haven't forgotten about Alexei." I didn't let Norm finish. "I still want to get him but I can live with killing him from a distance instead of up close and personal."

"Good."

"I prefer up close," I said. "But I want to get it over with."

"Even better."

"Do you think this will be the time?"

"No." Norm walked from the patio into the room. "I think

he's concerned about what happened in South Beach, especially after Tampico, so he's keeping his distance. If we're able to keep this from happening, he's gonna be pissed and want to get even."

"Come after me?"

"Yeah, but not personally," Norm said. "That's gonna make your life much more dangerous. Maybe kidnap you and take you to him. Or simply kill you and get it over with."

"What can I do to make him come after me?"

"Nothing." Norm shook his head. "You still don't understand. You want to do what Interpol hasn't been able to do for years. The DEA has a warrant out and he comes and goes on a whim. Hell, I don't even know Alexei exists. Maybe it's a name the Russian mafia uses to scare each other, like the boogeyman."

"I met him in Key West. Pauly was there."

"I know, Mick. You met a guy who said he was Alexei. I met a guy who said his name was Alexei. The only way I'd be sure there is an Alexei is if we meet him together and he's the same guy."

"You gotta be shittin' me!"

Norm's phone beeped. "How nice to hear from you again."

He listened a moment. "We have a P-51 and need it armed . . . fifty cal . . . yesterday . . . plane's in great shape, converted to a two-seater . . . Key West airport . . . only gonna use it once . . . yeah, you can rig it that way . . . four o'clock, see you there . . . look for a hangar with Cabanas stenciled on it . . . " Norm put his phone away.

"You're go-to guy?"

"Meet him at four," Norm said. "He thinks he might be able to rig something up if it's only for one-time use. Let's get some sleep."

"Do you think we can do this?" I closed the patio door.

"We have to do it, 'cause no one else seems to care."

Chapter Sixty-Six

I slept until 3 P.M. When I came out of the suite's bedroom, Norm sat on the couch, his Glock disassembled. I could smell traces of the cleaning liquids still lingering in the room.

"Bob and Pauly will meet us at the airport before four." He put the semi-automatic back together, slapping in the magazine and racking one bullet into the chamber, and then stuffed the cleaning rags, liquids and brushes into a cloth bag. "You sleep?"

"Yeah. You?"

"Let's go." Norm didn't answer me.

Since we left our overnight bags, I guessed he expected us to return.

Out in front of the Ocean Key House, people walked toward the music coming from the Sunset Pier that mingled with the rowdy sounds of laughter, which suggested a party environment. The sun hung in the sky, heading slowly toward Sunset Key. We grabbed a cab, told him to stop at Sandy's on White Street, and then to the airport.

When Bob and Pauly arrived, Norm and I had eaten our sandwiches from Sandy's and were finishing our *café con leches* at the picnic table in front of Cabanas' hangar.

"Has anyone talked to Freddy?" Pauly lit a cigarette.

"I left him a message," I said. "His voice mail said he's out of the country and would try to call back."

"Someone's gonna notice us messin' with his plane."

"You being the pilot with a plane here, run interference." Norm tossed his cup into the trashcan. "Can you do that?"

"Let's see what your go-to guy says and then I can try to figure something out."

Bob knocked on the hangar's regular door, opened it and went it. "No plane inside," he said, leaving the hangar.

The noise from the props got louder and drew our attention as a plane taxied toward us. The pilot maneuvered it to a free spot in Freddy's part of the airfield. The propellers stopped. A commuter jet landed on the runway, rattling the air with noise and turbulence, and taxied to the main terminal. The smaller plane's door opened and stairs appeared, followed by an older man in coveralls and a plaid shirt, wearing a baseball cap.

This was Doug Brian, Norm's go-to guy. He held the railings as he walked slowly down the steps. Oversized sunglasses rested on his nose, covering his eyes. Not exactly my idea of a CIA operative with special mechanical talents.

Instead of coming to us, he walked to the P-51 and circled the plane. We went to him.

"This it, Norm?" It was his only acknowledgement that we stood there.

"Yeah," Norm said.

"I need a stepladder." A two-day growth of gray hair sprouted on his weathered face. He had spent a lot of time outside. His shirt's collar was frayed and his overalls stained with grease and oil.

Norm turned to Bob. "Did you see one in the hangar?

"Wasn't looking for one." Bob returned to the hangar.

I wanted to introduce myself, but Norm grabbed my shoulder and shook his head.

"Someone's taken good care of her." Doug's attention returned to the plane. He adjusted his glasses, and ran his hands along the bottom of one wing.

"Not our plane," Norm said.

"Didn't think so. Not dirty enough for you." Doug wiped his hands on the coveralls.

"Not in our service."

"Yet." Doug grinned. "I'll need the hangar."

"No problem," Norm said.

"There's always a problem with you guys."

"You used to be one of us guys," Norm said.

"Don't remind me. We worked at it. You play with computers and hope the battery doesn't die. Like supermarket cash registers, nothing works for you when the power goes out."

Norm ignored his sarcasm. Bob brought a three-step folding ladder to Doug, who took it without a word of thanks and placed it in front of the machine gun channels in the wing. He climbed up and stuck his fingers in each hole.

With a racket equal to the landing planes', he used his feet to push the ladder to the backside of the wing and climbed slowly up onto it. Kneeling, he crept over the wing and stopped atop the machine gun channels. With a pocketknife, he appeared to stab the wing.

"What the . . ." I said.

Norm grabbed me. "I talk to him, no one else." He got nods from Bob and Pauly. "You need anything Doug?"

"I need quiet," he mumbled. "Can I get it?" Something on the wing opened, he stuck a hand in, brought it out, closed whatever it was that he'd opened and crawled off the wing. "Lucky son of bitch," he said to Norm, leaving the stepladder by the wing.

"Why?" Norm said.

"'Cause the barrels are still in there." He pointed at the plane's wing. "The gun box is empty but there's cable, so maybe it hooks up to the cockpit trigger."

"That's good news?"

"For you." He pushed his glasses back into place and gave the rest of us a quick once over. "The Agency scraping the bottom of the barrel?"

Norm laughed. "Why's it good news?"

"All I gotta do is jury-rig the guns and cables," he said. "Save you money."

"Jury-rig!" Pauly said.

"Who am I maybe gonna work for, Norm?"

"Me."

"Anyone else bothers me with useless chatter and my price goes up," Doug growled. "In fact, it's gone up a thousand."

"You haven't told us a price yet."

"Your bloomers too tight, kid? Let me make a call and I'll get right back to you." Doug walked away, his cell phone materializing from one of the coverall's many stained pockets.

"What the fuck?" Pauly moaned. "Jury-rigged?"

"Calm down." Norm raised his hands and moved us back

to the picnic table. "I told him on the phone the guns had to work once."

"This guy's good, right?" Pauly sat down.

"There's no one else I trust and no one else available," Norm said. "Unless you've got someone in mind, Pauly, we do it his way. And remember, Thursday's only a few days away."

"Christ, he's too weird even for Key West!" Pauly sat down. "I'll keep my mouth shut."

"Good," Norm said. "I'll do the talking, everyone else keep a lock on it."

We watched Doug stand by the plane as he talked on his cell. He nodded a lot but we couldn't make out anything he said. After putting his cell back into one of the overall's pockets, he stood there.

"Stay behind me and shut up." Norm got up and we followed, a few feet behind.

"Here's what I'll do for you," Doug said to Norm. "I can rig up two fifty cals, one on each wing. If the cables work, it won't be too hard. If not, I can rig the cables and they'll be good for a time or two. You said one run, right?

Norm nodded.

"My partner will fly everything in tomorrow and we'll get right to work." He looked at the closed hangar. "I assume you'll want me working in there."

"The plane will be in there tomorrow morning," Norm said. "Do you need anything else from us?"

"Give me the name of a good hotel y'all ain't staying in and show up when I call you tomorrow afternoon."

"What are we looking at price wise?" Norm grinned as he wrote in a pocket notebook.

Doug scowled. "With the grand added on for whoever that was that griped about my jury-rigging, my time, material and other expenses, you're looking at twenty grand."

"Will we be able to do a test run on Wednesday?"

"Hell, if the cables are in working order, you can test it late tomorrow."

"If they're not?"

"My price goes up because you're paying for my time and added materials," Doug said. "But I'll meet your deadline." He took the piece of paper with a hotel's name on it from Norm. "Hotel room is part of my expenses."

"Of course," Norm said.

Doug began to leave and then stopped and turned to Norm. "Schooner Wharf, ten o'clock tonight, we need to talk and leave the girls at home."

Chapter Sixty-Seven

Pauly rented a car at the airport terminal and we drove back to Old Town Key West. Norm was adamant that we not show up at Schooner Wharf when he met Doug. It wasn't a topic he'd discuss. Bob, Pauly and I said we'd wait at the Hog's Breath for him. The bar was only a short block from the Ocean Key Resort, and we weren't excited about being around the arrogant man, anyway. Curious, yes, like the magnetic pull an accident has as you drive by its aftermath, but happy to keep your distance.

Bob ran off to a cigar shop and we met up at the Tree Bar on Duval Street, across from Sloppy Joe's. We had beers, smoked and watched the parade of wacky tourists. Memories washed over me because drinks and cigars were a part of my life once. Some memories brought loneliness, and others came with smiles. Pauly kept to his cigarettes. Norm told stories about Doug, some true and some only rumors, he said. I half listened.

When Norm left, we had accepted his word that Doug was our best and only choice to get the P-51 guns working. None of us came up with an acceptable reason why the authorities didn't believe our warning about the attack on the cruise ship. That bothered us, but we sought solutions and had no time to deal with speculations.

We were a collection of diverse personalities, different in ways, and similar in others. At no point did anyone talk about abandoning our efforts to stop the terrorists' plane. I knew living with the knowledge that I did nothing, and people died because of it, would haunt me. I was not sure of anyone else's reasons, but assumed they were similar.

Nikki and Irish Bob were the bartenders at the Hog's Breath, Joel Nelson, Tim and Danny Carter had just begun the late-night show, when we sat at the far end of the bar. Julie and Alain worked the inside bar.

"Heard you were back." Nikki held up a bottle of Jameson's. "On the rocks?"

"Please," I said.

She took Bob and Pauly's beer orders while she poured my drink.

At ten thirty-five, Norm called my burner cell and said Doug wanted to meet me. Since he didn't say Bob and Pauly couldn't join us, they came along.

I made the walk from the Hog's Breath to Schooner Wharf Bar as if I had done it yesterday. All my fears of what Key West might hold for me after Tita's murder evaporated in the humidity. They hid in the mugginess but in the tropics you expect to sweat and get used to it or leave. I accepted that not facing my fears only made them more frightening.

For a Monday night in June, Duval Street was busy; sounds of patrons singing and shouting along with the band at Sloppy Joe's stormed onto Greene and Duval streets. New names appeared on old bars along Greene Street. The Conch Farm still took up a good section of waterfront and, as we walked past Jimmy Buffett's recording studio, the shops on Lazy Way were closed, but there were no empty spaces for rent, so business seemed to be good.

Norm sat with Doug at one of the large tables with a thatched roof, close to the boardwalk.

"Stay back," I said to Bob and Pauly. "We don't want to spook this guy."

They nodded and walked toward the bar.

Doug's aloofness had bothered me at the airport, so I said nothing and stood next to the table waiting for Norm to speak.

"Mick," Norm almost shouted. The band had finished the last set and the crowd applauded. "When I told Doug who you were he wanted to meet you."

That caught me by surprise. I looked at Doug, still in the same getup as he arrived in, minus the oversized sunglasses, but then that made sense because I hadn't seen an overnight bag when he hailed the cab.

"I remember some of your Central American stories." He'd lost the abusive tone he used at the airport. I leaned in closer to hear him. "Used to study them, especially after I found out you worked for Norm."

"I never worked for Norm!" The severity in my words came out before I could stop them. For years, I've fought the talk that I used journalism as a cover so I could report to Norm – in other words, the CIA – on the conditions and whereabouts of anti-government forces in Central America.

"It wasn't a fact," Doug said. "Just a rumor. But the stories had good info, so I studied them."

"I knew you'd show up in a watering hole sooner or later!"

I looked up and saw Richard Dowley, the police chief, standing erect in front of the table. He wasn't smiling.

"What part of call me with your burner number didn't you understand?"

Doug quickly evaluated Richard and then he turned to Norm. I saw a small nod of Norm's head, nothing more. I wondered if Richard caught it.

"Excuse me, I'll see you tomorrow." Doug stood and shuffled off past the stage, toward Caroline Street.

"Who was that?" Richard said.

"An old friend," Norm said. "Buy you a drink?"

"How about an explanation?" Richard stared at me. "You know that whatever it is you're involved in is really fucked. Right? I've had more federal agents in my office or on the phone with questions about the two of you than I really wanted. They weren't interested in an aircraft that might be crashing into a cruise ship. Then this afternoon it all stopped. Why?"

There wasn't time to answer. In all his scary infamy, the colonel walked up, ignored Richard, and banged his hand on the table. "Y'all didn't scram." There was laughter in his voice.

The patio crowd had slowly left or moved to the bar now that the stage was empty, but a few couples sat around, enjoying their privacy.

"You got something for me, right?" The laughter had gone and the question came with hardness. "Norm, talk to me!"

"I told you before, colonel, Murphy didn't keep the original?" Norm said in a controlled voice but I sat close enough to see the strain it caused him. "Can't give you what we don't have?"

"Suppose a broken leg or two would help you find it?" The colonel's tone kept getting harder. "I can arrange that! Or I can go see the priest, again!"

"Who the hell are you?" Richard yelled into the colonel's face.

"If you don't know, you don't need to know," he scowled and turned back to us. "You know better than to fuck with me, Norm. I don't play games."

"Are you threatening these men?" Richard placed himself closer to the colonel.

"Nothing gets by you, does it?" The Colonel turned to Richard. "I'm not threatening them, I'm promising them. But you, I'd gladly use a baseball bat on, so fuck off while you can still walk."

Think of the first strike of lightening in the night sky, how it rapidly flashes out of nowhere with a large raggedy bolt and is followed by the boom of thunder. Richard's two hands went up behind the Colonel's head and brought it down with such force that when the Colonel's head hit the tabletop our beer bottles shook, and would've fallen over if we hadn't grab them. Blood seeped from beneath the Colonel's head while Richard forcibly held it against the table.

"You, asshole, are under arrest for threatening a police officer." Richard reached behind his shirt and took out his handcuffs.

"You a cop?" The mumbled words came from the Colonel.

"I'm the police chief, asshole."

Chapter Sixty-Eight

The colonel tried to stand erect, his hands cuffed behind him, when Richard loosened his hold. Blood flowed from his broken nose, onto his shirt and the table.

"Someone call dispatch, for me!" Richard said.

"Better not." The words came slowly, as the colonel tried to tilt his head backward to stop the blood flow. Richard loosened his grip some more, but kept his hand in place.

"Call!" Richard stared at me. "Who is this asshole?" He looked at Norm.

"Your worst nightmare, Richard." Norm frowned. "Let him go."

"Not on your life! He threatened you and *me*!" Richard squeezed the Colonel's neck.

"It could be your life that's threatened, dumb fuck!" One of the colonel's three men said from behind Richard.

The colonel's men stood there, handguns pointed at Richard. The people around the patio took notice when the guns came out and ran toward Lazy Way or the bar. A few spoke into their cell phones as they ran and others screamed. Our table had everyone's attention.

Richard kept hold of the back of the colonel's neck, even after a quick look over his shoulder. "You going to call them off?"

"He don't understand, does he Norm?" The colonel's confidence came back. "Tell him."

"I don't have a lot of faith in Norm, so why don't you tell me, asshole." Richard ignored the gunmen. He stared at Norm, reading his expression to grade the seriousness of the situation. He had to know it wasn't good.

"Listen carefully to me," the colonel said. "My men can kill you, they can kill everyone at the table and maybe even cause collateral damage, and when the cops arrive my men will surrender, but before they're at the police station, a black SUV will stop your officers and men with federal ID will take charge of the prisoners. While the coroner's still bagging bodies, including yours, we'll be at Boca Chica on a plane and no one will ever hear from us again. We won't exist."

"He could be bagging your body too," Richard said. "Think about that, asshole."

"There's a difference." The colonel kept his head titled back to slow the bleeding

"And what's that?" Sirens' screams got closer.

"I don't care. You on the other hand, care about the people here. That's a police officer's duty. Do you think they want to die in Key West tonight?"

"Colonel," one of the three men called out. "Give us an order, sir."

"Yeah, give us all orders, *sir!*" Bob yelled loud enough to be heard at the bar.

Bob and Pauly had slowly walked up behind the three men and now they held their guns against the heads of two of the colonel's men. The man in the middle stared between the colonel and his two friends, keeping his gun aimed at Richard.

"Colonel, sir!" The man in the middle said.

The colonel slowly turned around. He saw that Richard held a Glock at his side. He looked at Bob and Pauly, and then turned to Norm.

"This ain't over." He turned back to his men. "Put the guns away."

Instantly, showing no concern for the guns held against their heads, the three obeyed the order.

"Richard, let them go," Norm said. The sirens were getting closer. "It'll go nowhere, Richard. They'll walk, just like he said."

"Get off my island." Richard unlocked the handcuffs and looked at his wristwatch. "In two hours I'm going to wake the base commander and if he doesn't report that you've flown out, I'm sending the SWAT after you."

The colonel smiled, holding napkins against his bloody nose. "Only the SWAT team?"

That caused his three men to laugh. Bob and Pauly pulled

their guns away from the men's head, but held them at the ready.

The four men turned and walked toward the boardwalk. They headed toward Duval Street.

Richard turned to Norm. Anger crossed his face. "Friends of yours?"

Key West Police cars stopped on Lazy Way, lights flashing, and then officers walked into the patio area. They looked toward the crowded bar and when the patrons pointed toward the patio, they turned to see Richard standing by our table.

Chapter Sixty-Nine

Richard spent forty minutes with the responding officers explaining that the men with guns were military police, it was all a misunderstanding, and the situation was not worth arresting them over. A number of customers had called 911 on seeing the guns and the cops responded, expecting the worst. Everyone, cops and patrons, was relieved no one had gone postal. Finally, as the police officers left, Richard spent about ten minutes clarifying the misunderstanding and apologizing for it to Evalena, the bar's owner.

"I apologized for you," Richard said when he came back to the table.

The curious crowd that gathered around the bar during our encounter slowly left and business got back to usual for the serious, late-night drinkers.

"Thanks." I didn't know what else to say.

"Who was that?" Richard stared at Norm.

"A loose cannon that doesn't belong here."

"Tell me something I don't know!" Richard tried to control his anger. "Who is he?"

Norm briefly explained to Richard about the colonel's intelligence background and work in Central and South America.

"What's he looking for?"

"The Russian diary, not the copies of Nadja's translation," I said.

"I called her and Burt when I didn't hear back from you." Richard sent the server away when she nervously approached offering a round of drinks from Evalena. "They were leaving for Delaware to pick up a boat and then sailing it to New Orleans for the owner."

That explained my not being able to reach them. Nadja, I'm sure, was happy to be away from all this.

"What's he want with it?" Richard looked at Norm, knowing I wouldn't have the answer.

Norm stood up and thanked Bob and Pauly for showing up and knowing what to do. "He isn't the kind of guy that explains himself," he said to Richard.

"You going someplace?" Richard got in front of Norm, to block his exit.

"Look around." Norm pointed to the bar. "People are still watching us, so it's not exactly the place to talk about this." He pushed past Richard.

We followed Norm onto the boardwalk, passed the Conch Farm and onto Front Street by the A&B Lobster House. All the restaurant bars were crowded and excited squeals fell from the rooftop bar of Pat Croce's Rum Barrel restaurant.

"Couldn't we at least take my car?" Richard tagged along, still wanting answers from Norm.

"Yeah, just what we need, to be seen in a cop car." Norm kept walking.

"It's unmarked."

"And nobody will know." Norm laughed. "Get real, Chief."

"Most people would like to know there's a cop in the crowd. Scare away those crazy shooters that you hear about on the TV news."

"Yeah, Chief, but wasn't it a cop that caused the guns to be pulled at Schooner?"

"Threats were made."

"Yeah, and guns were drawn," Norm said. "But it was Bob and Pauly that kept it from turning violent, not a cop."

"Where're we going?" Richard gave up the argument.

"The Ocean Key. It's after midnight, no one's around the pool." Norm said.

He was right about us having the pool area to ourselves, but a few couples sat on the patio of the resort's Hot Tin Roof restaurant that overlooked the pool and ocean, and the Sunset Pier customers continued to party, even though the crowd had thinned out.

The five of us sat around a table and Richard told us about the non-responses he'd received when asking about the cruise ship and the airplane attack. When he asked what we were doing about it, the table went quiet and the noise from the pier covered everything.

"What aren't you telling me?" Richard stared at me. "You're here, there's trouble, so you're doing something."

"We're pursuing options," Norm said and kept a straight face.

"Fuck you, Norm!" Richard squealed. He turned to me. "Mick, I'm losing sleep over this. Homeland Security isn't saying anything other than they are aware of the threat and the FBI isn't saying anything. It doesn't make sense."

"It doesn't make sense to us, either, Richard," I said.

Richard looked at each of us and frowned. "You're planning something illegal. Damn it, don't make things worse."

"Worse than crashing a plane into a cruise ship? Come on, Richard, be real." I wondered if he could think of a worse crime, I couldn't.

"The old man, dirty coveralls, he didn't smell like a boat mechanic." Richard shook his head. "He's part of this."

"Take a sleeping pill, Richard." Norm smiled. "We're doing nothing illegal and the old man is just that, an old friend I hadn't seen in years."

"Shit Norm, you lie real good. First of all, you don't have any friends other than Mick and if you did, they wouldn't be in Key West."

"Richard, I'm offended. I thought we were friends." Norm still looked serious.

"I think too many of your *friends* get put in the ground, Norm." It was Richard's turn to smile. "I'll keep you at a distance and figure if you're telling me something you're lying."

"It's late guys, I need some sleep," I said to stop the badgering. "Richard, will we see you tomorrow?"

"I'll call if you give me the burner number."

I read off the number and he put it in his phone. "I'm putting the city's marine patrol in the harbor before sunrise Thursday. As a last resort, I'll have two SWAT snipers on Christmas Tree Island."

"Not a bad idea," Norm said. "Fifty cal?"

"Fifty cal."

"You should put one on the roof of the hotel, you'd have two views of the plane." Norm was thinking aloud. "More than one opportunity to take it down."

His thinking reminded me of the battle by the hotel two years ago when Norm's people used me to bring Mexican cartel killers to Key West. He had snipers on the roofs of the hotels that surround Mallory Pier. It all started at a car wash and ended with a battle around the pier.

"I'll mention it to the SWAT commander. You agree with my plan enough to call off whatever you're doing?"

"Pursuing options is good fieldwork, Richard."

Richard turned to me. "He's gonna get you killed this time, Mick."

"Fuck you very much Richard and good night." Norm stood and walked away.

Chapter Seventy

I had six hours sleep, but it wasn't restful. I woke up with dreams diminishing in the darkness. I recalled obscure fragments that included water, airplanes and grease-painted snipers. None of it frightened me, but I woke with lingering questions I didn't understand or have an answer to.

Norm looked onto the harbor. "Restless night, hoss?"

"A little," I said.

"You made enough noise."

Outside, the sky showed robin blue and cloudless. Sailboats struggled in the light wind, but fishing boats rushed through the no-wake zone, wanting to pass Sand Key Lighthouse and get into the Gulf Stream for the big fish.

"Sorry. I don't remember making noise."

"I'm a light sleeper."

Dark circles puffed up below Norm's eyes, a melancholy smile did little to hide his concern as he stood there. I guessed he'd had little sleep.

"Richard said something interesting, after you left."

"Interesting how?"

"He said the Secret Service called and needed to meet with him Wednesday morning." My comment caused Norm to leave the patio.

"Why?" He closed the patio door.

"He doesn't know. The president's in Europe, the VP's in Washington," I said.

"It might have nothing to do with Thursday." Norm picked up his Glock from the coffee table, put it in the waistband at his back and pulled the shirt over it. "If the president or VP were coming, even unannounced, the Secret Service would've arrived long before Wednesday."

"Someone passing counterfeit money in Key West?"

"Richard say that?"

"Kind of group conclusion last night."

"Something to think about." Norm walked out of the

room. I followed.

"Where to?"

"Breakfast, while we wait for Doug to call."

We retraced our route from last night but passed Schooner and went to Harpoon Harry's. The usual morning breakfast crew of locals I remembered was still there, most of them, anyway. Kathy came to the table with my *café con leche* and took our order.

Keeping his voice low, though the restaurant resonated with conversations from all around us, Norm drank his coffee and told me about his late-night calls.

"I called Ed Scales . . ."

"Richard's CIA contact?"

"Yeah, him. He said there's no chatter on the cruise ship, or Iranians and Russians." He frowned and bit his lower lip. "There should've been chatter if only because of our document."

"What do you think?"

Kathy brought our breakfast.

Norm toyed with his eggs. "Scales said something. I don't like it. He didn't like it either, but said there's been a rumor . . ." Norm began to eat.

"What rumor?" I hadn't touched my food. Seeing Norm troubled about a rumor caused me to be concerned.

Norm swallowed his mouthful of eggs, sat back and took a drink of coffee. "Do you have any idea of how large a bureaucracy the Department of Homeland Security is?"

"Big?" I guessed.

"You don't know the half of it, hoss." Norm finished his coffee and as Annie walked by, he asked for a refill. "Hell, Mick, TSA is big and they're only a small portion of DHS. Secret Service is part of it."

"I didn't know that one. Coast Guard too, right?"

"Yeah. Immigrations and Customs Enforcement, ICE and FEMA and add to that sub-departments and agencies and the list looks like the phone book."

"So what's the rumor?"

"The budget for DHS is huge and with the cuts coming, some people are concerned that DHS will take many of them, so the military won't have to be hit so hard."

I cut up my eggs. "Where are you going with this?"

Norm had become uncomfortable with the subject. "Bottom line is there hasn't been a major terrorist act within our borders in years. Even Boston was a small event, compared to nine-eleven." Norm leaned in closer to me. "TSA security is a joke, something for the civilians to see so they feel safe on an airplane. It helps the public think they're protected and the politicians know this. Midlevel executives and other people at DHS are worried about their jobs if budget cuts go through. An attack on a cruise ship in U.S. waters would certainly prove the department is necessary and benefit its budget request."

What he said without being more direct startled me. Rumor, in intelligence circles, was that people in the right places would allow the attack on the cruise ship to happen, with loss of life, American lives, to keep a bureaucracy going, to save jobs, maybe theirs. Norm's boundaries on ethics were way out there, but he had his limits, or maybe they were rules he lived by, but he would never put innocent American lives at risk needlessly.

"It would explain, Mick, why our information has been stonewalled." He sat back up.

"I trust Pancho," I said. "The Coast Guard is his life. He passed the information on, I bet my life on it."

"And so did my CIA contact, and he got it to the FBI, too," Norm said. "But somewhere between here and D.C., someone or a group of someones has waylaid it. And they've got enough juice to come after us. My guess is they called in the colonel to keep us below the radar."

"That means CIA!"

"Lots of people from intelligence agencies got jobs with DHS when it was created, some from the CIA, DEA, and they all knew about the colonel. All the intel community does and that's an encompassing community."

I thought about the rumor and its consequences as I picked

at my breakfast. "We don't have time to chase down a rumor or be controlled by it." I leaned over my plate and spoke softly. "We keep on doing what we're doing, colonel or no colonel."

Norm nodded in agreement but I saw something in his expression that troubled me.

"What are you thinking?" I'd lost my appetite.

"Mistrust, Mick," he said. "We gotta mistrust everyone from here on in and that includes Doug."

"Doug? If he doesn't do the job . . ."

"I don't think he was compromised before coming." Norm didn't let me finish. "But the colonel watched me before approaching and he'll make Doug, he'll want to know everything about everyone I came in contact with. He'll know their weaknesses or scare 'em into cooperation."

"He could sabotage the plane!"

"No, he knows we want to do a test run, so the plane has to work. If someone gets to him, it'll be today and all he can do then is poorly install the guns or mess with the cables so the gun won't fire on Thursday, but work okay on Wednesday." Disappointment filled his tone. "They want us to think we're moving ahead, so we don't have time to find an alternative."

I realized why Norm had waited until breakfast to discuss the subject. If he'd been in the privacy of the hotel room, he would've lost it. I could see the anguish in his face and it worried me.

"Would he go along with the sabotage?"

"I gotta assume so. We have to come up with an alternative plan."

Chapter Seventy-One

Outside the restaurant, I called Pauly and was surprised when he said he and Bob had already moved the P-51 into Freddy's hangar. They were going to be around the waterfront the rest of the day, waiting for our call to meet up that afternoon.

Whisper-thin clouds rushed across the sky as if they were late for a date with the Gulf of Mexico. The sun was mid-high and promised a hot day, its rays already scorching the sunny side of the street. We walked on the shady side.

Norm was commenting on the window display at Fairvilla on Front Street, when his cell chirped.

"Be there in half an hour," he said and put the phone away.

"Be where?" I had only heard one side of the conversation.

Norm scratched his nose and squinted. "Doug wants to meet at the airport."

"His partner arrive?"

"Didn't say." Norm looked at his wristwatch. "Not even nine."

We took a cab from Duval Street. With people trying to keep track of us so they'd know where we were Wednesday afternoon, Norm said it was better to use cabs as our new form of transportation. Scooters hadn't worked for us, maybe cabs would.

Two regional jets were on the tarmac. I couldn't tell if they were coming or going. Private planes landed or took off, and a private jet shook the tarmac, preparing to taxi for takeoff. We walked through the unguarded gate toward Freddy's hangar. The large door stood open and Doug sat on a folding chair by the tail of the P-51.

He stood as we approached. "You didn't tell me the colonel was involved!"

He surprised us by being upfront about the colonel. I know I was surprised and could tell from Norm's grinding teeth, bit lower lip, and how hard he fought to keep his expression emotionless, that he was too.

"He ain't involved with us."

"Bullshit!"

We stopped on the front side of the wing, close to the large prop. Doug stayed by the tail.

"Wanna know how I know it's bullshit?" He hissed the words.

Norm nodded.

"He came to visit me last night."

"I don't know where you're staying."

"I didn't say you told him where I was."

"What are you saying, then?"

Doug walked to a small table that held a coffee pot, cups and sugar packets. He filled a cup, adding three sugars. I followed Norm as he approached the table.

"My price has doubled." Doug sipped from the mug. "Hell, if I wasn't here, I'd turn the job down now."

"Price is okay. I'll add the extra to your account today." Norm poured a cup of coffee and handed it to me and then poured one for himself. He added sugar and walked to Doug. I walked to the table, a bystander in whatever was happening.

"Like you gotta a choice."

"There's always a choice."

"Ah, a Norm truism." Doug almost smiled.

"What happened?"

"One of his men must have followed me from Schooner. I blame myself for that."

"Thanks." Norm appreciated people taking responsibility for their own screw-ups.

"The colonel showed up at my room, nice as ice cream on a warm apple pie, late last night." Doug drank his coffee. His right foot bounced up and down, on his toes, as if he was keeping rhythm to music only he could hear. "Wanted to know what you were up to." He looked at me. "Him too."

"What did you say?"

"That I was waiting for my partner to bring parts for my

plane and ran into you at the bar."

"He didn't believe you."

"Hell, no, he didn't. I didn't believe me, but it was the best I could come up with and was almost the truth."

"He ain't interested in truth. What happened next."

"He did something I'm told he rarely does."

"What?"

"He underestimated me. All he saw was an old man. He should've looked deeper. He started to be himself, you know, nasty, threatening."

"Didn't intimidate you?"

"Hell, scared the shit out of me! He had one of his men grab me by the shoulders. I thought, maybe he planned to rough me up. Took everything I had to keep from pissing my pants! I ain't been in the field longer than he's been alive." Doug nodded toward me.

"Where'd he underestimate you?"

Doug tapped his rodeo belt buckle pinned to his overall's pocket. "The inlay logo, detaches, and it's a small knife. As the colonel approached, I was able to take the knife out, stab him once in the gut, and the bum holding me in the kidney. I dropped to the floor and pulled my ankle gun."

"Pretty damn good for an old fucker." Norm smiled. "What happened?"

"I should've killed all three of 'em!"

"But you didn't. How bad were they hurt?"

"I made my own threats and the one I didn't stab helped the colonel out of my room. They needed attention, if that's what you meant, but a little stitchin' and they'll be shitty as ever. Blade's only three inches. Probably went to Boca Chica for attention."

"What about the other guy, the one you stabbed in the kidney?"

"He followed 'em on his own. Bent but walking." Doug grinned. "You know I never knew what the expression 'if looks could kill' meant until last night."

"They know where you're staying . . ." Norm began.

"Nope." Doug pointed at the back of the hanger. "I left seconds behind them and came here. I'll finish the job and be gone."

"He has three men with him. Did you see the third guy?"

"Fuck, no! He could've been waiting outside after the others left," he growled. "That's what I would've done if it was me."

"Me too," Norm said. "So they know you're here."

"Yeah," he grunted. "I have a suggestion for both our sakes."

"What is it?"

"You put some security on this place as soon as possible."

"Good idea," Norm said. "I got a question."

"How do you know I'm telling the truth."

"Yeah. How? The colonel can be persuasive."

"He can be surprised too. Okay, when I'm done, you fly the plane and shoot the guns before I leave. That satisfy you?"

"Almost," Norm said.

"What more do you want?"

"I think it's best you stay with us until Thursday."

"Do you ever trust anyone, Norm?"

"It's never turned out good when I have, Doug."

Chapter Seventy-Two

Norm and I discussed Doug's decision to stay at the hangar instead of a hotel. It seemed like a good option. We needed Pauly's expertise on hunkering down, being that he'd done it a number of times during his drug smuggling days, waiting out the searchers or shooters. Norm and I walked to the tarmac. It was noisier than inside the hangar but no one could overhear us and, after finding the listening station in Opa-Locka, Norm didn't trust anything.

"Jim Ashe can't give us anyone," Norm said after closing his cell. "I don't want him taking the guys off Padre Thomas. The colonel could see him as a weak link in all this."

Pauly had a strange collection of ex-military working for him and it was because of Rob Murdock, one of Pauly's crew, that I didn't die along with Tita. A sniper, Rob stopped the Russian shooter before he got off the third 20mm round into the *Fenian Bastard*. What they did for Pauly, other than occasionally save my worthless ass, we didn't discuss.

I called him.

"Is he gonna run?" Pauly needed to know.

"I don't think so," I said. "He'll feel better protected. Protection for him and his plane. We'll feel better, too."

"I'll have two men there before noon. Another two at midnight, to relieve them." He hung up.

I told Norm.

Norm began explaining to Doug what we were planning to do with the P-51 and why. I'm not sure what the reason was, but maybe he had to show Doug that he wasn't a complete hard-ass jerk, like the colonel.

"Hell, you should've told me upfront. I would've helped for free. I wanna do my part in stopping these camel jockeys." He took the last of the coffee. "You gonna have lunch delivered? 'Cause I don't want pizza."

Bob picked up cheesesteak sandwiches for us from Jack Flats and brought them to the hangar a little after noon. As we finished the sandwiches, two men with duffel bags approached. I always wonder why so many guys keep the military haircut after leaving the service. Habit, is about the best answer I've received.

They gave us first names and looked around the hangar, conferred by themselves, and came back to us. They wanted to know what we had planned.

"Waiting for a plane." Doug looked at his wristwatch. "Should be here at three with items I need. Some of those items we don't want crossin' an open tarmac."

The two men nodded. They understood or didn't care and went to their duffel bags.

Before that was settled, Texas Rich walked through the gate. I hadn't seen him since coming back to Key West. He smiled, his Houston Rodeo T-shirt hanging loose but the usual can of Miller Lite was missing from his hand. Like Norm, even in the Keys heat, he wore cowboy boots and jeans. Pauly's two men looked at me and I nodded. They relaxed.

"Nice to see you, Mick." We shook hands. "I've got two coolers in the truck. Pauly thought you'd need supplies for a day or two."

"Thanks," I said and wondered how Texas Rich got involved.

"Also, he thought there should be a third man here, in case you needed a runner for outside, or an extra gunslinger." He almost laughed. "You got a dolly or cart for the coolers?"

Pauly knew what we needed to keep off the grid for a few days and that included cold beverages and sandwiches. Texas Rich used Freddy's handcart and brought two large white coolers and a couple of shopping bags inside. The coolers contained soda, a six-pack of good Mexican beer, lots of ice and a variety of sandwiches, stored in freezer bags to protect them from cold and dampness. The shopping bags held potato chip packages, plain, barbecue, jalapeño and ranch. Pauly was thoughtful, if nothing else. There was at least three days' supply of food in the coolers.

Texas Rich met with Pauly's two men, unloaded weapons and walked the perimeter.

A little after noon, the heat inside the hangar got intolerable. With the large door open, the warm gusts from planes' spinning props and the noise of landings and take offs added to my restlessness.

It was hurry-up-and-wait time, again, and I needed to be doing something before I went stir crazy. Finally, I walked to the main terminal and bought a copy of Mike Dennis' "Setup on Front Street" and Jonathan Woods' collected short stories, "Bad Juju." Reading had always made time pass more quickly in Central America and Key West was about as close to a third world country as you could get and still speak English to the locals.

Norm and Doug were on the wing of the P-51 when I walked back. The lid of whatever compartment was up there stood open and Doug showed something to Norm. He walked to the cockpit, got inside, and he and Norm talked back and forth. They had their way to move time along and I had mine. I put a folding chair under the wing of one of Freddy's other planes, grabbed a Mexican beer, and read.

When I looked up, Doug talked on his cell and Norm came toward me. Even with the heat and constant airport racket, I had dozed. Both the books and the empty beer bottle lay on the ground next to the chair.

"Plane's here." Norm stopped and waited for Doug to catch up.

Pauly's two men and Texas Rich joined us as Doug moved ahead and directed the single-engine plane toward a spot close to the hangar.

"Do you know what he's got?" I said.

"It better be two fifty cal machine guns."

"Small plane," I said.

"Good things come in small packages, hoss." Norm smiled and I returned it. Doug was our Hail Mary Pass and the end-of-game buzzer was about to go off.

Chapter Seventy-Three

Doug didn't introduce his partner. The two of them unloaded beat-up cardboard boxes from the plane, placed them close to the P-51 and finally came off carrying what I recognized as oversized ammo cases. Two fifty-caliber machine gun parts in crappy cardboard boxes, who would've thought it. No one helped because Doug had snubbed our offers with grunts and growls. It made Norm laugh and me worry.

When the pilot cut the tape and opened the boxes, Doug took a folded paper from his overall's pocket and babbled to himself as he compared it against whatever he found in the boxes. The two men talked briefly and then the pilot left, headed to whatever secret, pre-technology scarp garden, compound Doug had hidden in the mountains or desert or maybe somewhere in the clouds.

"You didn't want to keep the second guy here?" Pauly said as the small plane taxied away.

"That's the agreement," Norm mumbled. He didn't like being questioned. "Doug stays with us until this is over, but his partner leaves."

"Doug expecting trouble?" Pauly slapped Norm on the back. "He must know you and trouble are hitched at the hip!"

"The first thing they teach you is your plan is gonna fuck up so always have an alternative." Norm never mentioned who *they* were, but he quoted them often. "Doug used his alternative for his partner."

"And I'd use mine for you, *amigo*."

"Sure you would, Pauly, just like I'd use mine for you!" Both men laughed.

I wasn't in as lively a mood, as I watched Doug stop next to the boxes. He looked as if he didn't know what to do next.

"Are we going to help or is he gonna do his standup routine again?" I pointed toward the befuddled man. "Is he wasting our time?"

I suddenly gave credence to the possibility that the colonel had compromised Doug and the waiting until three in the afternoon for the plane to deliver parts, was a delaying action. If the P-51's guns didn't work, or couldn't be tested tomorrow, we would be out of reliable options for stopping the cruise ship attack Thursday morning. I found it absurd that I considered using a World War II, P-51 to shoot down a terrorist's plane a reliable option. In reality, it was a dark, confusing and scary option. The only one left us. Doug doing nothing, saying nothing, was scarier, right then and there, then the colonel had been at Padre Thomas'.

"He knows what he's doing." Norm watched Doug too. "It might not look like it, but he does."

"But we don't trust him, right?"

"We don't trust anyone, hoss. That's the rule."

"Why aren't we insisting . . ."

"Because he's within his routine," Norm said. "He walked me through the job while you napped this afternoon."

"And."

"And now that everything's here, we'll see what happens."

"It's gotta happen damn fast, whatever it is."

Norm turned to Pauly and Bob, maybe looking for help in dealing with me or just to be sure the quiet duo were there.

"Don't look at me," Pauly said. "I'm leaning toward Mick's position."

"And you?" Norm pointed at Bob.

"Screw the plane," Bob said. "I think the Chief's plan of a couple of snipers is a better idea. One on Christmas Tree Island, another on the hotel roof, closest to where the ship docks, and there's no witnesses seeing anything. It becomes an unfortunate plane accident."

"Good point." Norm seemed to give the idea a thought.

"You get this antique in the air, with the guns working and what?" Bob moved closer to Norm. "You shoot the terrorist plane down? Boats in the harbor, people on deck of the cruise ship, on the docks, lookin' out hotel windows, checking the weather, or whatever. People see you. Where do you go? By the time you land, there'll be cops on their way. There's no deniability."

"Fuck deniability," I screeched. "If the snipers don't hit the plane right, it can still crash into the ship. Our way, we reach the plane on its approach and blow it out of the air."

"Last I looked, shooting down a private plane is a crime," Bob said. "It blows up from your shots or when it crashes, there goes your evidence. How are you gonna prove they were terrorists with a bomb onboard and that they planned to hit the cruise ship? And don't scream at me, I'm just asking."

I turned to Norm. "Can your people help?"

"What people?" He gave me a quizzical look. "I only have people when things go right, to take credit, not blame. I'm in the wind, Mick. I've told you that before."

"We still have to do it," I said.

Chapter Seventy-Four

"Do you need my help?" Norm saw Doug's bewildered look as he stood over the cardboard boxes of machine gun pieces.

Doug turned without smiling. "I don't wanna kill the plane, Norm, I wanna fix it."

"Funny, Doug. You can't do it alone."

"Nope. Can't and wasn't expecting to." He kept his stare. "Tall guy, in back, you know your way around a fifty cal?"

Bob looked surprised that Doug singled him out. He nodded.

"Ah, a man of few words, I like that." Finally, Doug smiled. "Your boat-bum attire doesn't fool me. I want him, Norm."

Norm looked at Bob and nodded. "Good luck," he said softly. "Do as he asks."

Bob walked toward the plane.

"Y'all can go now," Doug said. "Between us we'll figure out the phone and call you when we're done."

"You want us to take the security guys too?" Norm yelled as he walked away.

"Loosen the corset, Norm, it's unbecoming," Doug hollered back.

Texas Rich and Pauly's two security men met us at the hangar's sliding door.

"We're dealing with Russians," Pauly said to his two men. "They're sneaky and deadly, so be careful. You've got my number."

Both men nodded.

"Texas, something even looks like it's getting ready to go down, you call." He nodded.

"We should shut the hangar door," Texas Rich said. "Someone keeps watch outside, one walks around the perimeter and one in here."

"Just call, don't be heroes," I said. "And Bob is good too."

"I was counting on that," Texas Rich said.

"Don't let Doug get on your nerves, guys," Norm said as we walked away. The hangar door slid shut behind us. "We've got a little more than twenty four hours before the Feebs come after us, but you know they're looking for us now."

"You don't think they've found us already?" Pauly headed toward his rental car.

"Doesn't matter," Norm said. "If the plane's working we'll be out of here tomorrow."

Norm and Pauly discussed the car and Pauly returned it to the rental people in the terminal. We got in a cab and went to the Smokin' Tuna Saloon.

Angela, the manager, let Norm choose the table in front of the T-shirt shop. Norm wanted to see both entrances. We ordered beer and chicken wings.

"Pauly," Norm began between sips of beer. "You and I will take the plane up when Doug says it's ready . . ."

"You and Pauly?" I cut Norm off. "No way! I'm going with Pauly."

"You ever fire a fifty cal or sit in the cramped quarters of a small plane?"

"Let's cut to the chase, Norm." I could feel my face turn red. No way was anyone but me going to stop this and be the cause of fucking up Alexei's plan. "I'm going with Pauly. End of discussion."

Norm looked at Pauly, who replied by hunching his shoulders.

"This is a one-shot opportunity," Norm said. "You fuck up, the plane hits the cruise ship. There's no margin of error here, Mick."

"If the guns are working and Pauly heads broadside toward the plane, I can't miss. It's a twin-engine plane and bigger than a breadbasket." I took deep breaths and tried to relax. I should've known Norm would expect to be the shooter. He's been the shooter throughout this whole ordeal. I knew he was trying to protect me by keeping me from killing in cold blood, but this was different. This was mostly about saving lives and a little about screwing up Alexei's plans.

"It's not target practice, Mick. Planes are moving in opposite directions, there could be turbulence, speed variances. Hell, things could fuck up in an instant and you only have the one try."

I turned to Pauly. "Can you fly toward the plane, with whatever speed and turbulence?"

"Lightning could hit us, it could be stormy, but yeah, I should be able to fly at the right angle for you to shoot," Pauly said. "If the guns are working, we need to test them tomorrow in the Gulf. If I think you're having a problem, we let Norm do it. Okay?"

"No practice time, Mick." Norm frowned.

"I won't have a problem." I wanted to sound more confident than I felt.

Norm laughed, maybe to break the tension, as our chicken wings arrived. He asked for another round of beers and put a few chicken wings on his paper plate. "Hoss, we've had eight days of problems, why should the next couple of days be any different?"

I grabbed a couple of chicken wings and put them on my plate. I didn't have an answer for him.

Chapter Seventy-Five

We dipped the chicken wings into hot sauce and ate without talking. Angela delivered the beers and I wondered why, since she was the manager not our server. When she saw me looking, she nodded toward the saloon's writers' room, smiled and asked how the wings were. No one said a word, only nodded, probably because we all had a mouthful of spicy chicken and a hand on the cold beer.

Angela walked to the writers' room entrance by the bamboo bar. She stood there and beckoned me with a quick wave. I excused myself. Both Norm and Pauly must have thought I was going to the men's room, because they continued chomping away at the wings, discarding bones, and ignoring me.

When I got to the doorway, Angela grabbed my arm and pulled me into the room.

"I have something to tell you," she said when we were out of sight.

"You okay?"

"When you left here the other day . . ."

"We paid the tab, didn't we?"

"It's not about the tab, Mick." She kept her voice low.

"The guys chasing us make trouble?"

"No." She suppressed a laugh. "But the side door locked when you closed it and for a little while they didn't know what to do. They really looked stupid."

"What then?"

"The next day, some suits came by," she said. "I mean real suits, with ties, Florsheim shoes and socks."

"And?"

"They asked about you, after flashing Homeland Security badges. Wanted to know about a guy name Larry something or other, was he with you and what were you talking about."

"What did you tell them?"

"The truth," Angela said. "I hadn't seen you in a year, I said hi, didn't know who Larry was, the bar was busy and then you were gone, when I looked up."

"What did they do then?"

"Went upstairs to talk to Charlie and Donna, who never saw you, so they couldn't have said much."

"Thanks, Angela."

"That's not the reason I called you in here."

"Why are we in here?"

"I saw a couple of the suits outside just now, when I was in the kitchen, and I think they're coming in. One of them was on the phone."

I looked out the window onto Charles Street but saw no one.

Angela pointed toward the kitchen in the next building. "Outside the kitchen. You wouldn't see them from here."

From what Norm said, we had until midday Wednesday to leave town. Of course, that didn't mean no one wanted to monitor our whereabouts. It still pissed me off and I hadn't had my fill of chicken wings.

"Is there another way out?" I saw the room's two exits, the one I came in and the one that opened onto the main entrance, by the kitchen. It wasn't a good option.

"Behind the curtain." Angela moved a large curtain aside and behind it was a French door. "We don't use it as an entrance, but sometimes if the room is full we open it to help circulate air."

I took a bar napkin from one of the tables and wrote a note to Norm. "I want you to have someone take this to Norm."

Before Angela took the note, she unlocked the French door and looked outside. "They're still there." She left the door unlocked and took the note.

Norm and Pauly came into the room, licking hot sauce off their fingers, and checking their backs. I explained what Angela told me. I looked out the French door and the men were gone. I checked both ends of Charles Street and no one was there. People passed at the Duval Street end.

"Let's go." I was the first outside.

We headed toward Duval Street. The evening crush of

people and cars greeted us.

"Right behind us," Pauly said.

Norm and I turned to see the three men in suits coming in our direction. Like tourists from New England, we jaywalked our way through traffic and were outside the Lazy Gecko when the suits arrived at Duval. Why were they chasing us?

"I thought we had until tomorrow, Norm?" I headed toward Sloppy Joe's Bar.

Norm already had his cell out and dialing. "I'll ask."

The suits crossed the busy street and we turned into Sloppy Joe's. A band played on stage, the large service bar had people two-deep standing by it and the floor was so crowded you couldn't see the tables. Everyone seemed to be talking, singing along or arguing, all at once. The music wailed over the commotion.

"Follow me." I walked around the bar, having to push my way between people of every size, color and shape imaginable. No one seemed to pay attention to us as we jostled through. A normal bar crowd in Key West.

An employee doorway stood at the far end of the bar and went to the kitchen and backroom offices. A bouncer stood off to one side.

"We're supposed to meet Chris in the back office," I said to the bouncer. I knew Chris, he was the general manager and had probably gone home.

"Chris who?" The bouncer said without looking at us.

"Chris Mullins," I said as I passed him.

The bouncer nodded, more interested in keeping an eye on the crowd than us. We walked through and turned left, rushed down the narrow hall, passing the kitchen and servers with trays of food. Straight down the corridor at the back, a door opened onto the Old City Hall parking area. With a little luck, the suits were stuck in the bar, searching the crowd for us. We might have a few minutes to disappear.

"What's outside?" Norm said.

I told him before opening the door. "We go down Anne Street to Caroline double back to Duval."

"Find us a cab so we can get the hell out of here." Norm no longer had his cell open. "Something's wrong."

Chapter Seventy-Six

There must have been a city commission meeting because the Old City Hall parking lot was full and police cars stood stationed by the gate. To our left people on Greene Street rushed in frenzy toward Duval Street or the waterfront. Going through the parking lot, we entered Ann Street, keeping Sloppy Joe's and Old City Hall between Duval, Greene and us. We turned right.

"What do you mean something's wrong?" I stopped on the backside of the Curry Mansion.

"My sources complained about our treatment to Washington, and no one knew what they were talking about," Norm said. "They asked about the cruise ship threat, mentioning the document we turned in. Nothing! Someone has waylaid the whole project."

"What's that got to do with the suits?" Pauly said.

"If they're Homeland Security, they could want to arrest us." Norm held back his real thoughts, I knew from his tone of voice.

"Or what?" It was never easy with his scenarios.

"Or kill us," he said in a deadpan voice. "We've stumbled onto something and whether or not it succeeds doesn't matter, we're a liability now." Norm began walking toward Caroline Street. He pulled his cell phone out and dialed. "Bring the padre to Cabanas' hangar . . . we'll be there within a half hour." He hung up.

"What's going on?" I said.

Norm hailed a taxi, we got in and headed to the airport.

Norm sat in front. Pauly wanted to say more, but I pulled his arm and shook my head. We continued in silence. I knew that Norm's head was filling with possible problems as he searched for workable solutions.

The cab dropped us off outside the private terminal area of Key West International Airport. We all searched around, looking for anyone who might have followed us or looked out of place. The parking lot had few cars at that hour and no one lurked in the shadows. No one we saw, anyway.

Pauly's two security men met us at the gate. They had nothing to report. Pauly told them to stay together because he was expecting trouble. They smiled, touched their rifles and went into the shadows.

Texas Rich greeted us as we entered the hangar.

"We weren't expecting you," Texas said.

"Lot of unexpected things happening tonight." Norm headed toward the plane, calling Doug's name.

Bob kneeled on the wing and Doug popped his head out of the cockpit.

"Gone to shit already, hasn't it?" he called out and slowly stood.

"Could be." Norm stopped next to the plane's propeller. "How you comin' along?"

Doug stepped onto the wing, wiping his hands on his overalls. "I had to run new cables to the back seat so Red there," he pointed at me, "could be the shooter. The guns are in and I dry-shot 'em. The cable should be done soon."

"We might have a problem."

"Tell me somethin' I don't know, Norm."

"Not time to be a smart ass, Doug."

Doug and Bob climbed off the wing.

"Camel jockeys here?" Doug pulled a rag from one pocket and wiped his hands again.

"Not yet." Norm led him toward the picnic table outside the office. "But there are others."

"Who?" Doug sat.

"It doesn't matter." Norm continued to stand and waved us over. "The good news might be that they only want to arrest us."

"And the downside?" Doug looked up, expressionless.

"They want to kill us."

"My price is going up!"

"I'm not paying you unless the guns are working and we're out of here tonight," Norm said.

Doug looked at Bob. "Are the cables attached like I

showed you?"

"Yes and I double-checked 'em," Bob said.

Doug looked at his wristwatch. "It's a little after eight. You wanna be out of here at ten?"

"Want to be out of here at eight!" Norm grinned. "Nine would be good."

"Nine-thirty would be damn good!" Doug stood and took Bob back to the plane.

Chapter Seventy-Seven

Texas Rich opened the door, Padre Thomas and two of Jim Ashe's security people from JIATF walked through. Paul Carpino led the way. He was someone we'd worked with twice before; he's focused and good with an M-4. Why was Padre Thomas here? I turned to Norm, who sat at the picnic table.

"Why's he here?" Norm said before I asked. He read me so well, he knew what I was about to say.

"What are we doing?" I ignored his cleverness.

We nodded our recognition to Carpino.

"In a few minutes." Norm stretched and tapped the seat. "You might as well sit."

Padre Thomas came to us. He sat. "You know?" He spoke to Norm.

"I guessed, Padre."

"What are you going to do?" He lit a cigarette and when he couldn't find an ashtray, he looked at me. I said nothing and let him smoke.

"When Jim Ashe gets here, we'll work it out."

"Work what out?" The conversation between them confused me.

Norm's cell chirped. He answered it, listened and said, "Give it two minutes." He hung up and yelled at Texas Rich. "Tell the boys, Captain Ashe is approaching and not to shoot him."

"Let him in?" Texas Rich called back.

"That's the idea, Texas." Norm stood up. "Your boys gonna stay?" he said to Pauly.

"There's more if you need them." Pauly waited for an answer but didn't get a direct one.

"I need experienced, Pauly. Too many hot shots only add to the fodder."

"You've got my best," Pauly said. "They're all experienced."

By the time Norm crossed the hangar, stopping at the plane to say something to Doug, Captain Jim Ashe came in, followed by Pauly's two men, Rob Murdock and Wayne Bruehl. Norm greeted Ashe and the two men went back outside.

I hadn't seen Ashe since he almost got us killed off Cay Sal in the Bahamas. He hadn't changed, ramrod straight, military haircut and even in civvies, you wanted to salute him.

"I called Chief Dowley, he's on his way." Ashe said as a greeting.

"We need everyone here, Mick." Norm turned to me and again answered my question before I asked it.

A loud repeated clicking came from the wing of the P-51. It stopped, then started, and then stopped. Doug dry fired the machine gun from the cockpit.

Doug stood up, was about to say something when he saw Ashe and then quietly stepped onto the wing. He and Bob climbed down.

Bob went to the cooler and took a soda. He popped the top as he scanned the table and frowned at seeing Padre Thomas. He knew Ashe and the expression on Bob's face mirrored my confusion.

Doug wiped his hands on a rag from his overall's pocket and stopped by Norm.

Pauly's cell chirped. He answered it. "I don't think it would be a good idea to shoot the chief of police," he said. "Let him in."

Texas Rich opened the door, nodded to Richard and walked outside.

"Are you giving this party?" I said to Norm.

Everyone gathered around the table but Doug. He stayed back, not knowing who was who or why they were there.

Ashe explained to the six of us standing around, how he'd been stonewalled when asking about the document he witnessed Norm pass on to CIA agent Shirrel Rhoades and FBI Special Agent Bryan Paps. Norm mentioned his call from JASOC had much the same result. No one from the FBI or Homeland Security even bothered to return Richard's call.

"I don't know if it's related, but tomorrow morning I'm

meeting with two Secret Service agents," Richard said. "No idea what it's about and they wouldn't say."

"Let us know, when you can," Norm said.

Padre Thomas stood and lit another cigarette. I hadn't seen what he did with the first butt.

"I've got bad new and I've got worse new." There was no humor in Norm's voice. "The bad news is the Russian Mafia has connected Mick and Pauly to problems they had in South Beach and Mexico but I don't think they've figured out it connects to their involvement with the terrorists."

Norm doctored the information and I guessed it was to give Richard deniability if he needed it. Omission of facts is an important tool to a journalist. To someone like Norm, it was second nature.

"They're looking for Mick and Pauly and I don't think it's to talk." Norm let that sink in for Richard's sake. Norm was telling him there was trouble on the way. Ashe had probably been kept up-to-date all along. "The Russians know they're in Key West, so we can expect them to show up."

"It gets worse than the Russian mafia?" Richard said.

"If you can believe what I'm gonna tell you, it does." Norm went on to repeat the rumor CIA operative Ed Scales related, and then recounted the response we received when handing out the English translation of Alexei's diary and how the report seems to have vanished.

"I've no love for the lunatic fringe or conspiracy theorists," Norm sighed. "But an in-house conspiracy is the only answer that makes sense right now. Everything else leaves too many loose ends."

"It could be worse than that," Pauly said. "If you're right, what if everyone is in this together?"

"Everyone?" Norm looked puzzled and he doesn't confuse easily.

"Yeah, think about it. What Scales said, no attacks within our borders, so rumor has it that budget cuts will be deep and widespread within Homeland Security. Think of how big that operation is and what agencies it encompasses. Russian terrorists? Mexican terrorists? Mid-East terrorists? Why not put them in the pot together? You have the perfect clique for pulling something off within our borders, especially if they had help from people that knew the inside workings of government."

"Stretching it, a little . . . hell, a lot, actually," Ashe said. "Something like that would involve hundreds of people from D.C. to Key West. Too complicated."

"Stretch it more, ask yourself some questions." Pauly went on. "Alexei comes and goes freely, y'all know that, right?"

Norm and Ashe nodded.

"How's he do that? It's hard enough for some people to get on a plane with the fucked up no-fly list Homeland Security has. Why can't they catch a known, wanted criminal who doesn't seem to have travel problems? He's in New York, Miami, Houston and back and forth from Europe. How'd he avoid the no-fly list? Y'all know his aliases, have his photos, but he can't be caught!"

"You're saying officials in Homeland Security are more than aware of this." Norm's words were not an accusation or question, he was thinking aloud.

"It would fit with your scenario," Pauly said. "It would explain how things got this far so fast and why you've been ignored and now hunted. Someone kept the documents from going upstream and they're sending hit squads downstream! When it's over the Russians are perfect falls guys. Homeland Security double-crosses them, gives the Mexicans to the DEA and the CIA gets the Iranian connection, and all the credit goes to Homeland Security for solving the bombing. Now they're necessary and they need a budget to keep us safe! Washington will shower them with money!"

"All it costs are some innocent lives on a cruise ship," I said. "Collateral damage, you guys call it." I looked at Norm. "Shit happens, right?"

The hangar filled with silence.

Chapter Seventy-Eight

A few men lit up smokes after Norm's and Pauly's exchange, others joined Bob by the cooler for a soda, and a couple hid in the shadows, trying to find a way to deal with what they'd just heard. Americans betraying Americans isn't a topic we're prepared for. It's not something anyone wants to believe. It's easier to suspect Cuban or KGB hit men are responsible for Dallas than imagine an American sniper as the second shooter from the knoll. Only the lunatic fringe believed in conspiracies. That was easy to accept. People wanted to believe the government cared and didn't lie. People wanting to believe, didn't make it so and Norm and I had firsthand experience of that. Hell, we lied to friends in the hangar.

I saw Padre Thomas sitting on the floor, back against the P-51's wheel, smoking but he seemed to be using a soda can for an ashtray. Maybe he was talking with the angels.

Doug pulled Norm aside and Ashe talked with Carpino and his partner. I walked toward Padre Thomas.

"What were you and Norm talking about before everyone showed up?" I stood next to him.

He turned to me and ignored my question. "This is the plane."

"Didn't you see it in your dream?" The words came out snidely.

Padre Thomas smiled. "It looked smaller." He lit another cigarette. "Norm knows the plane has to be shot down." He stood and touched the propeller. "With this. All that," he pointed to the men milling around, "is unrelated to what has to be done."

"And you got this from the angels in a dream?"

"That's how I've interpreted the dream, yes."

"And Norm knows this, how?"

"I guess. He's been doing this kind of thing for years." Padre Thomas dropped the cigarette butt on the floor and crushed it under his shoe, forgetting about the soda can. "You know better than anyone, he chases drug lords, cartel gangs and now he's chasing terrorists."

"Did you see the terrorists' plane go down, in this dream?" I may not have been a staunch believer, but I believed sometimes, and not always for the right reasons. Padre Thomas' dreams were often the beginning of my nightmares.

"No," he mumbled. "But it must, if the angels say you can stop it with this."

"Did you see this plane afterward?"

Padre Thomas shook his head. "Too frequently, they only show me the answer."

"Excuse me, Padre, but I'm concerned about the overall outcome."

"You need faith, Mick, and it will be all right."

Norm and Richard waved me over before I could answer Padre Thomas.

"Before you go." Padre Thomas stopped me. "The other thing Norm and I know is someone is going to attack the hangar tonight. He's preparing."

"The angels told you this?" It was rhetorical and I didn't expect an answer. "How's he preparing?" Norm hadn't said anything to me.

"By doing this." He looked around the hangar.

I excused myself and took my concern to Norm.

"Richard's still talking snipers," Norm said as I got there.

"You're going to use snipers." Richard looked toward Pauly, knowing that the men working for Pauly were all ex-military sharpshooters. "Right? That's your plan?"

"You'll need a large caliber to stop the plane." I didn't want to lie so I avoided a direct answer. I needed to get Norm alone but didn't want Richard to notice my uneasiness.

"I've got SWAT snipers, Mick, that have been in Afghanistan. They know what they're doing. Shoot out the engine and how far can the plane go?" Richard wasn't asking permission, his words were a warning to stay away.

"Where are you putting them?"

"We were just discussing that," Norm said.

"I'll have the police marine patrol on the water for survivors, if any, and bomb retrieval. A sniper, maybe two, on Christmas Tree Island."

"You're assuming the plane's coming from the waterside." Until I said that, I assumed it too. Norm flashed a grin and I knew he'd already considered a land approach.

"Where do you think it's coming from, over Key West?"

"We don't know," I said. "We don't know where the plane is or what kind of bomb it's carrying."

"But you believe your document is accurate, right? Because, if we shoot down a plane that has nothing to do . . ."

"At that hour, there'll only be one plane headed toward the cruise ship. The terrorists will be on it, with the bomb." I was trying to convince myself about our accuracy, too.

Richard looked unnerved. His stare went between Norm and me. "I'm asking two of my men to do this. You have to be sure and if you're sure, then the things you just talked about are probably true."

"We're sure," Norm said.

Richard nodded and walked away, his message delivered but he was not a happy police chief.

"We didn't want to mention this plane," Norm whispered. "Doug has everything working. All we need to do is test the guns with live ammo."

"What's this all about, if we're not telling Richard, what are we doing?"

"Covering our asses. We may need people from Ashe. Richard, I'm not sure how he'd handle the truth. He might even try to stop us. He hopes we're wrong, but he can't afford to do nothing. He'd see our plan as a little extreme."

"When were you going to tell me about the attack?"

"What attack?" Norm said.

"Padre Thomas said you know we'll be attacked here."

Norm rubbed his chin and bit his lip. "I'm preparing. Forget the terrorists, for a minute, hoss. That leaves the Russians seeking revenge for South Beach and Tampico. You should understand how strong that drive is." Norm waited a beat before continuing. "They know we're in Key West, how long do you think before they figure out we're at the airport?"

"So, what's the plan?"

"You still want to go with Pauly?"

"Yeah, it's me."

"As soon as Richard leaves, you and Pauly take off. He knows a few private airstrips in the Everglades and you stay there until early Thursday morning."

"What are you doing?"

"Letting Richard run free with his snipers," Norm said. "Who knows, they may do the job. We also have to keep Padre Thomas safe from the colonel."

"What are you doing about the attack!" I wanted to yell, but kept my frustration in.

"Getting ready, preparing, like I said."

"And about us in the Everglades? How do we know what's going on?"

"We'll be in contact with radios Doug has programmed, while you're in the air. We're going to be your spotters, Thursday morning."

"Richard's snipers going to share space with Pauly's men?"

"I'm working on that," Norm said. "Probably not."

"What happens if one set of snipers mistakes us for the terrorists' plane?" This probability began to concern me.

"We'll have to see that doesn't happen," Norm said. "When he can't do anything about it, I'll let Richard know what plane you're in. Okay?"

"He'll know we lied."

"And he'll know why."

That was almost two days away. An attack at the airport, before we got in the air, had to be Norm's main concern.

"What if it's Homeland Security agents and not Russians that show up?" How would he know before the shooting started? Would it make a difference?

"Mick, I'm making an educated guess about an attack and,

hell, I've guessed wrong before."

"Norm, that doesn't answer me."

"I've no desire to shoot at American agents," he said. "Thing is, the agents are just as much victims to the assholes orchestrating this shit, as the passengers on the cruise ship, but we have no choice. We defend ourselves or we're dead."

"How do we settle the score, afterward?"

"If we stop this, the people who wanted it will slither back into the sludge of government bureaucracy and we'll probably never know who they are." Norm stared at me. "Live with it."

"If they succeed, how do we live with it?"

"The best we can, if we're alive," Norm said. "Either way, Mick, it's all over by eight Thursday morning. They win or lose, we're alive or dead. Only the two possibilities for all of us."

Chapter Seventy-Nine

Richard left the hangar after a brief talk with Captain Jim Ashe. What did they have to talk about? Snipers? Possibly, coordinating who was doing what on the water Thursday morning? As the attack neared, I got anxious and trust was the first thing affected. Norm's philosophy, as an operation progressed, was mistrust.

Bob and Pauly had taken a chart from Ashe and spread it out on the picnic table. Padre Thomas sat back down under the P-51. Ashe's two men went outside and joined Texas Rich and Pauly's guys.

"What've we got?" Norm said to Ashe.

The three of us went to the table that held a large, detailed design plan that took up most of the space.

"This is the plan of the cruise ship." Ashe showed us a set of pages with deck specifics under the first one, from the top deck to the engine room below. "I think all we need is the top page." The page showed a detailed drawing of the ship, looking down at the deck plan, and a waterline side view. He pointed to a blue scrawled line near the bottom of the ship. "That's the expected waterline when she comes into Key West. She's full of fresh water, fuel, whatever, so she's low in the water."

We walked around the table, circling like vultures checking out road kill.

"You've seen the plane," Ashe said to Norm. "What do you think it can do to this?"

"It can't sink it, but that's not the plan, anyway. Sunk, there's no dramatic photo op." Norm circled one more time and we made room for him. "This is a new ship, maiden voyage, right?"

Ashe nodded.

"The whole idea is to cause as many casualties as possible and get press coverage, graphic TV footage, before the noon news," Norm said. "This attack is simple, cost effective and bound to get them all the coverage they want."

"News helicopters from the Miami stations will be here

within an hour, two at the most," I said.

"Where does the plane hit and cause the most carnage?" Ashe nodded at me and then ran his hands over the plans. "It's a big ship, can they damage it?"

"Fire burns up, remember that." Norm leaned in and studied the plan some more. "Passengers on the top decks watching the ship come into port. First stop after an overnight sail, people are excited, curious." He pointed at the deck layout.

"Dive bomb the top deck?" Ashe looked surprised.

"No. They have a master plan, so what do they plan for? And remember, they've been planning this a long time. What would you plan for? Me? I'd want a sure thing and not be affected by bad weather, rain, wind, whatever would keep a lot of people off the top deck. Forget the top deck, look midship."

"Midship, five decks down?" I looked at the wide space filled with round portholes. "Lot of rooms, maybe people still sleeping or getting ready, so full with people too."

"Nope. What if the plane hits a support beam? No, they want to kill as many as possible and to do damage too, and to do both they have to get inside the ship." Norm pointed at the second deck of portholes and balconies. "You fly full speed . . ." Norm looked at Pauly.

"If they use the plane we saw in Mexico, say three-hundred miles an hour, if they have the distance and time, at least two, if it's a short run," Pauly said.

"Say two." Norm pointed at a balcony. "Nose aimed into this glass door at two-hundred miles an hour, the prop rips apart on impact, the wings break off as they hit the ship, but the fuselage, or a good part of it, goes into the room and maybe has enough momentum to pass through it, into the hallway."

"When does the bomb go off?" I said.

"The men in the plane are dead on impact; the plane is probably burning because it's full of fuel." Norm stabbed his finger at the balcony. "The fire may set off the bomb inside the ship or it could be on a timer to go off thirty seconds after impact. It goes off inside and the fire burns upward. The explosion kills people on that level and the fire would kill more and then burn the other levels. Panic would kill people too, so the news media would have a field day. Cell phone video would be on the internet within minutes, photos and the voices of panicked people, too."

"How many?" Padre Thomas had come up without any of us noticing him.

"No way to guess, Padre, but one is too many," Norm said.

"It could be a few, if something goes wrong for the terrorists, or it could be a few thousand, if we don't succeed," Ashe muttered.

"You have to stop these people," Padre Thomas cried. "You have to!"

"We plan to, Padre," Norm said. "At least we're gonna try to."

I thought of another of Norm's rules, plans fuck up! Always.

Chapter Eighty

"I'm putting snipers on both hotel roofs." Captain Jim Ashe rolled up the drawings of the cruise ship. "I know you don't think they'll come on the pier side, but it's where the passengers disembark, where the local authorities and dockworkers are. It needs to be covered, as a precaution."

"If I'm right about how the plane will hit, the hotels are too close to the dock and too high. They'd block a direct shot at the ship and the plane would have to come at an angle from above the hotels," Norm said. "To get the fuselage inside the ship, they need speed and a straight shot. On the other hand, nothing's wrong with precautions."

"Chief Dowley will have his snipers on Christmas Tree Island." Ashe turned to Pauly. "You'll have them somewhere too, but I don't want to know." He gave Norm a shake of the head. "If they succeed, it's a cluster-fuck, no matter where they come from."

Pauly remained quiet, giving Ashe his deniability.

"We'll stop them," Norm said, almost as if he believed it.

Ashe looked at the P-51. Padre Thomas sat under it, smoking, not seeming to pay attention to us.

"Where's the old man?" Ashe said.

We looked around and for the first time I realized Doug wasn't here.

Norm snapped his phone open and dialed. "Where are you?" Norm's grim look mellowed. "Get in here!"

"Did he get the guns working?" Ashe said, as the front door opened and closed.

Pauly looked at Norm, who shrugged. At that point Ashe was on board, arranging snipers. You can't fool some people. Maybe Ashe saw the obvious and knew. Or guessed. I wondered if Richard did too, but he chose to say nothing.

"We think so." Norm waved Doug over. "We'll know for sure later tonight."

"Keep me in the loop, I don't want my people shooting

down the wrong plane." Ashe smiled and shook hands with Norm. "It's a hell of an airplane!"

"It sure is." Doug walked up as Ashe turned to leave.

"Don't disappear like that," Norm said to Doug.

"You expecting trouble?" Doug ignored Norm's comments.

"Why?"

"The guys out there look like they're preparing to defend against Attila the Hun."

"Pauly, your two guys that came at midnight . . ." It was Norm's turn to ignore Doug.

"They're staying," Pauly said. "They brought ammo and they know Ashe's men."

"Time to test Doug's handiwork." Norm pointed to the hangar door and Bob went to open it. "This is gonna work, ain't it?" He turned to Doug.

"Don't abuse it," Doug said. "I attached the cables, but they ain't tied down inside the wing, so too much firing could be bad, might loosen and tangle them up and who knows what else."

Norm gave Doug a hard look of disapproval.

"Do you have the time for me to take the wings apart?" His words were challenging. "You got what you asked for, two fifty cal machine guns that only have to work once and briefly. Your boy there doesn't get trigger-happy, everything will work as I said. Or give me the time to do it right!"

"We're out of time," Norm growled.

"Who do you think's coming." Pauly pulled the blocks from the plane's wheels and had Padre Thomas get up.

"I'd eliminate Attila the Hun." Norm laughed at Doug. "I hope no one."

"Some one's coming." Padre Thomas warned in a deadpan tone.

Doug threw a glance at Padre Thomas that reminded me of a feral cat watching a marsh rat scamper across a vacant lot. He brought the look to Norm, as if asking permission to pounce.

"Padre, time is our enemy." Norm disregarded Doug's

stare. "The colonel wants to know where we are, thanks to Doug, and who knows what else he wants. The government has given us less than twenty-four hours to get off this rock and let's not forget the Russians. Given time, any of them can find us."

Padre Thomas expression showed a mixture of fear and confusion, but he said nothing.

"We've gotta avoid those people for the next thirty-six hours, Padre," Norm sighed. "The chances of that are slim so, yeah, someone's coming." He avoided talk of angels, but it was in the back of my mind.

"So, let's get the plane in the air," Pauly said as he and Bob lifted the tail and turned the plane toward the outside. "Anyone wanna help?"

Bob had opened the hangar door and Norm and I joined in pushing the plane. When it finally got into position so it could move to the tarmac on its own, we stopped. I looked and couldn't see any of the men who were supposed to be protecting the hangar.

Pauly climbed onto the wing and waved me forward.

"Pauly knows how to use the radios." Norm walked with me to the wing. "Shoot straight, Mick, there's no second chances on this."

I laughed nervously. "With all the snipers, I'm not sure we'll get within shooting distance of the bastards before they go down." I climbed in and Pauly followed.

The engine started and the noise drowned out Norm's reply, even though he stood next to the cockpit. I saw Padre Thomas send some sort of blessing to the plane. I've wondered during my misadventures in Central and South America, if God takes sides in wars. Why would He? War is man's stupidity, man is God's folly, or so I often thought.

I forced myself into the cramped back seat and the engine noise seemed even louder. Pauly handed me a headset and used his hands to tell me to put them on. The noise subsided a little, but not completely. A small mic extension poked out from the left side of the headset.

"You hear me okay?" Pauly said.

"Yeah, but I hear the engine better."

He closed the cockpit top and the prop began to spin.

"You see the wand on the floor?" Pauly had the plane moving slowly away from the hangar onto the tarmac. Hearing him was like talking to someone with a bad phone connection.

"Yeah."

"You push down the button on top of it, the guns fire," Pauly said. "When we get over the water, and away from the Keys, I'll make a quick dive bomb approach to the water, you test it. Keep away from it, otherwise."

"You know what you're doing, right?" I tried for humor but I think my nervousness came through instead.

"Too late, Mick. You should've asked that before we took off."

Chapter Eighty-One

Pauly didn't take the plane high and I asked why. I saw the island's roads and building too clearly. I wanted to know where the parachutes where, too, but knew if I said anything, he'd tell me I should've asked before we left.

"We're gonna fly below the radar," he answered me, as he banked the plane over the water. We had turned back toward the airport. "Did you see that private jet come in as we took off?"

"Yeah. Maybe it's Jimmy Buffett?"

"I didn't hear it try to communicate with possible air traffic." I heard concern in his voice. When the Key West air traffic control tower was closed, planes that came and went searched for other air traffic in the vicinity by radio, to see if any were using the airport.

"You didn't check."

"That's my point. I didn't check traffic because I didn't want anyone to know we were leaving. I'm stayin' off radar and no one needs to know I'm in the air."

"Can a jet stay off radar?" I knew nothing about aviation.

It was after one in the morning and there was little movement on the roads around the airport, but the surrounding grounds of the condo and apartment buildings were lit up as we approached. We had a shadowy view of the airport, but everything was recognizable. Pauly tried to radio Norm and received no answer while I was amazed at how close we were to the ground.

"Maybe they're sleeping," I said.

Multiple bursts of light, coming from Freddy Cabanas' hangar and the tarmac, caught our attention. Without saying it, we knew they were gunshot flashes.

"Shit!" Pauly said to himself and tried Norm again.

He kept the low approach and flew over the hangar. I could see people shooting from behind airplanes and others returned fire from next to the hangar. Engine noise was all I could hear.

"What are you doing?" Norm's voice crackled through my

headset.

"How many are there?" Pauly answered back.

"I didn't count 'em," Norm said. "They flew in."

We could hear gunshot report through our headsets, as Norm spoke.

"The private jet?"

"Yeah. Good target to test those guns on," Norm said. "If Mick can hit it."

Pauly banked and circled over the water. "Can you see it from there?"

I reached down and picked up the trigger-wand Doug had put together. Leaning forward as far as I could, I said, "I think so."

"Don't shoot, if you're not sure." Pauly headed the plane back to the airport. "We'll try to shoot down from above the jet and then I'll come back, lower, and you shoot toward the side of it. Hold the trigger for five seconds, count one Mississippi, two . . ." He didn't go on.

"I got it." I held the trigger-wand tightly, afraid to put my thumb on the firing button too soon.

"Once you've fired, I'm getting out of here, so be prepared for a quick change in direction and altitude."

The gunshot flashes continued and I couldn't tell who the shooters were. I knew our guys were spread around outside the hangar and Norm was inside, maybe with Bob. I wondered if Texas Rich came to their aid or was pinned down on the tarmac.

"Get ready." I heard Pauly's words through my headset. Engine noise still attacked my hearing. "I'm gonna dive and you fire."

I shook my head and realized Pauly couldn't see me. "Ready!"

I stared over Pauly's right shoulder, trying to see the nose of the plane. The jet grew larger as we approached. The plane angled down and Pauly yelled. I held the trigger button and counted to five. I saw torrents of explosive light erupt from the wings as bullets shredded the tarmac and moved toward the jet, obliterating the ground, as we flew closer. By the time I said five Mississippi, bullets had slashed into the jet's fuselage, and a few of the planes closest to it.

"One more pass," Pauly yelped as the plane banked over the water again. "Good shootin', Mick. We're goin' in low, and it won't be a surprise this time, so they'll be shootin' at us too. We won't have to get too close with these guns, so fire on my word."

"I'm ready." I saw the airport fence approach and hoped we were above it. I could see cracks in the tarmac. Men scrambled around the jet, aiming up toward us.

"Fire!" Pauly screeched.

I held the trigger button down and counted. Bullets ripped into the jet's fuselage and, as Pauly made a turn that propelled us almost straight up, the jet burst into flames. Pauly's enthusiastic scream reminded me of a wild animal and it came through the headset loud and clear.

"I think you ruined their morning, hoss," Norm shouted and sounded surprised. "Did Mick do that?"

"I helped a little." Pauly's voice changed from a wild animal's scream to someone with edgy laughter. "Casualties on our side?"

"I'll get back to you. Bob and I are going outside, but slowly."

"Padre Thomas?" I said.

"Saying prayers of thanks in the office, I hope."

Chapter Eighty-Two

I held tightly onto the trigger-wand, sat back in the confined space and tried to recall everything I'd just done. Even with the loud engine noise, I'd heard the jarring explosions as round after round of fifty caliber bullets spit from both wings, followed rapidly by fingers of burning light; an eerie radiance, in the shadowy night.

It frightened me as I recalled it, but at the time, as I pressed the trigger button, it excited me. My body tingled with amusement and it took an effort on my part to remove my thumb from the button, after I'd said *five Mississippi*. The seconds seemed endless.

Pauly continued his smuggler's treetop flying, skimming only yards above the water at a high speed, the chain of the Florida Keys to my right, as my mind wandered.

"How many rounds, do you think?" I finally said without fumbling the words.

"No idea, Mick. We'll ask Norm to check if Doug put enough rounds in for Thursday."

"Hadn't figured on that." What if the answer is no, I thought. The engine noise seemed louder. Maybe it echoed off the water below us.

"Not like we had a choice." Pauly kept the plane steady as we sped north.

"Where are we going?" I couldn't get it clear in my head that there was a reason we were going in the opposite direction of where we needed to be Thursday morning. I knew we had to hide but I couldn't get a grip on the senseless thoughts rattling around in my brain.

"The Everglades, east of the Ten Thousand Islands," Pauly said. "There are a few airstrips hidden in there. Short, dirt and gravel roads, but long enough to land on. Back in the day, I stopped a few times and usually there's a house or shed along with some kind of coverage for the plane. People too."

"You still welcomed?"

"If they don't shoot first because this plane scares 'em, I

think we'll be okay," he said. "I've got a cover story."

"Gonna share it?"

"We're flying to Key West to pick up boxes, and I mean a lot of boxes of Cuban cigars." He laughed. "It's still smuggling a tobacco product!"

I made myself laugh. I knew it was funny to him, from smuggling grass to Cuban cigars, but it was okay because they were both a form of tobacco. I knew what bothered me, too. I just didn't want to think about it. But I did.

"Did I kill some of them?" I thought I talked to myself and it surprised me when Pauly answered.

"Whoever was on the damn jet got toasted, for sure!" Pauly still rode a high from the attack. "For Norm's sake, I hope we got some of the assholes on the ground."

Pauly thought of it as *we,* and maybe he was right because he piloted the plane, but I thought of it as *me*, since I had pushed the trigger. I'd defended myself before. And I knew others died because of it, but shooting from a plane seemed different. Hell, it was different, but was it? I defended Norm and Padre Thomas; I might have saved their lives and the lives of others on our side.

"Are you slowing down?" I felt different movement in the plane.

"Yeah," Pauly said.

"Everything okay?" No parachute, no escape, I reminded myself.

"Couldn't be better. Are you okay? Seem nervous."

"Haven't come down yet," I lied but knew he'd believe me. "Why are we slowing?"

"Not sure I could find the landing strip in the dark, but don't want to be treetop flying in the daylight, either," Pauly said. "We slow down and maybe have to circle the islands before heading into the Glades. Five, there should be enough twilight."

We had close to an hour to go. Pauly hummed to himself, and the headset picked it up. Norm checked in but the distance between us didn't help the clarity. Doug hadn't expected us to be a couple of hundred miles apart when he set up the radio. Pauly and

I agreed Norm had said two guys were shot and Captain Jim Ashe had taken them to the medic on base. At least they weren't dead. Norm, Bob and Padre Thomas and the others had left the airport in the confusion following the jet's explosion. Most of the rest of the conversation broke up or was too muffled to understand.

"We will have a problem when we land," Pauly said.

Pauly's voice sounded as if he were on a bad phone line instead of a foot or so away, speaking into a headset mic. The loud engine noise made it impossible to talk without it.

"Problems only need a solution," I said and hoped there was some humor hidden in my comment.

"No solution for this problem."

"Great! What is it?" I knew there was no humor in my question.

"There's no cell phone coverage in the Glades, where we'll be."

"They gotta communicate somehow."

"Radio. No landline, no cell service."

"Maybe since you've been gone it's changed?" I could only hope. "How do we keep in touch with Norm? What if something changes?"

"We leave early tomorrow and check in as soon as we can make radio contact," Pauly said. "We'll be at least a half hour away, so if we got to abort, there's no problem."

I wanted to answer, but didn't, that we'd had nothing but problems since arriving in Key West. Off to the east, the blackness surrendered to the rising sun. Twilight couldn't get here soon enough.

Chapter Eighty-Three

Loud engine noise, I decided as Pauly flew so close to the water that I could see the swelling outlines the prop's motion caused on it, was like a bad relationship, in time you adjust. While Pauly circled the Ten Thousand Islands and tried to amuse me with stories of how, in his old life, he had survived worse situations than what we faced, I worried about Norm, Padre Thomas and the others. It was a waste of my time, since I wasn't in a position to do anything and wouldn't be for at least twenty-four hours. Knowledge may be power, but in my case, knowledge did little to keep me content, as the engine noise subsided while I escaped within myself.

The plane banked away from the islands and headed toward the sunrise.

"Can I help look for the landing?" I needed to do something.

"I know what I'm looking for, but, yeah, keep an eye out for a short road that goes nowhere."

I thought we'd been flying low, but Pauly showed me I was wrong as he brought the plane down to where I watched alligators slithering in the silt.

"Why so low?" I know I sounded concerned.

"Miami radar." Pauly avoided laughing at my nervousness. "No reason to chance it by being too high. I find the landing strip, I bring her down real quick, so stay buckled in."

As a sailor that's been in and out of Key West Harbor more times than I care to remember, I knew my way around the harbor well enough not to need a chart, but most other places that I've been to, I always checked charts. There was Pauly and, according to him, he's been out of the life for a while, flying into the chartless Everglades, looking for a smuggler's airstrip he hadn't used in years, and he knew he'd find it. Amazing belief in one's self, I realized.

The plane banked a few times as we made some kind of aeronautical grid across the Everglades. The gray of early morning allowed us to see the foliage of the swamp, watch the rivers and rivulets that wandered what was left of Florida's once vast wilderness.

"Three o'clock." Pauly's words crackled through the headset.

I looked toward my right, pulled from my reverie, knowing the nose of the plane was twelve o'clock, and just off the wing saw the short, very short I thought, runway.

"A hand glider couldn't land on that." I stared, trying to make the runway stretch.

"Ah, it's bigger than you think!" This time Pauly laughed. "See the house?"

"If you call it a house, I guess I see it." He circled the property tightly. I could see missing shingles on the shack's roof. "Where's the shed for the plane?"

"If you could see it, what purpose would it serve?"

The plane banked away from what Pauly called a runway, buzzed the house, and then turned and he began the approach. I watched over his shoulder as the ground rose up to meet us. When the wheels touched down, I half expected the plane would flip because it got stuck in the ooze. It didn't happen. I looked out the right side and all I could see was Everglades. The plane slowed and the green of the Glades seemed to go on forever. I checked the other side and saw two airboats tied off to a dock, but no runway. The plane took up the entire roadway, or, as Pauly called it, the runway.

As Pauly turned the plane around on the runway, all I saw was a wall of green.

"You got your rosary beads out yet?" The plane stopped, facing the direction we'd come in from.

I checked my wristwatch and it was 5:38 A.M. In twenty-four hours, we'd be back in Key West. But right then, we were in the bowels of the Everglades and two shirtless, barefoot men, carrying shotguns, walked from the house about fifty feet away.

"Friends of yours?" I said.

"You keep your gun ready, but out of sight if you get off

the plane." Pauly moved the top back, unbuckled himself from the safety harness, stood and waved to the men.

I looked at the two rednecks with shotguns and shoeless and wondered what Pauly meant by *if* I got off the plane?

Chapter Eighty-Four

The morning humidity of the Everglades swept in as Pauly slid the canopy back on the P-51 and got up. The air was sticky, a lot more so than the warmth of Key West. I began to sweat almost instantly and made myself a promise never to complain about Key West summers again.

Pauly climbed onto the wing and dropped to the pavement. One of the Bobbsey twins walked toward him, cradling the shotgun across his bare chest, while the other stood back, his shotgun resting on his shoulder, finger on the trigger.

"Marlon, Bernard, it's Pauly!" Pauly stopped by the end of the wing, kept in its shade, waved at the two men, and turned to me with his thumbs up. I doubt either of us felt that sure of the situation, but Pauly kept a good face.

The first man turned to his partner. "Shit brother, it's that redheaded spic!"

"You sure, Marlon.?" Bernard kept his finger on the shotgun's trigger.

Marlon moved closer. "Who you got with ya, another redheaded spic?"

"Marlon." Pauly laughed. "If you ever changed I think the world would end."

"Damn right it would." Marlon laughed and shook Pauly's hand. "That your bother?" He pointed to me. Pauly's strawberry blonde hair and my red hair looked alike to him.

"A friend," Pauly said. "Can he come down?"

"How long you figure on stayin'?"

Pauly looked at his wristwatch. "Less than twenty-four hours."

"Not like it used to be."

"Nothin' is, Marlon, nothin' is."

"Fuckin' government satellites probably already knows you're here."

"Ain't lookin' for me, yet." Pauly fell into their style of talk. "Maybe never will, if I'm as good as I think."

Pauly and Marlon laughed.

"What's so funny?" Bernard yelled.

"Can my buddy come down?" Pauly asked again.

"Unless he wants to sit up there waitin'."

Pauly signaled me to join them. I wasn't overly excited as I tucked my handgun into its holster, made sure my shirt covered it, and stood. I had hoped for a breeze or something as I got out of the cockpit, but it only got hotter.

When I reached Pauly, Bernard had joined him and Marlon, and the shotguns seemed more casually held, if that's possible. At least their fingers were off the triggers. Pauly introduced me and we shook hands as we walked away from the plane.

An air-conditioner purred from its window frame in the shack, but we sat on the porch. Once it might have been a comfortable, wraparound porch, but age and neglect had helped it deteriorate.

"Where you been? Jail?" Bernard said.

"Bernard!" Marlon scolded him. "It ain't none of your business. Mind your manners, Norm and Mick's guests."

"Just curious, is all." Bernard crunched up his face. "Don't mean nothin' by it."

"Truth be told, boys, I've been out of the business for a while," Pauly said. "And not because I was in jail."

"You get tired of working for the spics?" Marlon spit over the rail.

"Got tired of havin' to look over my shoulder all the time, yeah."

"Scary people," Bernard said.

"Don't hear much from runners anymore," Marlon added. "Seems they like boats not planes."

"No one comin' through?" Pauly stretched his legs and rested his feet on the rail.

"A few guys like you, once in a while," Marlon said. "They tell me to run grass they gotta use bigger planes because of bigger loads. Is it true?"

"Makes sense." Pauly nodded. "It's been five or six years,

but grass might've gone down in price, so a guy's gotta deliver more to stay even. Or maybe the price has gone up, so you deliver more 'cause you're greedy. Have you thought of makin' the runway longer? Deliver the grass here and use the airboats for deliveries to the side roads? Just like the old days!"

"Not really," Bernard said. "Don't like dealing with the spics."

In the silence that followed, I could hear sounds coming from the Everglades that I didn't recognize. Insects, I guessed, but I heard thrashing around and wondered if it was a gator or python. I didn't want to run into either.

"Why'd you stop here?" Marlon finally asked. "Out of fuel?"

Pauly laughed. "You ain't gonna believe it."

Marlon and Bernard stared at Pauly. I don't think there was much those two boys believed.

"Cigars." Pauly slapped my shoulder as if we were co-conspirators. "Right Mick?"

I nodded.

The two rednecks looked confused and I'm sure it wasn't the first time in their life.

"A guy is bringing in a shit pot full of Cuban cigars to Key West." Pauly began his cover story and I listened too. "I mean, he's filled his boat's cabin with them and one of his customers is an ICE agent, so he ain't worried about a customs check!"

"I believe it," moaned Bernard. "All them agents is crooks, if you got enough money to give 'em."

"Well, I agree, but that ain't my end of the stick," Pauly said. "Guys paying me $50 a box to fly his cigars to places like Atlanta and Raleigh. He says he's got one thousand boxes."

"In that?" Marlon pointed at the P-51.

"No, not that, not enough space."

"Didn't think so." Marlon smiled. "Seems like a lot of money for a box of cigars."

Pauly pointed to the plane. "That's my toy. But it got us

here too fast. That's why we stopped. The guy wants us at the Key West airport at five tomorrow morning and my toy . . ." Pauly hunched his shoulders. "It's too much fun to fly it at top speed. And I'm thinkin' of the payday on the whole flight."

"What do you need from us?" Marlon spit over the railing again.

"A couple of hours sleep where the skeeters won't get us, maybe something to eat and a cold drink."

Marlon looked at Bernard. Neither smiled.

"We don't got fuel," Bernard said.

"Don't need it," Pauly said again.

Marlon scratched his hairy chest. "We goin' gator hunting. Be gone a few hours, so you can sleep on the couch. Got two of 'em inside. You like gator burgers, that's dinner with cold beer."

"More than we could've hoped for." Pauly shook Marlon's hand. "Appreciate it and we ain't lookin' for charity."

"We ain't givin' any." Marlon's words were cold and tough. "Two thousand."

"Got a shower with everything, too?"

"*Me casa es su casa*, spic." Marlon and Pauly laughed.

"Could we get a couple of them beers now?"

Marlon and Bernard got up without responding and went into the shack. We stayed on the porch.

"What's with the spic shit?"

Pauly grinned. "They always called the Mexicans and Colombians spics and anyone that worked for them were spics, too. I laughed it off, back then. Some guys got insulted, made an issue of it, and I think they got used as bait on gator hunts."

"Good decision, *amigo*." I grinned as the Bobbsey twins came out, wearing shirts and work boots and carrying two cold beers.

"Be back in three hours," Marlon said. "Get some sleep."

Pauly and I swilled the cold beer and I swear the air-conditioner sounded as if it had been turned down.

Chapter Eighty-Five

The interior of the one-room shack didn't disappoint, but it held a few surprises. The air-conditioner looked new and Marlon or Bernard had turned it down low. I put it back on high. With the bare plank walls, gray with age and rot, the A/C had a tough job, but it was cooler than outside. The two couches looked better than I expected and mine was comfortable. That, or I was dog tired and my body didn't care. Large throw rugs with gaudy designs resembling ones I'd seen in Tijuana tourist shops covered the beaten down, exposed wood floor. Two tired ceiling fans that looked as old as the Everglades, circled loudly as they moved the air with deformed blades blackened with dust. Dirty windows did what they could to fight back the sunlight. The old, scruffy shack interior clashed with the few clean items within.

"There's new stuff in here for boys that aren't making money smuggling." Pauly looked around the room before he plunked himself down. "These couches weren't here a few years ago. Rugs neither and that's a new refrigerator." He pointed to a section of the shack that served as a kitchen.

"Maybe gator hunting pays better than smuggling." I lay down and let the cool air dry my damp body. I felt a chill and enjoyed it.

"It's not legal, so maybe you're right." Pauly lay across the couch.

I think even my dreams slept, because I don't recall a thing after Pauly mumbled something. I woke suddenly, thinking I heard airplanes. Maybe I had dreamt. Pauly sat up, too, and wiped the sleep from his eyes. I wasn't dreaming.

"Christ!" He jumped up and looked out a dusty window.

"What?"

"Airboats."

"Marlon and Bernard," I said.

"Probably, Mick, but they're not alone. Not with that much noise. Let's get out of here, now!" Pauly yelled.

I forced myself up and followed him out the door, running. The whirling motor noise became louder which meant closer. Pauly had started the P-51 by the time I got to it. I pushed myself up onto the wing as the plane started to taxi. Before I got inside, I heard gunshots. Even with the roar of the engine, the shots came across clearly. My headset lay in the seat and I snatched it as I sat.

"What the hell's going on?" I shouted into the mic.

"My guess would be Alexei's people." Pauly's voice hissed into my headset as the canopy slid over us. "Must be a good price on our heads."

"The Bobbsey twins?" I fastened my seat belt as the plane began to lift and then we were in the air. I had no doubt someone was still shooting at us.

Pauly banked the plane away from the shack and almost made a full circle. I heard the wheels lock up beneath us. "How many airboats?"

I looked toward the right wing and saw the creek where the shack's dock was. Four airboats below, tied off to the dock. I looked at my wristwatch it was almost 1:00 P.M.

"Four," I said. "How'd they get here so fast?"

Pauly took the plane higher and faster. I saw a group of men with rifles shooting toward us. Marlon and Bernard stood behind them.

"You got the wand?"

"You aren't going back there?" I picked the wand up off the floor and knew the answer.

"Give and take." Pauly laughed. He loved this macho bullshit, I didn't.

"We might be low on ammo." I didn't know that, but it sounded like it should give him second thoughts.

"Fuck it, Mick, I don't like being shot at or lied to . . . or betrayed. The assholes sold us for a bounty!" Pauly banked some more and I knew we were going in. "If we run out of ammo, I'll ram the terrorists' plane before I let it hit the cruise ship."

I believed him, but didn't say so. "How do you want to do it?"

"One pass, use five Mississippi count and we're out of here," he said. "We'll start in the yard where they are. When the bullets begin tearing up the ground, they'll be shittin' their pants and not shooting at us. The last rounds will go in the house. Five seconds, that's all."

"Tell me when." I held tightly onto the wand, afraid to get my thumb too close to the top button. The Everglades spread out before us, as I looked over Pauly's shoulder.

The plane started to descend, the engine noise seemed to get louder and the men shooting at us closer. Obviously, no one on the ground knew the P-51 was a fighter plane or armed.

"Remember, one Mississippi," Pauly said. "Now!"

I pushed down on the button. The two machine guns came to life. Even in daylight, I saw the quick flashes of explosive light follow the bullets. I could almost feel them burst out of the barrels in the wings. The men below scattered instantly. Some fell to the ground. I assumed they'd been shot. At the speed we were going, we flew over the fallen and those running probably at the same time as the bullets hit. The shack sped toward us as I fired and Pauly brought the nose of the plane up after we passed over it. I took my thumb off the button, turned and caught a glimpse as a piece of the roof caved in.

I laughed.

"What's so funny?" Pauly asked and flew over the scene again.

"Those rugs are dirty now," I said.

"The A/C's kind of useless too." We both laughed and briefly watched the men below run, thinking we'd shoot again. "Five seconds?"

"Yeah, I counted," I lied.

"So, in all, between the airport and here, we've shot less than a minute's worth of ammo, right?"

"I guess. Yeah, less than a full minute."

"We should be okay then."

"What are we gonna do for sixteen hours?" I knew we couldn't stay in the air because of fuel.

"Sugarloaf Airport," Pauly said. "No tower, and if no one's sky diving, probably deserted."

Chapter Eighty-Six

The realization of what had happened slowly sank in as Pauly flew the plane back toward the Keys. Two redneck smuggling-mules knew to contact the Russian Mafia when they recognized us. Well, not *us*, but Pauly. How far did the Russians' tentacles extend? I decided that there were no limits, no borders. How did you run from them? Them being Alexei, as far as I was concerned. You couldn't run far enough to be safe or long enough to be forgotten. I trembled with fear and excitement as the plane moved forward. Would my hunting Alexei turnaround and make me the hunted? Had it already? I was obviously in more danger, but also closer to Alexei.

"How long?" I adjusted my headset and spoke into the mic.

"You got some place to go?" Pauly's tone was playful.

I bit my tongue to hide my unease and laughed. "When we land, I need to call Norm."

"About an hour, maybe a little less. The Sugarloaf Lodge is next to the airport. We can get a room and some sleep. Tomorrow morning's a long way off."

"Leave the plane?" If something happened to the plane all our plans would be gone.

"You've never been to the airport?"

"I don't sky dive," I said. "I don't understand the reason for jumping out of a perfectly good airplane."

Pauly laughed. "At least you got a parachute when you jump."

"We still below radar?" I changed the subject.

"Hell, I ain't sure they've got radar in the Keys." Pauly continued to find humor in our predicament. "Think about it. Remember in '91, a Cuban MiG landed at the Naval Air Station and wasn't detected before landing? How secure's the air space around the Keys? That one plane could've destroyed the airbase and probably got to Miami before it was shot down. Luckily, the pilot wanted asylum."

"Comforting," I said.

"For a smuggler, it is!" He laughed.

The sky was pale blue, with a glowing afternoon sun on our right and a blue/green Gulf below. When we flew over boats, people on deck looked up and waved. Shrimpers didn't, maybe because they weren't shrimping.

"Do smugglers still use shrimp boats?" I wanted to keep my mind on something other than my fears.

"Not really," Pauly said. "Used to use 'em to offload grass from freighters in the '70s and '80s. Hell, there was a time in Key West where smuggling was more profitable than tourism is today."

"So I've heard. You were here then?"

"For some of it. Why?"

"The shrimpers didn't look happy when they saw us."

"They think we're checking them out. Maybe they shouldn't be in these waters, but on the other hand, shrimpers are not a trusting group, in general."

Norm's philosophy, distrust everyone and everything, I repeated it to myself.

The small mangrove islands began showing to the east and there were more pleasure boats below us. Pauly said we were in the Northwest Channel that boaters used to sail or motor up the west coast of Florida and then along the Gulf states to Texas. Of course, I knew that, but left it unsaid.

After a while, I caught glimpses of the paved, black string of US1, the only road in or out of the Keys. It continued to amaze me that Pauly flew without charts. He had to have an outstanding memory. I laughed to myself because I thought he'd better have an outstanding memory or we were screwed.

The islands got closer together and I recognized the Seven Mile Bridge. The plane moved a little to the west.

"Fifteen minutes and we'll be landing." Pauly's voice buzzed on my headset.

Every time I looked out, it surprised me how low we were. The plane raised a little and then banked east. I saw the Sugarloaf Lodge, a scattering of homes, some wetlands, mangroves and boulders, but I didn't see an airstrip. My seat belt was as tight as I could get it and I knew if I started peppering Pauly with questions, he'd only laugh. The wheels unlocked and went into landing position. I had to trust he knew what he was doing. The plane began its descent. There was water below us. Rocks in front. Mangroves to either side.

At the last minute, I saw the runway, as close to the water's edge and rocks as it could get. I breathed a sigh of relief.

"You okay?"

Damn mic, it picked up everything.

"Yeah," I said. "Just glad to be on the ground."

The plane touched down. I shouldn't have looked out, but I did and the runway seemed to be awfully short. I braced myself. The plane slowed, and then stopped. Pauly taxied between three smaller planes on a dirt patch off the runway. I supposed that smugglers were used to landing on short runways. I wasn't and probably never would be.

"Call Norm." The engine stopped and Pauly slid the hatch open.

"Do you think we can check how much ammo's left?" I climbed onto the wing.

"Wouldn't even know where to begin." Pauly worked with the instrument panel as he shut the plane down. "Better off to leave it alone. We know the guns work."

"Yeah." I dropped from the wing onto the ground. The air was still and hot. Only a faint hum from the traffic on US1 reached us. I dialed Norm. He answered on the second ring.

"You okay?" Is how he answered.

"Yeah. You?"

"We're all fine."

"We're at Sugarloaf Airport." I walked to the shade of a large tree. "Pauly said we're okay here until the morning. We might even get a room at the lodge."

"Great minds!" Norm yelled with a laugh. "We're at the Sugarloaf Lodge."

I looked at Pauly, as he closed the top of the cockpit and dropped to the ground. Did he know they were here?

"How come?" I couldn't think of anything else to say.

"We're out of Key West but it's only a half-hour to the port. We should be safe here for the night."

I told Norm what happened at the Everglades. He didn't seem surprised. Bob and Padre Thomas were with him. With everything coming down so drastically, he decided to let Doug leave. One of Pauly's men had died from wounds at the airport and one was still hospitalized. Jim Ashe's people came out okay and they were preparing to set up snipers positions around the harbor. He hadn't heard from Richard Dowley.

"Didn't really expect to," Norm said. "He needs deniability in case this all goes to hell."

I told Pauly where everyone was and then that one of his men had died. He took the phone.

"Who died?" Pauly said to Norm. He nodded. "Ross Thomas was a good guy." He handed the phone back to me. "I owe Alexei, too."

Norm had hung up.

"Get in line," I said. "What now?"

"A short walk to the lodge."

"The plane's okay here?" I looked around. There were three houses at the far end of the so-called runway. Water behind us, swamp to our left and right. A narrow road ahead, we took the road.

"At worst one of the regulars might check the tail numbers and Freddy's name comes out and they can't reach him, but they know him. The plane will be okay."

We passed tennis courts on our right and by then we heard the traffic on US1. The lodge was on our left. We booked two adjoining rooms. We didn't care but the clerk thought we'd like rooms with a water view. We thanked him and went looking for Norm and the others.

We found them at the Tiki Bar and Norm had two cold beers waiting for us.

"Padre Thomas called out your approach as you flew in." Norm pointed to the clear view of the Gulf of Mexico. "Said it was you, anyway."

Padre Thomas smiled, a cigarette in one hand and his Budweiser in the other.

Bob raised his beer. "Sorry about Ross."

Pauly took a long pull on his beer. "Thanks. Was it quick?"

Bob nodded. "I was feet away and he was gone when I reached him. I shot the bastard that hit him."

"Thanks, again." Pauly raised his half-empty bottle to Bob. "I'm hungry."

"Mangrove Mama's." I looked at Norm. "You driving something?"

"Yeah." He finished his beer. "The rental company's gonna give me an employee discount soon."

"It'll be all over this time tomorrow," Pauly said. "One way or another."

We all stared at him.

"We're gonna pull it off," he said. "Don't look at me that way. Come on, we're here, the plane's here and the guns work. What could go wrong?"

We finished our beers without responding and left for Mangrove Mama's.

Chapter Eighty-Seven

Norm and Bob gave brief comments about what our aerial attack at the airport looked and sounded like on the ground, and how they were all able to escape the scene before the sheriffs arrived. The airport fire department was there minutes after the jet exploded and the added pandemonium aided in their mixing within the airport crowd and getting out. They got to the parking lot with the wounded and dead and Captain Jim Ashe took responsibility for Pauly's two guys.

We ate and had another beer, while we discussed our plan for the morning, at Mangrove Mama's restaurant on US1.

"I'll be in contact with Ashe," Norm said. "He'll have spotters on the hotel rooftops and snipers on the two offshore islands. I still think the plane will make a direct shot toward the ship from between the two islands."

"We need to know as soon as the plane's spotted." Pauly finished his beer and refused a new one. "We're going to be out by the college, circling that end of Stock Island and can intercept the plane within a minute."

"Ashe has someone watching the radar and there won't be much air traffic at that hour. With the radios Doug left, you'll be hearing everything I do. When I hear from Ashe, you will too." Norm pushed his empty plate aside. "You okay on fuel?"

"Plenty for what we need to do. Am I gonna run into a problem getting back to the airport?" Pauly said.

"Get to the airport and get out. A car will meet you at the gate." Norm ordered coffee. "We need to decide on a time."

"I'll leave Sugarloaf at five-thirty."

"We'll leave at five-thirty." I corrected Pauly. He may not have been a team player as a smuggler, but this time he and I were a team.

"*We'll* fly out to the cut at the reef and see if the cruise ship is on schedule." Pauly nodded in my direction. "If we're lucky and see the plane too, it goes down there."

"Radar will show where the plane is coming from," Norm

said. "Wherever it is, it should go down as soon as possible and if it's away from land and witnesses, even better."

Everyone agreed. The sooner the better.

"Ashe and JSOC have been checking satellite feeds and can't find an unidentified airplane. So far, they all have flight plans," Norm said. "Some think the plane's in Cuba, others think it's on one of the cays off the Bahamas."

"Too far way." Pauly asked for a glass of water. "They want to do this, good weather or bad, so they're closer than that. A squall could screw up the air traffic between here and the islands."

"I agree." Norm asked for a refill. "Don't suppose there was a twin engine where you landed."

Pauly laughed. "Wouldn't that have been nice?"

My cell phone chirped and I saw Richard's name on the screen. "Richard." I walked out of the restaurant through the back patio and into the small parking lot.

"Don't tell me where you are." Richard's voice was calm but his words said caution. "You okay?"

"Yeah. Thanks. You?"

"I've had better days, Mick. I've got some news for you and none of it's good."

"I'm listening." I walked in circles around a parked camper and cars.

"The bad news is, Homeland Security has a BOLO out for you, Norm and Pauly for the disaster at the airport and an air piracy charge too. They spent half the morning in my office with a million questions."

"Air piracy?" That one surprised me.

"They say you stole Freddy Cabanas' P-51." I heard Richard take a deep breath. "Tell me that's not true."

"I can't."

"Norm somehow got the wing-guns working?" It wasn't really a question, so I left it unanswered. "You're going to shoot the other plane down?" Another non-question that I didn't answer. "Are you sure about this?" Richard's common sense still had doubt, but his policeman's gut knew the diary was honest. Now, the added mistrust of a government agency ate away at him.

"Richard, someone, probably in Homeland Security, is keeping the attack information on the cruise ship from reaching the right people. Tell me you believe that." I waited for him to reply. It took a few beats.

"Yeah," he sighed. "And I think I know why that cruise ship is the target."

"This is where the bad news gets worse?"

Richard's turn not to answer me. "I met the Secret Service agents this afternoon at Mallory Square. It seems President and Mrs. Clinton are special guests of the cruise company and plan to get off the ship and see a little of Key West. He's friends with cruise line board members and it's a great publicity stunt. National coverage, guaranteed."

"You're just finding this out?" I couldn't believe an ex-president's visit to the island would be kept from the local police chief. "Who's doing security? The ship's here for six hours."

"Secret Service agents did a walk through around Front Street and Duval, with the usual stops, Sloppy Joe's, Smokin' Tuna, Hog's Breath and a T-shirt shop or two and he wants to tour the Custom House Museum."

"Did you tell them . . ."

Richard didn't let me finish. "I asked if they had any safety concerns for the president or the ship. They wanted to know why I asked."

"What did you tell them?"

"I told them that we were always concerned for the passengers' safety and even more so now that I knew the president was onboard. They told me only a few people knew about the president's trip."

"Homeland Security knows?" I knew the answer.

"Top intelligence officials were briefed weeks ago and no rumor of possible threats to either the president or the cruise ship to report."

"We know better, Richard," I said. "You know the president's trip information trickled down to those that have kept the terrorist information from moving up?"

"I don't like it, Mick. I'm not a conspiracy believer."

"Do you have a better answer?"

"No and that's what's bothering me." Richard went silent for a moment. "I'll have Robert and his team on a boat and one other team out there at sunrise. Two crews, but it's real difficult to get a clean shot from a boat."

"You won't have to." I wanted it to reassure him, but it didn't.

Chapter Eighty-Eight

On the five-minute ride from Mangrove Mama's to the Sugarloaf Lodge, I told everyone what Richard had said about the ex-president being on the cruise ship. I've known Norm a long time and have never seen him so agitated because of information he'd received. I could tell from his lack of comment that something bothered him. Norm's not a quiet guy, never.

"You got something to say?" We'd pulled into the lodge's parking lot and I wanted to know what bothered him.

"Think about it." Norm's words had hardness to them. He locked the SUV. "You're suggesting that someone, more than one actually, if what Richard said is true, in the intelligence community is purposely allowing a terrorist attack on a cruise ship with an ex-president and his wife onboard. An attack that could kill hundreds."

"In a nutshell, yeah. We know our information on the attack has gone nowhere."

"It's not a nutshell," Norm growled as he nodded his head, unhappy at acknowledging the idea. "It's a wide net that includes accepting the possibility of a second shooter on the knoll in Dallas, and all the conspiracy theories about Bobby Kennedy, Martin Luther King and I am sure it's an endless list that includes visits by little green men at Roswell."

"You're forgetting another scenario," Bob said, as we walked behind the lodge and sat in beach chairs looking out at the bay, with music from the Tiki Bar in the background. "Coincidence."

Norm stared hard at Bob. "I don't believe in coincidence."

"Doesn't mean it don't happen." Bob stared back.

I turned to Padre Thomas as he lit a cigarette. "Padre, do you have anything to add to this?"

"Give me a break!" Bob said.

"No." Padre Thomas took a deep drag of his cigarette. "Only that you have to stop that plane."

Night was about to force the last of twilight into the Gulf

of Mexico. The five of us sat in silence. My head spun with concerns about tomorrow. I had questions upon questions but no answers. The answers were less than twelve hours away.

"I think I agree with Bob. Coincidence." Pauly lit a cigarette. "The president didn't decide to take a cruise at the last minute and the Iranians didn't just plan this suicide mission. The plan to attack the cruise ship took a lot more time than it did to plan the president's trip."

Norm agreed but did so slowly. "Yeah. The Iranians had to come up with the idea and then a location. They don't grow their own suicide bombers, so they go to Hezbollah. The plan involved the Mexicans and the Iranians didn't pull that out of a hat. Someone put a lot of thought and planning into this to distance Tehran from the aftermath."

"So, whoever sanctioned this attack from our government . . ."

"No one sanctioned this!" Norm didn't let Pauly finish. "Some assholes are trying to pull this off. It's not government-sanctioned policy."

"Norm, I didn't mean the White House or Langley." Pauly dropped the cigarette butt and held his hands up in surrender. "I meant, some people in an agency, probably have to be more than one agency, have sanctioned the attack and are pulling the strings to make it happen."

"With enough authority to make us fugitives," I said.

"I know guys in Homeland Security, worked with them," Norm grumbled, unhappy with his thoughts. "Good men and they wouldn't do this. Pancho? Do you think Pancho is involved?"

Captain Francisco 'Pancho' Santos, is the Coast Guard commander in the Keys and we all know and like him. I'd given him a copy of Alexei's diary.

"No I don't think he's involved," I said. "But that's a personal decision. What about your philosophy, trust no one, trust nothing?"

"You know anyone in the Secret Service?" Pauly lit another cigarette and so did Padre Thomas.

"Yeah," Norm mumbled.

"What would they do ahead of time for Clinton's visit?" Pauly moved closer to Norm.

"They'd have a car close by, maybe a police car, they'd have the local hospital on standby, with its best people in the O.R." Norm closed his eyes as he recited. "They have a number of routes out of the area to the hospital. Close locations of safety in case of gunfire, places they could defend."

"Not quick exit in Key West," Bob said. "North Roosevelt is dug up and one-way, Flagler is jammed all day with people leaving the island."

"Chopper." Norm opened his eyes. "Probably Coast Guard or Navy."

"Clear Mallory Pier and they could land one there," I said.

"Would do it ahead of time, be there before the ship came in." Norm looked at Bob. "Coincidence?"

"Richard didn't mention anything about a helicopter," I said. "You can't keep that a secret. Everyone's gonna see a helicopter at Mallory and they'd need the police to clear the area, especially the homeless at that hour."

"Say, for argument's sake, that this is coincidence. Whoever is keeping the attack off the books, now knows the ex-president's on the ship. Clinton will get media attention for stopping in Key West. If the ship he's on became a terrorist's target, that's worldwide news." Norm's expression grew darker.

"A win-win for both sides," I said. "The terrorists get world media coverage and all the intelligence agencies keep their budgets, maybe even get increases."

"You're forgetting the passengers," Norm said. "Some are gonna die and those that don't have to go through life reliving the horror. That's not a win-win for them."

"Well," Pauly stood. "We're gonna have to fuck up the bad guy's day, ain't we?"

Chapter Eighty-Nine

Pauly and I had adjoining rooms. Norm's was down a few doors and Bob and Padre Thomas shared a room at the end of the hall. Norm still had concerns about the colonel, especially after Doug had stabbed him, so it became Bob's responsibility to protect Padre Thomas. I couldn't have come up with that combination.

Norm knocked on my door at five A.M., then on Pauly's. We were both awake and ready. I'm not sure how restful what little sleep I got was, but nervous tension promised to keep me wide-awake for the next few hours.

Padre Thomas popped up in the hall without Bob. He wished us luck and pulled me aside.

"You'll do what you have to do, Mick," he whispered. "Have faith, you'll be okay." He placed the palm of his hand above my forehead, whispered a blessing, and went back to his room.

It was too early in the morning and I was too anxious to make sense of his words or blessing.

We didn't bother to check out of the lodge. Norm drove us the short distance to the airport and no one mentioned Padre Thomas. A gray dawn had pushed most of the night out, but Norm still drove with the lights on. The P-51 was where we left it. Shadows and darkness covered the small airfield. The rock border, at the water's edge, poked eerily from the fading night.

"I talked to Jim Ashe earlier." Norm stood with us by the plane. "Nothing on radar."

"If this was a perfect day for us, they would've called it off," Pauly said.

"Perfect days are like coincidences." The shadows almost hid Norm's grin. "Rare."

"Where are you going to be?" I'd never asked Norm what he'd be doing during all this.

"I'll be covering your asses." He laughed and slapped Pauly on the shoulder. "Shoot the bastards down, hoss, get to the airport and the car will be waiting."

His murky attitude from last night had vanished, or he kept it well hidden so it wouldn't affect the job we all had to do.

"To take us where?" He hadn't told me that either.

"I've arranged some faster transportation off the island." Norm said. "Good luck." He walked to the SUV.

I got into the plane, followed by Pauly, who did whatever pilots do at the instrument panel. He spoke the procedure aloud to himself. It meant nothing to me. The engine started and it must've woken up everyone in the houses by the runway and maybe at the lodge too. Pauly cranked the canopy closed and we began to move. My eyes had adjusted to the night and I saw the rocks at the end of the runway more clearly. When the plane lifted off, I swear I could've stuck my arm out and touched them. Once in the air, the wheels locked in upright position, tucked in tight to the belly of the plane. From rocks in front of us, we went to black water beneath us. I put my headset on and hoped to hear from Norm or Captain Jim Ashe.

I heard Pauly announce his take off over the headset and ask about other air traffic. Nothing came back. The plane kept climbing as it banked eastward.

"Flying on radar?" I was curious.

"They're gonna be flying low, so we'll fly high." Pauly explained the change in altitude and attitude. "They'll be focusing on the cruise ship, so we might go unseen until we're on the fuckers and shooting."

Sounded like a plan to me.

Pauly circled Sand Key but we saw no other planes and received no chatter on the radio. He pointed out the large, white cruise ship as the sun rose behind it off to the east. The ship had entered the channel looking like a floating island. Tugboats would take over on the last legs of the slow trip to Key West, helping the ship maneuver the narrow channel safely.

We kept flying eastward. Then turned south and finally westward and headed back to the island. The cruise ship made slow progress in the channel and it looked as if the sun might win the race to pier. We saw no other air traffic and heard no planes talking up their approach to or departure from Key West International Airport.

Pauly kept the plane high and made wide circles that took in Stock Island and the backcountry. It was almost six-thirty when the cruise ship approached the harbor.

"Spotters have noted the ship," Norm's voice warbled into the headset. "Ashe says you're on radar with some morning flights from Key West."

Pauly thanked him and said we had no visuals of other planes.

The rising sun reflected off the clouds and rippling harbor water. The ship was less than a half hour from docking at the hotel's pier. We could see movement at Mallory Square, but no helicopter. Two Coast Guard patrol boats wandered the harbor waters and stopped to talk briefly with the Key West Police boats' crews, while charter boats headed toward the Gulf Stream.

"Look to the southeast." Norm's voice carried urgency. "Southeast of the two islands."

Pauly took the plane higher and turned east. The sun cut our vision. Why hadn't anyone thought of that, coming at the ship with the sun behind it made it less likely to be seen. We put on our sunglasses and they helped but only a little against the sun's glare.

The tugboats pushed the bow and stern of the cruise ship into the dock. Men and women on the pier waited for the ship's crew to toss lines. The Coast Guard and police boats were prepared to stop traffic on the water, if it got too close. Only we paid attention to the twin-engine plane heading toward the cruise ship.

"Do you see it, Mick?"

"Yeah, Pauly, it's going to turn between the islands." Off in the distance it looked similar to the plane we saw in Tampico, Mexico.

"Once the ship's against the dock, it's a stationary target," Pauly said. "Norm called it."

"How long till they attack?"

"Go after it," Norm's voice bellowed over the headset. "You see it, go after it!"

"Yes sir!" Pauly mimicked Norm's shout.

Pauly flew higher and circled around as he headed toward the terrorists' twin-engine plane. It got bigger as it headed toward Sunset Key and Christmas Tree Island, and we got closer. We followed from above, the sun no longer an obstacle to our sight.

"How do we do this?" I said.

"I'm gonna dive down from above," Pauly said. "I'll tell you when. I want to make sure we're lined up right. No need to count this time. Keep shooting till the guns are empty, Mick."

"What if it doesn't go down?" The thought must have occurred to all of us at some point.

"I'll drop lower and you can shoot from the rear side. Okay? It'll go down!"

"Always looking for the alternative."

"My flyin' or your shootin' in question?" Pauly laughed.

"Where are you? Where are you?" Norm's voice crackled. "ETA."

"Two minutes," Pauly said. "They're gonna be close to the two islands when we hit them."

"Snipers are on the islands," Norm said.

Anchored boats of the live-aboards around and behind Christmas Tree Island no longer looked small and I could see people on their decks and on the charter boats. The cruise ship was so damn big the terrorists couldn't miss hitting it.

"Subject's plane will be in the drink in three minutes," Pauly said.

Pauly begin the approach as the terrorist's plane flew below us and toward the cruise ship. I held the wand in my hand and tried to keep from shaking.

I followed the diving nose of the P-51 as it drew closer to the target plane, from over Pauly's shoulder. The engine shrieked and the noise penetrated my headset.

With the wave of his hand, Pauly told me to shoot. I saw the other plane growing larger and pushed the button on the wand. I held it down and watched as bullets ripped into the twin-engine plane's fuselage and wings. The damaged plane lowered, but kept moving forward. I hadn't hit either engine. I pushed the bottom, again. Nothing!

"It's stopped!" I yelled.

"Shit!" Pauly pulled up quickly and banked east, causing the P-51 to shudder. He lowered the plane to the same level as the terrorists'. "There has to be ammo. Try again," he shouted as we approached from behind.

I pushed the button. Nothing! I slapped the wand against my palm and pushed the button but nothing happened. Slapped it against the fuselage, pressed the button.

"Nothing!" I yelled.

Pauly banked away and picked up speed as he turned again, this time at an angle to the other plane's tail.

"When we hit the water, get the fuck out of here." He cranked opened the canopy and air rushed in with a fury. "We're gonna collide!"

The P-51 picked up speed as Pauly angled in on the tail of the other plane. I didn't have time to cuss or react in the seconds it took the prop of the P-51 to tear into the plane's tail section. The P-51 pushed against the other plane and I felt and then heard the impact of the nose propeller, forcing its way through tail. The prop shredded into pieces, sending shrieking and grating sounds into the open cockpit, on contact. The twin-engine plane turned to the left, bounced uncontrollably and began a rapid decline to the harbor. The cacophony of the collision rattled around in my head, mixed with the rush of air. I looked toward the instrument panel and its million gauges and switches. Pauly used two hands on the stick, trying to keep the plane on an angled descent. I forgot to pray. We were going down. I didn't have time to see what happened to the other plane.

I looked up from Pauly's shoulder and the instrument panel. The harbor raced to meet us, its water shimmering with morning sun. The best he could do kept us at a forty-five degree angle of descent. An angle that would put us nose first into the water. He wanted a belly landing, but the falling plane wouldn't cooperate.

"Prepare!" Pauly screamed, pulling on the stick. "We'll

flip!"

There were only small pieces of spinning prop to blur my view, so I saw the sun's reflection on the water a second before the nose of the plane hit like it had fallen from the Empire State Building. The noise was indescribable. My body recoiled from the shock waves of the impact and it hurt like hell. It may have been water, but when the plane hit it, it had the strength of concrete.

The P-51 seemed to balance on its nose for a nanosecond and then flipped over. Instead of air rushing in, water flooded the cockpit. I tore off the headset and had to use my pocketknife to cut myself out of the seatbelt. I saw Pauly moving. His seatbelt was jammed shut too and had Pauly trapped. I pushed myself forward. I wanted to breathe, but knew I couldn't. I cut into the seatbelt at Pauly's shoulder. He turned and pointed upward. The plane was sinking. I shook my head and kept slicing. The belt split and Pauly forced himself out of the plane. I followed behind him. He turned once to make sure I was there. I wanted to breathe.

The last thing I remember was Pauly swimming toward me. The P-51 hit bottom, thirty feet below and I don't know what happened next.

Chapter Ninety

Noise rattled around in my head as I regained consciousness. I opened my eyes and dazzling sunlight forced me to shut them. Wrenching sounds echoed in my ears. I slowly reopened my eyes, pre-warned about the brightness, and squinted at what I faced. Water moved rapidly beneath me. I was leaned over the rail of a Coast Guard boat, dry heaving. My throat hurt, raw from the attempts to vomit. The rest of my body pulsed with pain. My head ached as if I'd battered a door down with it. The midair collision and crash had left a dull ringing in my ears. The quick motion through the water didn't help my nausea or aches, but the movement of the boat chilled me in my wet clothing and that I welcomed.

I turned, knowing there was nothing left to barf, and sat on the boat's damp deck with an intermittent hacking cough. Pauly sat across from me, smiled and nodded. I hoped that meant all we'd just gone through had brought success to our mission. I looked past Pauly and saw the large, white cruise ship safely at its slip. A Key West Police patrol boat raced along behind us.

I leaned against the orange padding that ran along the rail, making the 20-something-foot boat, with a pivoting machine gun mounted at the bow, look like an oversized inflatable. We sped past a large seawall and I knew we were entering the Coast Guard basin. When I went to stand the Coasty closest to me shook his head. I sat back down. The boat slowed and pulled next to a narrow finger slip.

The Key West Police boat pulled up on the opposite side of the slip. Both boats tied off and the two Coasties helped us off. We walked unsteadily up the ramp. Pancho stood at the top. He didn't look happy to see us.

"There's a chopper here to take you to the airport." Pancho's words barely squeaked into my buzzing ears, but I understood them. He moved closer to me and away from Pauly. "There's some pissed-off men waiting for you there, Mick. I think what you did was crazy. Heroic, in a sense, but crazy."

"Letting that plane crash into the cruise ship would've

been crazy." My words sounded muffled, even to me, because of my messed up hearing. "I wasn't being heroic, Pancho, but I am angry about how this had to come down."

"If the group waiting for you has its way, you'll be in Gitmo tomorrow and then you'll have a reason to be angry." I'd never seen him look so serious. "Be prepared for some heavy shit coming down, Mick." Pancho pointed toward the parade grounds were the helicopter waited.

The black chopper had no markings. I looked back toward the dock and the police officers had not been allowed to leave the slip. Coasties moved Pauly and me toward the chopper.

"Unmarked," Pauly said. "Ain't a good sign." He helped me in and then followed. Pauly looked none the worse from the crash and seemed to be hearing fine.

Two large men met us inside, black cargo pants, T-shirts, and muscles, and pointed to seats. One closed the door as we buckled up. I heard a soft swishing of the blades as we lifted off and wondered how long before I could hear properly.

No one spoke. Two of the men came to our seats and quickly tie wrapped our hands. It caught me off guard and I didn't even have time to protest. The man faintly said, "Orders," and went back to his seat. I looked at Pauly and he wasn't smiling.

Norm was supposed to have a car waiting for us at the airport to take us away from all this, instead the restrained hands made me feel like a criminal. It wasn't what I'd been expecting, even with Pancho's warning.

It only took minutes before we landed at Key West airport, close to Freddy Cabanas' hangar. The area where planes tied down, now served as a helipad. Pauly and I were pulled from our seats and dropped onto the tarmac. The chopper took off as we stood there, staring at the men outside Freddy's hangar.

I had an uneasy feeling as I looked at them. Soldiers with weapons at the ready, men in civilian clothing but with military haircuts and others that I knew would look out of place anywhere. Maybe spooks or Homeland Security aces. They spoke in small groups, but I couldn't hear them.

"Not much of a welcoming committee," Pauly said.

"I think they lean more toward a lynch mob."

Pauly looked around. "Where's the cavalry?"

We were both looking for Norm. "These guys are circling the troops," I said trying to sound macho.

Pauly pointed his bound hands toward the colonel as he broke from the group and walked toward us.

The colonel ignored Pauly and grabbed my shoulder. His grip hurt. "I'm going to enjoy interrogating you at Gitmo, shit for brains," he spit the words into my ears. "Do you know what you've done? You've given the terrorists a pass to run wild, to kill Americans. All your liberal bullshit thinking is going to get people killed. You just gave the Iranians the bomb!"

I wasn't sure what he was saying or what he meant. Pauly and I had saved the lives of innocent people on the cruise ship and maybe the life of an ex-president.

The colonel took deep breaths and then brought me in closer to continue his outrage, his breath hot and stale on my face. I'm not sure why, but I tightened my hands into a half-assed fist and swung with all I had and low-punched him in the stomach, hoping that was where Doug had stabbed him. From the shocked look on his face, I must have come close. He let go of me grabbed at his stomach and bent over. I hoped it hurt like hell and wished he'd gone to his knees.

Someone ran from the edges of the half circle and helped the colonel walk away. He turned once and I knew he was already figuring a way to get even. He knew my weaknesses.

A man walked toward us, ramrod straight, in civilian clothing. His weary face showed age, but I couldn't guess it. Late 50s or early 60s, maybe. His eyes were a ne'er-do-well brown and gray mixed with his faded blond hair. I looked around the tarmac again, then the hangar, but didn't see Norm.

"The colonel isn't a fan," the man said. His tone was cold but his words came out evenly with no emotion. "You've saved a few lives today. Maybe at the cost of your own."

Pauly and I looked at each other. We'd just been threatened.

"Who are you?" Pauly's words came hard.

We both stood there, dripping seawater and looking like drowned rats.

"Someone you didn't want to know." There was no smile just a robotic response. "I've got to clean up this mess." He turned to the hangar and the people milling around outside it. He pointed. "They're calling for blood. You've embarrassed them. A year of planning fucked to pieces by you two assholes. They were ready with the proof to connect the Iranians to this attack and Washington would've turned a blind eye, maybe even winked, when the Israelis nuked the bastards back to sand dunes and camels."

"At what cost?" I heard myself clearly, so I probably yelled. Pauly turned to me before I'd finished. "They were innocent people on that boat."

"War kills without discrimination," the man said. "Hemingway wrote after the First World War that politicians who declare war should have to fight it. But they don't." He ran his hands through his hair. "Politicians still make the decisions and it's men like me that have to decide the tactics. Sometimes, in war, innocent people die. No solider wants that, but it's unavoidable."

"Tell me, how does a terrorists' attack on a cruise ship, one you know about ahead of time, become unavoidable?" I said.

The man smiled but it was not comforting. He was one rung up the ladder from the colonel. He blew out a deep breath. "You are both under arrest for acts of internal terrorism." His face tightened. "You are under the jurisdiction of the U.S. Army and a military court will decide your enemy combatant status."

Pauly looked around. I did too. Where was Norm?

Chapter Ninety-One

His words came at me like a nightmare you can't wake up from. Some were clear and others difficult to understand because of my hearing, but the meaning came across, as it was supposed to.

"I wanna make my phone call," I said. "I'm an American citizen and have the right to a phone call."

His weary face brightened for an instant, like a sadist's before a ritual, I imagined. "Looking at you two, I'm guessing your cell phones are ruined. But, please, feel free to use them."

"There's a phone in the hangar office," Pauly said.

"Yes, there probably is, but we aren't going to the hangar. Also, I doubt very much there'll be a phone where you are going." He signaled and two soldiers came forward. "These men will escort you to the helicopter."

Pauly and I struggled to stay our ground as the men grabbed us. At about the same time we heard sirens and watched as police and sheriff cars raced into the parking area.

Someone wearing a gray suit broke from the crowd, ran to the man and quietly spoke to him. Police lights flashed, sending bursts of colored light over the area, and the sirens wailed and then went silent as officers got out of the cars. The flashing lights stayed on. I saw Richard step out of one car.

"You're a federal agent, for chrissake," the man yelled. "Don't let them in the gate, show them your badge. Use your authority, that's what it's for!"

The civilian in the suit rushed back toward the private terminal gate.

"Embarrassing, sometimes, who you have to work with," the man said. "Don't bother thinking the local law can help you. You're going to get on that helicopter one way or another. Unhurt, or with broken bones. The choice is yours."

Pauly and I said nothing but continued to be uncooperative.

"Let me explain it to you this way, you tossed the dice in this game and they came up snake eyes, you lose," he said. "I win."

"General!" a voice shouted from behind us. "You can't win the game without tossing the dice yourself."

We all turned at the sound. Behind us stood Vice Admiral Howard Bolter, a man I met once before with Norm. He was dressed in civilian clothing but the two dozen men backing him up wore green military fatigues and carried assault weapons. They had crept up behind us and caught everyone off guard because our attention had been focused on the police cars and the flashing lights.

For a brief second, maybe less, the general's composure lessened on seeing the admiral. He quickly recovered and signaled his men to stop.

"Pleasant surprise, admiral," he said without moving.

"Surprise, I'm sure," Bolter said as Norm walked up next to him. "I'm not sure it's pleasant for any of us."

The sudden silence sounded much too loud. Both men stared at each other and the looks they shared chilled me, and I think I shivered. What went through their minds at that moment will always remain a mystery.

"You seem to have two of my men in custody, general," Bolter said.

"You don't have jurisdiction is this, admiral," the general said. "These men are terrorists and I've placed them under arrest."

"Ah, general, you just rolled snake eyes!" Bolter and Norm moved closer. "These men risked their lives to keep cruise ship passengers safe. Maybe even saved the ex-president's life. I can document that they are working for me."

Norm moved forward and the two men sent to move us stood firm.

"You don't want to do this, general." Bolter nodded to Norm and he continued to move toward us.

The general signaled his men to stand down. Norm cut the restraints from our hands.

"You might be interested in this." Bolter handed the general a sheet of paper. "My office wrote up a press release for you and faxed it to me. It basically says a joint military and Homeland Security operation kept a terrorist plane from crashing into a cruise ship."

The general read the document to himself.

"You can add to it the connection between the terrorists and Iran if you wish, or not," Bolter said.

The general dropped the document and turned to walk away.

"And general, I am playing golf with the president this weekend and he'll want a full report." There was a trace of satisfaction in his voice. "I would issue the press release and then look into filing retirement papers, if I were you."

The general met with his men, while Richard, the police and sheriff deputies entered the area through the turnstile.

Pauly hit Norm on the shoulder. "Could you cut it any closer?"

Norm smiled. "I had to wait for the admiral's plane to arrive."

Those men I thought were spooks or Homeland Security walked to the parking lot and drove off. The general and his men got in the helicopter and flew away.

No exchange of words between either side.

"That's it?" Everyone's leaving surprised me.

"What did you expect, Mr. Murphy," Bolter said. "We saved your lives. Isn't that enough?"

I looked at Norm and Pauly. "They were going to let Americans die. And for what?"

"They would use the aftermath just like the terrorists planned to, to sway public opinion," Bolter said. "They've tracked this whole operation. They needed the news coverage of the death and destruction to go after the Iranians. To them, the attack was a minor event. Think about the coverage the Boston bombing got. This would've been a thousand times more and the American public would have clamored for blood."

"Why not stop it?" I shouted. "The FBI has done it a number of times."

Richard came to us and watched the helicopter take off.

"Admiral," Richard said. "This over?"

"Yes, Chief. The SEALs will raise the planes with air packs, once they determine it's safe. If one doesn't blow up, a barge will take both planes to Boca Chica. The Coast Guard will control harbor traffic."

"Do I need to be concerned, sir?"

"No Chief and thanks for the distraction."

"The least I could do, sir. If you want, I can throw these two in jail." Richard didn't smile.

"For stupidity, maybe," the admiral grinned. "For bravery, they'll receive my thanks."

Chapter Ninety-Two

Admiral Bolter thanked Pauly and me, again, and welcomed *me* to the fight against terrorism. I didn't bother to tell him my fight was with Alexei, not some jihadist. He assured us that the BOLO for our arrest had gone away and we could return safely to wherever we wanted. His plane and two helicopters were at the passenger terminal. That explained how they'd arrived without anyone noticing. Once the admiral and helicopters had taken off, the terminal's air traffic returned to normal. He had closed the airspace, just in case the general hadn't been cooperative. I didn't want to think about that.

Pauly made a call from the hangar and someone picked him up. He offered us a ride and looking like a half-drowned tramp, I was glad to accept it. Norm and I piled in with him.

Norm gave Tita's address to the driver and no one spoke after that, either. I had a million questions but had to sort through them before I asked for the answers. Pauly said he'd catch up with us after a hot shower and change of clothing, as he dropped us off.

Bob and Padre Thomas were inside the house when we arrived. They all wanted to know about the flight. I explained what happened at the Everglades, the Bobbsey twins, the Russians showing up and our escape. I gave what details I could remember about shooting at the twin-engine plane and how it kept flying toward the cruise ship. Autopilot, Norm assured me.

Finally, I told them what it was like as Pauly flew the P-51 Mustang into the tail of the other plane, the indescribable noise on impact and the few seconds we had to prepare because Pauly couldn't make a belly landing in the harbor. I remembered hitting the water, and how the impact felt like connecting with concrete, and said so.

I begged off after that, still damp from the crash and took a shower. Even though I had the water as hot as I could take, I felt as if I'd been swallowed in an avalanche.

I dressed in cargo shorts and a Smokin' Tuna Saloon,

North of Havana, Cigar Social Club T-shirt. I walked out of the guest room, barefoot, and found my friends sitting at the kitchen table with beers. It made me realize the afternoon had snuck up.

Padre Thomas got me a Harp from the fridge and I sat at the table. I took a long swallow and knew they were waiting for me to say something. I finished the beer.

"How could it happen, Norm?" I looked at him.

"A lot's happened in the last few days, hoss." His answer was elusive. "What *it* are you talking about?"

I laughed. I didn't mean to and it wasn't a laugh that followed a joke. "What *it*?" I yelled.

Padre Thomas stood, got behind me and placed his hands on my shoulders. "You don't yell at friends, Mick." His spoke softly.

I looked up and thanked him with a nod of my head. "How'd the last two weeks happen, Norm? How'd a handful of assholes keep the documents from reaching Washington? Who gave these assholes enough authority to hunt down American citizens and override local law enforcement? You want me to go on?"

Norm shook his head. "There's no easy answer, Mick. A lot of things happened leading up to this. Agencies got too big to control, thanks to September 11th. Good intentions lead to bad decisions by people trying to do the right thing. But that's not the answer you're looking for."

"Damn right, it's not."

"You think there's a political answer." He gave me that grin that said he knew things I never would. "Like when we argue politics. You a Democrat and you think I'm a Republican. Politics," he hesitated. "You think the president and congress make the decisions, the big day-to-day decision. But have you ever wondered how people like the general or the colonel have managed to stay involved for all these years? Or the department heads at the CIA, the FBI and other agencies stay long enough to retire? They're all bureaucrats, Mick. Hell the general's survived presidents and Chiefs of Staff changes, but he continues on."

"Can you cut to the chase, Norm?"

"Shit happens, Mick, and most times it rolls downhill." He stood up. "Anyone else hungry?"

His answer was blunt, cut to the bone, but to the point. I didn't like it. "So, what do we hope for? Where's our future?"

"We hope for more Admiral Bolters and fewer general and colonel clones."

Pauly knocked on the door and then walked in.

"Going to eat," Norm said. "You hungry?"

"Starving," Pauly said. "Where to?"

"How about we get some cigars at Schooner, maybe a drink and then do a few bars and eat a late lunch at the Tuna? I think we all need to unwind." Bob stood up and cleared empty beer bottles from the table.

On the way out Padre Thomas pulled me aside. "The angels took care of you, Mick. I told you they would."

"Yes Padre, with a little help from Pauly."

"No one can do it alone." Padre Thomas was the first out of the house.

Bob grinned. "You know he's crazy, right?"

"Maybe," I said.

"But he grows on you."

"Like mold. I need to talk to Norm. Give us a minute and we'll meet you outside."

"Sure thing." Bob walked away.

"You okay, now?" Norm looked serious, or maybe worried.

"I'm fine. A little overwhelmed with all this, but okay."

"Good. You did the right thing," he said.

"I know." I hesitated. Norm waited.

"You got something to say, say it."

"I haven't forgotten about Alexei."

"Neither have I."

"What's the next step?"

"Mick, he's no longer in Miami. Hell, he could've been here waiting to see what happened. No matter, he's connected

Pauly and you to his mission's failure. He'll want more than a pound of flesh."

"He's welcome to try."

"Keep your friends close, Mick. And be vigilant, because you're walking on thin ice with him and there ain't no ice to walk on in Key West."

"Are you going home, now?"

"For a few days, but it's business," Norm said. "I'll be back in a week and we can begin where we left off."

"I thought maybe I'd stick around here a little longer."

"Good to hear."

"One more question."

Norm nodded.

"How'd the admiral get here? How long has he been involved in all this?"

"That's two questions." Norm grinned. "He was in Tampa when I reached out to the captain up there. JSOC has been following this before we were even aware."

"And he did nothing? For chrissake, he plays golf with the president."

"One's politics, Mick. The other is reality."

"I don't get it."

"Politics is up front, media awareness, a show for the public. The admiral, he's a behind the scenes guy, you don't hear much from him or his team. You don't see headlines about what he does, usually, and when it makes the news, it's sanitized. But he's on top of it all. People like Bolter are our watchdogs."

I thought about what he said and nodded my head in reply. I couldn't think of anything to say, so I kept quiet.

I looked around the living room. Even with it almost empty of her belongings, I felt Tita's presence. It left me feeling lonely. "I miss her, Norm."

"Me too, Mick, me too." He closed the door as we left Tita's house.

THE END